NOCTURNE

Published by Aio Publishing Company, LLC.
www.aiopublishing.com

This book is printed on recycled and long-lasting acid-free paper.

All characters and events in this book are fictitious. Any resemblance to persons living or dead is strictly coincidental.

LIBRARY OF CONGRESS CATALOGING-IN-PUBLICATION DATA
Neuce, Jus.
  Nocturne / Jus Neuce.
      p. cm.
  ISBN-13: 978-1-933083-01-8
  ISBN-10: 1-933083-01-8
  1. Space colonies--Fiction. I. Title.

  PS3614.E555N63 2005
  813'.6--dc22

        2005002131
Printed and bound in the United States of America.

NOCTURNE

Jus Neuce

aio

Aio Publishing Company, LLC

Nocturne (a history)

THE COLONY PUSH

Earth's interest in not-Earth had always waxed and waned
with the fortunes of conflict, the psychology of politics,
the business of an increasingly ingrown global society.

An inward focus gave way to a desire for more.
An isolate planet orbiting a lonely sun was in its very existence
an Achilles' heel, unacceptably vulnerable.

Spurred by the race to identify habitable planets, Earth
breached its near interstellar neighborhood. Some of Earth's
finest minds seeded its exploratory ships.

Some succeeded.

A ship reached the edge of Earth's new grasp.
With anticipation built up over generations it saw a barren,
tidally locked, synchronously rotating planet in close tow to
its companion sun, a lone pair in a small red dwarf system.
The ship's inhabitants sent their message and settled on the rim
between permanent sunlight and the dark of night.*

But Earth's interest had again waned.

* See glossary

NOCTURNE

PROLOGUE

Before the explosion, when she and the audit group had come to the first food storage unit still blissfully unaware, Jenning turned her head and saw a tour group trailing some ways behind them.

A tour group.

Ridiculous, she thought. Did Chauncey really think that would work? The guide was fairly smooth, considering. "Primary food storage is in this section. This one here—" a point of the finger "—probably has a thirty percent capacity compared to the big ones. It's due for an update, next on the list. The big ones are already done."

They could have tried this earlier on, and it *might* have been effective. Way too late for it now, insultingly so; Gros Morne did not give tours—and this was no training. This was simply a little repetition wormed in, a different voice claiming what Chauncey had: an attempt at resonance delivered by an opponent who knew full well who she was dealing with—and there was the jab. *She* was no unsophisticate.

Though it had not been, yet, anything like yesterday, when she had hardly maneuvered herself out of the vehicle, stiff from traveling and wanting only her hotel room. Chauncey had arrived too promptly with the greeting delegation, had said, in front of them, with false quietness: The agenda that day was ambitious; would Jenning like the use of an electric cart? There would be no shame in it. Her age…

She thought to find something this visit, then. To say something with that much nerve—had to be designed to throw her focus.

The bays themselves were magnificent. She could admit that. Age-old limestone glistened out of the reach of the lights; the hydroponics units on the floor below were spotted with plants in full leaf.

Amazing that Kaettegut had produced *this*, when its buildings were slabs of uncolored cement—not a spark of creativity, of aesthetics.

But she was being unfair. Kaettegut did not have the resources Prime did, if she had to put her finger on it; long decades of that, and the population that resulted was unrefined, had a rawness of emotion. Even their highest officials had edges. Chauncey's smoothness was certainly intermittent.

"Main hydroponics are ahead." The guide's voice lost some of its volume as the tour group dropped further behind. One of the participants had slowed by one of the mechanical struts, was making a good show of examining it. Maintained as poorly as the much of the rest of the bays, no doubt, the metal rusted and bubbled under a cheap coat of black paint, if it was at all like the others.

Chauncey had gone further along, called ahead by an aide.

"Fine, ma'am?" Spoken to her now by a bureaucrat she particularly despised, a man whose fortyish face had more than its share of folds, of extra skin. It suited him, a simple panderer who had made it into the high levels of the Kaetteguttan government. God knew how their testing system was over here, but then, this one wouldn't survive in the rice fields. What was there over here not manual in *some* form, but government? "Ready to move on?"

A *crack!* It clapped hands over her ears, shocked all her nerves. She lost what the man was saying, he was no longer there—she lost all her weight, in a sickening instant, and she could not shout: her throat was stuffed with something hard and thick. *What*—

She opened her eyes. She thought she had: it was white instead of black. Dust clogged her nostrils, her mouth, her ears, bitter-tasting, bitter-smelling; her lips were coated with it.

Oh, my God. There was shocked silence all around her, the dust drifting down serene and light as fog.

She tried reaching out her hand to turn herself over. She was on her stomach; she could only tell because something pressed into it, hard and approximate to her own weight, which was too much, and she cursed it now, because she could not move. Her muscles were as insubstantial as the fog.

It was clearing. She could see a few feet ahead, with the direction her face was turned; she could not lift her head— Several feet, now.

There was a foot, some metal... She squinted. One of her staff? Someone awake? There was more—a calf, a hand.

At least it was intact. The remains of a hydroponics unit beneath it was not, and there was another shape mixed in with that, a stomach. Dear God, she could see a navel—the clothes were torn away, and there was something jagged and dark poking through.

The one on top was alive. *Not* her staff, not a tech—one of the tour group. Young, breathing very shallow, face resting on its side as if on a pillow; he might have been simply asleep, but for the surroundings.

"Hey!" she said, sharply. Ordering tone.

Nothing. She tried turning her neck again, and it creaked and protested, but it moved until she had gotten her nose ground into the floor.

She was not lying level. Under her arm she could feel metal grid, hard and unyielding, and chafing. The walkway—down at the level of the floor, at this angle, *good* God. Her leg, when she pulled, only came so far.

A flicker on the metal. *Oh, no—oh no, no, no. Oh, for God's sake—* She could not hear, but she could see it: fire, where there had not been any before, and she could not move.

PART ONE

1

Outside the floor lounge window Jargen Bay was a thin dark line. It would be blue if he were closer to it, smooth and slate-colored in the low light that was the bay and its surrounds. To the northwest there were plenty of lights on the edges, clustered, where the wild mussels clumped together on the mud flats sloping under the water.

Kellan sighed and put a knuckle up against the coolness of the glass.

Late, tonight. This floor had been quietly deserted an hour ago, in the slow, unnoticeable way that could happen. His job was still on the printer, creeping along at a pace the same as that at which a mussel larva must secrete a shell, but he had to get it done: it was due this week, and there was the conference in Gros Morne tomorrow, and the travel that would come with it.

He stayed at the window during the wait. To the northwest there would be the rafts and the long lines. He had not seen them in person, had last read about them nearly a decade ago, in his junior year of high school before he had taken the aptitude exams. He had wanted, then, to be on a boat, seeding and harvesting the mussel ropes.

When he had received his test results, the cold font that spelled his career field for him in less than a page, he had swallowed and sat there, knowing— He worked and pushed forms eight hours a day on the bland second floor of the Rue government office, with no chance at all for significance, to make a difference for anyone.

"You make a difference for me," Graham had said, the one time he had said something.

The refrigerator hummed along the wall behind him. He could hear it over his right shoulder.

He had to stop at the store on the way home. *That* was a comfort: home, secure, small in the sense that the office was not; the taste of warm food. Neither of them had known how to cook back then, but he had learned some since, so that he had a tiny set of dishes he could make very well, that were tender and flavorful and not very good for them, and the rest was passable. Graham's one expertise was a mean chowder; he was really better at the drinks.

He hoped the stove was working. It had been on and off for the last several months, just its age, but he hadn't wanted to replace it. It went with the place. To take it out would be to remove the gut of the rooms, and that would not be right.

He boarded the ferry for Gros Morne at the Cape in the late morning, with Graham, walking across the dock where the wind nipped across the water. He crossed his arms and tucked his hands into the crook of each elbow, the gusts lifting and parting his hair, cold.

The water wasn't all that choppy, though, and he was happy getting onto the boat, the deck shifting under his feet, a sensation both strange and pleasant.

It seemed stranger that their rooms would sit empty and dark even for these few days. It wasn't exciting, because it was only a conference, and those were rumored to be deadly dull. He had taken part in preparing for enough of them on his floor in Rue to taste the weight of that kind of boredom. Those kinds of conferences were for the outpost personnel, of course, the isolated individuals manning government offices who relished the rarity of in-person contact with anyone who understood the *importance* of their job.

Still, this would be Gros Morne, even if he and the others were only going so that the better ones could see to it they were filling out the forms right. There was certainly no special honor in being chosen, but it might be nice to be able to put a face to the names he saw on the reports and correspondence.

He looked over at Graham, standing by the rail, straight as if he barely acknowledged the movement of the deck. Stubborn.

That they permitted Graham to come for the trip, when he put in for it, had surprised him. He had known no co-workers going, though there were a few from other sections. And Graham had said he'd like to see Gros Morne, that he had the days coming from extra time put in at work, that he'd pay his own expenses.

It had made the whole prospect lighter, more secure—much more so, now. Graham could not attend the sessions, but he'd be there at the end of the day, one thing familiar.

The light was turning greener. He squinted into the wind—the east often had a greenish tint at this longtitude, but to have the rest of the sky infused with it, in every direction—a trick of light, probably, with the water and clouds. They'd pass the sea vegetation area, and he was eager to see that; the only time he had ever crossed the bay it had been dark and choppy, a storm coming from the east even as far back as the Cape.

That had been for the induction. He hadn't even been in the hotel, had been a part of the overflow and had been assigned to the extra room of an older woman. It had poured rain outside the window, water running down the streets in rivers and gathering at the bottom of the hill, angry and alone.

"Hey," Graham said, into the wind, but his eyes were toward him.

He lifted his chin, quirked his lip up a little.

They were alone on the deck by now. The few other sightseers had gone back inside to the rows of seats. Nothing really to see, once one had adjusted to the green cast to the sky and the stretch of the water.

Graham turned around and hooked his heel on the lower rung of the rail. Easily: "They'll probably give you some kind of tour. The food storage areas, all that."

"You're not going to find anything." It was an old theory of Graham's, going months back. Graham watched the media every day, analyzed everything when it came to markets, tried to make sense of it in the context of pricing. The rest was diversion, and irritation, because Graham could never find out if it was as he said, and when he did correctly track Jefferson's or Gros Morne's moves, the victory, Kellan gathered, was fairly hollow. Graham had won a number of grudging promotions—had to push for them—but beyond the office itself credit for anything was anonymous.

Not that the status necessarily seemed to bother Graham; it was more the lack of change. *Nothing moves*, he had said, more than once.

"They think she's doing it," Graham said. "It's *there*."

"And risk a Jefferson takeover."

Someone had, in the early days. It was in all the history books; no one was going to let anyone forget something as crucial as that. Kaettegut's administrator had done the unthinkable, though in those days things were wilder: everything hadn't settled out yet, power was still shifting and finding the wells where it could rest. Kaettegut would have been desperate, when it saw the way things were going.

A deliberately engineered food shortage, the only event Kaettegut had received credit for in the history lessons. Something nefarious.

It could not succeed. They had been fools to try.

"No one from Jefferson wants to come over here," Graham said.

That was flat truth, anyway. He put his hands in his pockets and drew up his shoulders. "They're not going to give us any tour."

"Sure, they will."

"A conference room. That's it." He should have asked for an additional day. The schedule left no time for any sightseeing, anything outside the ordinariness of two days' work.

The sea vegetation area was only a black strip in the distance when they passed it. He craned his neck, trying to see—no good. The dock drew up, and then there was a short wait at the station. The ground felt strangely solid under the soles of his shoes without the swaying of the water. He turned and looked back to the boat, but it was only the old ferry, a clunker.

He was surprised the train dropped them where it did, at an entrance into a long, flat tunnel where water ran in rivulets and puddled in the dips of the ground. In the middle of the tunnel's nowhere, though, there appeared a triplicate set of black French doors, with alloy plates at the base and behind the doorknobs.

He had thought—it would be the same as last time, they would have a hired room in some residence, had strongly expected an old woman very much like the last. Not entirely logical: there *was* the hotel, and there would be no overflow with so small a group.

"Did you know they had this?" Graham asked, finally, carrying his bag down the hallway after they had reached their floor. The bag jostled against his; the hallway had the illusion of width besides its sumptuousness, but the two of them barely fit side by side with their shoulder bags, and there were others behind him, so that he could not fall back for more space without being rude.

"I knew they had one," he said, only that.

He should not be surprised with this level of quality. The government had visitors from Jefferson, it was in the press sometimes, and what he might think was a luxury could not hold a candle to what Jefferson would think was ordinary, and what they might consider an insult. He let his eyes follow the walls, the wooden frames here and there around mirrors, vases, the occasional piece of wooden furniture against the wall. Not scrap wood, either, this was fine-grained, and dark—maybe a very well executed imitation, but that was cost in itself.

The administrator, of course, had quarters ordinary citizens could never dream about, he knew of *that*—and she had a reputation, she did not pander to Jefferson's visitors and received venomous criticism for it. This hotel had not been built under her watch, he was fairly certain of that. The alloy at the base of the doors, too, the molding with its extra paint caked on to hide the cracks, said it was very old.

Their room, when they opened the door, was immaculate: two beds with a narrow space in between and a starched smell rising, cool, from the bedspreads. There was a television on the opposite side of the room—he could barely see it where a cabinet door was cracked open.

He crossed over to it, pressed his palm against the cabinet door, ran his fingertips along the top edge. It *was* real wood, a kind and a use he had not seen, not even in the finest bookshelves. "Look at this!" he said to Graham, and Graham merely glanced over, dropped his bag onto the bed, and shrugged.

The first full day had been long.

The room was in Kellan's name—Graham stopped arguing and just used it to get whatever he needed, and reminded himself to transfer the funds to Kellan's account later. He was near the same age, could sound alike enough.

He'd bet the customers on the fifth floor didn't go through that. They rang for it and it came, count on it. *They* were Jefferson; their security was tight, the whole floor sealed off. He had found out from the desk clerk, a simple sort, naïve enough to be awed by those kinds of things.

Nothing to do with real security, any of that. It was Jeffersonian distaste, plain and simple, though Kellan had argued against it over dinner last night at the restaurant, his hair and their silverware burnished copper in the dim lights. It had been a novelty to walk downstairs and to be served, to have the food brought to the table by someone else—that was a Primean tradition, and what Kellan said Gros Morne had to offer, then.

Now Graham walked the streets to the west of the hotel. Mostly residential district: he looked to his right and there was another of the residential units, much the same as the others. Nothing of the individuality of their district in Rue—everything here was clean for the most part, this close to the government offices, but the walls were chipped and discolored here and there. A patch of some kind of fungi grew black on the wall of the next unit down, next to the doorway.

Gros Morne was grayer than Rue, more than he would have expected, and had a kind of apathetic dimness today with a heavy low-hanging cloud cover coming in, bringing the sharp tang of rain. A humid kind of cold made him put his hands in his pockets.

He *had* passed an anomaly not too far back, a sort of lounge restaurant similar to the hotel's with an exterior far too swanky for Kaettegut. That was another of Gros Morne's ways, he'd guess, to entertain and impress Jefferson visitors, to turn the image over on its nose. *See, it's not all backward.* There were metal fittings on the bottoms of the doors; the front was many-paned glass where it was not painted black over a cheap variety of wood, or maybe synthetic grain.

There was a noise, far off, quick and jarring for being so faint.

He stopped and looked around, but the street stayed quiet. He turned back, sighed, and kept walking. The hill crested maybe twenty steps away: Gros Morne was hilly where Rue was flat, and still managed to be the duller of the two.

There were voices, just snatches of them small in the distance. He turned again, and there were people coming into the intersection at the bottom of the hill.

Not just a few. He began walking back down the hill, rough cement where he had to watch his step more than coming up. There was something—*off*; the figures looked restless and fidgety, even at this distance.

The pattern was wrong, that was what. He walked more quickly, scanned as far as he could see: nothing elsewhere, but at the bottom of the hill the crowd was growing, had begun to lose direction, and one figure separated some from the rest. It dodged a few steps toward the far side of the street, stopped suddenly, and dodged several feet back the way it had come. A man.

Something was not right. He knew it in that instant.

He walked faster, almost to a jog. He could not hear anything distinct, but the crowd still grew, backing up like a sewer from the street leading toward the local access to the underground—he could see that, now, and the noise rose. He set his sights on the lounge bar; it would have the media on if it was anything larger than a very local disturbance. Not too far, if he could just get past this.

He made it down into the crowd. The faces pressed too close to him, disturbed and excited in a crisis sort of way, people asking each other for information, for clarification.

If it was something local and stupid… he gritted his teeth, shouldered his way to where the edge of the crowd had ended, and it did not end; it was spreading and trailing out new lines and clusters of people.

It took him ten minutes to get to the lounge bar, the concrete growing sharper and harder through the soles of his shoes. He could not get into the doorway once there—there were people already pressed up against the windows, straining to see the television sets, and the doorway was packed with arms and shoulders and heads, crushed together. He turned to the person nearest him, a man in coveralls, sweaty, too close. "What is it?" he said loudly, above the noise, and the man didn't look back at him, his head bobbing for a view of the television screens. "What *is* it?" he said, louder, and slapped his hand up against the man's shoulder.

Oh. He could see it in the man's eyes. "They don't know yet," the man said. "They said they don't know yet."

The hotel. He wasn't far; whatever this was, he could use a step out of it. *God.* Pack behavior.

He got to the entryway. The doors were locked, all smooth glass on the street side. He pounded on one of them with the heel of his hand, waited close in, because there were people going past in streams, and some were stopping to stare at the hotel, looking up at the façade above the entry, trying to look past him into the lounge.

A hotel clerk opened one of the doors for him with a key. "Come *on*," he said, and had the door closed and locked immediately.

"What the hell is going on?" His patience was trickling away more with every second, now.

But the clerk was already hurrying away, pocketing his keys. There was someone who looked like security personnel at the end of the hall.

He went into the bar—empty except for an employee, but the television was going.

Finally. He stood, and watched.

They were evacuating the hydroponics bays. *That* was something, a shock. He watched the people still trailing out of the access stair-wells on the screen, most of them already out if the streets were any indication. Earlier footage, then; one of the access stairwells close up, and there were people rushing out in masses, and some were covered in white dust. A spokeswoman's flat voice said they were evacuating the bays along the whole stretch, because they could not be certain how many there were—no explanation of what *there* was—and said security was on the scene at most of the storage areas, but it looked likely it was an isolated event.

Sweet Jesus. An explosion at one of the food storage areas, that was what it was. He leaned forward, and butted up against a table. He put his weight on its surface, on his knuckles.

The Jefferson delegation was underground at the time, on a tour of the facilities. That was next.

Oh, my God.

A *tour*. Where was Kellan supposed to be, in the middle of the day? He gripped the lip of the table, tried to think.

An agenda. There had to be a conference agenda— He kept his eyes on the footage, scanning actively now, looking for a shock of blond hair. He thought once that he saw him: a white-covered figure who had the same build, hair dusted white, and felt his chest lurch in relief—but then it was not him; the nose was not snubbed on the end the same way.

He whirled, chest pounding, and ran to the front doors, met up with one of them with a crunch—his shoulder, it was locked; it did not yield. *Damn it!*

The same clerk stood down the hall near the desk, looking in his direction.

No tour. *A conference room, that's it.* Kellan had said that, he remembered it distinctly, on the boat.

If he could get to the government offices—

He would know then Kellan was all right, could collect him. They could come back and watch everything from the hotel room. A food storage area—this was conversation for weeks.

"Sir." The clerk was there, and the door still wasn't opening. He pushed up against it; turned, furious. The clerk was a shade paler, but pulled himself up. A hand up, palm forward. "We all need to stay put, they're asking everyone to go back to their residences and stay put. We're fine here, there's nothing—"

The Jefferson delegation. They had been underground—lockdown, security, here. It shouldn't have taken him this long to figure that out. He spun on his heel, walked to the elevators, carefully, but when it opened on the second floor, he started running; couldn't get the door lock to read his card, then, and had to hold his hand still. It took an immense amount of control.

Inside, he said to the phone, "Call the government operator," and began searching, fast. He and Kellan didn't have much between them, just what the two bags could hold. A recording came over the phone speaker: no available line into the number at the moment. "Automatic redial," he said—*come on*, paperwork, anything that had an agenda...

He turned the television on. More footage. He kept an eye on that, went into the bathroom. A toothbrush, a razor—back out into the room. Clothes from yesterday; Kellan had kicked them under the bed.

No agenda, no paperwork at all.

Damn. He sat on the end of the bed, looked straight at the television screen and clamped his jaw shut. He was being a fool; Kellan would be at the government offices, that was by far the most likely, the most reasonable. It was what he had said.

Not that Kellan wouldn't love a tour of hydroponics—he had

tried to grow a planter of herbs, once, but without a sun lamp. Kellan might have tried for a tour. A question, a request, maybe they had the time...

Where *were* the offices where the conference was held? Anywhere near the explosion? Had it been limited to the hydroponics system?

"The line is still not available," the phone reported, and the blip said it had gone again onto automatic redial, twenty seconds between tries.

Relax. Relax. The bedspread had crumpled, hot, into his palms. He uncurled his fingers, an act of will, and the emptiness was unnerving; he leaned forward and re-clenched his hands into fists under his jaw, watched the screen.

Just the replay of the same scenes as before. A government spokesman came on, finally, looked into the camera and made a clear statement: there had been a small explosion at one of the food storage sites; it had done minimal damage to the food at that location and had affected no others. Security personnel were combing the rest of the facilities to check for any problems and would continue to do so, but had found nothing out of the ordinary so far, and did not expect to do so.

A slide replaced the spokesperson's face: a list of sections that had been cleared. No maps—intelligent, he thought, if there *was* something wrong, but the sections meant nothing to him without one. He memorized the list of sections and looked around, fast, for something to write it down.

The voice kept going. An investigation would certainly follow, and facts would be announced as they became available. The spokesman seemed even to imply that a small situation had been blown up into a fiasco. The spokesman would be back as more information became available.

The screen blipped, and—the spokesman was replaced with a special on sea vegetation farming techniques, a serene shot of the bay and the vegetation lying in clean rows, heaving with the movement of the water. Graham slammed his hands down, stood up, raised his fist against the wall beside the mirror and found it very hard to keep it back, to not destroy a side of the wall—made himself think, instead. He wasn't going to get through on the phone. No agenda, nothing in the footage.

The hotel would have back doors. A service exit, or the way they had come in; would they be watching the tunnel?

His mouth tasted of acid.

2

Chauncey closed her eyes. *Good Lord.* The departmental conference room stretched around her, the warm cabinets on the walls, real mahogany: administering the forestry division had its advantages. She stared at them until her eyes hurt, let the depth of the color draw her in and try to soothe her nerves.

Strange, to feel at once older and younger—off guard, inadequately experienced—than her four-odd decades.

One of her aides brought in a mug of hot tea, one of her own sets. The tea looked white against the pottery. "They're on the line," Rene said, not the gentlest of them, but speaking softly now.

And she had audio-only on the phone system. The videoconference system in this room had not been repaired, for purely budgetary reasons, since her predecessor had been here. "Put them on," she said to Rene, and wished for sleep. She had not had any for far longer than twenty-four hours, now.

She had sent a badly wounded delegate back to Jefferson a day ago, to the hospital there—her own people too, because Gros Morne did not have anything of that medical level, either in equipment or personnel.

Her own *people.* Hydroponics techs, simple people who worked with all their concentration on what they considered *their* plants. They'd be scared, terribly frightened. A strange place, a strangely lit sky outside the windows, people they did not know taking care of them.

The electrical unit had blown skewed, out one side instead of every direction, thank *God*, because if it had gone the way someone had designed it, the storage unit would have taken a direct hit: the control systems would have gone offline and they'd have lost a good portion of what was left after the dust and smoke cleared, before they could repair the system or move the food out. More people would have been injured, too, probably only a few with the way they were disbursed out in that section, but they were *hers*, damn it, and she would not send any more to Jefferson.

The burned ones—they would not be right again.

"Ms. Benner—" The man on the phone persisted in calling her that, no matter that thousands had graduated from Benner in her lifetime. In Jefferson the council members had the right to the surnames of their alma maters regardless of how many others had graduated, past or future.

She cut him off. "Nothing more here," she said wearily.

"We've waited the time you requested. We know you're in a difficult position." Just a thread of patience left, by the sounds of it, but they were trying. "You understand, we have staff here who have lost their partners. We have people asking questions. We've been *trying* to hold down panic, over here. That was a major unit, we understand."

"*Not* major." Again. She closed her eyes, shook her head. "A very small part of it was damaged. Food is *not* the problem."

"Jenning has given us—"

Jenning. She gritted her teeth. "Not minor, but far from the largest. It's *safe*. The losses have been very minimal. I'd like an update on my people."

"Ms. Benner, if you could guarantee no further breaches, it would go more smoothly over here."

If she had the energy, she'd be tempted to laugh. "I can't guarantee what I don't know," she said instead. They would send a team of their own over, of course, they would already have one assembled and no doubt on its way, made up of staff far enough down in levels that they could risk them. It would not be popular, not to those close to that staff, but in every other way it was crucial. Jefferson could not allow evidence to be swept under the rug by Kaetteguttan security, it *had* to send its own to guarantee confidence, and it would broadcast the action. Prime citizenry would not believe anything until its own people had conducted the investigation. That they were waiting so long to tell her—some convoluted logic, in someone's head.

"We understand," with a clearing of the throat on the other end of the phone line, "that the wiring was already in rather poor condition. That there were not sufficient funds allocated to the maintenance of the electrical system."

"I see. Jenning told you, I imagine." *Damned, damned woman.* Nosing far past what the previous audits had done, far past what was reasonable—and worse, she wanted budgets and documents delivered to the hotel, had read those nightly. *Very* carefully: "You're aware, I'm sure, of the size of our budget."

A pause. "Your budget is sufficient."

She cleared her own throat. More carefully still: "The size of our budget is one reason we're not talking by videoconference. One example."

"I imagine it's a simple matter of prioritization." Coldly. "We aren't in the habit of funding others' priorities. Experimental farming is woefully underfunded, for instance. Look to your government, Ms. Benner: it's burgeoning, while your product suffers. I don't think I need to remind you that you're in agriculture, that *that's* your purpose."

Well. She swallowed, and it stuck, hard, in her throat.

"I can account for every dime spent, of course. No, maintenance isn't well funded. I can show you why." *God damn it, money only stretches so thin.* "Call Jenning. I'm sure she's got the financial reports. I'll be glad to go over them with you."

"Talking with Jenning isn't possible right now. I'm sure you know."

"Of course." *Yes.* "She's not alone in that, of course. I'd *like* an update on my hospitalized, if I can."

Another pause. "Two are ready to be transported back. A team will—"

"Accompany them. Fine." She swept it aside with a wave of her hand. "I'll meet them at the dock."

She had seen the security footage. It was far from useful—the camera that had survived the blast gave only a partial view of the area, and from a substantial distance. She had sat in this room and watched it without any of her staff present, because it was something they would not handle well. The fire—when it started, in a far-off corner of the screen, her stomach had lurched. She had swallowed half a mug of tea to settle the acid. There had been cries, sickening.

The water jets had come on late, another fault in the system… but she knew the reason for that, the simple lack of preparation for something like this, because this had not happened even in her earliest memory.

There was nothing in the recording after the dust first filled the bay that shed any light onto the situation. She had edited the recording herself, cut it off after the dust had reached the ceiling on the screen, before the fire had begun—had given that to the security staff and to Jefferson. *This* version was hers, and sat in her own library back at the residence.

Her security staff was not well trained in investigation. But she had seen every thread of evidence they'd come up with, and they did not have the guile necessary to hide a finding—none of the ones on that duty. She had gone through their files and vetted them, individually, immediately after viewing the recording, when at last she had gotten back to her office and told Phoebe to guard her door, and Rene had been picking staff to keep the doors to the department secure.

She did not want, ever again, to walk to the window and look down at a melee like that swarming toward the building's overloaded, blocked entrance.

Someone on the tour had paused very near where the electrical unit was. She could not see detail at that distance, but she did not believe the person had done anything but look up into the cranny between the ledge in the cave wall and the strut. A head tilt, it looked like. An open access door to the wiring, perhaps? If the person had just *said* something—

But now two Kaetteguttans were ready to be transported back. Hell, *that* was something.

"The names?" she asked, and sat straight in her chair for one last moment.

The surnames were both Njelteberg. Two of the staffers in for the conference from Rue, then. She could not do much for them than transport them home to Rue comfortably, and regardless, they were not Gros Morne.

She crossed her ams and shuddered with the tiredness and the situation.

Graham was at the dock as soon as he got the news over the television. Two from Rue, on the way back. He clenched his nails into his palms, leaned forward in the chair inside the dock train station, stomach cramped.

It would be a while before they got here, if the media was right.

He looked up at the clock, kept his fists closed, taut, the semblance of control he had. Days of very little sleep, and he had dreamed during the snatches, nightmares.

God, that anyone had him like this! He had not seen it coming. Simple as that. He *should* have just kept to himself. Kaettegut was dull and it was safe, and he had one of the few jobs that provided any stimulation at all. He should have been content with that.

He had used to hate the prospect: the sameness, the dullness. He had dabbled in things he wasn't supposed to, that he shouldn't have.

Now he looked back on the apartment in predictable Rue, where trying to grow a planter of herbs was something different, and he *wanted* it back.

He shut his eyes, opened them, and there were the plain white walls of the station, the clock—still there, still the same.

They finally came. The boat came infuriatingly slow to bump against the dock, backed off, and cozied up to it again, the lapping water licking at the old hull... The two came onto the dock, and he vaguely recognized one of them—pale and freckled, almost colorless, a female, huddled into an ill-smelling blanket, walking bent and hesitant, and the other one was not in much better shape—his stomach, his shoulders felt sore and tired. Acid sloshed in his gut.

He took the train with the other group—Jeffersonian, not too hard to guess. He sat at the other end of the train car and did not look their way.

He had asked before. He went back to the government offices anyway, stood in the lobby and waited for over an hour.

"I *need* a pass. Just to the hospital," he said, when he finally got in front of the desk, and they did not ask him to sit; they exchanged glances with each other behind the counter, and finally one leaned forward, with only something official on her face. No feeling.

"There is no way. We told you."

Anger was swelling; his lower ribs hurt. "They won't let anyone with a relationship with any of the victims—"

"No." She didn't bother even with the *we'll tell you as soon as we know; they've assured us they will keep us informed*, the official line.

"And if one of them isn't doing so well—" *Good Lord.* He could not be talking that way; he could not listen to himself, could not let himself think like that.

She looked at him until he stopped. "No one is in danger of that. We'll be notified if they are." Mostly exasperation, but finally there was a hint of empathy, in a sigh. She leaned forward again, unclasped her hands. "We can't do for everyone what you're asking. Jefferson will not take those kinds of numbers. You understand. Go back to Rue—" she was searching her memory for his name, did not find it. "Get back to something normal."

He just looked at her. *God damn—*

She was losing patience. "We can reach you better in Rue." The excuse sounded pale, but she made no attempt to give it more strength.

Nothing, then. It could not have been any different; it would not have mattered if he had been like the woman the first time who had screamed and cried and had to be carried, kicking, from the room. He went outside, sat down on the curb, and looked with his eyes parched at the building across the street.

———

"What do you think?"

The question was directed at her. Quinn looked up. "Who, you mean?"

She wouldn't ordinarily sit across a table and converse with Stefan, with anyone of his sort. Age similarities aside, neither his tenure nor his affiliation warranted it; he was merely a peer delegate, beholden to Loren. From his few remarks in the chambers, even eleven years ago, he had quickly marked himself as an idealist, the kind the less experienced could afford to be. The less experienced were not in the position to do any damage skipping down that road.

His more recent commentary had not been sufficient to change her assessment. Of course, she did not expect anything otherwise, not from Ethics, no matter how much it was rumored he had lost touch with his own department.

But no one else was here yet; she had arrived to find Stefan sitting alone in the conference room. No staff in sight, as usual, but perhaps he didn't have any. "Coffee," she had said, coming in, settling her bag and pulling out the folders she'd need. "You?"

Stefan had blinked at her. "Thank you," he had said, and then, recovering: "That would be nice." With a smile. Her aide waited only for the *thank you*, and left the room for the kitchens.

"I think," she said now, putting her palms flat on the table—honesty— "it's fairly obvious who they were targeting. The proximity to food storage was a nice touch. It's doing what they hoped."

If he had any disagreement with that, any of his own ideas, he hid it admirably well. A little movement of the eyes to the right, but not a flicker otherwise. "Why, though?"

"Oh, a message. The current system's not as safe as most people would like to think. Fortunate, I think, that we're on a sufficiently small scale," she said, pointedly at the last, and left it at that. Offers of coffee or not, that was plenty of conversation. She opened the top folder of the stack she'd brought and frowned down at the map of the blast site. Stefan could take the hint, and he did; he was quiet.

She smoothed her hair, still tidy in its full chignon, and skipped back to the photos, still shots frozen from the only camera still operating. The gridded walkways had fallen along the right wall and in front of the storage unit. There, through the dust, was the almost indistinguishable form of what she knew was Jenning, from the briefing Jenning had given. Poor Jenning—she had almost smiled to see it, the first time, had covered her mouth instead. Beached, flat on her face. *Not* a position Jenning was accustomed to, and Jenning had been spitting mad when the doctors finally allowed her a visitor. *She* wouldn't want to be those doctors, not least the hospital staff, the nurses and underlings.

Jenning would doubtless get her chance for temper; for now, the Proteraiotita took *her* word for things. It would not be long before the doctors released her, and count on it, she'd be hobbling down the hall to her office the minute it happened, crotchety as any day.

Loren came in—*entered* was more true—only when all but one

councilor had arrived. She glanced at her folder to keep from revealing even a hint—crude theatrics on his part, but humility was how
one stayed out of disfavor, and for that reason was helpful. She had
not been on the receiving end of one of Loren's paybacks for what he
perceived as less than deferential behavior, though she judged herself
to have certainly come close. She *had* gotten a warning she'd not soon
forget; she had never gained that department back. It still reported to
Business, a minor division even with a delegate on one of the minor
councils and with strong leanings toward expansionism.

She would not be allowed to think of him as Loren, if he knew.
She had never slipped up in addressing him, not even in her most
heated moments, and she would not—he was Councilor Fifty, the
right to use the name of his school his privilege just as it was theirs,
but they did not do so with each other, even her. *Fifty* was another
rub, too. When he had succeeded to the chairmanship, all of Fifty's
alumni had received the slight rise in status and the salary that came
with it, and Loren did not forget that. He spoke at the graduation
every year, just that little reminder. Sickening.

She leaned back, watched him round the table and deliberately
settle into his seat—he would know that everyone was waiting, and
it didn't matter that the technique was old as his chairmanship. It
rankled those who believed in dignity and equality, the worse for the
repetition.

She tolerated him because she had to, but truthfully, might have
even if he were not so puerile because he had strong tendencies in the
direction of her contingent, no matter how much it was not said. Officially he was very much of the expansion party. It fit his penchant
for power to plough over the mountains in the Back, to shape the
world to his orders—but at heart he was as status quo as any of her
party's most ardent supporters. *She* came out ahead on the measures
that counted. She could count on that; she only had to frame it the
right way, to let him save face.

Nothing would be accomplished at this meeting; only the newer
ones would expect more. She sat straighter, closed her folder, and
folded her hands atop it.

Kellan opened his eyes.

There was a white ceiling. He lay on his back.

He turned his head. A window came into view, a single vast pane luminous with a kind of deep blue he had never seen in the sky.

No. Wait. On television: he had seen that kind of color there, when he was a student and had wanted, badly, to visit Jefferson, all the buildings glowing white in the lights, and the sky *that* kind of blue, all the time, darker than he could imagine living. The streetlights had to be on all the time, he had thought, for the people to see their way anywhere at all.

He could make no sense of the light now, in this situation. He had not visited Jefferson, had not seen this kind of sky.

He tried to turn his head to the right. *Oh, God.* Pain shot up and branched out into nerves all over his skull.

There was something stiff in his neck, anyway, that way. It felt like a steel rod, flinty and unyielding. He winced, and *that* hurt, aggravated the pain still radiating across his skull, so he lay still and it began to fade, slowly.

He was cold. That, he felt next; just his head, though, and he did not want to try to raise his head to look to see what he was covered with. He only forced his eyes down as far as they would go, looked past his nose and cheekbones, and could see his feet draped with a thin white—something.

His mind moved sluggishly. "Hello?" he tried calling out, and his mouth was dry like they had put cotton into it.

He did not want to try clearing his throat; still, his voice was a little stronger on the second effort. "Hello?"

Louder: "Graham? *Graham?*"

Nothing. There was only a whoosh of air above his head, steady.

3

One of the few times Prime would be watching Kaetteguttan media coverage—and Chauncey had no new information. Her stomach, on so little sleep, rolled queasily.

Rene sat on her right, in the room crowded with cameras and people. It had been an immense comfort to bring in *anything* of her own. Media was almost entirely Prime, though there was the one camera they still had to feed recordings to Media's studios in Grosvenor, when it was working. It stood in the front row. Media had tried to relegate it to the back, but she had won that argument, at least, because they could not very well transmit an empty podium.

She had to provide comfort to her own people, of course, that was the first priority, but what would be of most comfort would be to know there was some suspect identified and in custody in Prime.

She did not have it.

"I don't have any news," she said, simply, and put it out there. "Our security has turned over every stone—and it *has* been an internal investigation, for the safety of all, and by rights as it is our territory which has suffered. In regard to the food situation, most of you know that the supply is not endangered, but I say it again: only a minimal portion of a storage unit was affected, and was not one of the larger units." A break for emphasis. She let it stretch out longer than comfortable, but it was a point little regarded, and needed the extra space.

"We have been cooperating with allies in Jefferson and in Prime who also deeply desire to resolve this matter." She took a deep, strong breath. "We have been sharing and will continue to share our data, and I want to thank the medical staff in Grosvenor, who have responded to an emergency the size of which Nocturne has not seen in many decades. Our people are under excellent care. We look forward to the safe and healthy return of those remaining under care."

Jefferson did not have anyone any better trained. That had not stopped it before, but there was a first for everything. It was conceivable they worried the perpetrators were Primean, with Jeffersonian ties to someone important, and once that lid was opened—

Instead they put the pressure on *her*, made themselves look as active as they could be.

She'd *like* to be able to point her finger, definitively, to even an unknown party in Prime. The fact was she could not, that without results she could not eliminate someone from among Kaettegut's ranks. That was the double edge of the blade, and was now her own investigation. Since before coming into office she had become aware there were those who were not content, and that there were grumblings. None of her cabinet would own it, of course. It was always someone else's people.

Not hard to figure out why they were unhappy, of course. If they watched the media, if they had relationships with those who transferred over as renovation crew to Prime and saw what Primeans were living in, and consuming—it followed that they knew their place in the pecking order on Nocturne, and that Kaetteguttans had credit only with each other.

That was not spoken. What was, was that they were essential to life on Nocturne, period, and that the population would not survive without them, and they were therefore valuable. Every schoolchild's lesson.

"Questions?" She did not want to offer, wanted only to leave the room, but the whole of Kaettegut would be watching this, would be glued to their televisions. That was the important thing, the reason she had agreed to this at all, though point of fact, she did not have much choice.

"Will a perpetrator be found?" Someone in the back, asking for the benefit of his viewers.

"It's possible it will take a great deal longer than we hope for," she answered, and tried to keep the weariness from her face. "Nearly all physical evidence was destroyed. The investigation will necessarily have to take a turn away from the forensic." And again: "If *anyone* has information, even if it seems insignificant, I urge you to bring it forward to my office."

More of the same. She answered them, repeated herself more times than she'd like to count.

She did not know that she could really expect it of any Kaetteguttans, malcontent or not. It was too far out of the culture in this year, in this decade, in this series of generations. The simple momentum of time, of habits, had taken them all long past that.

Still, she would have said that of anyone, Kaetteguttan or not.

———————

Jenning's office, with everything set to her own preferences, gave her an inordinate amount of satisfaction. Large: she warranted a fairly spacious office, with space for shelves and a small meeting table, enough for two to have a comfortable discussion—three was a squeeze, with the piles on the floor. She did not permit her staff to straighten up in here, and they had left the piles intact, she saw with a small bit of pleasure, while she had been in the hospital.

No one had moved in on the opportunity, then. An unusual one, but people *had* died in office, and the ensuing, immediate maneuvers could be a terrible sight.

And that meant there had been no rumors of her demise. She could probably thank her direct superior, sitting in the chair opposite, for that.

Quinn did not often drop by for a visit. Quinn's nurturing quotient was near zero—she had seen Quinn's testing results like everyone else's before they got to that level—which meant Quinn was making an immense effort. If she could put her finger on it, she *thought* she could read a relief that she was back at the office, that she hadn't been lying dead on a collapsed walkway in Kaettegut.

Enough people had been. She had lost one of her own aides assigned to her from Safety for the agricultural audits, and she had gotten to know their ways, damn it, had become nearly as familiar with Clare and Ethan as she was with some of her own staff. Now there was only Clare, though she hadn't seen her. She had just known who was in the hospital when she was, in what numbers and in what proportion, and neither Kaettegut nor Prime had done well in ratio.

Her own legs were much the worse for wear. Swollen still, and she could barely move the right one. They had given her a *cane* at the hospital, and damned if she didn't have to use it.

"I received this," Quinn said, and pushed it across the table.

She looked and saw a name: Graham Long, on a request for a travel visa from Kaettegut; those were a dime a dozen. From Quinn, though... She picked it up, examined it, and the reason Quinn had handed it across popped off the second line. The pricing office, hell. "How the hell do *they* know what our levels are?" she asked, irritable, but it was intriguing, even if her head hurt.

A senior analyst, one with legendary tenure who had never made it into management's ranks, had died in office—and this application, from *Kaettegut*, said it.

It spoke of a leak in the pipeline, and more than that, for a Kaetteguttan to have access to that kind of knowledge.

She had lined up a Wright student, not a month from his exams, for the vacancy before she had left for Gros Morne. The office could certainly make do until then. Nothing to replace a senior analyst like that, but the pricing office would have already adjusted, would have planned its own promotions.

That this applicant—he was not shy; he implied the death right in the paperwork, up front. "It's yours," Quinn said, and stood up and tapped the table with the tips of her fingers. She had left the cup sitting there, still almost half full, but that was likely the limit of her endurance, and touching at that. "I'm glad you're back."

She re-read the first page after Quinn had gone.

It could be useful. Quinn knew her habits, her quirks; more important, Quinn knew what her quirks had done for the division. Status came from knowledge, iceberg-like, so that the more that appeared hidden, the better.

She looked into the records, and found easily the reason for the request.

She steepled her hands and rested the tips of her fingers on her chin. No downside, or at least there did not appear to be any. It would be extremely advantageous for her office to have that kind of detailed knowledge of Kaettegut food pricing—which could lead to knowledge of food supplies. An audit of a different sort, when the one mandated by law had gone largely nowhere, despite her efforts.

Chauncey had that one effectively blocked. Not this one.

Chauncey did not know. An ordinary travel visa, and it had gone through the channels too fast to have been held up at that level. He had been subtle, on their end. Not on hers.

She could approve the request for the visa as written. Not her name, of course. She could approve the real request while he was on this side of the terminator. Assign one of her contacts to it—see if he was worth the trouble, then decide.

She made a note to Audrey to sign off on it, no mention of the office, just an approval signature. *This* was her area of excellence—what paled in insignficance to others could be attached to an ever-widening web within her own scope, and it did not matter whether the person in question was ranked high enough to impress. Sometimes the little people got the job done best... properly guided.

It was a terrible sight. The hospital bed, the pillow—everything was white. Kellan's skin looked as if it had been bleached, as if the antiseptic air had been seeping into him. Asleep, it seemed his head hardly made a dent in the pillow.

There was a crease at the corner of his right eye, a stickiness that hinted of moisture. *God.* Graham wanted to rub it away. He kept his hands at his sides; the nurse was beside him. If he had been here—

The eyelids flickered. Opened, and even the eyes were washed out, pale, sticky.

"Graham?"

Quietly, as if he did not believe it. *Christ.* He reached over, put his hand on Kellan's wrist. His own palm felt hot against the coolness of the skin, the detached coolness of the whole room, the *air* of the place.

"Need your talent at the stove, old man. The chowder's getting old."

Kellan's lips quirked into a smile, slight, but the eyes warmed, much. A quick blink, a narrowing of the eyes; one side of the lips quivered, once.

"Hey." He squeezed his wrist, hard. "I'm here. I'm here, all right? I'm not going anywhere. You're going to get better."

Kellan closed his eyes, tight. His jaw clenched. He took a deep breath through his nose, finally, opened his eyes again, and they were dry, under control. "I—"

He sat down on the stool, leaned forward, clasped his hands on the bed. The nurse was still there; she had just moved back, blessedly discreet. "The place is lonely without you," he said, honestly. He made his voice strong, something solid.

"Graham." As if he still didn't believe it.

He should have been here sooner, he should have—

But Kellan looked at him, and went calmer. "I—was in the explosion. The accident. I don't remember much."

"It's all right. You don't have to."

He nodded, very slightly, faced the ceiling again, and closed his eyes. His hand moved; Graham put his own on top of it, but Kellan pulled out from under it, closed his fingers around *his* wrist. "You'll be here," he said, eyes still closed, and his grip was not as weak as he might have guessed.

"Right here."

His breathing slowed. Graham looked to the nurse; she nodded. Quiet, so that he could hardly hear her, and had to rely on reading her lips, some: "That's a lot, for him. Come on."

He went, but he stayed in the floor lobby.

———

Stefan took the turn north of the ferry dock, often took walks out this way when he needed to think, when what he saw at the table of the Proteraiotita needed digesting. It smelled *clean* out this way, the baseness of humanity washed away with water and the scent of it.

Windy today, and the river this evening did not reflect the sky as it often did, a calm mirror extending to the opposite bank with the bay beyond—today it was almost as choppy as the bay, and dark. He did not imagine it was all that deep, just enough to buoy the ferry, perhaps.

Here, they had done a decent job terraforming some very hardy grasses. Dark, of course, always, but that was the way when there was still a sizeable population, high-ranked, who could not tolerate more direct sunlight due to genetic predisposition—and might be a problem if the expansionists were successful. There was little problem with a trip to the pitch-black of the Back. There *would* be a problem, for some of them, visiting what was constantly exposed to the sun.

He turned and looked back at the white-lit facades of Jefferson, at the wide, empty boulevard lining the tributary that ran through the center. *His* Jefferson, his Nocturne—and all his colleagues on the Proteraiotita could do was squabble.

They seemed to have taken the explosion in without surprise or emotion or regret. He could hardly look at the photos they'd been given, enlarged without any mercy, and yet Quinn had sat across the table from him and thumbed through them, looked at them in detail, and not a line had creased her lips.

The more senior ones... Steel-haired old Decheran would not betray any life. The only emotion he had ever seen out of her had been anger, hard as the logic she used. She had sat there impenetrable with the others at the head of the table.

She had been passed up for the chairmanship even before Fifty's time, he had heard, but then, he could not imagine she had ever been a real contender, no matter that she headed the Back—what was a sizeable population. Perhaps that was some cause for her shell.

Quinn thought his party had some part of it. So the lines the explosion had drawn were widening, spreading like the dust had in the photos. Departments that were part of the same Jefferson, of the same divisions, regarded each other differently. Colleagues did. *He* looked at Quinn warily, now: who did not know whether the status quo party had not had something to do with it? A warning of what would happen if the race were permitted to grow—elegant, probably, in their eyes. Why not do it on a small scale now, before it could become too large in scale, while they could still handle it?

Fortunate, I think, that we're on a sufficiently small scale, Quinn had said.

They could not handle it. It struck at the heart of their survival, it had torn away part of the infrastructure surrounding a food unit, and *that* was tearing at the base of humanity. Maslow's hierarchy of needs.

It was not his party. Not anyone accepted in his party.

Perhaps they had come too far. The councils had been of three minds for so long, he had made the mistake of believing it would continue indefinitely, when he knew better, that the nature of the conflict would not allow the parties to parallel each other for long. If the expansionists were in power, they made inroads the others could not take back—only abandon.

This—it made him want to say *stop*, even if it was only a whisper. He could not see order torn apart. The system in itself was beauty, the scheme of things that produced white-lit structures like this, that had settled Nocturne and produced a society that had lasted this consistently.

Everything fell. That was the lesson of history, and that was his area of specialty, the route he had taken to Ethics. He had seen, in the database texts, too many Earth civilizations battle their own decay— and the best had survived only in parts. Rome with all its might and faults had survived only in memory, and falsely: the most powerful nations had still thought to imitate it up to the day his ancestors had left, but by then they had lost sight of what it had really been.

They were fools, here, to believe they were any different—but they did believe, and were reassured because a century and a half had not proven them wrong. They thought themselves on a steadily ascending slope, when that was not the way history worked: history took a series of steps forward, and tended then to fall back, badly. Humanity did it to itself—the parties on the outside, and on the inside.

Haste was the danger: ill-considered and rash reaction to provocation from outside, common thinkers who had no business threatening that which was great.

But no one would understand that, think the way he thought. He was another number added to the table for the expansionists, a reason for Quinn or Decheran to sit with faces wiped clean of any reaction.

4

The first time he stood, Kellan had smiled enough that teeth showed. Wider still. It was enough to make Graham's heart stand still for a second, and he had returned the smile. No words.

Walking was different. Kellan struggled with it, forced himself when he was too tired and he couldn't lift his foot far enough off the floor to avoid stubbing it. The first time, he had tried to do it with only the nurse's assistance, and Graham had grabbed him just in time.

He had put Kellan's arm around his own shoulder. "It's okay," he said, had almost Kellan's entire weight back against his left arm, and Kellan looked away, eyes closed, teeth clenched, and he could *feel* the mortification. "It's *okay*," he said, again. "It's okay. Let's just go back to the bed, you want?"

A nod, eyes still closed, teeth still clenched.

Even then, the nurse had to come and get the other side. Kellan wouldn't look at him, didn't talk, just let them lay him down, let the nurse arrange the sheets, lay there breathing hard.

Now he accepted the shoulder, didn't even need the arm around his back on his good days. On his good days, he was too ambitious, walked too far and then he did *this*, trying to come back. "Easy," he said, looking down, watching the feet. There was the additional indignity of bare feet and a hospital robe, every day. He maneuvered his arm around his back, bolstered him that way. Kellan's head hung down, hair blocking his eyes.

"How long?" he asked the nurse, privately.

"It's just exercise. His muscles need to build back a little. That's all."

That wasn't what he meant. It was still enough of an answer, enough to make his stomach lurch. He hadn't been thinking about it, hadn't *let* himself think of it. A matter of time.

He wouldn't wish for Kellan to stay here, to wake up every day and remember, and face this—not for any reason. He told himself that.

———————

It wasn't the lack of freedom, or the recovering, so much—it was that they touched him, anytime, examined and moved him as if he were an arm, a leg, a torso. They *handled* him. The most private functions, and they were right there—worse, affecting patience, when they did not want to be there.

Some of the nurses had become more human. When he had begun trying to walk, a few of the nurses had begun to look at him and *see* him, a kind of startled pity. Still, that was as far as they got, and he had grown used to it, and looked to the day he could leave the room, walk out and leave it forever, with an intensity that kept his fingernails hard into his palms at night, when it was quiet and they had long ago drawn the blinds and left. They hadn't trimmed his fingernails or given him anything with which to do it; they had gotten long and strangely white, and hurt his palms.

When Graham had appeared... With Graham came the drafty, empty smell of the streets of Rue, the warmth of the apartment when the stove was on—sanity. Graham, his sameness an unthinkable comfort, calm, level-headed.

He looked for *those* visits like a drowning man.

The rest of the time he stayed still, responded to nothing except when they spoke to him and wanted an answer. That's what they wanted. No good getting upset, he had internalized that early on. He strove to get better; any instructions they gave him he did, prompt, and as close as he could to what they said. He ate the food whether it was palatable or not.

Only with Graham could he show any emotion. He was embarrassed when he did, but it was an enormous relief, and he was *human* again, someone who had mattered. Maybe.

He knew how insignificant his life was, then. He had done nothing that anyone else could not do. Someone did it for him these days, back at Rue, and probably with no difficulty.

He warranted visits from one person.

The nurse came to change the sheets, made him sit in the chair beside the bed while she did it. He watched, and sat as straight as he could with the chair curving around his back. It was small things: if he was diligent, he would be stronger and could leave. The headaches had gratefully faded away, had left just a dullness. He told them, and they did not release him, but they did write it down.

Oh—to sit in the apartment, to turn on the stove for the heat and the smell it made, and feel the cushions of the sofa, feel something yielding instead of hard. Everything around him, familiar.

Something like that—he shook his head to clear his mind.

They hadn't even told him what was wrong, what his injuries were. Maybe he was going to be here a long time; maybe they had done surgeries and he wasn't going to be able to live like he had before. Maybe—

"Hey." A smile in the voice. He turned around, quick, and Graham was here early; either that or he hadn't been calculating the time in his head right.

His heart lifted, all the same.

Graham had a package, a plain paperboard box. He walked in the room, and the nurse finally finished and left. Graham sat on the end of the bed facing him, and he was glad he hadn't been slumping, that he had been sitting like he had some strength. "What's that?" he said.

Graham handed it across. No smile, but his eyes were not cold. "Something I should have thought of," he said.

He took off the lid. His head was going a little light—he had been sitting a while, now, and the effort it took to stay upright, to not surrender to the curve of the chair, was starting to cost him. A muscle to the right side of his lower back began to spasm, twanging like a violin string. But there was paper, real, in his hands; he unfolded it to the side, and there was something— Fabric. He went to lift it out and it slid through his fingers, slippery, black, but some of it was still in the box, and it did not slide all the way to the floor. He was grateful for that.

It was a robe. He realized it when he saw the cuff, where the material doubled under, heavier; black and smooth under his fingers. He looked up at Graham.

"Something so you don't have to be everything they want to make you," Graham said.

He opened his mouth. Looked down at the fabric in his hands. "Thank you," he said. It was inadequate; he wanted to say more, but his mind produced nothing he could use.

"You're welcome."

He could make it to the bathroom. He clutched a fistful of the fabric in one palm, put both hands on the arms of the chair, strained every muscle getting to his feet, and kept his face smooth with huge effort. Six steps to the door with the size of *his* stride, and he made it inside, bent over and gripped the sink in the tight space—there was not enough in his arms, and his left leg buckled. He let go, and his left shoulder hit the wall behind him with a loud thump, and then it was pretty much over, but his rear took the majority of the impact.

Cold, hard floor. His buttocks stung with the shock. He leaned back against the wall, put his knees up, clutched the fabric in both hands and put his face down in it. Frustration welled up in his eyes; he squeezed them shut until they hurt, dug his knuckles into his forehead. *God damn it.*

"Kellan? You okay?"

"Fine," he said, through the material, as loud as he could. His head hurt, something jarred loose. *Oh, God. Oh, God.* He felt very much like crying, just the unfairness; he would not.

He got his hand back up on the sink. His legs were stronger; he used his arm only for balance, and got himself up so that he was leaning against the wall. He unwrapped the hospital robe, the material limp and white and pale, and struggled to get his shoulders out of it. Sweat gone quickly cold glued it to his skin, so that he had to peel his arms out of it. He stood there a minute more, breathing hard, letting the sweat dry.

The new robe went on easily, felt like cool air. He looked across at the mirror, and by God, he had some *presence*, some color—even thinner, he looked stronger just for that.

"I like it," he said, before he walked out, and he felt foolish coming out, but Graham's face broke into a smile and that made him feel better, that alone.

He got to the bed, tried to sit up straight on it, and gave up. He leaned back against the metal bar of the headboard where it met the wall, and looked at Graham sitting there in the chair. "I'm sorry," he said, and wanted to shrug, but could not do even that. "Not a good day, today, I guess."

"You're not going to be here much longer." Graham looked at him, bent forward a little. "You're not. You're going to be out of here. Matter of days."

"They told you that?" His voice lifted too much on the last syllable, and betrayed him.

"Yeah." Graham looked down, made his hands into fists, pounded the top one into the bottom. He looked up, and gave a smile that wasn't quite right. "Hate to tell you that, now that you're so nicely dressed for here."

He *wanted* to ask if there was something wrong with him, if there were parts that wouldn't heal. He couldn't bring himself to—didn't want to know if it was *yes*, maybe. A reason the doctors hadn't told him when he was getting out, and what they had done... Or maybe they had, and he didn't remember. "I really like it. It was really thought—"

Graham dismissed that with a flick of his wrist, a turn of his head. His hair had grown; there were strands starting to creep down his neck. "I should have thought of it before. I'm sorry."

For days afterward, sitting there in bed, Kellan looked down at his sleeve and it was the only intensity in the place, the only real pigment. In the bathroom, washing his hands, he looked up into the mirror and the figure there had a surprising amount of grace, some force.

Graham had known. Without him saying anything. He sat back against the pillow, nights later, and closed his eyes.

So.

This was something she could control.

Jenning read the report. A minor thing, but it was always either one of her side projects or a particularly conflicted individual that held her interest, and there were not, usually, enough of either. Her job could be tedious: too much of a good thing, a flaw in the system for someone like herself, who tested for variety, and they thought that a job like this gave it to her.

Many samples of the same thing, in the same field, did not variety make. Fortunate in a strange way, she supposed, to get the head audit assignment, and probably another reason for it. They were sometimes not so single-minded. They could surprise. And there were the occasional tidbits from Quinn, who perhaps after all knew her better than was comfortable.

Graham Long was fitting in nicely—not socially, not at all, but he was picking up the methods and procedures of the wholesale pricing office. Her staff contact had made an inane note at the bottom—*intelligent*, when she needed no telling. Good grief, what field was she *in*?

The important thing was that he was leaking information left and right, just with the assumptions he made while learning the new system. Kaettegut food pricing worked entirely differently, in a sphere of its own; she had not expected that. She gathered from the report, this far, that they did not produce the same levels of food in each sub-segment each year, did not remotely follow population levels, as she might have expected. They selectively raised demand every season, a lower level here, letting an oyster bed lie fallow there.

God, how long had Kaettegut been operating like this? *It* had been taking everyone else for a walk, and had hidden it in the numbers, in excuses. She had believed them. Mussels were living beings: they sometimes thrived and sometimes did not. Their best experts studied, they were constantly refining their practices; meanwhile, some seasons the shells were smaller, and Prime was happy to have them at all.

They *planned* it. They harvested early, she would bet.

So. Graham Long *was* worthwhile, and not a bad bet, even if they got nothing else but this, while he was learning. A minor figure, in all appearances to others very minor, but she had learned to collect small arrows, no matter how insignificant. They had a way of turning. She was this high up in Organization's hierarchy for a reason.

She was not so foolish to believe that the cooperation would keep on at this level. His key was in the hospital. The minute it wasn't, the minute he had lost that back to Kaettegut, things would change. His was the type that would shoot itself in the foot. He had done other things, she would bet on it. He wasn't what they wanted on this side, alone.

But that was easy, and would have some political mileage of its own, too, for her. It would be very little trouble to have the hospital delay his friend's stay long enough to run some tests. He would suspect nothing except that they were testing his brain function, and it might not be so bad for him that they did.

She'd have to mention it to Chauncey only once; it would embed itself on its own, would rankle Chauncey to no end.

The additional rest would do his friend good. There would not be any inordinate stress in the testing. She glanced over her files, selected those tests she thought helpful and listed them. She had her favorites, of course, the ones she could interpret at a glance—read a series of numbers and letters, take it in combination with codes from other tests, and *know* a subject down to his most basic motives, what was most precious to him.

Some believed the human race to be vast and varied, unique; she knew better. At their basic design, there were only so many kinds.

This would be inexpensive in the large scheme of things. Both of them would be. Kaettegut had made itself important, and if others did not realize it yet, they would be knocking at her door soon enough. Quinn would want the data; Quinn would want to sit at the table with her folders and look knowledgeable, to hold back some and dole out little bits of the other.

Quinn might have information to ration out, and Quinn might not—from her.

5

Clare sat, now, had sat in the same chair, in the main room, since she had gotten over the worst, when she finally *could* sit up.

They had not recovered yet either—everyone, the people who walked past outside and lived in her district, and she still saw it in the media, when she could bring herself to turn on the television—but it had changed. In the beginning, it had been just horror, and the nurses and doctors had been careful with her. People had looked at her and their faces held conflict: the same horror, but sympathy, too, and it had been the only consolation she had.

Now—now it was all about *them*, the other had passed, and she and Ethan were just names, and Ethan—*Ethan*—an unfortunate mark in a quick, historic event. No longer human, no longer someone who had fully existed and passed them on the streets.

Now it was would *they* have enough food, was there enough in reserve to make up for the loss of the unit?

She should have been beside him. They had worked together for so long, had been the only two from Safety ever since the audits had begun, the way it usually was.

She had been next to Jenning instead. Behind. Ethan had gone forward to check something out, she could not know what, but that was normal, that was the way they worked. She *had* been looking to him, to see if it was an item worthy of their joint consultation. She had her comfort only in that. He had not—gone on alone, she had been with him, her focus had been with him. Someone who knew him, his soul, who cared.

She had used up all the moisture in her body when it had seemed her eyes would never run dry, the days running together. The recent past had lasted for years rather than weeks. Longer than all her time in Safety, when she had first met Ethan, when she had been that young. Seven years between her and that, now.

Even the apartment, this room—was an insult, foreign and empty: she had spent far more time at Ethan's place than hers, always had. His had been so much more convenient, and one could see the water from the windows, where it was still the bay and the river berms had not yet formed.

They weren't going to find the responsible party. She was not sure if that upset her or not. She *was* angry at who had done it, who had stolen everything from her; she would have choked away their life, precious to them—but there was no official announcement, and no focus. Regardless, that was not what mattered, what mattered was gone.

Jenning read through some of the individual questions, delayed looking at the codes of Graham Long's friend until she had milked the full value out of those things she needed.

There was an inordinate fondness for the familiar. It encompassed home, relationships—everything, perhaps, but his career. Kaettegut had done badly there, and that was telling in itself, to get that kind of rating from this kind of individual. They had only a certain number of openings, she would wager, pre-set needs, and did not have the flexibility to deal with that, with anomalies born of wrong ratios. She had expected more of them; worse, she had wrongly assumed they produced largely one kind.

Lord. An interesting study. She'd love to be handed Kaettegut in a textbook, a case study with everything laid out in black and white and the topic only academic, distant—not just across a narrow bay which was, in the north, all too easy to cross. On paper it was fascinating.

Home, and relationships—it did not appear he had many. They had tried to delve into that, but they were not expert test administrators, all they had given back was that the system did not accommodate it. Not necessarily *accommodate*, either—something they could not pinpoint, and *accommodate* was what they used. She could see that tendency in their notes, the mark of an amateur.

Well, that made her job easier. It wasn't what she expected to see, and was certainly not what Graham Long would want to see, she would speculate.

Graham was the one who would make the request. His scores for initiative she could guess to within a few degrees. That he had very few defense mechanisms against the limits of society, especially in Kaettegut, she would easily wager.

He did not. She almost forgot, she had so strongly anticipated it, and the request for the pass from the doctors a few days later startled her.

She was not wrong. She sat then at her desk and tried to figure it, and *that* was not without pleasure, but Transportation needed instructions, and there were things to do.

———

The pass came before dinner. The nurse sat it on the table in an envelope, set a small bag down beside it. "For you," she said, and smiled thinly, which was her way. Kellan didn't often have her; she seemed to be a substitute of some kind.

He waited until she left to open the envelope. It was not labeled, and not easy to open; when he did, there was a pass wrapped in a statement with his name on it, all his identifying information. *Gros Morne*, it said, and the date—tomorrow.

He read it again, and breathed. It did not change.

Finally, *God*, at last! He wanted to get up and pound the wall, expend his new energy. He swung his legs over, instead, and picked up the flimsy bag with his heart beating fast. It sagged with its burden, and *that* was his clothes—clothes from home, he did not know how. The fabric was strong and substantial to his fingers, almost not real, after everything here.

He didn't wait even to close the door of the bathroom. He hung the robe on the edge of the door, pulled everything on, and looked in the mirror. Even finger-combing his hair it still hung in his eyes, but by God, he *recognized* himself. Normal, not injured, not a patient stuck in a room. Shoes, too—not barefoot anymore, warm.

When Graham came, he was waiting. In the chair. He held up the envelope, smiled to see the reaction on Graham's face. He had folded up the robe and put it in the bag, tied carefully; he was taking that with him.

"I got it," he said, and handed Graham the pass. He could not keep his face straight. "Going home."

Graham's mouth was set: strange. He had expected much more. "Are you okay?" he asked—stood up, offered him the chair. "Sit down."

Graham stood there, finally gestured to the chair. "No, no, you take it," he said, and that, stiffly; he sat on the bed, and gestured to the chair again. A smile, not natural. "That's great."

He was working too hard at it. Nothing was natural in his movements. Kellan stood there, finally sat back down, and looked up at him. Waited, his heart beating too fast. *God, what*— Graham wasn't meeting his eyes. "What's wrong?"

Graham just smiled, looked away.

"Where's your pass?" he asked, then, because it came to him suddenly that Graham was not participating, there was no—sharing involved. "You have one."

"You're well," Graham said, and tried looking back at him, and smiled again. Too wide, this time. "God, look at you!"

"Stop it!" He had the arm of the chair in a death grip; his knuckles were standing out. What to say—what *was* this? "Where's your *pass?*"

Graham opened his mouth. Closed it. Shook his head. "I transferred."

"What?" Only it came out weak, when it had felt like it had burst from his lungs. The chair no longer mattered, there was no comfort in gripping the armrests harder. He shook his head to clear it. "No, you didn't. God damn it, Graham, don't mess with me!"

"It's not that big a deal."

"You're working in renovations. That's what you want me to believe? You *transferred.*"

"Things were a little—strange. The explosion. It's changing a lot of things."

"And they're taking transfers, now?" He was on his feet before he knew he was, could hardly feel the floor, and then he was next to the wall. He hit it, as hard as he could. "Damn it, Graham! Don't *mess* with me!"

There were two nurses in the doorway. They wanted to know what was going on; *he* could hear nothing, there was just a buzzing in his ears, and Graham had his palms up, was trying to talk to them, to calm things down, to keep them back. They didn't, and one had his arm in both hands, then, and they were calling someone. Did he want that? Was he going to calm down or not?

"Graham, damn it!" He threw the nurse's hands off, and then there was another one, a man, in what seemed like only seconds. He filled the doorway almost, huge, his clothing very white next to his skin.

"Can I talk with you outside?" Graham asked, very politely, to the other nurse, the dark one.

The new nurse was nothing. He threw *his* hands off, tried to make it past, but Graham and the other nurse were gone. "Graham! Don't—" The chair back hit him, hard, and the man was leaning over him, breathing fast, and not pleased.

He waited. He was shaking. He looked at his arm on the armrest, under the grip of the nurse, and *it* was shaking. He pulled it and his other arm back, slowly, looking at the nurse, and the nurse permitted it, and he crossed his arms hard against his chest and did not look up again.

Graham would come back in. He had just asked to speak with the other nurse, that was all; they had just stepped into the hall. He waited, and his heart was racing, dangerously.

The new nurse sat back on the bed. He could feel his eyes on him.

It took too long. He still waited, and now he had gone cold, and was shivering with that. The nurse had gone over to stand by the doorway; he didn't move, himself.

The other nurse, the one with the thin lips, finally came back. The newer one permitted it, stayed there and watched. Kellan looked at her, and stayed where *he* was. "Can I talk with the other nurse?" he said, as calm as he could, and his voice was hoarse; he cleared his throat, and when she looked at him dumbly— "The one talking to

Graham."

An odd look. "She went off her shift a *long* time ago."

She might have hit him in the stomach. He stood up without feeling it, stood there looking down at her, and she only said, in a voice as if she were speaking to a child, "Are you done with all this? Or you still need us?"

He could not think. He only shook his head. She left, the male nurse too, and the door closed behind them. Clicked.

He went over to the envelope, took the pass out and sat down with it crumpled in his fists, rested his knuckles against his forehead. His head was pounding.

There was a thought, cold. To the bone. They hadn't let them have visitors from home. The way they didn't let them have travel visas but in tiny numbers, and only occasionally. Things that Graham had said back home, that the administrator had once even implied, on television—Jeffersonian distaste. They didn't rub shoulders.

Oh, God. What could he do, what could he *do*?

The matter, of course, came straight up to her nearly first thing in the morning. Her staff knew to forward it without overmuch delay.

Raining outside, damned nuisance: the public vehicles' rain guards were flimsy and rain got inside anyway, and had this morning. Her left leg was still damp up to her hip. She did not want to go back out into it. One look out the window told her it was drizzling, now—better, but not ideal.

"Call a vehicle," Jenning said over the intercom to Gabrielle, her most personal staff member, the only one she entrusted to *that* duty. "I'm going to the hospital. Have Orlando take a trip down, too, when he has a minute. Main lobby."

So it came from a different quarter. She had begun to wonder, had half thought she'd be dealing with Chauncey on this one, and that would have changed the game considerably.

She hobbled down to the lobby, and there was Gabrielle, with her umbrella at the ready, and a blanket for good measure. "You're still covered?" Gabrielle asked, and she had a bag over her shoulder; doubtless it contained more wrap if she needed it.

Her injured leg, of course, Gabrielle meant. The bandages could not get wet. She hadn't had time to unwrap, regardless, not yet. "I'm fine," she said, and Gabrielle gave her a look from beneath her eyebrows, but she would not push it.

The leg was getting worse. When the nurse came to change her bandages, the lacerations were thickening, reddening, swelling. The doctors wanted—something she would not give. She would *not* walk into public with a piece of leg that was not hers; it would be a visible sign to those who had done it, and to those she would not lend any satisfaction.

The ride to the hospital was jarring, but the blanket served its purpose—though she hated to be seen riding this way, a blanket over her lap like a damned convalescent. The hospital had a portico, thank goodness, better than her own building had, and she was out without any help from the driver, thank you, and hobbling into the exterior elevator with its thick metal doors: one small mark of truth, she knew now that she'd had her own extended stay.

There was the same bright hallway on every floor. She had to use her cane—not that she would rather not, if only to spite the doctors—and finally, as far from the elevators as almost they could put him, came to the room.

The same white walls as hers. No one got better treatment here. Graham Long's friend was sitting in the chair, its back to her—she presumed they had given her the correct room number—had turned at the sound. He stood. "Ma'am," he said, and his face was not its natural color, that was easy enough to see.

At least he had some manners. Large as life, a young man in weekend clothes, and really—a face unexpectedly with some merit, some aesthetic value. The stress marred it some, pulled his skin tight and dried the pores, but the basics were there.

She might as well have been the hospital administrator. It was clear he did not know who he addressed. "You're running a risk," she said—and he was; a brain injury, and this on top of it, could get him relegated to neurology, and those cases did not fare well. She leaned heavily on her cane.

His eyes went to the left, then back to her.

She might have laughed. That *this* one was capable of talking any game to this hospital staff—implausible, she would have judged, but it had made it up to her level, and so he had convinced someone high enough to have that kind of priority, or someone with influence with such an individual. They should have seen through it. He *thought* he was under severe pressure; he was not.

Some training was due. They showed themselves poorly.

Ah, well. She rubbed her hands; the rain and humidity had swelled the joints. "Well?" she said, and put a sharp tinge on it, and waited.

"Are you—? I need to talk with someone who—"

He had that guttural pronunciation they all had over there, that made her recoil. An association, unwilling, from all the damned audits. "You can start with me."

A pause. "I need... I can't go back. A transfer."

He didn't know what he was talking about, plain and simple. A transfer, indeed. "You and a hundred other applications we get in a year," she said. That might have been stretching it, but it *was* the intent, after all, behind those she had seen. "What makes you deserve it more than them?"

He looked to the left again, wet his lips, looked back and tried to meet her eyes, and failed. "I'm already here."

Better, he meant it. She allowed herself a laugh, at that. A second one. *Ah,* that was nice. Open the lungs a little.

The emotions were going across his face one at a time—insult, hope. Completely untrained: a small pleasure, easy, on a rainy day. She made her way over to the end of the bed, leaned against it, and pointed to the chair. "Sit." And when he had: "Why don't you tell me *why* you want to stay. —And don't waste my time. There's a hauler leaving in a half hour. I can have you at the dock by then."

He looked faint, at that; tried to recover, licked his lips. "I have a good friend here." He looked at her, and when nothing happened: "He transferred here, to help *me.* I was in the accident, I didn't have any—"

"Did you ask him to come?"

"No!"

"Then he did it. Let him work it out himself."

Nothing verbal in response. He sat there, appalled, and stared at her. Opened his mouth, closed it, opened it again. Finally, "I don't know—"

"Maybe this was just a good opportunity for him. There *are* a lot of people who want to come over here. It's not only the renovation folks, you know. We do have other transfers from time to time, though they're very rare." Emphasis on that, for him. "Usually artisans, but he's useful, a pricing liaison. We were short one in that office."

Another lick of the lips. He started to shake his head but stopped. Hesitantly: "They say you don't like us."

Ah. That showed some sophistication. "Who says that?"

"Why didn't you let us have visitors? Why did he have to get a *transfer* to come over?"

She laughed, very dryly. "*I* wasn't allowed to have visitors." Which was true, at first.

That was a setback. He looked at her again. "You were in the accident?"

"That's how they refer to it around here, isn't it. Yes."

He looked at her a good, long while. He had lost some of his posture; his shoulders went forward, as though his stomach pained him. Still, he was thinking: his eyes went out of focus, went to the side. Finally: "You have a need for artisans?"

"I said we transfer them occasionally."

"I can work with the renovation crews. I like working with—with my hands, I can learn fast."

He was speeding back up; she had gained nothing, he had gone back to square one, dropped all the facts and implications that were not convenient. Typical, all the more disappointing in someone who had shown a glimmer of logic.

"Slow down. We're not talking about renovation crews. We're not talking about you staying."

"You said I've only got a half hour. Listen. I know I can do it."

Ah. Still, she tightened her gaze on him, made it less than patient. "I told you not to waste my time. What do you think? I've got to look at supply and demand. I don't have time for someone to apprentice an office worker in a line of work like that, even if I were inclined to consider your request—which I'm not, because you've given me no reason to, and I don't think you're going to."

A breath. "I can do whatever you need me to, to stay. Or send him back too."

That simple. *Hell.* His tests hadn't shown anything like this.

"Why don't you ask your government why you didn't have any visitors? It wasn't just me. They didn't ask."

That one found its mark. There was doubt, sudden, in his eyes, and as immediate, a struggle to stay focused, to ignore it. More than that, though, in the tension in his muscles, his nerves—corollary information, even that little bit, was too much. A mistake, on her part. His immediate need simply eclipsed all else. For his doggedness, he was not equipped for this.

Still—give him credit, it was more than a renovation laborer would have done, and she had heard stories of them. *Those* started and ended with shouting, mindless. She did not need any hysterics—this was enough, and there was much more at the office that called for her attention.

Perhaps a slight facilitation, even if she was out of practice—she had time enough for that, and it could prove useful, down the road. Help and hinder, both, if she did it right, and that would leave her the most options.

"You and I have much in common, you know." He had hardly enough focus to look surprised at that, but there *was* a thread. "The explosion. —Do you remember it?"

He had clenched his hands, wanted, clearly, to go back to the topic at hand. Still, he shook his head.

"It was different than you might think." She modulated her voice, the pace of her speech; this had been one of her best techniques. Somewhat of a legend: she had been able to cast a spell, back then. "You know what I remember most?" And when he only looked: "Silence. Just *silence*. You know, it's strange, how something so terrible can have its own beauty. It rescues you—when you think of it, you think of beauty, instead of pain. There was nothing painful about the event itself for you, was there? You don't remember any?"

He shook his head.

Details would be unspeakably precious, even just one or two. "The only light was from the curve in the tunnel back behind us, that far away. I could see it from where I was, and it was white, that far over there, and quiet, and perfect." She paced her voice a bit slower yet, could afford it. "There was dust in the air, like powder. Do you remember? The limestone had turned to dust, and it was falling like fog. So slowly—you could hardly see the movement. Where it settled, where it touched you, it was cool. It made you think it wasn't real."

He was seeing it: his eyes had already begun to turn. He *wanted* to know; this was something he did not have, and he sat still for it, let the rest go, for a minute, for this. He would *not* get it again, not from anyone, not from anyone with her skill, certainly.

Any story, any imagination worth having... The mind could heal itself, more simply than anyone would admit. Point of view. Nothing more, sometimes.

Could harm itself, too. "*You* were there. Yes, I could see you, when the dust had fallen enough. We were all white with it. There was a man, too, a tech, I think, and the way each of you had fallen—I couldn't see him as well with you there, you understand; you covered part of him. Natural as if you were sleeping. Both of you were still and quiet—I could see you breathing, and see the equipment had come apart, and had gone through him before he knew it."

He was not breathing, just listening. All his attention, eyebrows drawing in.

"He hadn't even known, I'll bet. Just working, for him; a tour for you and me. We weren't too different, you and I, not then. None of us were." It was not untrue, in the very grand scheme of things; she could grant the dead that.

She stopped. A time to breathe, for him, to let the room come back, the walls. For herself, too, if she allowed herself to sink into her own memory—but she did not, not on any more than a superficial level, where it was comfortable. *Careful...* a needed reminder when she had not tried a facilitation on an experience where she had been personally involved.

"You see?" She leaned forward, touched one hand with a finger. "You see?"

He just looked at her. She smiled, drew back her hand.

"Please," he said, simply, finally, and looked at her. He *was* struggling. "Let him come back with me."

Damn. But he was still in that facilitation, was struggling to pull himself out of the memory and get back to where he had been, to this. More central to him, then, than she would have thought.

She shook her head. "We need him. He has a job here. It might be something good for him. Think of him, what he wants. Do you really know him?"

"I won't interfere."

She sat back, contemplated him for a good deal longer than she preferred: she was done, this was the way she had always been. A quick end to the interview, ostensibly for the subject, when that kind of illusion was necessary. "I'll make some calls." And, a neat wrap-up, a way for it to linger, for him: "You've seen, now. Remember."

The way he was, some of this would no doubt help. The rest— would ensure that if there *was* an anomaly in his friend's lack of initiative, it might not be there now.

Orlando would be in the lobby. She really shouldn't give him, in that condition, to him. A little more time alone would not hurt. He'd be out in plenty of time, the workday would have ended. A sedative, perhaps. She made the note in the elevator, dropped it by the nurse's station on the main floor, held up her hand. "Orlando." He looked up, sitting in a lobby chair.

When they came through the exterior doors the rain had stopped; there were only puddles.

6

The videoconference equipment worked now. Jefferson had found it convenient to have a working unit there to link to, and so found the means to repair it.

Chauncey grimaced when word of the call came in. Rene came to tell her, and brought a cup of tea into the conference room to ease the nuisance of it. "Thank you," she said to him, and faced into the camera, and Jenning's face on the screen. Jenning, who must have recovered, from the looks of it—to whom Jefferson had turned, no doubt thinking Jenning was a familiar entity.

Jefferson felt the pressure, and turned and applied it outside itself. *That* had been its answer, so far, not much to inspire faith in the system. "We still have crews working on most of the sections," Chauncey said, and kept nothing out of her voice she did not feel. "Good God, Jenning, I've had to pull techs from eight sections down. We're repairing the damage on top of maintaining everything else. I don't have the staff for this."

"It's been enough time. Every unit needs to be operating."

"That may be, but we don't know what may trigger another explosion, if there's more like that in the wiring. Damn it, Jenning, we lost our staff in there too."

"You're not permitting your own hydroponics staff in there." Her face didn't change.

This was touchy: Jefferson *might* be using Jenning as a familiar contact, but this was audit territory, and Jenning knew the layout better than anyone else they could get. Jenning, count on it, would be aware of it, would be looking for a slip in the heat of an emergency, a slip she would certainly bring up later, when it seemed to have been all but forgotten. *That* was Jenning's way. Odious woman. "They're getting into three of the major storage units. Those have been cleared. That's enough to get us through until we can make a determination."

"And food production?" A little rise in the voice, careful. "You think there's not still panic? People are going about their daily lives, yes, but it's a thread. If they knew we were talking about three *units*, we'd be talking riots now. You know that."

"There will be enough. We're talking about safety. They're still playing footage of the burn victims, Jenning! *You* send your staff in with that kind of ammunition hanging over your head—you wouldn't, and you won't. You know as well as I do that Jefferson won't take another incident. You want to talk about riots?"

"We *need* everything reopened, Chauncey. We've got our own issues in our districts, all the way through to the Back. That's our answer."

"Then find out who *did it*. Release that." There were times when even a videoconference was just damned inconvenient. "You know, don't you? You already have your results."

A bark of a laugh—enough to close the eyes, to give a second's worth of recovery—but that was all it gained. *Damned* woman. "Your people could have done it most easily. They had the access. You say nothing shows on the recordings. And the timing—your people don't like the audits, do they?"

She was long past reaction to that sort of tactic. "Then say so."

A long minute. Jenning took the opportunity to talk with one of her own staff, someone off screen—that was a good sign, more of a reaction than the first, if it took turning away.

But for an instant she had the stomach-lurching certainty, too, that she had hit something she did not want, something Jenning knew—but there was already a nerve there, she might have hit it instead. Jefferson could not release information of that kind, after all, even if it were true. They worried about riots: let the threat come from within Kaettegut, within the source. *Oh, God*, let it be external. *Not* Kaettengutan. It would tear up what had—

Jenning was facing her again on the screen. "Your last patient isn't returning."

Christ. She was off-center in another direction, now. Her hand went to her tea.

Think. On life support, then, or worse. The last one. She had needed that last patient, had been waiting for it, did not want the public relations fiasco something like a death meant. The last *one.* She framed the word carefully. "Why?"

Jenning shrugged, took a sip from her own cup. Black ceramic, typical. "He asked not to return."

She took a breath. *Good God. Rene—* she needed the files. Bluffing? Jenning would not hesitate, not at this level. She would know she could verify it, a matter of time. "I see. And you didn't solicit that."

"I have two nurses who say it was unsolicited."

"This is his citizenship. He has a post here. I'm not going to permit this."

"The hospital did some extensive testing—scans, a battery of cognitive tests. I can tell you the injury wasn't a factor." That, a last little twist.

Petty, and she still took pleasure in it.

Rene was at the door. She glanced over, and he had a note in his hand, held it up. *Fifty.*

Damn, and damn. No time to review the files, the topic would have to wait until later. Fifty was a hard one to reach. He made calls, did not take them. "I have another call," she said to Jenning. "Councilor Fifty. He's aware of this, I take it?"

Point scored, from the flitting of an expression across Jenning's face. Small comfort... She disconnected the line. "Rene, pull up the files on the last one we have over there. Have the staff go over it."

He looked at her. "Priority?"

"He asked to stay over there." Not so surprising, really. Plenty wanted the additional comforts Prime offered. That someone would take advantage of this situation to do it—that was.

But that was Jenning, pushing her damned buttons, and this was Councilor Fifty, and she needed her wits about her.

She clicked acceptance of the waiting call, heard the door close behind her. Rene would handle that, and well, without any leaks. One sentence was all she had to say, after this many years of working with him. A Vessup, an untraditional choice, and one of the better decisions she had made. "Councilor," she said.

"Ms. Benner," he said. Coming from him, it could come across as a slight. *He* was never anything but Councilor Fifty.

He did not consider the minor councils of much importance, simply that, and inclusion on the Ligotera was all that was permitted to Kaettegut. Agriculture was officially under Environment, never mind that she oversaw six major departments, two under what Environment, the largest division, itself oversaw. He continued, "I understand repairs have been progressing."

A completely different tone. She guarded herself against that: despite the arrogance, Fifty had a way of taking one off guard, of relaxing a person. The undefended might well put their trust in him in an instant's time. He had won his position on votes for over a decade counting, and she could certainly see it: some handshaking, an offer of help whenever they needed it—effortless, though she judged him the type to come through for an individual constituent, if only for the public relations value. Or perhaps—the ego value.

Regardless, not a man of subtlety. For every consecutive term he had chosen Stefan Coubertin as one of his two peer delegates—from Ethics, a heavy-handed message since Ethics was already represented in the lower councils. She knew that much.

"They have," she answered. "Slowly but steadily. The staff has been doing admirably here." The first time she had spoken with him, she had not done well. She cringed to think of it. Consummate professional, or some kind of good/bad routine he and Jefferson were running, although she very much doubted *that*, the representatives she had spoken with, she suspected, were at far too low a level to attract Fifty's notice.

"I'm sure they have been," he said. "I'm certain you won't mind passing on my respect to them. Truly remarkable the way everyone has come together, isn't it? No one has any experience with this, but this is the kind of thing we're seeing. The medical staff over here have been particularly impressive. They don't often see this level of thing, you know."

"Hopefully not."

"They really came together. I know you're as proud of your own." He rubbed his nose, appeared to suppress a cough. "I'm afraid, Ms. Benner, I called only to assure you again of our support, and to offer you our resources should you need it. I understand your wish to control your own facility, but please, if you're short-handed, permit us to send just one or two people over. We have specialists in areas that might translate well to this sort of thing."

"I think we're doing fine. We have enough storage units up to more than ensure continuity. It buys us enough time to thoroughly check the other areas—which I know you'd want." She winced inwardly on the last, but Fifty played this way, which meant she did, too.

A nod of approval. "That's absolutely right. Take your time. Just let us know if you need any assistance, and I'll have someone to your specifications over on the next ship."

"Thank you."

He gave a final nod, and the screen went blank. She leaned back in her chair, swiveled to see the door open and Rene coming in. "Good Lord. I don't know which one is worse."

"How'd it go?"

"Fine. He's ridiculous." He'd be putting the pressure on his staff to get someone over here *now*, she'd bet, to worm their fingers into every nook and cranny they could find, and their arrogance coming across full bore.

Stefan combed the report, always did. The students habitually made a summary for him, spelled things out in simple bullet points and the ever-present definition footnotes for even the basic terms—*telomerase, senescence,* but he did not need it. He had started out learning the definitions with simple order and determination, had assembled a custom medical dictionary on his home computer, largely unnecessary to him by this time.

In reality, of course, it was only another lingo, far more specific than ordinary language, yes, but still only jargon. They liked to hold the market through that just as other professions did, their secret key card.

Funny how humanity was, how cliquish, how self-protective. Against another intelligent species, it would make a fine defense. It made divisions, now. Divisions made possible what he did, though: everything could be made useful, no matter the design.

He could be more patient than the others on the council. Fifty's position was secure and with it, his almost equally so. For now. He had other irons in the fire to that end, but for the time being he had played his part to Fifty's ends, to that design.

A single human being could matter. Not always in the way of a Loren Fifty, whose self-protectiveness and ego successfully masqueraded as rhetoric, but one could matter.

To others, perhaps, the entire history of Nocturne followed a straight line, more and more advanced. It was *not* a line. It was a dot. They had not advanced, they had not fallen back. That would have been saying much, except that Prime had not started in such a lofty position as was taught in the schools. Excellent ideals, of course, but the reality was they had in-fought, in-bred.

The report in his hands showed that the medical students had made a small progress. Ironic, really, that they did so well—the fountain of youth, and the young were the ones making strides.

The more radical and very long-term arm of his project had dabblings in human tumor cells: another small alliance, this one from those who were earmarked as probable candidates for the Science department, itself a stepchild of its division, where only the immediately practical was well-regarded and there was not enough patience for pure theory. Medical staff did not ordinarily deal well with the kind of mind-leap it took to create what they fought against in the field.

Slow progress was fine. He saw that they were funded where it was not expected, merely that. He could not keep major news from bursting. Small steps were exactly what he wanted, and consequently he kept the funding to those levels. Care could do a great deal.

He folded the report into his attache case, locked it.

Graham could not work. He had been an idiot to think he could. He sat at the desk with the pricing readouts they had given him on his screen, and could not do even the simple formulas. He lost the thread on the second or third step even on the simple ones.

He rubbed his forehead, his scalp, and that didn't help things. He looked like hell; he knew it, they had looked at him when he came in and *they* were no experts at hiding their thoughts.

He was unfamiliar with the layout and the services of town, still. He knew only the way to the hospital and what was along that route, did not know if the restaurants served anything like liquor here, where even to buy it, where the stores were located. He had eaten at the hospital every night.

God. What did he think, living with Kellan?

Kellan did not know how he felt, had no idea. He had a fair idea what Kellan would think if he found out. No, better this way: he had known he would not say it, that he could not, or he would lose what he did have. Just—it was frustrating, more so with time passing, was getting more *physical,* and he perhaps did not want to go any longer.

With this happening... he *could* get out, memory pristine and unruined, and move on. He'd not make this mistake again, would eventually find one who wouldn't mind.

—Who wouldn't be Kellan, would not be anything close to Kellan.

Five o'clock came, and he had gotten only a small pile done, the simple ones. He was embarrassed. He pushed them all far back into the inbox without organizing them. He hoped they were right, at least, the few he had done. Ordinarily he'd never have any doubt, but he looked back on the day and instead of a series of clear equations and logic, there was muddle, all that his mind had produced.

It was simple. He had trained his mind to do it, to appreciate it. Numbers. Logic. Theory. It got him through, most days.

He pulled his jacket from the chair, put it on, and fumbled even the sleeve. Here it was colder, maybe due to the humidity of the water so close. This office was not far from the port, he could see the water from the windows along the wall near the stairs.

He stopped by the windows today, let others go by behind him. From here he could not hear the bay, the waves. The dock did not reflect in it, too dark; the seawall, the land, everything was black where there were not streetlights. He watched the small chop breaking against the dock's side, a small, shivery line of white.

He took the shuttle back to the residential district. He had begun to get used to its awkward configuration, the benches pointing forward and to the side and to the back, the roof that did not keep out rain if a person sat on the wrong side. Gloomy out, now, heavy and slate-colored clouds hanging low in the east, and the smell of rain lingering. The whiteness of the shuttle car jolting along in front of his was brightened against it; the light in the roof of the driver's car far ahead was blinding if he looked at it. He looked out at the dark instead.

They had given him fairly nice quarters. He had equivalized it in his mind, knew not to react wrongly because on Kaettegut there would never be something this nice: he did not need to be too impressed. For here, it was by no means the best, and in one of the lesser districts close to the warehousing peninsula.

He got out at the stop there, when he was not accustomed to do that, and that was depressing in itself. He took one step, and turned around and got back on before the shuttle started up again, while others were still getting off. The majority would get off at the next stop, he knew that from experience. The better area, he had supposed, from looking at the houses from the shuttle every night before, the streets were better lit, and there was more detail, even latticework on a balcony here or there. More levels to each building. Same smooth walls as his, though, with rainspouts that worked—they all worked here. All the houses had shutters here, too, against the storms; he had looked at his and they did look like they would work, even if the latches had been painted many times over, symptomatic of their age.

"Where do you find stores for food here?" he asked the person on the bench behind his, facing the opposite direction, because he was closest. *No*— "Where do you drink?"

The man turned, looked at him, put his arm up on the bench back so that they faced each other. Some surprise, but they all had that: his face was not familiar to them, and there was the accent; he knew where he stood, had figured that since he put in the application. "Everything's in the north section," the man said. "Not the next stop, the *next* one. That's all the businesses."

"Where the restaurants are."

A nod, encouragement, though it wasn't confident because of what he had asked. "Thanks," he said, and the man turned back to face the other direction.

He got off at the correct stop, and wished then that he had stopped back at the house to get his heavier coat. He had purchased both when he had picked up the robe for Kellan, his only expedition into this district, and not far in. They dressed a little differently here— he would need to come back again, had been putting it off. A little bit of denial.

It had rained earlier; the puddles seeped into his shoes and made the air colder. He walked, anyway, blocks' worth of restaurants and retail establishments with the gold of their interior lighting drizzling onto the wetness of the pavement outside.

He found a grocery at last, when his feet had grown sore. Small, with an awning, and in a part of the district that had begun to get closer to the residential district, and less well-lit. He went inside, knocked his shoes against the mat, and looked around. Tight shelving, florescent tube lighting that hurt his eyes after so long outside; one of them was blinking, and that was worse.

There were a great deal of spices. Many empty spaces: he supposed they were conserving because of what had been on the news, the talk about still-unopened storage units in Gros Morne. He found some canned oysters and picked up a stack of those. "Your drinks," he said to the store manager.

"In the back."

He was the only one in the store. He went to the back and there was a small section, less than one shelving unit, but it had distilled stuff, it would do the job. The prices were amazing; he had paid double for some of the same drinks in Rue. He got some cheap soju— cheap even by these standards, but a big bottle.

The street lights had dimmed by the time he got home, after a long stop by the river, and no one had bothered him; he had sat on the bank where it sloped, with the bottle open and welcome. Now, he suddenly could not *wait* to open the canned oysters, was past hungry. He got in the door, sat on the stairs next to the downstairs neighbors' door and peeled back the top, and scooped them out with his fingers. The oil ran down and made a mess and he did not care; that was the benefit of liquor, if he let himself feel it. He didn't feel soaked, either. His feet were wet, but he could only tell if he looked.

He unlocked the door at the top of the stairs and let himself into the main room. Dark, and that was fine. He left the lights off and went for the sofa that badly needed upholstering. Antique nothing; it *smelled* bad, but it was as good as anything else now. Kellan would have looked at its frame and been astonished that the trim was real wood, the way he had been awed at the hotel in Gros Morne.

There was someone *there*. He picked it up only after he had slumped down on the sofa, careless.

The voice was familiar, even so. "You're late, aren't you?"

"What are you doing here?" He made it as flat, closed his eyes, shook his head.

"I got a transfer."

Okay. He could clear some of the liquor's effects, practice, and then he was cold, and damp again. Kellan was over by the window, sitting on the *floor*, for Christ's sake. He could see silhouette and dim street light shining in through hair that was way too long now, and dried wrong.

This was not happening. "How did you get here?" he said.

A long silence. Then, almost offended: "I'm glad to see *you*."

"Damn it!" He was across the room and hitting the light switch, and the room was too bright; it hurt behind his eyes, but he didn't stop. He had Kellan by the shoulders, wanted to shake him, hard— could not, not with his injury. He stopped himself in time. "What did you *do?*"

There was no resistance. Kellan looked at him.

"Where are you supposed to be? *Damn* it!"

"Here."

Too flat, still. He looked again: Kellan was drugged with something, that had to be it, and if that were so, how he could have made it this far did not make sense. Just—trouble. He leaned back, softened his voice. "Tell me what happened."

"I talked with a woman." Kellan looked out the window, still, and his enunciation *was* a little off. Finally: "God, she tore me up."

"What?"

"She made it so I could stay. She said she'd make some calls."

His thoughts went in too many directions. "Who? What was her name?"

"She didn't say." And when there was only silence, an offering: "She had that kind of authority, that's all."

"Kellan." He knelt there on his level, and did not know what direction to take, what to do. Neither of them at full capacity, and Kellan could *not* be here legitimately. —But nothing could happen before morning, could it? He could think then, he would have resources tomorrow, at the office. An organizational chart of some sort, the work database. "Listen. Why don't you get some sleep? There's a bed in there, I can—"

"I've been sleeping all day. Some kind of sedative. My sleep cycle is way off." Kellan looked back, more directly this time. "You do this every night, here? Drink like this?"

"No." He stood up, backed off; he probably smelled terrible, of canned oyster oil. He could taste his own breath.

"All right. I'll take the sofa, though."

He went and got some blankets, without any more presence of mind. He had one replacement set in the closet. No extra pillow. He got it ready, and Kellan stood up, dutifully, and in the full light of the street lamp he did not look good. No color to his skin, and his hair clumped together in cords, just hanging there. The room was cold; he had not kept the heater on, since only he had been sleeping there, and not much. He did not know the policies here on electricity or where the thermostat was, had figured he could find out later.

Lord. A fine mess. Too much alcohol in his own blood, Kellan still coming off some kind of sedative—but he felt a buzzing in his veins that was not the type that alcohol produced.

He went and got the blanket and pillow from his bed. Kellan would not know.

In the morning he woke up shivering, and he still had his jacket on, all his clothes. No pillow, just his wadded up coat. He groaned, crawled out of bed—remembered.

In the main room the window shade was still open, and Kellan *was* there, asleep on the sofa, the blanket almost over his head.

7

Another damned meeting, and this time Quinn could not see the reason for it. Not regularly scheduled, though granted, few of the others had been in the past several weeks—but this one Loren had called, short notice, when he had not called a meeting since the one immediately following the Gros Morne incident, impeccable timing on that one, impeccable concern, even a touch of alarm. Rather fiery rhetoric for the public, of course, afterward, but Loren's truer reactions he showed to the council.

True*r*. Not true.

Jeri Tasco sat two chairs down and across the table, bookended by Andrew and Stefan, and favoring as usual a slight shift away from Andrew, in the angle of her chair. Blank expression today; she looked to Quinn, gave the merest hint of a lift of her left shoulder—a shrug.

Jeri had not been able to find out the purpose of the meeting, then, either.

And there was Loren—the usual entrance; he had stopped inside the doorway this time, was directing one of his aides regarding a cup of coffee— Moira, in her usual brown, the gentlest of Loren's immediate aides and third in line because of it. She brought the coffee a few minutes later, slipped the cup and saucer onto the table in front of Loren and faded to a chair adjacent to the cabinetry along the inside wall.

She would take the minutes, then, not Gwen or Tevin, who usually did it.

Loren slid the saucer closer, surrounded it with cupped fingers, and for a moment she worried he would taste the coffee, drink it, swallow it, while they all waited—but he straightened his shoulders, instead, looked down the table, each side in turn. Quickly, this time: he meant business, evidently.

"I won't spend time on courtesies," he said. "Something that has not been said in the immediate crisis, but is become starkly apparent—and I know it has occurred to all of you—is our dependence on the current system. In an area our size, in our situation, districting has been efficient. When it comes to agriculture, districting originally gave us the best and most efficient use of our personnel and energy resources." He lifted a finger. "Originally."

Oh, my God. He was going ahead with it, then, had changed his mind and decided to push through, now that there was space enough between them and the botching. Damned discourteous, of course, that he could not have told her beforehand, that he would begin it on his own, but it was something, damn, it was something!

"Something like this—shines a light on the weaknesses in our system," he said. "More than one significant weakness, I'm sure, no matter how much we try to plan, but agriculture is *not* an area where we can afford a vulnerability. Taking into account the need to find more raw resources in the Back, perhaps what we've got isn't the most efficient any longer." He lifted the cup, finally, with two fingers crooked around the handle, took it to his lips but did not drink—only looked over the rim, then set it down. "It doesn't take a crisis like this to point it out, of course. Here's where I'm not going to offer any pleasantries. I know some of you aren't going to like it. It *has* taken a crisis like this to point out the need to the public, and if we're smart we can turn even a tragedy into something that will move us forward. And when I say *us*, I mean the population under our care."

She leaned forward, intertwined her fingers on the surface of the table, and listened.

"We have the start of a contingency plan, at the least. I had not brought it to the attention of the council because we did not have a sufficient success rate. This has been purely in the scope of Environment, at this point, with the cooperation of one other division."

She consciously did not straighten, did not change her position. *What the hell—*

"A few years ago we set up, purely as an early departmental exper-

iment, a handful of small agricultural stations. Outside Kaettegut."
He nodded to his left, toward *Decheran*, she realized with a shock.
"They're right outside the dock area in the manufacturing sector."

A murmuring began and rose in a wave down the table. She looked
across to Jeri, to an expression as jolted as her own.

Loren lifted a hand. "We also set up an experimental program—
cultivation of cold-water fish grown in open water, rather than in
hatcheries, in the mining sector. We haven't—"

She sat still, did not look at Jeri any longer, looked instead at the
surface of the table, the smooth, polished wood. Could see, barely,
the reflection of light on it, beside her hands.

God *damn* him. This was why; *this* was what he had been doing,
this smacked of expansionism. He had fed her into his own damned
plans, and she had played right into it.

She stood. Straight spine, very carefully controlled—picked
up her folder, still unopened, swung the chair back away with her
other hand, and stepped away from the table. She heard, behind her,
Loren's voice say, "Councilor," and saw Moira before she reached out
and opened the door, and Moira's face was a mask of genuine distress.
She turned her head, just slightly, and in the corner of her eye caught
Jeri standing at the table, picking up her own things, sliding a pen into
her own folder.

She took a risk with this, something she could not repay later.
She felt nothing, merely a coldness inside her chest, moving up her
throat. There was Adrienne, in the hallway, coming out from the
aides' room; she handed the folder to her for safekeeping—she would
not go back to the office, not where Loren could reach her easily—and
kept walking. "Councilor," Adrienne said, and pointed back along the
hallway with her eyes.

She almost kept going. She turned at the last second, and Jeri was
by the doorway to the council room, was holding the door open, with
Joseph beside her, and Kate Daschen came through.

A chill rose up her spine, branched out at the shoulders, tingled
at the roots of her hair. She stopped, and Kate looked directly at her,
nodded, and walked down the hallway the opposite way. Jeri still held
the door; she turned back, and Adrienne fell into step with her this
time. "Tell me who else comes out," she said, sideways, to Adrienne,
and Adrienne paused at the top of the stairs while she continued.

She did not know where she was going. Home, she supposed, perhaps to a restaurant, no matter that it was mid-afternoon and they might not be serving, and there would be observers.

Adrienne caught up with her in the lobby. "Avery and Marcus," she said, simply.

The status quo and all of the resourcists, then, save Decheran. Of *course* not Decheran, who had those stations and that experiment in her territory, but even with Decheran the rest did not have a quorum—irrelevant now, because there was no vote meaningful, the action had already been taken. A walkout, on the other hand, was rare, would be reported in the media for weeks whenever the issue was discussed—and it would be, it would be announced to the public with much fanfare by one Loren Fifty, whether he had her support or not. He had timed it this way: the public would support it wholeheartedly, after the Gros Morne crisis—and she had *played into his hands*, damn it!

The gain, for him, had evidently been large enough for a betrayal of this scale. *She* had no recourse, of course, beyond the standard party line, and he had known it.

He could have worked with her, could have brokered a deal to let those stations stand—though she would not have accepted it. Not *that*. On the Back's land—that was the slippery slope leading directly to expansionism, out of their immediate control, false proof that it would work. Something on their *own* lands she might have supported, on the warehouse peninsula, perhaps, something that would have served as a real contingency plan while the management culture changed in Kaettegut.

Jeri caught up with her in the lobby, and walked out with her into the humid chill. "It can't be stopped, if it works," she said.

"We're on record," she said, with her lips still tight. She stopped, turned, and put her hand on Jeri's shoulder, firm. Gave her a direct look.

Jeri looked at her, nodded.

"I need to think," she said, and lifted her hand, turned toward Adrienne: "See that gets back to the office. When the media calls, my comment is this: 'Due process of vote was ignored, and has been ignored for the duration of the project. Experimental projects of a scale affecting the whole of Prime are not the sphere of any single department.' I'll have more later."

Joseph would look for guidance; she saw him coming down the stairs, through the window. She looked to Jeri again: "We'll meet in the morning. My conference room, if that's all right with you. Six-thirty, breakfast. Make sure Joseph knows. —Careful with Kate." Which meant, *I'll handle that.*

"Six-thirty," Jeri said, and nodded, and went.

That was loyalty, the first to follow, deeply appreciated; Kate's departure was in line with the issue itself, and emphasized—magnified several times—that she had more to consider than her own betrayal, that she could not afford to be short-sighted.

Loren *needed* her cooperation. She had taken a risk walking out, yes, but she represented far more than herself, and he had perhaps forgotten that.

Going back to work was too much, she should not have tried it so soon. There was Ethan's empty seat and station across from her, and moving the plant between her and it did not work. Her own chair and station and belongings were the same, too, a reminder: the rock she had picked up during an audit assignment. Ethan's signature on papers in her files.

Clare put the paper back into the file, touched the signature at the last moment. He *had* been here. He *had* mattered.

She went to the floor lounge, quickly, and faced the wall with its painting of the darkness of the bay on it. The artist had painted who knew where—she did not recognize the stretch of rock outcropping in it, when almost all of Prime that had that kind of lighting was flat.

She was proficient. Every review in her file showed high ratings. She *thought* she had a reputation, a good working reputation. Perhaps some bargaining power—she hated to think of it—as a victim of the explosion, too.

There were several personnel in Audit who had been in Gros Morne as well. Jenning had been. Those were the departments—she and Ethan had not dealt with most of the Audit staff, though, they had worked with Jenning.

She could not think of the room at the hotel in Gros Morne, the only place where they could get away from the plain *work*, be themselves.

No. Focus. She looked at the painting, held her head still.

She had been comfortable working with Jenning. Jenning was highly respected in her field—they said no one had exceeded her, if she believed those rumors. Jenning had power, more than anyone else she knew. Jenning could facilitate a new assignment if anyone could.

She heard noise behind her, the refrigerator opening. She turned her head, and there was a supervisor she did not know well, from the other end of the floor—looking at her. "Are you all right?" the woman asked.

"Fine," she said, and lowered her eyes, and turned and went back into the work area.

At work Graham had the same problems spread out over his desk, and he could not concentrate again; his thoughts refused regulation, took abrupt turns—damned hope always at the forefront, confusion, questions—who *had* Kellan had spoken to?—dread. They would find out Kellan was still here, that he hadn't taken the ship back to Kaettegut, out of their hands, out of their hair. They would undo everything, after he had gone through a day and some hours of a hope of recovery and life going on. A more interesting life, he had consoled himself; access to much, much more, if he could satisfy at least the brain, and possibly more, depending on what they had over here, underground, that kind of culture.

But—*God, she tore me up,* Kellan had said. Who could even think they had the right to tear at a hospital patient who could not *walk* within weeks of today? Worse, someone like Kellan, someone made to live in Rue.

He had not handled the situation right at the hospital. He had been too wrapped up in himself, that was what, in his own damned emotions. He had gone in intending to hide behind a face that hadn't failed him in *other* things, damn it, had relied on that with blind faith. Never mind it was Kellan he had been talking to, who had seen him every morning, who had seen him on the floor in the bathroom after he had tried eating oysters that had been in the refrigerator too long, because he was too stubborn, had picked him up and dragged him back to bed and given him a bowl.

He had seen what he had caused, this time.

They had given Kellan a false hope, and he would not make it worse. That Kellan thought he would stay was clear. *He* had no job; they would not let a Kaetteguttan who was not even Gros Morne into their hallowed administration, no matter how low the level. Rue, God, *Rue* must be provincial to them, an outpost. They were polite here, but this was in the office portion of the warehouse district, and he had some specialized skill. He could pick up their formulas, the theory, even if he hadn't been taught it in school, not the way they used it.

Not Kellan. Kellan just pushed papers, straightened up and sent through things others had already approved. His most major assignment had been to put together a procedures binder, a step-by-step affair that would train new graduates coming into the outpost system, that would reassure Gros Morne it was being done the way they wanted.

That was as close as Kellan had thought he would ever come to Gros Morne. A *damned binder*, he had said. Kellan would not be of any use to them here.

Now he sat at his desk and got nothing done on a second day.

He went down the hall, stuck his head into the tiny office Ted worked in, who had done most of his training. Not much younger than him, he *would* have thought someone just barely expendable for that sort of thing, but Ted knew his stuff. "How do I turn the heat on in my unit?" he asked, when Ted looked up.

"At home?" Raised eyebrows.

"I haven't gotten around to it yet." They knew nothing of him, he had guessed that the first day. He was just an assignment from somewhere higher up in the tiers—a Kaetteguttan, yes, there was no hiding that, but they did not know from where. He could have been from Gros Morne, from the central office, some kind of exchange project.

"There should be a utility closet. You adjust it there." Ted swiveled, leaned back in his chair. "Mine is near the front door. Toward the front of the house. You know."

"What are the rules?"

Ted's eyebrows drew close. "What rules?"

"A temperature limit. You can only have it on at certain times?"

"No. Just what you can afford. You have to be careful because the energy price levels fluctuate once in a while." Ted stood up, came over, and clapped him on the back. "You must been have been freezing, man! You didn't have to wait this long to ask."

"What's a good restaurant?"

"Well, all right." Raised eyebrows, but nothing worse than that. Ted rocked back on his heels, put his hands in his pockets. "Cisco is decent. They've got great seameats. Just ask what's in season." He stopped, looked at him. "I guess you know what's in season. —Cynthia!" Much louder. "What's the best place to eat?"

There was a wait. Then, just a voice trailing down the hall: "Osiake."

Ted looked back at him, and that implied something. "She likes the spice thing."

"How do I get there from my place? I'm about a block off the first shuttle stop."

"Well, Cisco— I guess they're both in the northeast part of the district. If you catch the second shuttle, it's not that far. Cisco's at Dali and Ellis."

"Thanks."

He went back down to his desk. He did not have an office—well, not like theirs. There was another desk in his room, empty, and a wide doorway without a door, and stacks of boxes and papers to the right that said this had probably been a storage room or an old mail room.

The day crawled.

He had done worrying. He told himself that. Kellan was here; he had an extra day, when he had not expected that.

He had *not* expected anything like this from Kellan. If he let himself think about it—

There was nothing that way. Kellan would go back to Kaettegut and this would have been useless. He would be in the same situation as the night before, with the same bottle of soju. Maybe worse. That Kellan had come as far as he had—

There was something he had misinterpreted.

He rubbed his temples, took a sip of the stuff they drank over here. Coffee, they called it, but it was not like the coffee he knew in

Rue, or in school. This stuff was black as the water down by the port, had a film always floating stagnant on top no matter how fresh out of the pot it was.

He took the first shuttle, even though that was leaving earlier than most of them did and Ted's office light was still on, down the hall. There was only a handful of people on the shuttle by the time it came, but then a good number got on at the warehouses closest to the end of the district—they perhaps did that every day, because only a few had ever boarded at that stop the other nights.

He halfway thought, on the way home, that he would open the door and find just the blankets on the sofa.

No. Kellan was there, thank God, sitting on the floor against the sofa with the apartment's tablet attachment in his hands, the blanket wrapped around him. Same clothes—of course; he had no others.

"What about your transfer?" he asked, shutting the door.

"They called. They said they'd be by tomorrow."

His stomach sank, at that. Tomorrow, then.

Focus. "I found out how to turn the heat on. Sorry about that. I have an extra jacket you can use."

A half-smile, the first he had seen since the last day at the hospital. "I'll take it," Kellan said. And encouraged, he offered: "A little colder on this side."

Kellan was watching *him* for cues. That was enough to shock, to make him straighten up. He went to the closet, got the coat out, glad it was the heavier one. All day in this clamminess— The sheets were folded and put in a pile with the pillow, a neatness not typical for Kellan.

The utility closet was in the corner of the room near the windows, near where Ted had said. He found the switch, turned it on and set the gauge. "Hopefully when we get back this will have warmed up a little," he said, and went through the route in his mind. Kellan would be able to take a rest at the shuttle stop and then on the shuttle before walking through the business district. It wasn't *that* long ago that Kellan could not make it down a hallway; he had to remember that, looking at him like this, normally dressed.

"Where are we going?"

"Dinner." He had gone out early in the morning and found some cream of rice, at least, had left that on the counter. "I've noticed— It seems like people here eat out a lot."

It had astonished him, actually, the number of restaurants. All of them full, too.

The coat didn't look bad on Kellan. He was thinner now, after the hospital, and that helped some with the fit.

"How did you get down here?" he asked, outside. Kellan was looking at the houses, at the lighting, at the sky. Near black, down here this much further west, much less luminous than the sky Kellan had looked at outside the hospital window.

"They took me. They had kind of a public vehicle."

A public vehicle. *That* wasn't seen all that much, even over here. He had seen one outside the hospital one night.

"They have shuttles over here," he said. He hadn't seen anything like it in Rue *or* Gros Morne. "A car like that pulls seats."

Kellan was going to stand, when they got to the shuttle stop. Kellan was imitating him, watching *him*; he had already forgotten. He thought of saying something but sat down instead, and Kellan sat too.

God. This was strange; but Kellan trusted him, probably, to know the ropes over here, probably thought he had gotten to know the territory much more than he had, when he hadn't even found out until today how to turn on the heat. He hoped the rooms were warmer when they came back, did not want to have to try to find someone to fix it, and if this *was* going to be Kellan's last night here— He determined to have a good time, to look like it at least, because Kellan would not if he didn't.

"When they come by tomorrow," he said, "if you have time, call me. Tell the operator you want the wholesale pricing office."

"Okay." Simple as that.

The shuttle came. He waited two stops and got off at the business district, and Kellan followed. Now that they were here, he thought twice of it. The main avenue was Ellis; it stretched ahead, made an S curve, and bent north, out of sight.

Kellan was walking fine, for now, was looking around at the buildings. Quite a bit different here than anywhere, if he took the time to look: the architecture incorporated more glass so that light spilled out of the ground floors, gold as he remembered it. Everyone here was content, cozy at their tables eating, that was the subliminal message. They had an entrepreneurial class over here that was much different than anything they had in Rue, and this was evidence of it, right there.

He began to worry when they had passed several such restaurants, when the S curve was far behind them, and he still had not seen a cross street named Dali, and no sign of Osiake either. He'd take either one, though if Osiake was as spicy as had been implied, it might not be such a good idea to take Kellan from cream of rice to something with that much bite. "You doing okay?" he asked, and looked for any sign of fatigue on Kellan's part.

"Wish it were warmer," Kellan only said, but his breath was coming much shorter. He had his hands in the coat pockets.

He was *not* going to imply anything, not after Kellan's humiliation trying to walk the hospital hallway. If they didn't come to it soon, he'd turn back. It didn't matter if Kellan knew he didn't know the territory as well as he was acting, not against that.

There. He saw Cisco's sign up ahead, where the avenue began to curve again.

"Here we are," he said, and turned aside when they were close.

They had to wait a few minutes for a table, one in the middle of the room but far enough away from the one large group dining; that was good. The smell of warm food mingled with that of hot drinks, of people at the end of their workdays, fresh again for dinner. He sat, read the menu, and looked over at the next table. A woman there had a large, oblong plate of mussels, black-shelled, steamed open. She lifted one, tried to work the meat out with her fork, and a thin, melted butter sauce dripped down. He ordered that. It came with a side of rice, a small black bowl piled high. It steamed up, warmed the underside of his jaw and the side of his face.

"Who was this woman you talked with?" he asked, and carefully made his voice neutral.

"I was thinking about that." Kellan had been looking in the direction of the window. "She said she was in the accident. I *know* she was."

"She *was?*" There were no more than two dozen injured in that, good Lord, *that* had to be providence.

"She said she spent some time in the hospital, that she—wasn't allowed any visitors either." A frown, between the eyebrows. "She walks with a cane. I don't know if it's from that."

All he had to do was find the footage, then. "She's older?"

"I don't know. You think she's old, at first. After a while you realize she's too—sturdy to be as old as you think. I don't know. I guess that doesn't make much sense."

"Maybe it's the cane."

"Maybe."

More carefully, even though Kellan had loosened up some with the food, with the atmosphere—it didn't help that they were sitting in the center of a room full of people, but no one was paying attention to anything but their food, their own conversations— "You said she tore you up."

His gaze went back down to his food. "It's nothing."

"I don't— I've never heard you say anything like that before."

A fork, speared into one of the mussels. "I guess I was shaken up, still. I thought—I thought I wouldn't be able to stay."

The first part didn't ring true. The second did, too much so. "Kellan." He laid down his own fork, looked across at him. "You can go back."

"I've known you a long time. Been friends."

"Everything you know is over there. I know your job isn't all that great, but you know people, you know where everything is. Hell, it's warmer."

"Everything *you* know is over there too."

"I'm—different than you." Kellan was going, regardless. *He* didn't have a choice; if he did, in this moment, he would talk differently—a new start, maybe Kellan could get something here that was more interesting than government work in Rue. This was a first, for himself, too, eating out at a restaurant like this over here; he didn't have to do it alone.

He should not. He should ease the way; Kellan would be carrying some guilt, the way he was. The first mention of the word *transfer,* and that would have been it. "I'm someone who likes things different. Change isn't bad for me."

"I know." An aversion of the eyes. "I know you're like that."

"Kellan. I didn't mean—"

Kellan put his fork down; it clanked against the other utensils. And looked at him. "Did you do this because you wanted to? Transfer here?"

He eased the air out of his lungs. He was going wrong at every turn, now, but he would not lie, not on Kellan's last night here. He *would* undo everything he had just done— *Christ.* "No."

Kellan stood up, and that was unexpected, too, but there was nothing in the movement to alarm, and he was still polite. "Excuse me." And, mumbling, before he moved away: "Restroom."

Oh, hell. He sat there and looked at the remains of the mussels. Gone was the attractive presentation, the careful placement. It was a graying jumble of garbage for the disposal now.

He waited.

He stood up, finally, put the cloth napkin down beside the plate. He walked toward the back, found the restrooms, and opened the door, and found Kellan leaning on the sink, arms straight, head down. His knuckles were white against the metal. "Kellan," he said, and Kellan jolted, turned his head. His face was— "What's wrong?"

"Nothing." But he didn't try to hide it: his skin tone stayed the same. *That* was something. There were white streaks radiating across his temples.

"What *is it?*"

Kellan opened his mouth. "Nothing. She just knows—her stuff, that's all."

He put his hand on his shoulder blade, applied some force. *I'm here.* Slowly: "What happened? What did she say?"

The door opened. A man took two steps in before looking, before realizing, and his face changed. He almost stopped, thought better of it, and went into a stall. Graham dropped his hand.

"I'm being stupid. That's all." Kellan turned on the water, ran his hands under it, shook them dry. His head was back down. He didn't look in the mirror.

He wasn't going to let this rest. For now, yes; this wasn't the place.

At the table, the food looked worse. The butter had congealed. He sat back down, deliberately, and changed the subject. "I *wanted* you to have a good time. Your first real meal for what, weeks?"

"It was good." Honest. "The first real taste I've had in that long."

"You want dessert?"

"That might be taking it a little far. Thanks." He patted his stomach, even if he looked queasy doing it. He leaned forward, put his elbows on the table. "I'm sorry. I think I— I haven't done much thinking about the accident. Meeting someone else who had been in it—it's been making me think. That's all."

Oh. God. He crumpled the napkin in his palm. That made sense; he hadn't been thinking—a lack of sensitivity on his part, one more time. He had to think. *Think.*

"I'm happy to be here. When I think—I might not be here. To come through and be walking again, like this, to be sitting here eating."

"It would be better for you to be in Rue. To have everything the same."

"If everything could be the same, I'd be over there. It can't. This is fine."

He *didn't* want to let him go back to Rue, not like that. He had thought, he guessed, that they had taken care of that in the hospital too. Foolish thought. They had not supplied even the most basic of mental comforts, that a *robe* had been an anomaly there.

He didn't want Kellan back in the hospital, either, much less so. All the same—he could argue that he wasn't recovered, not by a long shot. That wasn't the reason they had approved his visa, of course; they had little idea of the reason he had applied, and would not care. He had no bargaining power, he brought nothing to the pricing office that they could not get in someone else, eventually, if they did not have anyone now that they could not transfer. Still—

Except that he knew what he was doing, that he had rationalized like this before. He was grasping at excuses, that was all. Kellan *would* do better in familiar surroundings, not where everything was strange; this was not the time for a career change, for everything in his world to shift.

For himself, he was at the same place he was before, where he had expected to be all along, and it was time to deal with it. Nothing new.

"What do you think of over here?" he asked. Something light.

There was a visible relaxation on the other side of the table. Kellan toyed with his fork, thought it over a while. "It's different. It seems a lot more crowded. All these places share walls, like here. And it's dark."

"Yeah."

"What's it like working over here?"

He thought, a few seconds, considered. "They do things differently. They have the same economic theories, the same base— I guess they have a lot more going on over here, a lot more elements that have to mesh, and then they've always got a wild card in us. They haven't known how we do things in pricing on our end."

"You tell them?"

"They haven't thought far enough ahead to ask, yet."

Maybe *that* was his advantage. Once he got to know their system—he could have it working much more smoothly in conjunction with agriculture.

He *did* have a bargaining chip. It wasn't all that small. More efficiency in what was already a very efficient system, hell.

He looked across at Kellan, at the shape of the face, the forehead, the jaw. Kellan, still blast-shocked inside, and not even a bandage put across it by any of the hospital staff, *God*. Rue wouldn't bother to do anything, they weren't trained to think that way. The other explosion victims— He thought of the two getting off the boat at the dock at Gros Morne, the way the pale, freckled one had walked, wrapped in that blanket.

"I'm sorry," Kellan said. He picked up a fork, pushed a mussel shell around with it. "It isn't such a big thing."

"No." Good Lord, he'd better guard his facial expressions more than *that*. "I'm sure it's not."

8

Jenning was not sure what made her think of it.

She had turned on the media in her office, had it running in the upper right-hand corner of her screen while she worked. It was all still the walkout, the news of the experimental food stations—the populace still hanging onto the news of a contingency plan. *Bah*. Experimental food stations were no contingency plan, not until years and decades of success had been reached and passed.

She had been mulling things over in the background of her daily work, at the subconscious level, a longtime talent to simply let things settle themselves out.

One—Kaettegut had been manipulating the food levels, here and there. How long was not the question; if and how long Jefferson had known was that.

Two—Quinn had sent *her* to Gros Morne. Someone of *her* level, her particular area of expertise. Someone from outside Audit, one of the under-the-table arrangements that could be worked out now and then between allies.

At the time she had assumed that at that point Jefferson's auditing teams had gotten nowhere. Could be that Quinn *had* known, or suspected, or it could simply be that agriculture had grown more important of late.

She stopped working, and leaned her chin on the tips of her fingers.

Quinn had been here. In a show of support—she had been naïve to believe that for a second. A twinge of regret, *that* was what that visit had been.

With the advent of Chauncey Benner, with a handful of no-good years in office under her belt, Kaettegut had grown too big for its britches. That much was certain. For the status quo contingent, that was not acceptable; no change was.

Quinn had watched her deal with Chauncey, step by step. Quinn had, she would bet, known about the food production tinkering, and *she* had found out about it late—when she prided herself on knowing as soon as the first word came out of a mouth. Still, she *had* found it out. Few others knew, that she could likely warrant.

There had been tampering in the wiring, was Kaettegut's report. It had blown a fairly major electrical unit—and it had been fortunate for a good many of them that it had blown skewed. And if that was so, she had leaned toward it having been designed for a scare. Singe the food storage unit, that would have been enough.

Perhaps it *had* been an accident waiting to happen. Poor maintenance on the wiring, along with much else in hydroponics—but add it to the timing, that *she* was there, that an entire Jeffersonian audit team had been there. Add it to the fact that the low budget allocation to maintenance on the wiring had been in her own reports—that Quinn had been the recipient of those reports, that the report might have gone further than that—to any colleague allied with Quinn on the Proteraiotita, really.

A smokescreen, that Jeffersonian delegation. Including her.

She breathed, deeply. Her door was shut, as she preferred it: no interruptions unless her staff judged it imperative, and by this time they were very prudent.

The Proteraiotita had not come out with any results, when it was politically beneficial that they do. No, someone was blocking things, Unofficial suspects—of course. Rumors flew. The major councilors would be careful to keep those in control, to defend their own.

That was what Quinn had been doing. She *had* been moving, under the scenes, simple damage control, likely guiding some of those rumors herself. Her own staff member, settled cozily in Organization, untouchable for an investigation; and Administration operated the audit teams, and Quinn had the most influential contact there: Quinn had long made sure Loren Fifty's former department had what it needed, economically and in personnel levels.

Her own division. *Quinn* was who had done it, had caused that explosion, had somehow had the electrical system rigged, and now-Quinn sat pretty and *she* sat with a damaged leg and more than that, that she could count.

Chauncey walked out onto the porch, stood and blew on her tea, and the moist heat came rushing back against her lips, her chin.

Gros Morne had signed a travel visa for one Graham Long. That was standard.

They had *not* signed a transfer.

It was not hard to figure out the reason for the application or for the transfer: her staff had found Graham's visa through the records of his roommate, who had been in the accident.

Gros Morne's signature on the travel visa—was damning. It lent legitimacy, and she gritted her teeth, looking down at it. The usual office, they would not have known, they just followed directions and procedures, had the lower scores in aptitude, lower than the government office in Rue got, where there had to be *some* independent thinking.

Kellan Long's situation—was distinctly different. There was no signature. He had been transported over in the midst of an emergency with every other person involved, an exception, a clemency. For them to take advantage of *that* put them into a poor light. A little public relations could be very effective, if she chose that route.

A little divide between Prime and Kaettegut—

Jenning might have had a chuckle that she had said she would not permit the first transfer. She was accustomed to that. The snickers might die down a tad, the first taste they got of that on the media.

No. She was thinking recklessly. She leaned back in her chair. But then— *What the hell.* Starting her staff on a plan or two besides what Jefferson handed to her—might not be imprudent.

Consultation, that was the thing. A say in one's own fate, without having to listen to rumors spread in the media. Agriculture held two land masses, for God's sake, dwarfed Jefferson and Grosvenor, and still they turned it until it might have been a leper's colony, safely over *there*, held at a long arm's distance across the bay. In its best light, insignificant and small to the average Primean, because what they could not see could not matter, that was only human nature.

She had read, as part of her graduate thesis, about a process in the mess that had been old Earth. A quick mention, a minor history point, but delving down—the working classes had been against the higher, and the higher against them. Unionization, the process had been called, and there had been a skirmish or two at least, but it had worked for a time. She had pursued it as a curiosity as far as she could, but had gotten no further than to determine the unions had fallen, eventually, that they were not mentioned in writings only a century or so later. Now, she wondered—

Foreign concept, with its logic twisted exceedingly, but she had never forgotten it.

She could, of course, appeal the transfer decision. It might not be disadvantageous to start with that. Useless, yes. A transfer required only two signatures: Organization, on Jefferson's side, and Environment. Whether Agriculture signed for its own was beside the point, Agriculture belonged to Environment, and anyone outranking her there could override her signature or denial, and had done it before. It rankled every damn time, had never become easier.

An internal appeal or a full council appeal, was the question. A council appeal would stir up the most dust, but Environment had long been solidly expansionist, which probably made it the natural ally of Fifty, and that meant the appeal would end with Fifty. Fifty would certainly back his ally rather than its stepchild.

Internal, then. It would serve the same purpose, and perhaps best if it were more quiet. She could point to it, that *she* had been loyal to her division.

She had been planning on using the return of the last patient as an event, a closure, when she could not announce the guilty party. There still had been no information on that, and that meant that there would not be.

She made a mental note to ask Rene to set up a meeting with key staff. Not her cabinet, by any means. She did not trust all of them, not by a long shot, and the more troublesome ones would only turn it into a bevy of accusations, a headache. She could just see Murray Lerkenlund quivering in his seat, too angry to be coherent, the way he could get.

She took a sip of her tea.

She did not have a choice. She could only work with what she had, and if this was what some Kaetteguttan had done to clog up the system she had carefully arranged—well, she could come up with a decent alternate plan. She'd not be controlled by what others did, only by what she did herself, when she *had* to pay it.

Jenning was not so shaken that she could not work.

There were not many options, but there were implications each way of which she had to be careful. This was no time for pure reaction.

Still—a move of her department to another division was inviting, would make a statement, certainly. Such a thing was rare, but not impossible.

She had another request sitting on her desk. One of her aides from the Gros Morne audits, the surviving one. Clare Daschen.

A bad time for it, when surely there would be turmoil—and if she made the initial move, and it did not succeed, very probably there would be dissolution of the whole department in the name of reorganization. Quinn did not suffer disloyalty, could be very hard on just the hint of overmuch cooperation with another division, and what she was contemplating would certainly be that. For Clare to come in during a time like that, in a state like hers—she understood the reason for the request, and for that reason it was too much risk.

All the same... it might not be such a bad time to ensure she retained such inside knowledge of Safety, regardless, and Clare would have contacts there.

Clare had proven herself able in the limited fashion the audit process had allowed. She and Ethan had, level-headed both, but still that paled against the potential such an alliance with Safety could bring. Even a small one could prove useful in some negotiation down the line, a piece of information, and small alliances could grow, given the proper care.

Of course, if she *did* succeed in a move, too, a spot in her department could be very secure.

Clearly Clare was not well where she was. She approved the

request on Clare's copy, with a note, and sent a separate feeler in Safety's direction.

She valued her own. They had been loyal. She had staff who had been with her from the beginning—Neil in particular, and Audrey; she saw that they were treated well. Taking on Clare... She did not work in grief counseling, though she had done facilitations, plenty difficult, in other areas. No doubt she'd fumble, some, but better hers than someone else's hands, by far.

Clare did not have any training in what was relevant here, but she *had* masqueraded very well as an aide in Gros Morne, could just as well do that here.

Graham went to the office. If he did not, it would say too much.

He had thought, had changed his mind more times than could keep him sane.

He knew there was a docking schedule, days when ships came in and went out: Grosvenor's pricing system hinged on it. He had not tried accessing external parts of the database outside simple department lists, did not know if it had an alarm built in if he made a misstep somewhere, but he had a user identification number and a password for his own system, and tried that first.

It worked. He was in. He looked at columns, green on black, primitive, and an entire world flowered open to him.

He sat at the desk and just looked at it, at first. Tried navigating it, and that was simple, too: there was the Back, more sections than he would have thought possible, both mining and manufacturing—but then, the Back had been only something remote, something in the textbooks, in the rough-panning films of history class. Somewhere in the backs of their minds they all knew it still existed and operated, but here were *names*, crew rosters, vehicle records.

He sat in a tiny section of the populated area of the planet, that was the way it really was.

There. There was a shipment of sea greens coming from Kaettegut. It should already be—he looked down the list—the ship had docked yesterday, was already unloaded. It would be taking on consumer goods now for the return trip.

His heart sank.

Damn it. He closed his eyes, kept his back to the door.

Well, he had expected it; it should be no surprise. *Calm down. Relax. Think.* He opened his eyes, scrolled down until he had found the departure time. Another ship was scheduled to be in from the Back later in the day, there was little room in that.

He worked through lunch. Cynthia stuck her head in the doorway on her way out. "Damn, you're a workhorse. You can eat, you know."

"Later," he said, and did not turn around. "I'm finishing with this."

He did not get a call. He had been listening all morning; the longer it went on, the worse it was. He thought his nerves jumped out of his skin when a phone program blipped, but it was not his, it was in an office up the hall.

He had told Kellan to call *if* he could. He reminded himself of that, picking up his things when it was time, putting on his jacket.

The air felt humid as usual when he stepped outside the building entrance. He was lucky in the placement of the pricing office, in the neck of the peninsula, so near the dock. He had seen—people took their lunches down to the dock, sometimes, ate out on the empty pier under the lights sometimes when there was not a ship in. He would not look so out of place.

He had found the woman's name, hadn't slept much the night before, but it had been time well lost: Jenning Crote, a crusty old piece, judging from the footage. He had her office contact information in his pocket. They might not pay any attention to him—he had the idea of more extreme measures, if he proved weaker than he judged himself; the Kaetteguttan crew might back him up on something like this—but if he bluffed right, they'd take both Kellan and him to her office. There would always be another boat. He could make his argument, his offer.

No. He was stronger than this. It was not as if he were left with nothing.

Why, then, was he shaking? He pulled his jacket tighter, hunched his shoulders into it. There was the ship, black water lapping against it, and he could only see where the lights spotted down—early in the preparations to cast off, but it would not be long.

The dock itself was empty. They were moving the last of the units up further. He walked past the forklifts, in the midst of the smell of *wet*, onto the slick puddles of the pier.

One of the deck hands was checking the upper holds, one by one, quickly. The latches clattered and snapped shut.

The boot soles squeaked when the man came over to the railing. "Yeah?" Guarded.

"Have you taken on any passengers, this run?"

Surprise, and a visible relaxation. "Hey! Kaetteguttan, eh?" And, slower, a little narrowing of the eyes; he probably did not look like part of any renovation crew, which meant he should have been standing there with dock paperwork, except that his inflection did not have the smoothness of a Primean.

"Yes."

"You looking for passage?"

They'd take him on without a pass, probably, even if it meant depending on him for the credit, on his position level to be able to afford one. He shook his head. "I have a friend going over soon, maybe today. You taking anyone?"

"Nah." The man had lost interest, then, was already turning away.

Well— He stepped back, walked back to where the units were stacked and leaned against one, where it was dark. It was getting to the end of the lunch hour; the fork lift operators would be back to finish the job in a few minutes.

He waited, watched all the approaches, and once a group came down, on foot—but those were the fork lift operators, and he relaxed, some. He *tried* to.

They did not see him. The forklift lights came on and lit up the sky around the edges of the units behind him. Engines whirred. The boat pulled away, finally, slowly—he thought his nerves had already had it, but this twanged at them, would not stop. Someone could still call out; it would take five minutes at this rate for the ship just to get far enough to turn, and it would still be within easy range.

It took a full fifteen minutes for it to move out of view. He watched the stern's light blinking, sharp and white in the dark of the sky, until it had rounded the tip of land jutting out into the channel and had gone.

He walked slowly back to the office. There was no dock over here besides the Back's, if he knew correctly, and anyone would have to get to *it* through this one.

What the hell did this mean? He had not done anything; he *hoped* Kellan hadn't. Kellan was not built to withstand anything like what he had met with the first time, not after the injury—and no matter the recovery from an event like the explosion, there was more to what Kellan was saying, he knew at least that much. Kellan said things the way they were; he was not good at downplaying, at anything that was other than the bald truth.

No. He had just understood it wrong. There was another dock, maybe up near Jefferson.

They would not let Kellan stay. Kellan didn't have the skill or the knowledge to bargain his way into something like this, and he had already begun to get a measure on the woman who had done it; sympathy had not played a part in any shape. Of that he was certain. The rest—he had time to find out, and he was going to, it was going to carry him quite some time, a distraction he would sorely need.

God. They had taken even this from him, finalization, the kind of knowing that came from seeing it happen with his own eyes.

Inside, he climbed the stairs wearily, felt like nothing else but going back to the apartment, on foot if he had to, falling into bed. Not enough sleep, but that had not affected him like this before—he'd had the self-control to keep it from doing that, but not today, not now. His nerves could only take so much. His skin crawled, exhausted.

The secretary called him back when he had gone past her station. She looked through her notes. "Your friend called," she said, and read from her screen. "Kellan Long."

It took a great burst of self-control to turn where he stood, to stay in the spot. "When?"

"A half hour ago, probably."

A half *hour.* He had been at the dock. "Did he say anything?"

"Just to tell you he called. Are you feeling all right?"

"Fine. Thank you." He went down the hall to his office and sat down, numb.

God *damn* it. Just to know what was going on, what was happening, would alone be worth everything he had over here.

It was a strange, cool relief to Clare to be at a job again, in new surroundings. *This* was bright, the rooms well-lit, and there were people everywhere, faces she had not seen.

Yesterday she and Gabrielle had toured Jenning's department itself, met the staff—all on one floor, several in small offices. A Jeffersonian department, especially one in Organization, ranked that kind of space and privacy, Clare supposed. In Safety they had been out in the middle of the floor in desks, with partitions and piles blocking the view of other desks if they were lucky.

Gabrielle—she could not quite read. Older, extremely accomplished if her reputation in the department meant anything. No matter who was being introduced, they straightened up at the sight of Gabrielle, treated her with the utmost of respect. It could be intimidating—she could admit that to herself, but Gabrielle was on the other hand courteous and protective to a fault. She did not trust that, yet.

She was being shown Organization's central offices today, a quick tour—Gabrielle termed it *Quinn's area*, with an informality that surprised. There were things there that the rest of Organization lacked, videoconferencing and presentation equipment, an exercise room, training facilities. Most of it was in the adjacent building, connected to this one by a shared lobby. She had walked through the security station, past metal detectors. Jefferson had such things, though from the look of the guard monitoring the station, it was simply routine.

This hallway was busier than any of the others. The women who passed had for the most part pulled their hair up and out of the way, pragmatic. The dress was definitely a large step up from Safety, in its snug seat on the warehousing peninsula, safely out of the way.

Not that any of them had been complaining. It could be a blessing, with none of the expectations *this* place shouted.

There was a bank of elevators, the doors all of burnished metal. Gabrielle shifted to the other side of the hallway to pass those waiting there, and she followed— Something of Ethan caught her eye.

It wasn't him. Confusion stayed, but there were two young men standing waiting by the elevators, that was it: the shorter, slighter one had dark hair similar to Ethan's, and next to him, the blond one— there was something, the chin, maybe, or the way he held his head.

"He's Kaetteguttan," Gabrielle said, next to her, with just the barest disguise of distaste—Gabrielle had followed her stare. And, continuing, "There's only the storage room down here that we'll ever use. Most is upstairs. You'll need a code to get in."

The elevator doors were opening, anyway, but she could not stop looking, still, even over her shoulder.

Oh— It shook her. She had not expected it, when she should have. There were going to be times like this.

It was going to happen again. She did not have the fortitude yet, she was not *going* to have it.

It went well at first. Kellan had been nervous, sitting in the apartment waiting for them to arrive. He had called Graham, and the phone system had worked the way Graham had said, but Graham had been out of the office and the secretary had not known when to expect him back.

The same car had come, but it had been a young man who knocked on the door, who said his name was Orlando, and whose slightness made him seem safe. Only him, too; there was no one else out in the car except the driver, who did not speak and did not seem connected to Orlando.

"Where do you work?" he asked, on the way. It seemed strange sitting close to someone he did not know, especially in the dark that was the sky over here, but the car was small and there were only the two seats, unless he wanted to sit next to the driver. "I'll be in your department?"

"No, I'm from Organization. Getting you set up," Orlando said, and there was an openness to him that *seemed* wholly natural.

And then there was a ferry. He hadn't expected that, but he saw passing it that the ground between the restaurant district and Jefferson was wetlands, not passable by anything but the ferry. It ran along a river separated from the blackness of the bay to its west only by low berms, lit by the ferry's running lights.

The ferry did not rock, only hummed; the river was smooth, strange for being next to the bay. He could see small chop breaking out that way occasionally, past the berm. "Usually people just get their assignments, but you're new over here," Orlando said. "My department head felt it would be better if I helped get you oriented."

"Thanks," he said, and that *was* nice, that was far more than he had expected.

"You'll meet her, maybe. We're stopping over that way; there's some kind of formality she wants you to take care of. Sign some paperwork, probably."

"Where *is* my assignment? Is it okay to...?" He had very much hoped it would be in Graham's office, but he was no economist. His scores in those classes had been fairly average. He did better with the numbers themselves where there *was* no theory: straight arithmetic, algebra, accounting, and that probably wasn't enough to get him into pricing. Maybe the renovation crews after all; he had offered, he had said he learned quickly.

But that made him think of that conversation, and that opened up too much. He stopped, just looked at Orlando, kept his mind even and smooth.

"Audit. It's in Administration. A good division to be in."

Audit. His mind blanked on that.

"It's not far from where we're going, just across the street. You'll be taking the ferry every day. It can get crowded—I'd recommend the earliest one, if you can stand to get up that early."

Not near Graham's office at all, then, and another government job. Still, it would not be worse than what he had been doing, probably, and it was maybe better that he not take on any big changes, as Graham had said.

Still, he had hoped—if not for Graham's office, for some variety. His lungs felt deflated. He breathed in the river air, and it did not help much, the air too heavy with the humidity.

His scores must have pointed solely to government. He was suitable for nothing else.

"What do they audit?" he asked.

"Everything. Wholesale, mining, the ports—you name it. Audit's kind of small, but it's solid."

He could see Jefferson from a long way off. Its buildings were white, solid, the exteriors lit with levels of electricity Rue had not ever seen. It made him take in another breath; he had seen Jefferson on television, just like that, glowing—but not from *this* angle, approaching from far off on a ferry, a river beneath his feet.

He was going to work in it now, see it every day until it was commonplace. *That* was something to get one's mind around.

When they started walking, from the dock, seeing it up close—he would not have this first-time experience again. The walls and columns stretched up and towered above his head, and at this range he had to squint against the whiteness, the brightness of the floodlights. He felt newly the chill in the air—Graham had left his heavier coat for him, and that helped. For a second he felt lightheaded, and no one else was walking and staring at the buildings. He put his head back down and looked straight ahead.

"I know," Orlando said. "Gives you hope that this planet might have some culture, huh?"

"It's incredible," he said, and it was the truth. His first glimpse of the hydroponics bays, with its rows of machinery and light, the metal grids of the walkways—*that* came close, but nothing else in Rue, anywhere in Kaettegut, compared.

And he was surprised, then, that he had remembered that, the hydroponics bay, a full visual memory, not just imagined.

"Here," Orlando said, and turned into an entrance in a building squared off in its corners, its windows. No columns or even ornamentation, just white stone.

Inside, it was warmer. The lobby was a vast three-story affair; here there were columns, rounded and simple, and the floor stretched slick under his shoes, white stone polished to a sheen, with small diamonds of black. Orlando went to the left, through some kind of checkpoint—he had not seen one like it—and he followed. There was an attendant there who looked at him as he went through, and looked away.

There was a wait for the elevators, and then they were in an upstairs hallway carpeted thickly in dark green, when nothing else had been carpeted. There was a logo woven in white and beige where the hall opened into a reception area. "This is Organization, my division," Orlando said, and nodded down at the woven logo. "We're on Councilor Rhodes' floor."

One of the three councils, then. In Kaettegut he had not followed the membership of the councils, except to know that Agriculture sat on the Ligotera, one of the minor ones.

"In here," Orlando said, and indicated a double doorway with his hand: the left door was open, a conference table visible through it, and tall-backed chairs. And inside, there was thick, dark wood—just the tabletop had to cost ten years' salary. The double doors and chair bases were sumptuous, together had to cost almost as much.

"This is our director," Orlando said, and he looked over to the end of the room, following Orlando's arm. "Jenning Crote, Aptitude."

His knees went weak. *Oh, God.*

"Nice to see you again," she said, didn't bother with the name. There was the cane, gray metal. He looked toward Orlando and felt only panic. His fingers seemed stuck to the tabletop, frozen, but there *was* the open door just behind him—

"If you could sit here," she said, and her voice was as dry, as humorless as in memory, where he had thought he had gotten it to finally stay. She indicated a small screen, propped in front of one of the seats, and that chair's back seemed suddenly too tall, too encompassing.

She was starting to sit down—two seats down from the screen, at the head of the table.

Orlando was looking at him, his face gone to confusion. "Is there a problem?" Jenning said, and it was not a question; it had annoyance in it.

"I'm sorry, what—what did you need from me here?" He looked toward Orlando instead. He could talk if he did that, if he didn't look at *her.* The room, the thick chairs absorbed most of his voice.

"Well, it's rather strange, but there's no reason not to permit it, if you don't object." She arranged her things carefully on the tabletop, looked across at him. "Your administrator would like to speak with you. She's received your paperwork to stay over here."

God. He was not up to this; he could not hope to win, against her. And this—? *To stay over here.* He had thought— "I want to stay," he said, and his stomach was churning, badly.

"Of course." A small smile, what was meant to be soothing, but didn't reach the eyes. "You don't have to talk with her, if you don't want to."

He had no idea what that meant: if to talk would be hazardous, or to refuse. Had the administrator not signed off on his paperwork? He thought—this woman had said she would make some calls, she had made it sound like it was done. "What does she want?"

"Just to talk, apparently. There's no harm in it. You don't have to agree to anything."

He went to the chair, pulled it out just enough to sit in it, faced the screen. No choice.

"Good. Don't worry. If you have questions about anything, you can ask me." A nod to Orlando; Orlando went out the doors, closed them behind him, and that was much worse; he was in here, closed in with just her. He wanted to protest, to go back out and ask Orlando to stay—he folded his hands together, clenched his fingers in on themselves. The screen came on. Some initial code, and then—the face he had seen nearly all his life, on television, was there on *this* screen. The series of dark pinpricks to the side of the nose, the hair drawn back tight into the chignon: Chauncey Benner, whom he had not ever known to step outside of Gros Morne, in Kaettegut.

"Kellan Long?" she said.

He only nodded, could not seem to find his voice, did not want to say anything wrong in any case.

A tight smile, as little reassuring as Jenning's. "Are you alone?"

He did not turn his head. He looked at Jenning and saw the beginning of the slightest shake of her head.

"I need to talk to you privately. I've already discussed this with the parties on your end. You should be alone. Do you understand?"

Jenning's face had gone ugly. He leaned back in the chair, away from the screen, away from her, and had the table edge in a death grip. "I don't—" He looked at Jenning, back to the screen. *Oh, God.* "I'd like her with me."

"It's not part of the arrangement. You can talk with her as much as you like, afterward." The tone stayed moderate, reasonable.

But he had done right: Jenning's face had cleared with his response. She stood, and for that she used the cane, and came and stood behind him, and his back muscles tightened painfully in anticipation of a touch, or her breath on his neck.

"I appreciate you're in a new situation," Chauncey said, and was looking at him. "I know you probably don't feel certain of anything. Is that right?"

With Jenning behind him— He flinched. Nodded.

"It's all right. Nothing is going to change, if you don't want."

"I'd just—like her here. There's no one else." He had no idea what turn to take, *this* might anger her, and he felt a jolt of panic. Did she have to sign his paperwork for it to be approved?

"Good God, Chauncey, he doesn't have to talk to you at all. Let him be."

"You know—what I think." There was a small threat in that, he could feel *that*.

Jenning was leaning down; he heard it, could feel it, and recoiled inside. The hand came down on his shoulder and rested there. "I'd like to stay." Sincerely, and to him. "I'll be outside. If you have any questions, you only have to step outside the door. There's nothing that's going to happen that you don't want to. You understand?"

He nodded; he had his eyes locked on the screen edges, for support. The contents had blurred. The hand lifted. Cool relief rushed in behind it and chilled his shoulder muscle.

Silence. He was almost afraid to turn. He did, finally, and the room was empty. The chairs stood like sentries in a row down the side of the table.

"Kellan?"

Chauncey Benner was still on the screen. He turned back. "She left."

"All right." A pause. "I'm less refined than she is. I hope you'll understand me anyway."

What did *that* mean? He nodded, anyway; one less person to make angry.

"Are you feeling better? Are your injuries all healed?"

Concern, when he had not expected it. He examined her face, the lines on it, the eyebrows, and she *looked* as if she meant it. He still did not know how to answer—what she meant, what she wanted to know. "I don't know how long it'll take. They didn't really tell me that much. I feel a lot better."

"I'd like to have you back here. I haven't filled your slot at the Rue office yet."

A stab; his stomach might have flipped over. It began churning again. "I—can't."

"Your friend transferred. That's why?"

Even more unexpected. She *knew*? He nodded, just that.

But—no, Jenning knew; there was the conversation in the hospital, and maybe the animosity between the two of them was not real, an act, politics. *God*, could they not leave him alone, leave him out of it? He was nothing, just a transfer. Jenning had said—

"Did they tell you why they approved his transfer?"

He swallowed. Were they allies, or were they not? Should he say— "She said he was a pricing liaison and they needed one in his office." He hoped desperately he was not making trouble for Graham.

"How do they treat him there?"

More focus on Graham. He *was* making trouble for him. "I don't know. He hasn't said."

"I hope they treat him well. I'm sure they do." A smile; she made it appear loose, but it was not. "They don't often transfer any of us over that way. I don't know any outside the renovation crews."

That was a question mark. "She said they do. It's rare. She said something about artisans."

"A different part of the renovation industry. Not much removed from the crews."

He did not know what to say to that. It contradicted— Insane to be making conversation, regardless, and who did he believe? *Oh, God.* What did she *want*, what had he done?

"Ever heard of one of them transferring over here?" And when he didn't speak: "Anyone from Jefferson, or Grosvenor."

"No." Where was this leading?

"Why do you think that is?"

Graham had said— He had not heard anyone else in Rue imply it. He was supposed to say—? He turned and looked at the room again. Empty. "Everyone knows," he said, only that, because he could think of nothing else.

She nodded, slowly, oddly, a cue he could not interpret. "Why do *you* think so?"

What was she leading him toward? "I guess— I don't know how to say it." He did not feel it, anyway, over here except that there was maybe—a sense of being in the better place, the things newer, the nurses' confidence that they were right. Wider windows, like in the restaurant, where people felt confident being seen. "Just that they're right, I guess."

"Pure human nature." She leaned in toward him. He could see her hands folded under her chin. "Anyone who does things differently—that's not as good."

Just a nod; that might keep him out of trouble. Still, he turned it around in his mind, carefully.

"We *are* different, of course. We grow up differently, have different resources, our focus is different. —When you were in school, when you were very young, what did you think about doing?"

No one had ever asked him, except for Graham. He hesitated.

She waited, raised an eyebrow. A corner of her lips curved: an encouragement.

It seemed as far away as another lifetime. Still—she waited, and she had asked; she looked interested. "I wanted to be on one of the mussel boats," he said. It felt strange, saying it. He drew his shoulders in, near embarrassed.

Another nod. "Why?"

She was *pleased*. He felt a coolness in his chest, strange, and spread his hands, looked down at them. "I don't know. To be so near—to be in the water, to feel the currents, to feel life—in your hands. Real things." He looked back at her. "I guess that sounds kind of odd."

"No. It doesn't." She was serious, more so than before. "*That's* what we are, Kellan. *That's* what makes us different."

Unexpected, a third time. Still, his chest expanded some, and he felt he could breathe, again. He had said what he had not told anyone but Graham, what one was not supposed to say when the aptitude results and assignments came out, and she had not laughed; she had not put him down.

She had made it sound like—a strength, something worthy.

"I want you to remember—this is why I asked to talk with you. Remember who you *are*. It doesn't matter where. Keep that with you."

He was beginning to feel regret, miserably so, but that—strangely mixed with pride. If he could go back— *No*. He could not.

"I can stay?"

"If that's what you choose. Is it?"

She sat and looked at him, and he—he could not say it, but could not *not* say it. Either way, a loss, in her eyes, with what she had said: less than a person. Not truly of them. He could not meet her eyes for the moment; he looked down, and the light reflected in the dark of the table, the glorious wood. "Yes."

After the call, he sat still, with his hands curled and resting on the table. The chairs across the surface faced him, blank.

9

Six sat at the table, finally, when Loren took his seat with an uneasy glance at Quinn. She had not made the recovery of any semblance of their former relationship easy—had only gone this far after she had determined, thoroughly, that the status quo and resourcists had made themselves heard by the general population.

And there was this situation.

She was wary, this time. She did not hide it.

She'd had a time of it, still, convincing him to leave Marcus Gouman, head of Terraforming inside Environment, out of the meeting in favor of Gallagher Crote. Marcus's presence even as a peer delegate of the Proteraiotita would tilt the balance too much toward Environment, and they would have lost any advantage in confrontation... and she *did* intend to confront. Agriculture was Environment's department, and to see an appalling display like this—spoke of a lapse on that division's part not typical of Meghan.

Gallagher sat now on the other side of the table. Controversial, yes, to extend a meeting like this outside the council, but Gallagher's presence on the Ligotera with Chauncey Benner could be strategic. There was little danger that a Ligotera councilor would serve to beef up Environment's presence significantly.

Only she and Loren had seen the recording. The others sat there, only Decheran and Meghan with enough experience to keep their faces blank, and it was shock enough that Meghan failed. Gallagher, for all his service to the Ligotera, was still a novice here; judging from his expression, that council operated fairly differently.

Andrew Edmond of Administration only looked to Loren: typical reaction from a bland man. Edmond was not a school renowned for creativity, and for Andrew to carry the name—fitting. But for Andrew to sit two seats away was her concession for the inclusion of Gallagher, and not a bad bargain. Loren merely desired a simple ally, an old habit of stacking the deck.

"Care to explain?" Loren said drolly, careless of a subordinate's presence, which itself put Meghan into poor position. Quinn could feel that from across the table.

"I don't know." Shortly, almost flippantly. Meghan had eyes hard to read, near black; they revealed nothing now. "Nothing leading up to that."

It had been much too close to comfort that Chauncey Benner had used that particular prop—a reasonably intelligent subject, she had not chosen a renovation laborer, but—that *particular* choice of subject. Jenning had handled that transfer as well, had only told her afterward, but she had consented. Jenning could have good instincts, one; two, it was well within her latitude as far as it was related to the Graham Long transfer.

It had certainly extracted a reaction, more than Jenning had predicted. But *that* meant there was a nerve there to be touched, and that meant Environment's management structure, nothing short of solid for decades, could be questioned. Lucky, perhaps.

She had to be careful in her wording. There *was* a member of another council here. "Did she question the transfer?" she asked, and kept her fingers light and placid on the cool surface of the table.

Meghan appreciated that far less, that was evident in the eyebrows, in the stare. "She filed an internal appeal. It's in process."

"How long ago?" Loren asked. Gallagher's head was turned, watching Meghan: this had his interest.

"A few days." A twitch in the turn of the head to face Loren, impatience.

More than a few days, then. A silence. Loren simply steepled his hands; the implication was there.

Environment kept Agriculture isolated, and in consequence, had isolated itself from Agriculture and all that Kaettegut represented, and that's what they were seeing now. Two things: one, this Benner was not her predecessor, no matter the similarity in name and implied in that, education. Two, this Benner had *some* instincts, which did not spell any comfort for a management structure caught off guard and out of touch.

She and Loren had been aware of the first, had been far ahead of Environment—and that should not have been so. Of course, she had not expected anything in *this* form, and that was a deficit on her own part. Jenning had given her the data, and both had failed to interpret it correctly. She had been amused by Jenning's outrage, when Jenning was not at all accustomed to treatment of that sort, and Jenning had not seen further than what was in front of her face.

Jenning still did not. This was evidence of that.

"Anywhere else this might have come from?" Loren asked, looking at Meghan, and had unsteepled his hands.

Hmn. Where that was going—

"I don't want to speculate," Meghan said. "I would have appreciated an opportunity to see this before a meeting had been called. A fair chance to do my own investigation."

"I'll speculate," she said. Another stare from Meghan, at her, coming more quickly this time. "Behavior out of character—isn't really beyond the pale, is it? No one has been named in the explosion. Is it unnatural for Agriculture to feel the eye is on *them*? —Let's not forget, it's far beyond what Benner's had to deal with." She turned, crossed her own hands on the table surface. "If anything, I'm surprised this is the first we've seen of it."

Gallagher nodded; a more urbane model than Jenning, for both having come out of Crote—but then, Gallagher was the far younger graduate, and things changed. "That's natural."

"That's bullshit." It was the first time Decheran had spoken, and was typically coarse. "*Listen* to what she's saying. 'Ever heard of one of them transferring over here?'"

Everyone knows. She could hear the answer in her head; she did not need to see the transcript to remember it. Short, efficient.

"She put it where we could see it," she said, and dropped all pretense. "It's a test."

Loren looked at her. To Meghan. "It's Environment's problem, isn't it? I trust it won't become ours. I believe there *is* some talent in your division. I don't have to emphasize that this needs to be fixed."

Christ. She kept that out of her expression only by force of will.

To simply turn it back over to Environment—that *was* what he was doing. The bottom dropped out, and she had only begun.

Loren saw this, then, simply as emphasis, not the agreement she had thought they had, not at all. Worse, the likelihood of damage control on that was close to nil, not with all of them sitting here, and that sternness on Loren's face—she knew better than to challenge him in those cases, no matter the favors owed.

She kept her mouth closed, her fingers still light on the table.

She caught Gallagher outside the door, in the hallway. "You sit on the council with Benner," she said, and kept a quiet voice, calm, nothing to attract the attention of the others, and still she had his full attention. "I think you don't let an observance pass you by, am I right?"

That worked, easily, a combination of her influence and the prestige of the council on which *she* sat. "I've noticed some things," he said, and kept walking, and had his eyes on her.

Nothing significant, if anything, presumably—but he would now. "I'd like to have lunch. Tomorrow?"

"That's fine." No pretense of even checking his calendar.

That was the right way to play her. Some cause for confidence. "Wonderful. I hope you don't mind eating in, in my office. I've been busy. —I believe that when a committee is in Environment's territory *you* chair it. Is that right?"

"I don't think Agriculture has ever chaired a committee." A slight implication, a point of defensive pride, on his part—the Ligotera's history, what he considered should be well known.

He *was* Crote: the same kind of education as Jenning. She let displeasure show in the corner of her eye, in the turn of her head... just for an instant; he was not stupid. "That's what I need to know. I'll see you tomorrow, my office. Noon is fine."

She'd postpone whatever it was she had on her own calendar.

Outside, the wind had picked up. Outside—far, far earlier than she had expected to be. She let the breeze blow her hair back from her forehead, a welcome briskness after the meeting.

Had she anticipated Loren would consider the meeting simply as pressure on Environment, she'd have been able to counter it ahead of time—but then, Loren's simplicity could hide plenty, to someone who was accustomed to dealing with minds that worked in layers, in branches. Loren posed a challenge of a different sort, and one for which she was not well designed; an irony that *this* was who would last as chairman for eleven years.

The devil you know... If Decheran had been successful in her bid—she did not need to think of that.

Kellan sat on the sofa, head in his hands, the room his alone for another couple of hours: they had taken him back here. Someone he did not know, who did not speak much, this time.

He should have asked. He had been handed the opportunity, and he had not been able to think straight enough. He had been floundering and had *missed* it.

He could not sort it out. His head hurt, not a headache like the kind he'd had in the hospital, but close.

If he could have just asked: had Kaettegut failed to ask for permission for visitors for those in the hospital, or had it not? A simple verification. If Jenning had him believing that to Graham the transfer might have been purely advantageous, if she had him doubting *Graham*—

She had acted as if she had been his friend, when she had been the only one in the transaction that he had known at all. And she *had* become familiar, in a way that almost meant safety—for the space of a few minutes, a flip he could little comprehend, only knew that he had felt it.

God. To be in Kaettegut again, with nothing to worry about, and no chance he'd see Jenning Crote again.

Jenning clicked off the connection with a distinct displeasure.

For Quinn to choose now to question one of her assignments—the timing was just bad; she was irritable today, and wanted nothing more than to go home, sit by the electric grate and warm her feet, and breathe, and *then* perhaps get some work done.

It was not only that, if she admitted it. The Benner call had not gone well. Damned woman had given no signals—and now, perhaps, *she* paid for it, with Quinn.

Frustration on Chauncey's part was natural in retrospect, of course, when Chauncey had damned little to work with, but to see *that* coming?

So Kellan Long had been transferred, a done deal. To *Travel*, to an obscure subsection long ago shrugged off to the dimmest corner of that department's back office—in no small part due to the lack of social skills on the part of the man who headed it, who had one employee left to his roster, if he still had even that.

Lord knew why Audit hadn't been good enough, that Quinn wanted him *there*. It was an overreaction to judge him even a pawn, in her opinion; Chauncey had made her statement, and was done.

Although—Quinn had suffered to *ask* her to file the paperwork. Poor consolation, of course, when for practical purposes it was already done. But damn it! he could have been useful in Audit. Perhaps nothing like his friend had been, but she could use a little extra largess in her own departmental negotiations, soon.

The idea was not outlandish. There were reorganizations, occasionally, usually initiated by the Proteriotita chair. She'd have to get a division head to suggest it, of course, and that might take some doing, but her department did have its value, much more than before.

It came down to two candidates: Iain Burton and—Stefan Coubertin.

The shock waves would go through all of Jefferson if she pulled off a merger with Iain, who headed Business—particularly since Quinn had lost a department to them years back. The thought did give her pleasure. But that would be a downgrade: Business only had a seat in the lower councils.

Stefan Coubertin was another story. If Stefan played half as brilliantly as he did as a mere peer delegate on the Proteraiotita, there was potential.

He was dabbling in things. It had been hell to dig that up even with her resources, and she did not know what it was yet, except that it involved the medical school. There were small, telltale signs of funding where funding should not have followed.

From his modest place on the council, Stefan Coubertin had turned some events—without anyone realizing it. A herding mechanism, if she had to put her finger on it: a respectful suggestion here and there, what only seemed logical, and they agreed to it, for what they should have been thinking. *God.* Remarkable, and if Fifty ever realized, Fifty would have him off the council in seconds.

There was the problem with Robert Wright, councilor of Education, who had not yet named a successor, but she might be able to massage things there, from the right position.

Yes, there was potential for a partnership, and conceivably for a wholesale relocation.

In that regard, the brouhaha over the Benner call might prove to be a timely distraction, depending on how long it lasted—and from this vantage it did look to last. Chauncey was playing them like a string, if anyone cared to ask *her,* and they were permitting it. Far better to let her handle it, who knew Agriculture's administrator much better than its own division did.

Agriculture had pushed itself into places it had little mattered before, *that* was the situation—but she would wager Chauncey Benner was only dabbling. Chauncey did not have the tools to play past that.

10

Kellan put his bag down inside the front door before he had taken another step. Graham had the heat on, thankfully. Graham left to himself preferred things cooler and could take even the brisk days outside with just a thin jacket. Not him. His first purchase had been a fleece marinac parka, with a hood that he could zip up enough to cover the back of his neck. Days like this, when it was raining, it got slicked down fairly fast, and he was already shedding it with his second step.

"How's it going?" Graham was in the kitchen, always made it back before him; *he* had to wait for the ferry in Jefferson and then the shuttle.

"Okay. Thanks for turning on the heat." His hair was more than damp. He headed straight for the bathroom closet, took out what he needed, began toweling off his hair and his hands on the way back to the main room. Friday, thank God, after a second week of newness and hard work. They had not bothered with an orientation or anything like the friendliness of Orlando, whom he had not seen again.

"Well, it's Friday." Graham came out with two hot drink glasses, handed him one. "Sit back, relax. —You should see the prices on soju over here."

"Expensive?"

"The opposite. I can't believe I paid for it what I did, back home."

He kept the towel on his shoulders, sat down on the sofa—Graham hated the sofa, he knew that now, thought it old and frail, but *he* liked it. It had the character of the old apartment in Rue, not the bulk of the stove, but something—venerable.

A sip of the soju gave a nice burn in his throat. It steamed; he tipped one hand over the glass and let it warm his palm.

"Has the old guy warmed up at all?"

He gave a short laugh. "Not at all. Worse, I think."

How *anyone* like his supervisor had kept from being transferred— but then, they probably could not find a more out-of-the-way location for Thomas Gouman, where he could do the least damage. He understood now why travel visas were approved so rarely. Travel had to be the least important department in its division, and anything outside official visa business—which the glossier women up front handled— was relegated to piles of physical paper and interoffice envelopes in the back, where his office was.

That he had an office—*that* had been something, he had only ever had a desk before, not even a full cubicle; but this one was tiny, enough only to fit a desk and a chair and a credenza with piles of papers on it and below it and beside it, with a warped door that had to have come from the remnant pile and a cabinet behind his head, that he thought might come crashing down. He had opened it on his first day, and that had been a mistake: the shelves had groaned with the shift of weight, and the files inside began sliding until he could not get the cabinet door shut and almost all of it was on the floor, covering his feet and the chair casters.

Thomas Gouman was related to Marcus Gouman somehow, he had heard, beyond having gone to the same school. He'd had to look up Marcus Gouman in the media archives to find out who *he* was, had only inferred from the coverage that the man had a reputation for being contrarian, that he was of a party different than those of his superiors, who had made their division a bastion of expansionism.

Political parties. That was something entirely new. They were mentioned in the media, of course; media coverage extended to Rue and the parties were big in election years, but he had paid it very little mind, it having no practical impact in Rue or in Kaettegut of which he was aware. He did not know if Chauncey Benner had a party affiliation, even if she did serve on one of the minor councils in Jefferson.

Graham already knew about things here; it was time *he* knew it, maybe had to know it, because he had no idea the practical impact it could have on him in the workplace, or if people discussed it in social settings.

"Do I need to have a political affiliation over here?" he asked, and looked at Graham, who sat on the floor to avoid the sofa.

Graham laughed. "They asked you, at the office?"

"Not yet. Do they?"

A shrug. "They haven't asked me. I think we're—so far alien, they don't think we'd have one, I guess."

The light wasn't strong, inside; they didn't keep it so. It felt too strange, with such a large window, and with the location on a block others walked to get to their homes. He looked, hard, at Graham, tried to read his expression. "Seriously?"

"I guess. They know I'm Kaetteguttan."

Would it always be like that? "We don't look any different."

Another shrug. "I think they just know."

He had not thought he had been any different than the most of them. He thought back, tried to think of himself saying something, meeting his supervisor for the first time. He shook hands like any of them. Thomas had not shrunk back or looked at him strangely, Thomas had worn the same displeased expression he'd had with any-one else, with one of the women from the front who stopped back to ask a question, with the one other person in his department, the most reticent man he had ever seen, thin and afraid of any contact.

The women up front—of course they spoke in a more polished way, but that was part of their persona, their superiority. They were the public arm of the department when someone called or came in. Orlando's speech had been very refined, if he thought of it in that context. He *was* a little different in that respect.

"What's Chauncey Benner's party affiliation?"

"It's not really necessary for Agriculture to have an affiliation, I don't think." A kind of wry humor, a little flat.

He started to ask—and stopped. He could reason some things through on his own without pestering Graham for everything.

No social settings, then, he could assume that: it would not be expected of him.

Coming into Travel, that first Monday, after no word on Thursday afternoon or Friday... He had been a good deal confused, at first, had expected to go to Audit, had been afraid this was more of the paper-work ploy, and that somehow he was going to end up with Jenning and a conference room again, but no, no one had come by, and by the end of the first day in Travel he had almost felt secure that he *was* assigned there, that he was not going to have to see anyone outside of his new department, and that department unimportant. Gladly so, in that context. He had come in on Tuesday, and worked at his desk for two hours undisturbed, and had been relieved.

Yesterday he had found there was an exercise room in the building. Rue had not had anything of the kind. He had been afraid he was supposed to have an identification card or something similar to use it, to even enter, but there had been nothing at the doorway, and only one person in it, a man, who only concentrated and did not look at him.

He thought he might start using it. He would never haul in mussel ropes, would never be mistaken for the ones who did, but even just recovered he was *stronger* than Jenning, whether or not she could take him apart.

Still—he hoped not to see her. He worked in the same division, he knew that, but he had found out, one of the first things, that her department was in an adjoining building, and that she had not ever had occasion to visit Travel.

Here in Grosvenor, with Graham, he felt far more secure. An obscure address, in an obscure part of town, far from Jefferson.

"Do you like it?" Graham asked.

There was weight behind that question. He looked at Graham, who had drunk all of his soju, and sat there looking at him, and had some investment in the answer.

He read the worry. "Yes. I do," he said, and made his voice firm, though he had *not* really liked much of it. There was the novelty of working in Jefferson, the exercise room, there was coming home at night, and the meal at the restaurant. He focused on that. "If there's better weather tomorrow— Do you think we could go to that restaurant again?"

Graham's face cleared some, at that. "The same place? We could try something different."

He thought it over; could see the black shells of the mussels, the walls painted in their vivid orange-red so that the room seemed snug and warm, for its length. "The same place. If it's okay."

"Yeah. That's fine." Graham understood him, sometimes; this was one of those times, and was solace.

Her own main room was a far too infrequent sight these days. Chauncey stripped off her jacket and laid it over the sofa back. "Television on," she said.

She had set it to the educational channel last night, and left it at that now. She did *not* want to hear any of the news or of the part Agriculture would surely play on it if Meghan Truong was acting true to form. Media did not have a seat on any of the councils, but Environment had long had a hold on it—how, she was not sure. She did know that even the educational programs tended to focus on Environment's programs, to highlight its accomplishments a little much, and to downplay its failures—and it had some, not insignificant, Meghan being prone to taking risks. The terraforming of the area across New Bay, for one, which opponents had said from the first received insufficient light, even for the degree to which specialty grasses and plants had been reengineered—she knew that much from her tenure on the Ligotera, gossip when Gallagher Crite was not in the room and they thought her preoccupied with papers or the coffee pot.

Meghan was good at squeezing in negative angles in the media, with the result Agriculture looked less than competent, to intrepret it charitably—that was the usual way, and Meghan took it because it *did* chafe. That Agriculture lacked in intellect, that—implied—its people were lesser, good for manual labor and for little else. That was a tactic old as the initial settlement, when the colonists diverged and took the natural route, and refused to use the sperm banks, to subject their population to selective breeding like a litter of animals.

No, the whole of Nocturne was built around the ones who did use the genetic banks, continuing the sin of the first of the two ships, and the sun-adverse disorder of one scientist on that original ship—whose daughter had lived to see the planet—spread through that population and now its time-removed descendents. The capital still sat just off the terminator, everything flanking *it*, and the expansion discussions were largely moot, no matter how much commotion the parties stirred up. There were still those, highly placed, whose DNA very no doubt included that predisposition, because, she understood, lineage was still very much a sign of status. No one was going to settle out of their reach, *that* was the real bottom line. That left viable expansion to the north and south for a strict number of miles on either side of the terminator, and even that space diminished rapidly with Nocturne's temperature bands.

There was the Back, of course, and beyond it—but the miners and factory workers who lived there did so at significant credit to their salaries, and because their aptitude suited them to only that, by careful design. Few others would be willing to expand that way, into the blackness and cold, and the resourcists did not want to grow the population, of course, to go with the expansion. Smaller, more numerous communities where there were rich resources to be found, to be shipped back to Jefferson and Grosvenor—that was the idea.

Her staff would have a report ready, the appropriate sections recorded straight off the media broadcast, if there had been any mention of Agriculture. She could deal with it in the morning.

For now, she sank into the cushions of the sofa, let her head fall back into the padding and relax. The pounding in her right temple worsened, but would subside if she stayed still.

Well. As a feeler, it had been successful beyond her expectations. Judging from the reaction time, Jenning had walked the recording to Environment as soon as she had it. Jenning, who, she knew now, worked somewhere in *Organization*, whose councilor was all but in bed with Loren Fifty—a truly odd coupling, given the opposing political parties.

Did she regret it? As an opportunity, it had ranked up there—she could have done the same thing with any of the renovation transfers, but that would have lacked finesse. A laborer's reaction might have lacked subtlety to the extent that Environment's reaction would have been far worse than this, that she might not be sitting here.

Her delivery had been exact. She had been pleased, a combination of what was natural and the experience she had already gained—*Jenning* had given her the rudimentary training, although Jenning would no doubt refuse to acknowledge that even in an empty room.

Environment, unfortunately, showed no sign they had read any other potential lines of action in the conversation. Subtlety was not Meghan's art, and that had spread down through the top levels of the entire division. Subtlety was not rewarded. Boorishness was.

Foolishly, she had believed upon first coming into her office and onto the Ligotera, that Agriculture's status as a department of Environment would serve her department well. She could almost laugh aloud, at that.

And far from it. Agriculture's status as Environment's *stepchild* had helped her, at least in small ways. She had more than half a mind to put that into gear, to take far more advantage of it than she had thus far—but that required patience, and a wait, because the others would hang back from whomever Environment punished, and publicly.

It was one more reason she did not look forward to the convening of the Ligotera. Ten days away, and the reception would no doubt be very cold.

The worst was that this had given her entirely too much food for thought, and she needed, damn it, the time to digest it. To look the options over and decide—unexpectedly tempting. This was ground Agriculture had not trod for decades. Agriculture complied, it did not make decisions about anything outside its routine operations.

She stretched. The headache had receded some to the rear of her consciousness, and there was—if she wanted to think that way—a fairly wide future spreading into its place.

Kellan went down to the exercise room during his lunch break, when the buildings emptied and half of Jefferson seemed to be out negotiating and collaborating over the tables of the restaurants they had around here—nothing like Cisco, nothing as common or relaxed as in the business district; instead cold as the whiteness of Jefferson's edifices and his building's slick lobby floor. No one ate alone there—the ones who did ate in their offices, as Thomas did. He did.

No one was in the room. He read the directions posted on the first machine, lay on the padded bench and positioned his arms the way it instructed. Lifted, and it was too easy. He adjusted the weights and tried again, and he had gone too far, he had to strain to lift the stack the several inches shown in the diagram. He left it there, anyway, pushed it up as many times as he could, was chagrined to find it was not much.

No matter. It was his first time. He could be patient.

He tried all of the weighted machines, with an eye to the time, tried an inclined bench, too, figured that was for crunches or some such, and that was the most difficult; his abdomen and the back of his neck burned.

The room seemed much warmer by the end of the lunch hour. His hair had dampened at the roots, and his temples were pounding—he should have brought clothes to change into, he had not been thinking. He did not have clothes like that over here yet, though, had not thought to look for that, when he was using Graham's advance for what he *had* bought.

He went down the hall, found the restroom diagonally across from the elevators, went in and turned on the sink faucet, and ran his hands under the water and through his hair, got it back into some kind of shape.

Even with the blood in his face, though—suddenly he felt *solid* again. Not injured, not weak. The ground beneath the soles of his feet answered back where he stood. He was real, with a core in there. Not everything had been blown away in the accident, in the disappearance of Rue and all that it had been.

The secretary came down to his office. That was unusual in itself; Graham turned in his chair at the sound of her voice, and her face, too, was a mild mixture of surprise and interest.

"They want you in Jefferson," she said.

So. A little inevitability, a slight consternation. He did not move. "Now?"

"This afternoon. They said to ask for Gabrielle Rhodes, in Aptitude."

He would not give her the satisfaction of any information, any reaction. They'd be discussing it while he was away, count on it, and probably afterward, and Ted would likely be in the center of the conversation, his office the center of the rumor mill. He simply stood, reached for his jacket, and put it on. "Thanks."

"Do you know what it's *about*?"

"No." If it was Jenning Crote—and Aptitude *was* her office—she'd expect him right away, if he read her right, and even in the impersonality of the media she was not hard to read.

Outside, he walked to the shuttle stop quickly, hands in his pockets. Another windy day; there was a major storm broiling in the east, it had been in the weather reports, and had been leading news this morning. And—*damn it*, Kellan was just beginning to settle in, even if Prime was not interesting to Kellan, or different, but foreign—and *now* he got a request from Jenning's office.

Kellan's questions had mostly regarded what he was supposed to do or say. That, and that they had been to Cisco's twice, and that he had received a request for his chowder—said Kellan was not trying to keep from standing out, necessarily, but that he was trying to construct a home, that he was trying to put up the parameters where they should be.

Damn it. Jenning's timing was nothing less than accurate; he should not have expected less. Kellan had not taken the hauler to Kaettegut, no, not while things *and* Kellan were in flux, when Kellan had only tentatively made his decision. Now that Kellan had something invested in it, had made progress, real progress—yes, Jenning came calling.

He *had* expected less. He had thought he had gotten by, that they both had. Kellan had been hard to read that night a few weeks ago, but he had understood that Kellan had talked to someone in administration in Agriculture, in Chauncey Benner's office, and that it was official, he was staying.

He had been deluding himself from the first day of his transfer; that had become conspicuously clear the moment he did relax. He had *not* been ready to walk away; had they sent Kellan down to the ship a few weeks ago, during that lunch hour, his reaction would have been stronger and far less calm than he had tried to give himself credit for; certainly it would have lacked any polish. He had been fortunate they hadn't: Jenning's timing might be impeccable on Kellan's end, but it was not on his. He was calmer, and he knew now far more what he was working with in the pricing office.

It took an ungodly amount of time to get to Jefferson. There was a directory and a map on the ferry, which he had not ridden before, and he consulted that, found Aptitude located fairly near Jefferson's second ferry dock.

Kellan would work in the building next to Aptitude, if he had understood his description correctly. He could stop by, see Kellan's office—but he did not know what would be his own state of mind after the meeting, and if it was at all off— Just the fact that he was in Jefferson would be a red flag to Kellan, who did not need any of the anxiety. No, he could not visit.

That Jenning had done what she had to Kellan in one conversation—was something he would have to put to the back of his mind; he could not afford emotion.

"Gabrielle Rhodes," he said at the reception desk in the lobby, which appeared to be shared between the two buildings. The footfalls of every staff person walking across the marble floor clipped and echoed behind him.

Just who he would be dealing with first, in a Rhodes, was significant. Rhodes was one of the three prominent schools over here, especially for government, and reportedly tended to produce finely precise minds; its leading light sat on the Proteraiotita and had a reputation for brilliance. It was far different reading these aspects over here, of course, where it was live, but it could be more useful here.

He was escorted to the elevator banks to the right. No conversation outside the introductions and the very efficient handshake—a single pump, and a quick release. He stood in the elevator and looked at Gabrielle Rhodes out of the corner of his eyes: she was one step in front and to the side, and had the disadvantage of being required to turn her head to see him.

She did not. She had long hair, and she did not wear it up as most of the women in the lobby had, a combination of burnished blond and a very light gray, from all that his vantage point gave him. She smelled of some kind of warm fruit, slightly musty, probably the twenty years or so that separated him and her.

She kept her hands folded in front of her. He kept his the same. The doors opened; he followed her out onto a floor that was nothing like the slickness of the lobby, but rather showed the structure's age. Judging from the worn carpet and the furniture, this department received the same level of funding as the pricing office did, though it *had* warranted far more space.

He was seated in a small conference room. He folded his hands on the tabletop, waited like that for a good deal of time, but that was fine; he kept himself on a very even keel, did not let his mind wander other than to examine the walls and the odd textured paint used, a striated gray which did not at all mesh with the variegated carpet.

Gabrielle at last reappeared and sat across from him, placing a tablet in front of her. "This is fairly standard," she said, and clicked a button, and handed it across to him. "I know you've been through it before, but we don't always have the most optimal access to Kaetteguttan records. We appreciate your patience."

He looked down at the screen. Two open radial buttons sat beside two sentences: *Worrying about unfinished work interrupts my leisure time; I would rather just get it done. / Work is necessary, but I don't let it interfere with my leisure time.*

"What the hell is this?" he said, and put the tablet back down on the table, not carefully.

"All the permanent transfers undergo aptitude testing. Your file will reside over here now."

"You pulled me out of work for this." He did not attempt to sound convinced, or friendly. *I have a meeting with your department head,* he thought of saying instead, but that would give him away. Jenning would hear everything he said, no doubt.

She returned his gaze, offered nothing else.

"I need to be at work," he said, a bluff, but he picked up the tablet. Not happily. She pushed back the chair, stood, and was not pleased; the veneer of thin neutrality was beginning to disintegrate. She said nothing, only closed the door behind her, quietly, with a click. Very controlled, that was commendable, at least.

He answered several of the questions, looked up, and the door was still shut. He stood, turned—turned back, rested his palms on the lip of the table. *Damn it!* Jenning didn't talk to him without having every bit of data on his psychology, that was what. He could only guess hers; his was going to be down in black and white, neatly coded, his insides butterflied open.

Her territory, her game, and he could do very little about it. If he did not take the tests, he was not even a player. Skewing the results— he was not trained enough. It would show up in neon lights, and he'd be out of the game again.

He sat down, picked up the tablet, and— *Wait.* He put it back down, sat there with his fingertips light on the the tops of his thighs, and his mind going cold until it could have matched the wind chill in the Back.

Kellan had said— *Christ.*

She'd had Kellan tested, too. Hell, he would not doubt it, not for a second. Kellan had gone in there expecting nothing but an encounter with another nurse, another doctor, and she had taken his data and known exactly where to go, must have flayed him apart with it. *She tore me apart,* he had said. Drugged, at the time, but still plain.

No wonder Kellan did not talk about it. She had gone right to the very personal, no damn doubt, and to repeat it—would be to lay himself bare.

This was her tool. Preparation—and why not? She had the luxury, she had the clout, and she was not the type who would enter an arena without every advantage to which she had access on her side. That was not the way they played, here.

Where he was, that meant, then, was not as simple as it seemed, either. Pricing was part of a division—what division, he had not even thought to wonder—and if his office was close to the goods it priced, it did not automatically follow that it was separated from Jefferson in philosophy as far as it was in distance. There were almost certainly things going on there of which he had not been aware. He had been learning the theories and the computer system, ignoring the real weight, the human systems which could have impact on him here. Ted and his damned simple, good humor had disguised what he would otherwise have looked for.

His mistake.

But there was no use wasting time on that, not this minute. He was here, and he would be far more of a challenge than Kellan. Less emotional. Far more controlled, because if he was not, he'd find it very easy to go for *her* jugular, and if he did not have the advantage of seeing her data first, he could damn well figure it out.

He picked up the tablet, pushed in another answer, and made himself breathe, and slow his heart rate.

He would ask. She would know he knew.

Hours. They ran him through every kind of test, until it was evening and he was hungry and thirsty, and Gabrielle offered him nothing, kept him in the room with the door closed. He was beyond late;

Kellan would not know where he was, and he was *not* going to ask to make the call, not here.

She opened it again, and at last she was not carrying another disc. If she had any sympathy for him, it did not show. "You're done," she said, and, "Thanks."

That was it. *Thanks.* By the time six o'clock had come and gone, he had known he was not likely to see Jenning, and that was a tactic in itself. "That's it? I can go?" he asked, just to confirm, and made it casual.

"That's right."

She might have had to stay late, herself, for him. She was patient, if nothing else, if there was no warmth left to her.

He picked up his jacket and walked out of the room, and down the hall to the elevators. She did not come this time. No doubt she had called the security guard at the reception desk to advise him of his exit; the guard was already watching as he stepped out of the elevator. He said nothing, passing him, just went through the doors, and outside the wind had picked up, was whipping down the largely empty boulevard. It lashed at his hair, his neck.

He had to wait an interminable time for the ferry. At last the lights came around the bend and slugged, slowly, in his direction.

The heat hit him full in the face, coming up the stairs to the apartment. Halfway welcome, this time; his skin was raw from the wind. He put his card into the slot, and Kellan was right there when the door clicked, pulled the door open to let him in. "Where were you? Are you all right?"

His face was probably red, and as striated as the walls in the conference room had been. His nose was running; he ran the back of one cold hand across it. "Fine. Just terrible weather."

"What happened?"

"Paperwork. Hours of it." He pulled off his coat and looked to the kitchen. No promising aromas, only the smell of the heating system and that damned sofa, pervading the entire space. "Do we have any of that chowder left? I'm starved."

"I can warm something up. I didn't know what time you'd be back." Kellan was already heading for the kitchen. "It's too late for me to call the pricing office by the time I get here. Nobody there picking up."

Kellan *had* been worrying, then. Damn Gabrielle and Jenning that they had waited to call him, when they had *known* how long it would take to complete that number of tests—and he was not slow.

"Did you have to take all your aptitude tests again, when they approved your transfer?" he asked, and made it casual.

"No." Kellan had a drink ready, came out and handed it to him: soju, cold, but it would warm the stomach nicely. "They tested me some in the hospital, I guess, kind of similar. For brain function, though."

They had no pride, then.

But Kellan was looking at him sideways, suddenly. Some anxiety. "Is that what you were doing?"

"It seems they have to rebuild my entire file. Why they can't get it from Rue—Agriculture *was* one of Jefferson's departments, last time I checked." He swilled half the drink down. It filled his stomach for one long, gratifying moment, and stung pleasantly in his throat. "Relax. Just formalities. They said they do it on the renovation crews too. Probably Kaettegut's stuff isn't good enough for them."

"I guess." Not at all convinced.

"Really. I didn't even warrant a supervisor." For all of Gabrielle's pedigree, her manner *had* struck him very much as a staff member accustomed to moving subjects through the tests, or through the department. "I think it was just an assistant."

"Oh." Some success, judging from the look on his face. He moved back to the kitchen. "I'll warm up some of the chowder. God, you look like hell."

"Thanks. Seriously."

He ducked into the shower, and the hot water helped a great deal, even if his stomach still clawed. *God.* That they had given Kellan those tests—in the *hospital*—burned, and he could not let it, or at the very least had to put it behind everything else. He still had to face her; Jenning wouldn't pull him in there for that for nothing.

She'd not call him in for another series of days, he'd bet. Would let him stew.

He toweled off, dressed, and Kellan had the chowder already in bowls, with spoons, ready to eat. He sat down at the table, glad again for the heat, with his hair wet.

Kellan took a bite, even though he must have already eaten. "If you ever have to come up that way," he said, and didn't look at him, "stop by and see my office. I'm on the third floor. You go left when you come into the lobby."

He had heard about the supervisor; from *this*, he gathered Kellan's office was not all that great.

"I'd hoped you'd get something better here," he said, simply, and meant it.

"Actually, I think I can maybe make a difference, where I am. A little." He looked up, and he was being honest. "I was thinking this week—my part of the department processes the travel visas for Kaettegut. I can maybe move some of them along faster, get more approved."

Kellan's mind still focused almost entirely on Kaettegut, then. He lowered his cup to the table without drinking from it.

"There was something I wanted to ask Chauncey," Kellan said, further, and was eating with vigorous enough appetite.

It was *Chauncey* now. "What?"

"Did they not ask—if people from over there could come over to visit the people in the hospital. Partners, friends, that sort of thing."

Partners. His stomach nearly froze, then clenched. He made himself sound calm. "They didn't."

Kellan looked at him for a long time.

"At least I don't think so, from what they said. I tried." He balled up the napkin in his palm, already damp from his skin, from the shower. A little hesitant, but now was as good a time as any; he did not often get openings like this. "You had said there wouldn't be any tours. You didn't come back to the hotel, and I didn't know— Maybe, I thought, they had kept all of you in the government building. They finally showed footage, and there were mobs at its doors. There were mobs at the hotel entrance, too, on and off. I couldn't find an agenda in the room."

Kellan had put down his spoon. A strange expression—it *crawled* onto his face, slow. "I didn't—" And finally, "I should have called."

"Kellan. You were in the *hospital*." But there was something in that, in the surprise— He let go of the napkin, put his palm on the table. "But, my God, did you think I wouldn't care? This—that you seem surprised!"

He looked down. "I didn't think—"

"That anyone cares about you?" His heart had begun pounding; he had never gotten this close. *Back off, back* off. "We don't really need to talk about it. I assume my actions speak for me."

The moment had gone awkward, very much so. Kellan stayed where he was, though, in the other chair, and only played with his napkin, had crumpled it. "It's why I stayed." And, "I really appreci-ate—"

Oh, God. He had not meant to put him in this position.

Still, he thought of continuing—his self-esteem could certainly take it, when he had lived on a starvation diet, willingly, for years—but there was too much risk. Too much. "Why did you want to ask the administrator that?"

"I just—they told me, that's all. I wanted to get it from the source, hear if it was really true. They didn't tell you anything?"

"No." Flatly. And: "Who did you talk to in Chauncey's office?"

A frown, of confusion. "Chauncey was who I talked to."

That raised his eyebrows. *What the hell?* He opened his mouth, for something stupid, when suddenly he could figure it out, easily. The media brouhaha surrounding the return of every patient, the way they trumpeted it across the news—the two coming back, in blankets, at the Gros Morne dock. There had been cameras, he had not had the presence of mind to notice, had not focused on anything but the boat, on the figures disembarking, but it had been on television. There had to have been cameras.

Good Lord. Kellan not coming back—he would have to check the media reports, but they had all gone back, every Kaetteguttan who had survived. Putting it together—*his* transfer had been nothing. No one had known, though they must have told the Rue pricing office something; he doubted they cared, overmuch.

Kellan's transfer was a political statement. That was the long and short of it, and he had thought of none of it. Last he knew, they had been keeping count. They would not miss that. "She asked you to come back," he said.

Kellan looked at the wall. "She asked what I wanted."

He was truly at a loss. No way to interpret things, not enough information—spinning, free, and suddenly he did not know why Jenning had called him in.

"Christ," he said, and did not realize he had spoken out loud, until he saw Kellan looking at him.

And Kellan had not said yes. Must not have—Kellan was still here.

Never mind. He could figure that later, needed a change of subject until he could reason it all the way through and could look at the media surrounding the Kaetteguttan returnees, did *not* need any more emotion.

Kellan had been in longer than most of them. He did not know any of the details, if Kellan had been in the position to be injured worse, had just landed wrong, had hit something wrong. Head injury, he knew that from the nurses.

"I thought—if Gros Morne cared, they would have asked for us to have visitors." Kellan looked past him, over his shoulder, for a long minute. "It *seemed* like she cared, on the phone."

"We can't know everything that goes on. There are probably things we have no idea, political things. Power structures. They might not have been in the position to ask." He got up, went into the kitchen, found the remains of the chowder leftovers, and waited while it warmed, and talked from there. "There was a lot of speculation. I think they thought at first it was targeted at the Jefferson delegation."

"Did they find out?" Kellan put one arm over the back of the chair, turned to talk to him.

He had to shrug. "I haven't been paying attention, much. I'd catch things on the television in the hospital lobby once in a while, that was it. They hadn't found anything back then that I heard."

A slow nod, a little disappointed—but he might be reading that into it. "They were in front of us."

"The Jefferson delegation?"

"Yeah. I didn't see them close up, but our guide said they were from Jefferson."

The timer beeped. He took out the chowder, went back to the table, and spooned more into Kellan's bowl, and here was a change of subject: "Not much of a dinner. Maybe we can go out later this week. There's got to be a store with more than canned oysters and soup."

He'd had a time finding the ingredients for the chowder itself, had purchased it at the same store, and only by talking to the manager. The clam meat had been in the back, in a storage room; he had the impression the manager had been saving it for his own. Still the fears about the food shortage, even if one could not tell at the restaurants.

Kellan finished chewing his current spoonful; he had hardly waited for him to refill the bowl before taking it. He *hadn't* eaten, then. "I think—you want to try a new place?" he said.

That was progress. He sat down and leaned back in his chair, pleased. "I've heard of another place. Osiake. A little spicier."

"That sounds good."

It *was* progress.

Chauncey Benner had asked Kellan what he wanted, whether he wanted to stay, and he was here, still, weeks later, even with his commute and his job, and an emotionless supervisor.

Still—that he had talked to *Chauncey,* and all that meant.

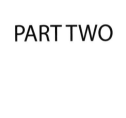

PART TWO

11

Kellan took a breath, and knocked on the door.

Thomas' office was full of paper, stacked everywhere—on the credenza behind him, on the desk between them, towering in the inbox so that it threatened to fall over. The room was as cramped as his, or it only seemed so because of the crowding, and there was a peculiar smell of *age* in the room—not emanating from Thomas himself, who was probably not yet into his sixties, but from within the cabinets and papers.

Thomas had, the message was, been there a long time.

The chair was uncomfortable—Thomas grunted for him to clear it, and Kellan put the paper in stacks on the floor, as neatly as he could. He had the request in his hand, freshly printed. Here, the printers worked much faster, and there were less of those with whom he had to share it.

"I can't get the system to take my authorization code," he said, after the courtesies, all of which were on his side, and not entirely comfortable.

"Kellan." Thomas leaned on his hands, took his eyes away from the computer screen for the first time, and really looked at him. "There *is* a quota."

"I thought we could override it."

"You can override it to a *point*." He made a gesture, tired. "An override is for very—outstanding cases."

"I think this is outstanding." Thomas could have deactivated his code, put some sort of limit on it. The thought had entered his mind;

the code hadn't worked for longer than this, but he had not said anything. He started to pass over the papers; Thomas did not extend his hands to take them—they hung, awkward, and he finally set them down, gently, in the midst of the other papers on the desk.

Thomas leaned back in the chair. It creaked. "Kellan. I appreciate where you're coming from—" a little, rare attempt at diplomacy—"but you've approved requests in one *month* we don't normally approve in a year."

Perhaps it was because there had only been two of them in the department, and a towering backlog, kept in a separate room, crammed in piles on top of the filing cabinets of legitimate business from another department. Only Thomas, grim in all the other duties he must have as a department head, and Emory, slow and deliberate, who had not said more than one word to him in the weeks he had been here, and that one word in passing, in the hall. They did not have department meetings here, or at least there had not been one yet.

If Emory got work done—he did not see it. The piles of paper stayed at exactly the same height. He hadn't ever gone in Emory's office, would not, because it would be an invasion of privacy, but *he* had looked in when he had gone by, when it was empty.

"I thought maybe I'd get through the backlog," he said. Thomas had not noticed the piles diminishing, probably, had certainly not thanked him for it. Thomas rarely went by the storage room, kept to his office, from what he had seen. "There were requests in there from a while ago." He did not say *four years*, which was the case in what he had found.

Thomas leaned a bit further forward, on his hands. "One of the things you'll need to learn is that Gros Morne does not discriminate. It approves everything. It doesn't matter if there's a pressing need or not. Schoolchildren, adults, doesn't matter. *They* make it our job to differentiate real needs from the frivolous request."

Is that why they had not considered *his* request? Frivolous? "Not all the schoolchildren get to come here," he said, because they *did* give the schoolchildren priority, and from what he had seen, rarely approved the adults.

"For a reason. A quota. A quota that's there for a reason, that has a purpose. In case you didn't notice, passage on the water isn't easy, it's *haulers*, for pity's sake; we have one accident and there's hell to pay. —For another, they all want to see Jefferson, and the lawmakers here have work to do, work that's hard to do when you're tripping over children and tourists. You don't see the average resident up here much, do you? *They* don't come up."

Graham had come up. Once. Maybe more than once, if Graham hadn't told him everything.

"Regardless." Thomas had his hands up in the air, now, for an instant. "It isn't us that sets the quotas, and it *isn't* our place to change the numbers. I'm sorry. It's the way it is."

"But—" Thomas had not so much as glanced at the papers. "I think it's an extenuating circumstance. She's old, she's above eighty, she just wants to see—"

"There's plenty of filing and paperwork to do. I appreciate the enthusiasm. It's a change. Just put it where it's needed."

Damn it. But it was no use, that was clear. He stood up and took his papers from the desk. "Thank you. For seeing me."

Out in the hallway, he wanted to put his fist through the gray walls. Eighty years old, not in good health—she might well not outlast the bureaucracy over here, could die before her paperwork was ever moved up. Schoolchildren, at least, got to come over, some of them—but in school, he had not appreciated the things he did now; who knew, if he *had* been privileged to see Jefferson, if it would be more than a distant memory of a time under supervision, when he had to behave? A vague memory of white buildings.

He would put her at the top of his list, for whenever they reactivated his code. It *was* deactivated, blocked, something; Thomas had as well as confirmed it.

More filing. *His* office was clean; he had spent days organizing it, when it must have been used as a storeroom before he came, and then had moved things through, had not let his desk get to the condition of Thomas' or even of Emory's, who was at least tidier than Thomas.

His desk, when he got to the sanctuary of his office, was not empty. The imitation wood grain, mustardy, of the surface next to his computer screen held a slip of paper, torn evenly off at the top.

He sat. Picked it up, and it was of finer paper than the usual variety, the mark of the highest levels. The scrawl was hard to read, thin and slanted well to the right—*Kellan*, he made out, and the rest clicked, mostly, into place. *Hear you're getting along. You know you can see me anytime you have questions.*

And the signature at the bottom, less readable than the rest—a *J.* Two squiggles, a long one and a tail. ...*Jenning.*

His gut went cold.

No one had been in the hallway. No—he had been too upset to notice; he thought there wasn't, but his desk had been empty when he had left, and he had been in Thomas' office for only minutes.

He stayed glued to the chair. Swiveled a little, looked around the rest of the office, but it was as he had left it, not a paper out of place.

He should leave, should find something to eat. His stomach was empty and that was not good, not after the denial by Thomas, not with this.

He could not leave his office. He stood up, took the few steps to the door, closed it.

She had not sent it to him over the system. A *note*, a physical note, on physical paper. Had *she* delivered it?

No matter what—she would know where his office was.

You know you can see me anytime you have questions.

He had, that once, considered her presence something—almost positive. Briefly, but it was there.

No. Jenning had said, when he had been at his weakest and in the hospital, that he had—killed a man. *He hadn't even known, I'll bet. Just working, for him.* One of *his* own, in the way Chauncey Benner had talked, Kaetteguttan, a man who might want to see Jefferson, who could be in that stack of papers on his own credenza, for all he knew.

God. He hadn't been awake, it was just where he had landed; he did not remember any of it, did not even remember the sound of the explosion, when there must have been one.

Had the man been awake? Had he struggled, and been unable to get up, because of *his* weight?

She hadn't let it go. And she wrote him a note, now, hand-delivered to his office; he looked at it again, saw again *hear you're getting along.* Heard from *whom?* Who had told her anything about him?

He set the note down on the top of his inbox. Carefully.

He *had* to get something to eat. Coffee, at least, and the coffee machine was down a hallway abutting this one, not far from his office. She and anyone in her office would be too busy to wait, and his stomach felt queasy, needed *something* in it, if only liquid.

He put his head in his hands, for a minute, tried to get his stomach to settle. He stood, finally, and opened the door, and the hallway was empty; he took two steps out, forgot to close his door until he was already turning down the abutting hallway and the light from the floor lounge made a slight rectangle on the floor where the hallway was between lights.

He put the spout of the coffee pot against the mug. It clattered, not as bad as he would have thought, though, and he was grateful.

That could be his filing project. He'd find the names of all who didn't make it through the accident, and all who did, and see who they were, and what they were about, what they were like. How old the man had been; had he simply been a tech?

He had not mentioned any of this to Graham, would not. Graham had watched him early on to make sure he could walk the distances to the restaurants and elsewhere; he did not need to hand anything else to Graham to worry over. Graham asked him careful questions about his job here, somberly casual, and he answered; that was enough.

He stood and drank the coffee there, in the floor lounge, and tried to calm his nerves.

Her room's window overlooked the trash area, was apparently just outside the hotel kitchen because there were piles of discarded oyster shells that had gone gray in the wind and with age. Worse, the flue from the stove must be venting below, because the smell permeated even the glass.

This—showed a little more finesse than Chauncey had anticipated. Meghan Truong had a sense of irony after all, to place her within view of discarded food.

She was in a northern corridor of the Grosvenor business district, this time, near enough to smell the dark wetness of the mud flats separating Jefferson and Grosvenor. They had not put her into Jefferson's small hotel, and that was a message.

But this location was near to all the restaurants, at least. She'd have a selection this time, something different, none of the ubiquitous glass-walled, zinc-tabled eateries of Jefferson. Her schedule would allow it, they could not so monopolize her time around the clock, and she was here for the week.

That was something she missed on Kaettegut, even with its abundance of fresh food, where the mussel laborers regularly brought home daily harvests from the sea, drawn out of the water and on the table only an hour or two later—but it was just what talent local to that kitchen could cook. There *were* no chefs. Gros Morne had a couple spots for the visiting dignitaries—only in the central government district, though, and those were staffed with cooks, nothing of this level.

Not so here. Everyday people ate in the restaurants here, every day it seemed, especially in Jefferson. Offhand luxury, the way Prime had other things. Truly *finely* prepared food.

The air was far chillier than the temperature gauge read, now, as was usual for Prime with its humidity, so flat and close to the water. She drew her black scarf from her bag, a previous Grosvenor purchase—looped it lightly over her head, wrapped the rest around her neck and secured it in her collar before she had made it to the front doors. There was wind, evident in the blowing hair and quick pace of the few people passing outside. The door sucked inward on its own vacuum when she first pulled on the handle, and she had one breath before the wind hit. There was the smell of bitter—spice—in the air, too, she could not quite define it.

And there was Rene, standing at the curb with, of all things, an umbrella opened against the wind. He turned and fell into step with her, and the umbrella went to the rear. The constant buffeting against the scarf ceased. Wind only pushed at the small of her back, at the back of her knees.

"Good morning," she said, and cared very little if they looked out of place with an umbrella—the residents here might be used to this kind of weather, but she was not.

"Morning. We're not far from the ferry stop." He had the collar of his coat pulled up, the odd worsted trench coat he had purchased on the first trip here, and had brought over ever since. And, "Environment is still angry?"

Their hotel location and the particular location of the rooms had not been lost on him, then—although he'd assume the appeal to Environment was responsible. He had processed it. "I suppose," she said, and left it at that.

The wind blew. The walls of buildings were a deep blue where the light from the street lamps did not fall. That anyone could live in such a place... She had long thought the renovation crews crazy, that they *watched* for openings in Prime, and were more organized about it than most of Kaettegut, excepting, probably, Murray Lerkenlund's seameats operations.

Two more had transferred, now.

These were small signs of an epidemic that had been going on for years, simply that. It had started with the colonists against the first settlers, the vaunted scientists. They were still fighting patterns set by the long-ago dead, that was the bottom line.

But she had been thinking more on unionization.

The unions' flaw, in hindsight, had been their own management. Over time, it became that they were run by men little different from the powers the workers were battling—in some cases worse, and that was appalling.

The concept had been true.

That it had not worked— *Power corrupts*, was one possibility. Or the original organizers did not have sufficient resources, and got into bed with those who did, and it went downhill from there.

Kaettegut had its strengths, not least its distance from Jefferson—but it was not just that, it was natural light, however dim, it was tolerable temperatures, it was its *people*. If their intelligence was different than what the Primeans held as their birthright, it was *not* less valid.

That renovation crews waited for openings in Prime—offered layers of feedback. First, they had believed the propaganda, their portrayal on the media. Second was the known difference in values. Luxuries were ranked far higher than the integrals: Jefferson, with its white-lit buildings, its business district with its true-plumbed walls and flawless windows glowing gold, was simply *grander*. Most all was old on both sides, and both were renovated time and again—but the best talent on the crews went to Prime, and the cracks in Kaettegut tended to be stuccoed over, the shape of the trowels still showing, from what she saw. A quality problem *and* a budget problem.

There was value in being unique, even so, to have and be something nothing else Nocturne had—and that was what the crews who watched the openings board did not see.

12

Kellan tried to fit the chopsticks into his fingers the way they should go. Osiake was busy tonight, the start of a weekend, people feeling freer to spend more time out eating. The bar near the front entrance had been packed full when he and Graham had come in.

He had seen Chauncey Benner. In person, from inside the lobby of his building.

The Ligotera was meeting. Of course. All of its councilors were in town, those from the Back and Grosvenor along with Agriculture. He had not expected to see any of them, could simply forget sometimes that he worked now in the central hub of government.

She had gone by outside on the sidewalk, in a group—he vaguely recognized another man from that council, from the footage to which he had never paid enough attention—but it had been *her*, vivid in a violet-blue scarf dark against brown skin and fastened tight against the wind. She stood at least a head shorter than all the rest, but she'd had more presence. The others walked; she *looked*, and every person got the same glance, the same quick evaluation.

It had made him feel—something he could not define, that he could not define even here, now, sitting safely in Osiake with Graham. Only that it paled the note from Jenning about which he had been worrying; and he only remembered it when he had gone back up to his desk.

He had not told Graham about the note. That evening Graham had fortunately been preoccupied. There had been no questions, and time had gone on, and there had been no reason to bring it up—

though he considered, now, and there had perhaps been enough time gone by, and nothing else had happened. Graham would perhaps not worry as much.

He did ask, trying to lift the chopsticks to his mouth without losing the bite, without shooting food to the right or the left of the table—he was unpredictable in the direction it went— "Did they ever call you back to—you know, for more testing?"

"In Jefferson? No." Graham was largely focused on the food; he had become proficient with the chopsticks more quickly, but still was no expert. "I'd have come and seen you if I had. I still will, if you want."

You don't see the average resident up here much, do you? Thomas had said. They *don't come up.*

"Do people here go up to Jefferson, much?"

Graham shrugged, took a sip of the tea and drained the tiny cup in the process. Osiake was not big on large helpings, except for anything that had to be eaten with chopsticks—there was an abundance of *that* on his plate. "I don't know. It did seem like a big deal that I got called up there, I guess. The secretary."

Disappointing—no answer there, then, and he had not built relationships with anyone else that he could ask. He did not think he was going to; here things were insulated much like on the other side. One worked with people, and knew the co-workers on one's floor. The women in his department were too polished, too cold; Emory was as close to lifeless as anyone he had met.

He had been using the exercise room at work nearly every lunch hour. He did not often run into anyone there, but it got him away from the empty floor lounge, gave him something to *do*, a purpose—but now he was the more glad of it, in that it had been a long time since he had felt shaky walking to Osiake or to the grocery, no longer felt his heart beating smack against his ribs. He had carried back a good quantity of groceries one night and it had not felt like *that* much.

"I got a note from Jenning the other day," he said, and took a break from the chopsticks. The owner was coming around with new carafes, replacing the empty ones on each table; he watched, because theirs was empty.

"What?" Very understated, and said over a bite pinned between Graham's two chopsticks, but Graham could look alarmed, and did, and his heart skipped a beat. A mistake.

Too late to take it back. "It was on my desk. On paper. I don't know who put it there; I was in Thomas' office for a few minutes." He fiddled with his cup, made the few drops of tea roll around the bottom. "They would have said something if it had been *her* that dropped it off, wouldn't they? The women at the front?"

"What did it say?" Quieter.

"I still have it back at the office. In the credenza. It said—" he could still *see* the writing, in his head, "—'Hear you're getting along. You know you can see me anytime you have questions.'"

A small silence. Then: "Well." Graham bent over his plate, concentrated on pincering his next bite.

He waited, and when there was only more silence: "She's too important to be delivering notes herself, isn't she? A staff member, right?"

"I'm sure." But Graham crumpled up his napkin, put it beside his plate, and laid the chopsticks along the other side. "Nothing before that?"

"No. Nothing."

Finally, somewhat strenuously: "It's okay. I'm sure—I don't know what she's doing, Kellan, but you're here, you're doing well at work. Don't worry."

People talked around them. He wanted more tea; even the mildest of Osiake's food tended to be salty, and he could handle a cup far easier than the chopsticks. He drank more than he ate, here; ate the bulk of the food at home as leftovers, when he had access to a fork.

Graham's face showed concentration. But after more thought, he said, "You know, she might not be a bad person to know."

He thought before the next. He had thought a longer time on this, had still not decided. Maybe now— "She was in the accident. I told you that. I didn't tell you—she told me about it."

A dead silence, for a long second, and then the proprietor was at their table. Very sudden, and welcome, with the tea, but that made his statement colossally bad timing on his own part. He should have been watching, should have noticed the pattern the proprietor had been making around the tables, and waited a few more seconds. A slight bow, from the man. "Good dinner?"

"Yes," he said, "excellent," because Graham seemed struck, had gone into a different mode entirely.

"Glad to hear," the proprietor said, and bowed again, and moved off to the next table.

He took the carafe, heavy now, and hefted it. Poured himself a cup, and filled Graham's cup, too.

"She was awake. I—wasn't, didn't know."

He was not getting anywhere, was not deluding Graham. His careful demeanor—he wanted Graham to be calm, to take it for what it was, nothing else. Graham was going on different cues: he had his fingers hard against his palms, on the table, behind the plate. "What did she tell you?"

"She told me what it was like. Dust falling. She said it—was beautiful, actually. She couldn't hear anything afterward."

A little relaxing of the fingers. Not much. *Graham* did not view Jenning as benign, then, despite what he might say, did not see her as someone who might have been a victim, too. *He* only did—halfway. Maybe not even that. "That wasn't all she told you."

"No." He put his own napkin beside the plate; there was still plenty of food, but he would take it home in leftovers, the usual; regardless, he was not going to be able to eat more tonight. His heart was pounding, now, for all that this had been delayed, and to see Graham's reaction, and to not find it friendly. "God, Graham, it's not my fault. I didn't—"

"No." Graham started to lift a hand, thought better of it, pulled back. "God, no. It's not."

The food he *had* eaten felt distinctly unsettled, in his stomach. He should not have brought it up, then; had been right to leave it where it was, to question his own judgment in telling anyone of it, of what he knew.

He could have been content, not knowing. Still—when she had started to tell him, he could have said something, could have stopped it. He had thought it. He had not done so—knowingly. He had gone in with his eyes open, by his choice, and she had done what he had given her permission to do.

He was *not* sorry for knowing. For what had happened, for what he could not take back.

He had not found a file for the man. He had no idea where to look to find the names of those injured in the accident. If he could, and the man had ever applied for a travel visa—precious information would be offered, on the form: why he wanted to visit, his age, a snapshot of his career.

"You said she's maybe a good person to know." He tried that, and it fell flat. Graham did not take it, would not be distracted.

"Did she make you feel it *was* your fault, Kellan? Did she?"

Graham knew there was something there, then, the way Graham always knew; he had never hidden things well. He stumbled over words for a second, blanked— "No. Just..." And tried again: "Let's talk about it later. Okay? It's all right. I shouldn't have brought it up."

But Graham looked at him, and was not going to let it drop, and he *had* brought it up.

He looked down, at the food growing cold. "There was one part I— That's all. I know it couldn't have been my fault. Not my decision."

"God." Graham had his wrist, now, never mind the restaurant and the people. A tight grip. "What? What did she say?" And, "Tell me. Good Lord, Kellan, it's *me*."

He shook his head, and let his wrist stay where it was. "Nothing can help it. It's just there."

A pause, when Graham was not often speechless. But then: "Kellan, everything I've *seen* in you, this—she wasn't there to help. I don't know what this is about a note, but it's *not* what it says, face value. Not help. Some kind of—" Frustration; Graham was forcing words that weren't quite there, and it was an about-face from what he *had* said. "I don't know why she'd care, why we'd make a difference to her. She should have left you alone."

Graham *wanted* him to tell him. It was there, in his face, in his expression. Maybe morbid curiosity, even; he could not put that past any human, even Graham. "Can you just be a little, a little more friendly?" he said, not smoothly. "I wanted—God, I don't know what I wanted, telling you. Just that I don't like to have things that I don't—"

Graham stood up. Took his wrist with him, and he stood up, too, in confusion. Other were looking. He pulled his wrist back; it released, too easily.

That set in. He regretted it, immediately, but Graham was already across the floor to the doors, and gone, and others were looking at *him*, now, alone. The door swung shut, slow. He sat back down, took a breath, put his napkin back on his lap, looked determinedly at his food. He could very little take the chopsticks and eat, under scrutiny; he took a drink of the tea, instead, still hot. His face felt equally so.

Graham did not lose his temper, Graham was level-headed in the worst of situations.

It *had* been his fault, then. This, at least. He had said it wrong, he had picked the wrong time to bring it up, and Graham had wanted to know all of it. Of course Graham would want that, he could not open *this* box and expect Graham to be satisfied with half-information; he should not have said anything at all. Should especially not have dumped this on him here, in a public place.

The proprietor was coming his way, another carafe in his hands. At the table, the slightest bow—the proprietor doubtless did not want controversy in his restaurant. "I hope things are all right."

"I— I'm sorry. I apologize for any inconvenience." He wanted to ask for a carton for the food, for what would last him a couple days. He could not, now. "I'm very sorry. The bill?"

He hated to leave, still. The tea smelled acidic but calming; he might do better to stay, to give Graham time. Inconvenient to live with someone, certainly, in situations like this.

The owner went to get the bill, in any event, and that left him time to take another cup, and ordinary conversational volume had returned around him, at least.

Oh, God. He had miscalculated, badly.

He signed the bill as soon as it came, stayed for two more cups of tea, and went back to the restrooms, through the tables. Faces looked up at him, faces with curiosity, some furtive, some open. He smiled at one, a tight smile that was all he could manage; to his surprise, the person returned a small one.

Someone understood. He felt better, washed his hands when he was done, dried them, and walked out with his head held a little more erect, even if he still felt stares against his back. The doors closing behind him were an immense relief; he stopped, and sighed, and let his head fall back.

Now. Where to go? He could still taste the tea toward the center of his tongue. The wind had died down, at least; he could last some time out here, walking, and that had maybe be best: some time to walk it out, to think how to go back home, how to repair anything he had done.

Graham wanted him to tell him. He could not; this was too intensely—much. There *was* no help.

If he could only remember! *Had* it been a choice, in a millisecond, to lose consciousness? An easy way out when all was surprise, and unknown—trust that someone would find him and do right by him, the way he trusted Graham?

It did *not matter*. He could not stop what had happened, could only hope the man too had been unconscious, that he had not felt anything metal driving through him, any pain—had not felt his life ebbing away.

Oh, God. Please let him have been unconscious, and not to have cried out for help, and received none.

He did not let himself think of such things. He had carefully segmented it off, increasingly well with more practice, and more practice still.

He was walking toward the river. The other way, at least on the maps, was Jargen Bay, and across it some distance there was Kaettegut's northern province, and not far into it, Rue. He had never gone that way, could not think why not; he considered it for a minute, but his feet carried him to the river, along the newly familiar ways.

It was all behind him. *Behind* him. The accident, and the man who had been impaled, and all that went before that. He did not look that way.

There was, in a recess in the walls lining the street ahead, a vague shape. Someone sitting. Rare, at street level; he tucked his hands deeper into his pockets, hunched into the coat, and veered a little left, for space—not enough to offend.

"I'm sorry," the shape said, when he had gone almost past—*Graham*, Christ, and he jolted.

Graham did not get up. *Drinking*, was the first question that entered his mind, and he pushed it away, there had not been quite enough time—but he looked, and the alcove was wet with something—no, a drainpipe was leaking its water there.

Graham had been letting his hair grow, hadn't cut it since the hospital, when he had first noticed. It was getting long, now, enough to hang in his eyes; more obvious here in the dark of the alcove.

"Are you all right?" he said, and did not know whether to squat down to be on his level, or to offer a hand, because Graham stayed where he was and made no sign of rising.

"My fault, I guess."

"Are you *all right?*" He did bend, a little, and looked, but Graham did stand, then, and was tall again.

And Graham seemed more himself again, like that—some. "I didn't mean to embarrass you. Back there." He glanced back the couple blocks, toward Osiake.

"It's okay. It was all right."

"Look. I think—I *know* I did wrong. I would have negotiated for you, and you wouldn't have ever had anything to do with that—that—God *damn* it, Kellan, if I had known, you just never would have talked with her. That's all."

"It's not just her." He gave him that, in the awkwardness of the setting, wished it were something else besides an alcove on a street, that it was the restaurant again, with the hot tea, and that none of this had happened. "It's the whole thing. She only told me what happened."

"And she said something about me."

He considered, very briefly. "Yes."

Graham dropped the rest of the pretense, then, and that was discomfiting, more than he wanted to admit. "Kellan. Just tell me what she said."

He looked down the street, at the lights gleaming off the plate glass, the metal of the drainpipes, of the light fixtures themselves. On the occasional puddle; they must have washed off the street or the buildings, because it had not rained for some days. "Back at home," he said, finally, and knew he had not thought it through enough, but Graham had not given him that look before, at the restaurant, *raw,* and he didn't look right, still. "Most everything."

Graham hesitated, but there was relief with it. "Home," Graham said, and started walking, and had his own hands in his pockets, and did not look as if he wanted to talk, then.

Graham would want to know the rest. He should not have let him know there *was* more. Stupid, and he *had* said it, and now he could not go back on it.

It was only—he didn't like keeping secrets, not from Graham.

This time he had just wanted to work through it on his own, and had worried—he would offend Graham, because she *had* said things about him, and he had almost believed them. Stupid, but it was what he had said the first time, and what he could recognize, even at this distance—she knew her material, and she was head of the aptitude department, which dealt with psychology. That she had made him feel safe with her there, too, for a time, in that conference room—that more than anything spoke to her skill.

And Graham had said she might not be a bad person to know, and maybe that *was* true, even if she was like that.

The shuttle's seat was white and cold, the breeze from the cars' slight velocity made worse by the proximity of the river and its cold water, but it was comforting, too, in the thickness of the air.

There might be a fog by early morning. He was beginning to attune to the weather patterns, if nothing else.

Their street came, finally, and Graham still said nothing. They came to the street-level door, and the stairs, and their own door, heavy and black—Graham opened it, let him past, shut it, and leaned against it. Looked at him.

"It's okay," Graham said, in a tone that *was* reassuring.

He let out a breath, made his shoulders relax. Went over to the sofa and sat down, at least, and rested his elbows on his knees, his chin on his hands. "Hard to remember all of it," he said.

"It's okay."

He took another breath. From the beginning; Graham would ask, if he did not start there. "I told the staff I needed to talk to someone who could—let me stay. I don't know what they call it over here. She came after a long time. She laughed at what I was asking for, but she didn't leave. She wanted to know why I wanted to stay."

Graham was concentrating; the lights were not on, there was just what there was coming in the window from the street, but he could see two dark eyes, not blinking. A little stricken, at the last.

"She wanted to know if I had asked you to come over here. When I said I hadn't—she said you made the decision, and you'd work it out yourself, and that maybe you wanted to come over anyway. A good opportunity, she said. And that they were short one in the pricing office, and that they didn't just transfer renovation crews, though that was most often." Chauncey Benner had contradicted it—*a different part of the renovation industry.* Dryly.

He blew air out through his cheeks, leaned further in on his fist, on his knuckles. This was maybe *not* the best idea; Graham was looking increasingly angry, but Graham had wanted to know, and was going to have it one way or another. "I found out she was in the accident. She said she and I had a lot in common because of that. She asked if I remembered it. She did. She described it for me."

"What did she say?" A dangerously level tone of voice, and it was still dark.

"She said—she said it was beautiful, actually. Like I said." He said it louder than he should have, but he was still defensive; halfway wanted to fade into the sofa back and disappear, but the other half— he was getting it over with. It *would* be over, and Graham would know. "Very quiet. Dust floating, and where it touched skin, it was cool. She thought it wasn't real. She remembered seeing me. She said it looked like I was asleep."

There. That was all the further he was going to go, because the rest— Perhaps, after all, he wished Jenning hadn't told him. She could have told him only that, and it would have been enough.

Graham stood there and did not move; it was as quiet then as it must have been to her, back in the hydroponics bay. She must have been deafened in the blast; he had not thought of that before, but that would explain the silence—maybe they had repaired his own eardrums before he'd even woken. Who knew all that they'd had to do, to all of them, to make them right again?

"I did not," Graham said, with evident restraint, "come for the opportunity." A little silence made the words hang in the air. "I *made* the opportunity so that I could get here. I was—afraid they might not take it."

"Why did you leave?" he said, and hadn't intended to ask that, not now, but that Graham said *that*—it just made him angry, suddenly, that's all. "You went out of the room to talk to the nurse, and I waited. They didn't tell me until later that you had gone. God, Graham!"

"I told you. I said I was wrong." Graham took the doorknob in his grip, behind him. "I wasn't going to do it like that. I thought—I hadn't expected you to have that kind of reaction, it surprised *me*, and I thought maybe the more I stayed, the worse I would end up causing. I told the nurse—"

"Not that." *Damn it.*

Graham's turn to take a breath, a deep one. "Because—" He left the door, finally, came over and sat on the coffee table facing him. Reached out and took his hand—strange—and pressed it between his palms. He pressed again, and let go. "Because that was the arrangement. I knew it when I did it. They weren't going to let *you* stay; I knew just trying to get my own transfer over here was a risk, and I was surprised they took it, but I had something to bargain with, and they did. That's all. They weren't going to reverse something like that. It just came time to pay."

"You weren't going to mention it to *me?*" There hadn't been only one person in the equation; *he* had been there, and he thought he did matter, in something like that. *He* thought.

He leaned back, put a little space there, and wanted more.

But Graham was leaning forward, Graham wasn't letting him have any. "God, Kellan, do you know what it was *like?* —I told you I couldn't find out where you were. When I finally did find out—it was hell, that's all. I couldn't get any information—they said everyone had been sent to the hospital over here, there was no word on what your condition was, *I* didn't know they weren't sending bodies."

Oh, my God. He had not thought—he shut his mouth and sat there, and it did not answer it, quite, but he was appalled.

Graham stood, and maneuvered around the coffee table, went back to the door. Some distance, when he *least* wanted it, now. And damn—he had his hand on the doorknob, again, and he was opening it.

"Graham," he protested.

"I need a walk. A cold dunk in the river." A little wry humor, but there was not much in the eyes. "At least you asked. God, Kellan, I did *not* come for the opportunity. I know—I guess you could have thought—the things I said, about change, they *were* true, but they weren't that."

He stood. "I'll come."

A small gesture of Graham's free hand, the one not on the doorknob. "By myself. —It *is* true, I don't mind something different, I could have used more of it, but I never planned to come over here. I just wanted—well, I didn't want you thinking I'd been sentenced to hell. That's all. I would not have left Rue."

He felt suddenly stricken. "It's all right, isn't it? Over here?" Squeezed in at the last second, before Graham could open the door.

A small smile. "It's fine."

Graham did open the door, then, and left, and at least he was still wearing the jacket. Kellan looked to the window and it had fogged with the humidity.

He was standing by himself in a dark main room, then. He stripped out of the jacket, laid it on the coffee table, and sat where he was.

His heart was beating too fast, now, knowing he could not take any of it back.

13

Robert Wright's office was enormous, set in the corner, traditional except that Robert liked to stay near his staff, wanted to make sure they were always working, if Stefan had to guess.

Robert sat across from him now, lips tight, reading his report. No small talk, nothing political, no matter that almost every Education department head was expansionist and talked about things amongst themselves. He would have *liked* to hear Robert's thoughts, for his part.

Perhaps Robert did talk to the others. He was on the council with Robert, an opportunity, but Robert had never treated him as a partner or anything close to it.

The expansionists had their eye on Kaettegut's northern province for the first leg of expansion. He had been in those meetings just as Robert had. Barren now, but if Marcus Gouman's department was succeeding at last with the northern patch—Kaettegut posed less of a challenge, at least. There had been talk of canals, which got into the wilder side of things, and Marcus was staunchly resourcist: he would have to be convinced of the value of the project, Meghan Truong or no.

—And now Chauncey Benner had stuck her hand into the gears and skewers of the machine, had made Quinn and the status quo party more essential, and her *own* division head less so. Chauncey Benner would be ground up between those two, much less Fifty. Unfortunate timing, when she could have no idea, and the phone call showed it.

Robert grunted and looked up from the paper. "You're working with Consumer Affairs on this?"

"Yes." Of course: Consumer Affairs and Business were his biggest customers of late. Of the two, Robert did not mind Business.

The expansionists had to stay on that course. No, more than that: things had stalled, had been stalled for a while, and they needed to get *moving*, needed leadership that was—bolder than Fifty had been so far.

He looked at Robert and wondered. Always did.

The life span research he supported was designed for the right leadership, once it was in place, to ensure there was continuity between the quicker-lived generations, that they did move forward, and with careful and deliberate design.

They could assume nothing about time, but they *were* making assumptions, just in the way they thought. *He* thought in the long term, on the other hand, and in terms most were not comfortable thinking, but that needed to be considered, by someone.

He looked across at Robert, at the white hair and the deep lines on an otherwise robust face. Fifty would eventually be gone, and plausibly Robert within a lesser number of years, and he had that long to get himself into this office.

That was not probable.

He knew it, had known it longer than he had wanted to admit. He had misplayed things. His advantage was his council seat, and that was not guaranteed even under Fifty. Once that was lost—

He could stay in Ethics, of course, leading his department. Tiny in numbers, and as ineffective as those numbers.

He hunched his shoulders.

"All right," Robert grunted, and handed the paper across the desk, back to him. Robert swiveled his chair sideways, reached for his computer, and that meant he was dismissed. Stefan sighed, and stood.

Graham picked up the plate, rinsed it, dried it with the hand-towel. Routine, simple actions—a comfort, sometimes.

He had been shaking. He had come closer than he ever had—he had said some things he might reconsider now, in a saner moment, had taken Kellan's *hand*, for Christ's sake, had pressed it between his, twice. And Kellan had not pulled back; there had been no resistance at all.

He had gone too far. He *had* no excuse.

In the restaurant, when Kellan had pulled his wrist back—he had been completely outside propriety then, and Kellan had been well within his rights to do it, in that kind of setting, in that kind of reaction. Still, it had stung, more sharply because he *had* taken the chance.

He had left Kellan in there to clean up the mess; Kellan, who was still feeling his way through, trying to fit into a new setting.

Kellan's hand had been warm, in the main room, for having been out in the cold not long before. Warm, and firm, and he just should not have done it, because he knew himself, he knew he would not be content once he had started, and he *had* started.

As far back as the hospital— other people had acted. Naturally. He had *made* Kellan act, by his own lack of it.

Now Kellan sat in the apartment some evenings, when Chauncey Benner was covered by the media, and watched the reports without so much as blinking. Kellan *wanted* Kaettegut, another thing that would not be satisfied.

Oh, God. He was stuck, that was all, he was standing here in the kitchen with the greater part of his body that wanted something that it could not have, the way he was used to it, only—

The television was on in the other room. "Volume up three," he said, because that might help. He had gotten by with such simple distractions before—when, damn it, it wasn't just physical, either; it went deeper.

The television volume rose.

Kellan would not tell him all that Jenning had said. There was something she *had* said that had done something—Kellan had mentioned it, but from his behavior from the first, too, there were signs, and if Kellan was still stinging from it—damn it that men could not touch, at all, that he could not help— that words were empty. He felt that acutely. He had tried to make his words count, being all that he could use, had put emphasis where he could, had *argued*.

No, he was not being honest, not even with himself. He did— *Wait.*

There was an image on the television screen. He clipped the

kitchen counter getting into the main room and in front of the television. —It was the freckled girl, the one he had seen disembarking the boat at Gros Morne. Colorless still, and her photograph on the screen was not moving; it was an old shot, with a tight smile, and they were speaking over it. They were saying—

The doorknob clicked, and the door came open. He looked, and could not rearrange his face fast enough.

Kellan stopped in the doorway with his hand still on the knob. "Graham?" he said, and moved to the front of the television set, then, and looked.

"Suicide," he said, before the announcer could repeat it, and felt sick to his stomach; that was the snatch he had caught, and there was no way to change it. He should have turned it off the instant he heard the click of the doorknob, damn it!—now Kellan stood beside him and looked on, with the reporter's continuing voice, and all that came with the story.

Good Lord. They were expanding on it, and his first thought was: *they don't have the right.* It was too intensely private, *her* life, and there were others, too, who had gone through it, and did not need to hear this. One of whom— He opened his mouth to instruct the television to power down. "Don't," Kellan said.

He stopped, and sat down, then, Kellan still beside him, an arm's reach away—who was looking at *him.* "What?" Kellan said, but as if he wanted to know.

He thought—but Kellan wasn't telling him everything, couldn't, and that wasn't the way he wanted it to start to be. He could give him something. "I saw her," he said, and looked only at the television screen. He shrugged. "I saw her come off the boat back in Gros Morne. I had heard two people were coming back; I had hoped one of them was you. She was wrapped in a blanket, and she was—very pale. I felt bad for her."

Surely there was still some speculation—they could not know she had done it, that she had done *that.* Not for certain, not this fast.

But the reporter was quizzing the other man on the screen, and there came out that she had been one of the burn victims, that she'd had burns over most of her body. Kellan refocused on that, on the screen. And that explained the blanket, and even the lack of hair: the hair in the photo on screen was longer, but he had seen her, and it had been cropped close to her head.

Kellan sat down next to him, and that was worse. "It's the people," he said, because the two men on screen were discussing that, that she'd had difficulty fitting back in, that she had not ever done well after the accident. "God."

"Did you know her?" he said, then, because that seemed the right thing to say, and Kellan *could* have known her; the tour had presumably been for the conference attendees, and there were others from Rue.

Kellan shook his head.

They were going to have Chauncey Benner on. They had to plan on that. Chauncey Benner would make a statement; *she* would have some sense to make, better than this, at least—and that would be the best thing for Kellan. "The administrator will have something to say about this," he said, and: "Okay to turn it off? Okay?"

"Okay."

"Television off," he said, with some relief, and Kellan's eyes had acquired something at the mention of Chauncey. "Chauncey will be reasonable," Graham said, and it was only *words* again, damned words, near powerless. "Not everyone reacts like that. Damn, who knows what it was, for her? Everyone's different."

Kellan stood, finally, and took a few steps, and then was out of his range of vision. There was the sound of a door closing, quietly: the bedroom door, if he had to guess; he twisted, and it was. The bathroom door was still open.

Damn that they were still lodging here, as familiar as it had grown. Kellan still had the sofa for a bed, no personal space for him, no privacy for something like this.

They hadn't shown the burns, at least. After the reporter had gone into what he had, he would not have doubted it.

He reached forward, turned the television on manually and muted it. Watched for Chauncey Benner; that would mean the most to Kellan.

Nothing. He sat for a half hour. The streetlights finally dimmed; they dimmed the final time at ten o'clock here, and stayed at that level until the morning.

He stood, finally, stretched bones that had already grown creaky from the stillness, and went into the kitchen. There was crab soup in the refrigerator, leftovers. He warmed it on the stove, waited, patiently, and poured some into a bowl before it began to boil. He found a spoon, carried it all to the door, tapped.

No answer. He nudged open the door, and Kellan was lying on the bed, the only furniture in the room, with his arms behind his head. It took another minute and a closer vantage to see Kellan's eyes *were* open, and looking at the ceiling, before they rolled to the side, and to him. He held out the bowl, with the spoon already in it. "It's hot," he said.

Kellan closed his eyes, opened them, shook his head. Sat up with some effort, and leaned against the headboard, and shook his head again.

"I know."

He did *not* know. Of course. He was not one of them; Kellan was, and who knew what had been going through Kellan's head? Nothing from Chauncey Benner; that was worse. He did not mention it. "I'm sorry," he added.

Kellan reached out and took the soup, at least. "Thanks," he said, and looked to think to add something else.

"No. It's okay," he said, because he had a fair guess what it would be, and went to the door and put his hand on the doorknob. "Stay in here tonight."

"No! It's yours."

"It's both of ours. No argument, Kellan. I'll be on the sofa. All right? Just the pillow."

Kellan considered, a long time. Finally handed him the pillow with his free hand; balanced the hot bowl in the other. "Thanks. Sorry."

He went into the other room, retrieved Kellan's pillow from the neat stack of pillow and blankets, tucked to the right side of the sofa, as far out of sight as Kellan could make it. He brought it back in, and did not want to even look, again, now that he had delivered the soup. He made himself do it, to meet Kellan's eyes. "You'll be okay?"

Kellan nodded, and made a show of wedging the pillow between his back and the headboard, and blowing on the soup to cool it off. "Yeah. Just thinking."

He wasn't going to eat the soup, likely, from the look on his face. He appreciated the effort: to get Kellan moving, even a little, helped. "I'll be in the other room," he said, in case.

Not for that, not in something like this, though he had little hope he'd be able to talk him through this kind of situation.

———————

Chauncey had come—almost—to the end of a long day, after a series of long days, the constant Ligotera sessions. She took a quiet look at her watch under pretense of shuffling some of her papers—her sleeve drew back just enough if she held her hand a certain way. They had long passed dinner.

Gallagher Crote sat beside her, nearly an arm's length away with the way the chairs were spaced. He glanced at her movement and smiled very slightly with one side of his mouth, in like opinion.

Gallagher had stuck closer this council round than he had before. For both being Environment, they were occasionally grouped to-gether—but this went beyond that. He had sat next to her at lunch at every one of the restaurants, could do so unobtrusively in this group, who had no one eager to sit next to the other.

The staff could not come into a closed session. The building's kitchen staff had come in to bring dinner, and later to take it away, and the session had gone closed shortly after that, with the result that there were still coffee cups and used utensils lingering on the sides of the saucers here and there.

Tonight it was a personnel issue. Shipping had a quarrel with an employee directly in the line of Owen Pace, administrator of Manu-facturing, and when the distribution system did not go smoothly—yes, the smallest personnel issue came before the council.

Gallagher Crote stayed aloof, for the most part. Now he folded his hands under his jaw and leaned in to watch Shipping take on Manu-facturing, for what would surely have Decheran involved in short order, and the entire point moot.

Rebecca Wright, who—say this, knew her furniture—had little to say for mercy. Competence was key for her, that was how one worked *her.* "Ridiculous," she dismissed Owen's defense, at one point, with a wave of her hand. Straight down to the core. "Either he gets the job done or he doesn't."

She would not be needed until the vote. She settled back in her chair and wished for more coffee. They had drained all the carafes, and Jefferson did not offer the kind of tea Gros Morne made. Galla-gher likewise sat back and folded his hands atop his stomach.

They took an interlude at last. Her eyes had gone dry—the clock neared midnight, but tomorrow they only had the half-day session, and then it would be Gros Morne at last.

Rene was in the hallway. That surprised: he generally sat back in the lobby with the other aides. She took one look at his face and was alert, quickly. "What?" she said, and took his shoulder with her hand, and turned him so that he walked with her, paced comfortably between the others. Automatic. "What?"

Rene looked at her, his face drawn tight. "Sophie Njelteberg com-mitted suicide."

"What? When?"

"It came across on the news a couple hours ago. I couldn't inter-rupt the meeting. I tried."

A couple *hours* ago. "I need Media," she said, and kept presence of mind enough, at least, to keep walking, to not disturb the line of councilors and their aides streaming down the hallway, to match pace with them. "What have they been saying?"

"It's heavily Kaetteguttan coverage at this point. They've been running mostly that."

Meaning they were letting Kaettegut hang itself with its own rope, when Kaettegut's media personnel were naïve and plenty of the pow-ers on that side would be glad to give their opinions, Murray Lerken-lund foremost of them, almost certainly.

And herself not reachable—*oh, hell.*

Media personnel would be in the lobby. "Who did they send?" she asked.

He looked away, first. "I've left messages."

Her mouth dropped, slightly.

They weren't taking his calls. What— But she could not afford emotion, frustration, right now. Rene looked past her at the wall and said nothing.

Sophie Njelteberg. From Rue, but Sophie's face just played well, had played well all the way through, to a media who was eager for images and a population that was more so. Plain, pale, square-faced Sophie Njelteberg, whose shyness reached past the cameras. Her staff was to have kept all but the official photos off the air, but the ones that had broken through generally had included Sophie. Of course.

For being from Rue—less her concern, previously. Everything, now.

"Why?" She was still walking, and here was the lobby, where they could stop—and her legs did not *want* to stop, she wanted to keep moving, to work the nerves out of her arms, her legs, her rib cage. They jangled, at a rest; she crossed her arms and clutched them close to her chest.

"They're saying she couldn't fit back in." Rene, bless him—all facts, that was how he handled situations, and how she did, and he expected her questions, and had the answers already there. He said the next carefully: "They're saying she was transferred too soon, that we didn't have the resources to handle something of that level."

"That's ridiculous." Sophie Njelteberg needed *home*, the way all the survivors did. She had seen the exterior, at least, of the hospital where they had been taken, and its entrance, all concrete where the supply rail came through and where visitors entered. Large windows on the upper floors, most lit to some degree, but everything sealed inside—no way for air to get in except through the steel doors of an elevator and the one wide set of glass doors.

She could go to the media buildings down in the business district. Except—the closed session had not ended, and she could not leave. "Does this building have videoconferencing capability?" she asked.

"Upstairs, but it's locked and shut down. No staff available that knows how to run it."

Damn, and damn. There were chairs lining the wall of the lobby, away from the doors. The other doors were closed for the night, by all appearances. "Over here. A written statement, and you hand-carry it down there. You stay there and you knock until they let you in, you hear me? I want the first interview slot they've got after this. At the hotel, whatever. Let them name the place."

He had already prepared the paper. *Paper*, when there was working videoconference equipment upstairs, and a lobby perfectly fine for an in-person interview.

"How? First." She settled in the chair, sideways, and there were looks in her direction. She had not hidden her reaction nearly well enough.

He pulled in his lower lip, but did not flinch from the answer. "She walked to the bay from Rue. They found her in the water. She'd been there a couple days."

"No one noticed?"

"Not at first. She was staying home most of the time. She hadn't had at-home care for a while."

Air filled her rib cage, and settled heavily. "Say this: "This hurts us all. I—no, say *we*, grieve deeply with Sophie Njelteberg's associates and friends. She was one of us, and will remain one of us, and we will not forget." She thought it through, played it back.

"Anything about an investigation? Or the accident?"

"They know it's the accident. I'll address the investigation in the interview. They'll ask." She held out her hand for the pen, and the paper, and signed it large—because they might film that, and her signature meant something, if not her face, and her posture.

14

Work in Travel had, surprisingly, become another respite for him. Not free from danger, if another note happened to end up on his desk or if God forbid, Jenning or one of her staff decided to visit, but that had become a little more remote over time, and it was *not* home, with everything that had happened there over the past few days. Here was his desk, badly and falsely grained, and the cabinets and credenza full of papers, familiar. His own space.

He was making progress on his work, too, had organized the applications in order of priority for when he could edge one or two past the system again. It had to be only a matter of time; he had gone too fast, that was all.

Here he could set his brain on automatic and fill it ordering things in his cabinets and drawers and in the storage room, and taking his share of the incoming backlog. No one expected him to socialize; Thomas and Emory were recluses, and the glossed-over women up front had lumped him in with them and did not talk to him, either.

Home was still a relief—it had just begun taking on associations, and he did not know how to break that. There had been the news of Sophie Njelteberg—she had a name, now. He had missed that coming in late on the announcement, on the pallor of her face in the photo, the paleness of *Graham's* face, when Graham had just heard the announcement himself. Graham had seen her, had been very near her if he had seen her coming off the boat.

Graham was clearly concerned for *him*. He had been watching the coverage in the mornings, coming in on the ferry, where Graham could not see him do it.

There had been no little blame put on Gros Morne. Sophie Njelteberg had been physically, badly burned; there was nothing in Kaettegut to compensate for that, they said, to counsel her or help her fit back in, and she would not be normal again.

He felt—something he could not quite identify. He must have passed her, must have come in or out the street entrance in Rue at the same time as her more than once, but the floors didn't interact with other floors, not at his level.

He would have—*would* have liked to have met her. He had thought that, seeing her in the footage: there was the vulnerability, the way she had walked.

He could guess what had greeted her on her return, could guess that no one had known what to say and so had said nothing, and there had only been silence whenever she walked in a room, or, at best, the conversation continued along and did not acknowledge her. ...That was if they had let her go back to work at all, and if they hadn't, that might have been worse.

He had thought himself unique, when he was only one of a number.

And as insensitive to Graham, *God*, as he could have been. Sophie Njelteberg and the conversation in the restaurant before, one on top of the other. Graham had seen Sophie—while waiting for *him*.

Graham had said he had gone through some hell back then. It had been for longer than the day Graham had described, if he had been afraid they would not take his transfer request, if he had seen Sophie come back. That implied time— God, how long had he been out, at first?

That he did not know, that he had not thought even to ask— Had he even *thanked* Graham for paying what he had?

As far as he could remember, he had lost his temper and punched a wall.

He rested his head in his hands. What Graham even—but Graham had still been decent, all the way through, had brought him soup the other night and would not take back his own room.

"Phone," he said, and did not move. The phone program came up. He had not thought of *this*; damned but he was slow. "Call the hospital."

Sheer loyalty, maybe. "Hospital," the receptionist's voice came across, and he scooped up the earpiece, put it in. The department didn't need to hear this, and he had not had the foresight to close the door.

"My name is Kellan Long, I was a patient there a couple months ago, and I'd like to request my medical records." It was getting on well *more* than a couple months, now.

He sat through a number of transfers, and finally reached the correct department, and a voice came on. He repeated his request again.

"Those records are restricted," the voice said.

"They're *my* records," he protested, and held his hand over the earpiece: someone was pushing a cart a little down the hallway, and making noise.

"It's departmental policy."

The tone did not give him any hope. He pushed a question in before the man could disconnect the line, and stumbled over it in his haste. "I just want to know how long—how long I was—what day it was that I first had a visitor?"

The line disconnected, anyway; after, he was fairly sure, the receptionist had heard at least the beginning of his question. He took out the earpiece, tossed it across the desk; felt like throwing it across the room, instead. Hard.

Damn it! His own records.

He could ask Graham. Maybe that would finally show a little sensitivity; he could apologize, and it would open up the conversation, at least. He could prove that he *did* think of such things, he was just slow. Very slow.

He wished he had not gone to the conference. That he had seen the list of names and made up some excuse to stay back, to work on something else he could show as more pressing. To have arrived at the dock late and missed the ferry, himself and Sophie Njelteberg.

He would not have have caused that kind of distress; he would have been far from the tech who had fallen. And that could not happen. He could dwell on that for as long as he wanted, and every morning he would wake up and find it not true.

———

Chauncey came to her own office at last. She took a deep breath and let it out, slowly, leaned against the door behind her—and behind it at least ten concerned faces, which had been looking up from their desks.

There was a tap on the door. She felt it through the surface, in her shoulder.

She opened the door a crack, saw Jocelyn's black-haired-framed face, and a cup of hot tea in Jocelyn's hands—strange to have this coming from her, whose desk was across the room and *not* near her office in the way that Phoebe was, and Phoebe being the one who normally took care of that sort of thing. Jocelyn held the cup in both hands, and pushed it through the crack in the door like an offering. "Some hot tea?" she asked, and the concern was still there in the expression.

She smiled. Took it in both of her hands, which let the door swing open several more inches, and took a sip—very hot, but very good. "Ahh," she said, and watched Jocelyn's face relax, some. "You've no idea. They don't have this over there. I'd been wishing for some, this time."

"I imagine," Jocelyn said, calmly, but then gave a nervous laugh, shot through with relief. She ducked her head, face reddening.

Phoebe was coming from the direction of the department doors, having secured things—and spied the cup already in her hands, and Jocelyn standing there. "I'll need to call a meeting," she said to Phoebe when she had come close enough, and did not have to smile for Phoebe's benefit, though she put more confidence into her tone than was warranted. "Give me thirty minutes. Send me the list of everyone who can make it, department-wide."

"Yes," Phoebe said, who for being young at the start had risen quite quickly *because* she was not frazzled easily, was simply competent. She'd had her pulled from one of the customer service departments on the first floor—which one, now, she could no longer remember.

Phoebe made a simple gesture, not unkind, and Jocelyn stepped back. Phoebe reached and closed the door for her.

Rene would be with her bags, seeing them to the residence; he'd be back in a half hour at the most. He would attend even if the trip over on the hauler had been exhausting, the way it always was, the cold spray of the water, the heaving through the widest part of the bay where the water rolled. There was nowhere comfortable to sit, and she did not demand it.

There had been the growing light in the sky that meant *home*. That had been welcome, as welcome as the tea steaming on her desk now, welcome as the hills rising from the water. She had been to the northern province a few times, but it had never spoken to her the way Gros Morne had, the hydroponics bays nestled inside those hills—but then, she had grown up here, and Benner was not far east, where the hills grew a bit taller. The northern province—stretched mostly flat and barren where the seameats and rice industries and the desalination plants did not line the western and northern shores. Environment still made its faint efforts to engineer land crops in the low light of the eastern side, of course, and the experimental fields rimmed that side, but the train took a straight route up to Rue from the dock and through the most barren land, spotted only with the holding tanks and pens of the fish hatcheries. Environment itself did not work *there*, of course, on the eastern side or anywhere in Kaettegut. Its scientists simulated conditions inside their comfortable laboratories in Prime, and dictated instructions to the Kaetteguttans in the fields, little better than laborers. A small handful of those handled the sensitive work of the mixing of nutrients, the observing, the sending of data back to almighty Prime.

The farming unit was not much to Jefferson's liking, not long decades ago, and not today. Oh, things grew, now and then, but they tended to be frail and bent, and suitable so far mostly as bitter herbs. That was a delicacy, these days: de-shelled mussels steamed in the anemic leaves of these plants, made limp and only slightly less bitter in the heat. Not many could stomach that, even if she had seen it fairly frequently enough on tables in the Jefferson restaurants.

Good God. What was she going to do about Sophie Njelteberg? Her staff might believe she would lead with a firm hand on the rudder, that the problem would be solved, that the dank suspicion Kaettegut had been swimming through in the last week would dry up, when an extra *week* spent with the media in Prime had done next to nothing.

Oh, they had played the written statement, yes, and she had obtained interview slots the next morning, but by then it was too late and there was nothing she could do to turn it. Heaven knew she had tried. A small personal tragedy had been blown up into *that* and had taken on a life of its own, when, damn it, there had been no other news to push it out of the way, and that had left plenty of time for speculation. And even that was suspicious in its timing, when Environment made much of the news on a regular basis.

She leaned on her hands, elbows on the desk, did not swivel to look out the window at the view.

She would *not* change her course. She would continue it more subtly, on her side and in person, in handshaking across the province if she had to—both the provinces. She had been mistaken to consider the northern province not truly her own, had let Murray Lerkenlund turn her off from what was hers, when he controlled only a small portion of it.

She would visit Sophie Njelteberg's Rue. A good, solid visit, *before* she had things settled here. That was a move guaranteed the attention of that populace.

Prime wanted its food, its constant little innovations courtesy of Environment's science department, the new and improved species of mussel, or of this, or that. Prime wanted to eat in peace without the reminder of who was in the pantry, who might be picking those mussels out of the water in shirtsleeves, and sweating, and throwing those mussels onto salted and dirty decks. *Jefferson* certainly wanted that, ate the finest of what the world had to offer in its restaurants.

But there they were, Kaetteguttans, in the pantry.

There were staff to whom she had not given sufficient responsibility. They could fill in for the ones to whom she gave the key assignments. Phoebe would come with her. Rene would want to accompany her, would not feel comfortable otherwise, but he could best be of use here.

Only she wished for her own residence and her own furnishings after so long, to sink into the sofa and watch the rest of the world on the television screen.

Rue was not what she had remembered from her only other visit, years ago. The government office with its buff-colored stucco and row upon row of reflective windows, the rowhouses connected with each other by firewalls, yes. The wideness of the streets, not at all.

Rue's top officials were shrewd, oh, quite aware of Rue's image, the way all of Prime saw it outside of Kaettegut. She picked that up on the tour of the government office, of the quickly-familiar cubicles and desks, the barren walls.

Phoebe, for all her competence, was not quite the same as having Rene along. Jocelyn and Dominic trailed far in the back while her guide droned on about government operations on this floor. The staff gave little pretence of working while they went through. They sat frozen, turned their heads back to their screens and desks after glances altogether too long.

Phoebe took mental notes: she saw that in her obvious concentration. It *had* been a good idea to bring her, to bring Jocelyn and Dominic, who had likewise not been outside the southern province, and Dominic was already in his lower forties. Stocky for that age—no stranger to good food, perhaps.

Rue was the most aged of the settlements on Kaettegut, outside the hydroponics bays and limestone mines themselves. Rue had been built, in its core, five years after the second landing, when the first schism had taken place. Rue was older than Jefferson, on which construction was not begun for another twenty years. The first ship's population had still huddled in Grosvenor then, a paltry number.

They reached the top floor, at last, looked in on the far nicer offices of the top officials, whose office walls offered the only color in the building: rich cinnabars, mustard yellows. Of *this* area, the guide glowed with pride.

"Now," he said, turning, and rubbed his hands together. A breath. She hoped he would offer a few minutes in the chairs and sofa of the lounge. Rue's government offices were not so small, particularly when one saw every corner, every filing cabinet. But—"Have you thought as far as dinner, yet? We'd like to get something arranged, if you'd give us an idea what you prefer."

Rue did not plan things on the spur of the moment, if the rows of cubicles were any indication, that the top officials could not stay with them for most of the city tour. "We haven't given much notice," she said, and inclined her head in apology. "Whatever you can arrange is fine."

"It's fine. Fine. *Any* preference at all?" And from the expression on his face, she guessed a preference would very much help.

Her goal was to be visible. Just that, this trip, to give these residents an idea they *were* important, that they warranted a visit where her predecessor had very seldom been, if ever. To honor what was very much Kaetteguttan—was not a bad idea. "I think," she said, "I've heard the salmon is excellent here, very fresh. More so than in Gros Morne."

"Yes." But he was pleased, his eyes said that. "We'd be glad."

What she'd *most* like, more than that, would be the chance to talk with some of the staff who sat at the desks and cubicles. Not someone ensconced in an office: regular staff, who worked hard every day, who went home to watch the media and cook dinner. It should go both ways. She was visible to them, that was fine, and the message. *She'd* like the time to get to know them, even for precious few minutes, in their own setting. "Have you any local teas?" she asked, when the guide made to prod them toward the two elevators. "A local specialty? Something I could take a few minutes in one of the floor lounges you showed us. I'd like to talk with some of the staff."

It set him back no little bit. He stammered, looked to the receptionist sitting ensconced behind the low wall of her station. She looked at him, and stood, moved into a room behind her station.

Oh. "Downstairs, please," she said. "In one of *those* floor lounges, some of that staff."

Jenning made the decision: a relocation, a new home in Education, and with it Stefan Coubertin.

If she did not care for him in person, there was time to change; she would not overextend her position, not in the initial exploration.

Stefan would push for the move once he saw the advantage. Whether Stefan had sufficient relationship with Fifty to get much of it done without Robert Wright's help or not would soon be seen. But Robert Wright should be pleased at the addition too, if he was not a fool. To pull a department like Aptitude that could facilitate a full expansion agenda, given the reins—he would be crazy not to take it, and to fight for it.

She had mapped out the rest of her department's advantages

rather nicely, paired them up with every reasonable angle. Every side project, every contact in all those departments, was an additional bargaining chip, far more useful than before taken in this light—all the way to the tedium of every damned agricultural audit. *That* slotted, by the way, neatly into an improved relationship for Education with Environment, because Education, with her in its ranks, could solidify Kaettegut's position for Environment, when Environment's slot above Organization was tenuous at best.

She had examined Chauncey Benner close up, was accustomed to dealing with the woman, knew her better than anyone on the damned council did, and now, after all the study, significantly better. She had a thick file full of analysis, and she *could* guess Chauncey Benner's next move, had foreseen exactly that kind of quote coming over the Njelteberg girl's suicide.

Environment would find such knowledge very useful indeed. Education's stock would rise. So might Stefan Coubertin's.

If she liked him.

This was an entirely new game—and Chauncey had not stopped playing, contrary to Environment's belief. Environment felt Agriculture was under control, standard Environment ego, from the rumblings she saw in the council and between the lines in the media, a foolish position by Meghan Truong.

No one had expected Sophie Njelteberg, of course. Plain, unassuming, quiet. Certainly after her death they had gathered all the footage they had taken of her, mostly group shots, and discovered belatedly how very well she played. Kaettegut had been skewered, no one else, a fine case of blame-shifting to the victim.

Chauncey would answer. She'd have to do it differently than she had on the media: no simple interviews or statements this time. Visuals against visuals, if Chauncey had any sense, and one of the other victims would work. *Any* Kaetteguttan in the accident.

That meant Kellan Long stayed here, quietly, in Prime. Just in case, because if he was only a government staffer he was still one of them, and she had say over that when she had little say over anything else related to Kaettegut, now. He was no Sophie Njelteberg, but she had seen him in a hospital room, in the kind of atmosphere that produced. Yes, he could play to the cameras, too, put in the right circumstances.

His companion was an interesting case, a delight, really, of a kind she rarely saw at that level, where the calculating ones were so few. His coding was on the screen, minimized: fiercely protective, both of himself and what he valued. He could be useful, long term, where he was. Pricing was one of the lower tiers in Economics but it was key, and it would by no means be disadvantageous to have another contact there.

"Gabrielle," she said to the intercom, but Clare's voice came back instead, after a moment: "She's gone downstairs." And, "Do you need anything?"

"No. Thank you. The schedule just seems to be a little off."

"She's gone down to pick him up. Less than five minutes ago."

"Very good." She clicked off and leaned back in the chair, folded her hands below her rib cage. Clare had been a good acquisition; she was more than satisfied. It *had* given her the hoped-for entry with Safety.

She closed down the first file. There were footsteps outside, then, and a tap on the door. "Jenning?" Gabrielle's voice said; Gabrielle's habit, to notify her that it was her, and not anyone with her who was unexpected.

"Come in." She swiveled in the chair behind the desk.

So. Graham Long was tall and lean in a rather rapacious way, and maybe of some particular descent; they mixed in Kaettegut, did not plan things, and she could not identify any of the ancestral lines on that side except to say that some were distinctive, and some were not. Narrow face—and a great deal of self-control, already evident, which said he had not reached the level where self-control truly *was* that. Gabrielle stood aside, a practiced gesture in her introductions. "Graham Long," she said, and: "Jenning Crote." No more than that; not necessary.

"Thank you, Gabrielle. Just coffee for me," she said, and got to her feet—without the cane. To him: "Anything to drink?"

"No," he said, and was already taking in her office, the shelves of files, the stacks. *Good.* She moved to the table, sat in the chair that faced the door and indicated the other with one hand. He took it, and the wariness was there despite his efforts: he did have some distance to go.

She waited for the coffee in pleasant silence, with her hands folded on the tabletop. Synthetic—this wing of the building did not warrant the warm wood of Organization's central hub, or Quinn's floor—but it was more solid than it looked, and white, and spotlessly clean in comparison with the piles on the carpet.

Graham likewise folded his hands on the table, and continued his scan of the office.

The door swung back open, quiet, and Gabrielle brought in the whole coffee service—carafe, two cups, all the accruements—and set it in the center of the table. *Good girl.* "I'll be right outside if you need anything else," Gabrielle said, a little reminder for Graham's benefit.

Jenning poured herself a cup of coffee, black, and poured the second cup. Took her first sip: pleasantly hot. "Your friend requested his medical records," she said.

He did not take the second cup; it sat where she had placed it. "When?" he said, only that, and timed well, but he had *not* mastered his facial expressions. He projected calm, yes, but any real relaxation was gone with that one sentence, and there was plenty beneath that surface.

"Yesterday." Another sip, slow. "Any idea why?"

"No. Do you know?"

Ah. Barbed, that, but well delivered, softly; he would have convinced someone less experienced. And he had *not* known, then.

Delaying his reaction, too, that was quite obvious; he would leave the department and the building and then think it over, likely—suppressing things until then was the difficult part, and if she drew it out long enough, if she used some skill, he would not make it that far. The interiors were easily cracked if one knew where the keys were. Depending on the level of practice, the exterior showed the damage or didn't, but the exterior was only a thin guard.

"On his part—any thoughts as to why Sophie Njelteberg did what she did?"

He considered, and looked her over; that she had not answered had not escaped him. Finally: "He didn't say much."

An honest answer. Likely he considered it the best approach, to get what he needed. Still, she was unexpectedly pleased, and reshaped the conversation to accommodate the turn.

"What little did he say?"

He took the cup, then. Fingered it, did not drink from it, and looked across at her. Carefully: "Why should I tell you?"

She allowed a small shrug, a fine, ironic counterpoint to what she could put very bluntly. "Because I'm responsible for him staying on this side."

"Your office approved his paperwork."

"And yours."

An easily read reaction. He looked down at the coffee, this time stirred it with one of the spoons, and that too was masterful, considering. "Why?"

"We could use you. I told your friend, we were one short in that office."

"I came in at mid-level."

She gave another small shrug. "You disrupted the chain of promotion a bit, yes." And: "Have you found things uncomfortable?"

"No." Too much emotion in that syllable, then. He was losing a little bit of his steam; credit him that it was not more. Few of his kind could carry on this conversation at this kind of level, called to *this* office. A few sentences was all she typically got before the façade crumbled.

"Good." Another sip. "What did he say, then?"

He was reluctant, that was evident. That, and he was still thinking on the other. Finally, though, and very slowly: "He said it was the people."

"Meaning?"

"I don't know."

That was intriguing. "What are the people like over there?"

"I don't know. People."

It was an honest answer, for him. She could have laughed. "Different than people over here?"

"Not really." He looked up, and she looked back at him and did not move, except for her fingers on the cup. He would have sighed, then, but suppressed it. He settled a little more back into his chair. "A little more provincial, I guess. More closed."

She nodded approval. Better still.

More coffee. She took her time, watched him over the rim of the cup. He matched the gaze for a few seconds, then looked down at his hands, refolded them on the table.

"I could get help for your friend," she said, at last. "This department is not without resources."

"He doesn't need it."

"You said you don't know why he requested his medical records. Isn't it possible you don't know everything that's going on?"

The body language changed; some muscles tensed, even while settled back into the chair, peculiar—a reminder, he *was* foreign. Not altogether like the ones she had met at Gros Morne, either; not that posture. "Why?" he said, and the tone was mild and utterly contradictory.

He was from the northern province. She had only been to Gros Morne, had not seen even its surroundings. She had made an assumption, there, that Rue was Gros Morne in miniature, or that it aspired to *be* Gros Morne.

Dangerous assumption.

And an additional insight into Chauncey Benner—who governed what she considered *her* people, and not a department of the whole. Chauncey had said it in the midst of crisis and stress, her most immediate reaction, and for that, the truest: *She was one of us, and will remain one of us, and we will not forget.*

One of us. The key to Chauncey Benner was her people.

Well, here were two of them. Not typical, either of them, the way the renovation crews were, but perhaps more valuable in that they *were* different. Still—she made a mental note to tell Gabrielle to pull up the paperwork and perhaps set up a session with some of those crews.

She took another sip, this time of coffee already growing cool, and set the cup down, a small *clink*. Refilled it from the carafe. "We're civilized," she said, after another sip, biting hot again. "Relationships. That's what it's about, on this side." A little truth for him to play with.

He sat there and digested *that*, no matter that the posture had lost none of its very particular strain.

"Why don't you think about it? You know how to get in touch with me." She smiled, thinly, over the cup. "I'm busy, sometimes, but I'll get back to you. If it's an emergency, you let Gabrielle know."

He watched her reach across and put the cups back onto the tray next to the now-lighter carafe. Tidying up: that was a signal to the end of the meeting, and his face showed some alarm, then; mixed, and became complex. He stood, even so, and reached for what was already cleared, an automatic act of courtesy, and got credit for it without doing any of the work. Not unclever.

"There's not going to be any emergency," he said, at the door, when he had seen he could draw it out no further.

"That would be good." Pleasantly dismissive.

She did not worry once he had opened the door and closed it behind him. He would be escorted downstairs, equally pleasantly, to mull it over out in the cold air and wind.

The water welled up where the hull cut through it,.Graham could see the billows, swollen and unhappy, in the lights of the ferry.

It had not gone at all as expected. Not at all. He had expected—that she would go for his jugular straight off the bat, the way she must have with Kellan. That he would offer what he had to bargain, and that she would laugh at it, likely, but the negotiating *would* happen. She would be direct, would not waste time to trivialities or small talk.

She had sat there with coffee, and sipped it, and come at him from behind. She had held herself in a way that said *trust me*, and he could have very easily fallen into it if he had not known what she had done to Kellan... if he had not sat in that small conference room and taken test upon test at the hands of her assistant.

She *was* good. *She just knows her stuff*, Kellan had said.

Kellan had not mentioned anything, maybe just wanted to keep it to himself—but what could he want with his medical records? Was there a concern that knowing his records would clear up, something related to the news of Sophie Njelteberg?

A nerve twitched in his neck.

That Kellan had said nothing—it stung, simple truth. It put more tension where he had been trying to keep it down, and to be more open, for his part.

He could not ask Kellan about it. Kellan would want to know how he knew, and he could not tell Kellan that Jenning had that kind of access. ...And *that* was a good question in itself, a damned good question.

He remembered, late, that he had told Kellan he would stop by and see him if he was in Jefferson again. He almost stayed on the ferry and went back—but the tension was still there, it was pounding in the back of his skull, then, and not just twanging nerves.

He went to the house and sat on the bed instead. Kellan would not be home for a while, had said he would stop on his way home for groceries.

Jenning had not even brought up the pricing office. No—only that she had approved his application, had stuck to the line that they'd needed someone, and when he had challenged it, had simply not answered. *Have you found things uncomfortable?* she'd asked, only that, and that had put him off his guard some, because it *was* concern, for him, when he had not been accustomed to that.

Were the records connected in any way with the Njelteberg suicide? Just that. Just *something*, some indication from Kellan.

He would still be called upon for what he could do in the pricing office, with what he knew of Agriculture and its system. This had likely only been preliminary; perhaps a simple flexing of power, to let him know how far her fingers reached. And how civilized she could be, if she so chose.

It gnawed at him. God, *was* Kellan all right?

Kellan had not been asking questions so much. *That* was different. But physically—if he looked just purely analytically, Kellan was becoming fitter here than he had been back at Rue. More consistent food was the reason, maybe, eating out at the restaurants most nights instead of relying on their collective skills at the stove. A lot more walking, back and forth.

There was no need at all to request his records, then, unless it was something that didn't show. Headaches, Sophie Njelteberg—maybe Kellan wondered if there was something wrong with him that had gone wrong with all of the victims, and just showed in Sophie. God help him.

He wanted to ask. He could not. He could *not.*

Christ. *Jenning* had him thinking like this, had the sheets crumpled up in his right fist, had put him where there was no way out. She'd known the way his insides were settled, how he worked, and if he had managed not to cue her somehow in some other way, it did not matter. This was proof.

15

Sitting at the dinner table with the bay a thicker line to the west dark beneath the clouds and officials to her right and left, and surrounding Jocelyn and Dominic where they sat, a table away—Chauncey realized: these officials looked to Gros Morne more than she had known, differently than she had known.

And were no fools.

This was the private home of the top government official, on the far west side of Rue, where only the most well-to-do lived. To see the bay like this—was privilege, in Rue. She gathered that.

This home was built to take advantage of that view. There was an open terrace on the roof, shielded from the weather only by what appeared to be flat metal sails, an extravagant architecture unique to this residence, of all the places she had seen. She sat now at one of four long tables beneath those sails, in the glow of lamps placed in the center of the tables and on the stuccoed railing-walls.

The seafood was indeed fresh. And it wasn't only fish: dishes of garlic-sauced mussels sent steam up into the sails and skies, too, and there were trays beside the lamps littered with oysters. A shucking knife lay at her left hand, on top of a napkin.

She should not eat so eagerly. The sauces were rich and would give her trouble in the morning, if she was lucky, rather than the middle of the night. Still—the fish flaked under her fork, no knife needed, and she had *not* had food quite as fresh as this, no matter the wonders of the science of food storage and shipping. Every bite felt silky on her tongue; the mussels slid slippery down her throat in a paroxysm of flavor.

There was more tea of the kind she had sipped in the government offices, talking to the staff. Earnest faces, all of them, memory evoked by the unique flavor—she had not had it in Gros Morne, and it was both more bitter and more creamy, and managed somehow to balance. The liquid was pleasantly warm now, in the very cool draught of the rooftop terrace. She was fortunate there was not a brisker wind.

Phoebe sat across from her, coppery hair blowing in the wind—she had left it pinned, but the breeze had pulled out tendrils until very little must have been left in the roll. Her face was pale in the lamplight but happy, and she was ripping into a difficult mussel teeth-first. Chauncey had not noticed before that Phoebe's top row of teeth were a bit large for her mouth, though straight, and unexpectedly charming. Amusing, at the least, to see Phoebe's stiffness gone in favor of appetite and taste, and conversation: the officials on either side were far older, but not less in their own charm.

Jocelyn, it was evident, did not know what to make of the hospitality and the honor. Funny to see her staff like this, human. Perhaps she *didn't* regret, after all, bringing them instead of Rene. His insights would have been keener, no doubt—but this trip did not require as much discernment. She could relax here, and see all the signals, see exactly what was there on the surface, and match it up to what was beneath it.

She had not overplayed her hand earlier, after all, with Jefferson. She had been accurate, precisely accurate.

They saw Sophie Njelteberg, her actions, as a blot upon them. "Jefferson sees us like that," the official to her right said, in question: Satonori, if she remembered correctly, who occupied the cider-yellow office back at the government offices in the heart of Rue. "That incapable of dealing with our own."

She swallowed a mussel, wanted to sigh instead, to blow air out of her cheeks. "It's just media. They blow things out of proportion."

"The rest of the population doesn't know that."

"Some of them do." And that was true, whoever had been pulling the strings behind the scenes, at the very least. Anyone on any council who had ever been quoted.

"The average person doesn't. Including ours."

Far more sophisticated than she had expected. She had *expected* provincialism, a blind following of the directions Gros Morne provided.

"What do you think they thought—what was our image, before this? Before the crisis." She was careful not to say Sophie's name. That was a political fireball, here, almost an insult, and not for the reasons she had initially suspected—more for a lack of discipline, almost of loyalty, on Sophie's part. That she would take that action and let it reflect on the rest.

He allowed a wry smile as he bent open a more reticent mussel. Careful action, careful words. "You tell me."

"Honestly—I'd like to hear *your* thoughts." She took another bite, another buttery brown mussel. "Your seafood is outstanding."

"Thank you. I'll pass it on." Satonori put his own fork down, leaned on his elbow. *He* could take food like this for granted, living here. But he had bitten, it would after all be too awkward to refuse a direct request, coy or not. "You see the lights over there? Out there."

She followed the line of his arm, his finger. She had to crane her neck to see over the half-wall of the railing, but blinked and saw a distant glow of lights, outside the pools of light the lamps cast here.

"That's one of the seameats communities. Little more than a street or two, they're like that, all along the coast to the north. Salty. I've been there, duties, this and that. Someone was over there today, picking this up." He pried the flesh of a mussel out of one of the black shells, lifted it, let his lips close around it. Swallowed. "That's what *they* eat. Jefferson."

She put her own fork down and looked at him.

He looked down at his plate. Shrugged, smiled, and said nothing.

She had expected more. "An honor, if you look at it a certain way. There are some restaurants over there that *boast* of these mussels."

He wiped his chin with the napkin, smiled, and reached back to the buffet tray for another plateful. "But this is a celebration, a time to enjoy your visit. You're enjoying it. That's a great pride to us, you know."

He was very high-ranking, to be resident in one of those offices. "I've stayed away for far too long," she said. "A mistake of my predecessor, and I've made the same one, until now. I'd *like* to know. It's very possible I don't think as you might surmise."

"You do have a reputation. It's precisely why I don't need to be

blunt." And, heavy with implication: "Your visit here—is quite welcome."

"That was part of the reputation."

A long interval. He ate, swallowed. "Say that we'd be glad to have
you representing all of us in Jefferson."

The bite in her own mouth turned just that little bit sour. "You
believe I represent you—that *I* promote that image."

Another dab of the napkin. He used the same tone of voice, light,
nothing to draw attention: "Not implicitly. There are some who do."

"Murray Lerkenlund's department." The synapses moved, snapped
together pieces and fragments. Stray flotsam, she had not realized she
had stored it. Now— *Damn!* Had he gone this far, up here? And to
what end? "Seameats. Anyone else?"

He showed a little amusement, that she found very little humor-
ous—and that hid truth very thinly. "That's jumping to conclusions,
don't you think?"

Subtlety, social graces—the very base of diplomacy, in the view
of most, but a waste of time in her view. Oh, she did it when the
situation forced it, a tiresome dance of words and phrases, of body
language. With the media recently, certainly.

Rue operated that way. *That's* how they talked, then, up in those
offices. She had not expected that of them, either—would have except that they had given every indication of being otherwise, had
turned her expectations on its head in other respects. She folded
her hands on the table, before a plate that had become littered with
shells. "I see Murray once a quarter." She shook her head. "I'm—not
surprised, from this angle. A shame he hasn't come forward with this,
of course."

Damn it, to what end? The administrator's post was not elective.
A Benner graduate, always, chosen purely from aptitude scores and
graduate work. Oh, not the most intelligent—a unique set of apti-
tudes and interests for an office where management and organization
were the most important things, and politics second. Her predecessor
had not entered office as he had left it. He had performed outstand-
ingly in day-to-day administration, but at politics he'd wholeheartedly failed. Politics had ground him down, the same that made every
Kaetteguttan aware of his image in the world, but closer, more keen.

She had not asked Gallagher what her predecessor had been like on the council. Gallagher had not been accessible until recently. Until recently, to ask would have been to reveal weakness.

Murray Lerkenlund, on the other hand— There was little to grind him down. *There* was the spirit, the pride she longed to see in a Kaetteguttan, paired with the wrong ego, and taken to the wrong levels. Murray dismissed the cabinet meetings as an inconvenience, and ruled his department as an empire.

And there was the key.

"What else has he been saying?"

Satonori had grown uncomfortable, that was evident in his fiddling with the handle of his mug. "I can't really speak to the views of someone else. I can speak to my own."

"Just the externals."

A direct gaze, this time. "I can't." He set the mug on the table, carefully, one side, then the other. "Rue will support you. If our residents know you hear them, that you've been here, that you'll come again."

"I'll come again. They can count on that." *You can.* "You're somewhat isolated here. I know that."

He gave a small smile that had no mirth in it. "Somewhat."

She sat back.

She'd like to leave, now. The piles of shells had grown on every plate, thank the heavens. They were starting to clear the silverware. The plates in the middle of each table were largely empty.

She looked to her mug, and there were two sips left, perhaps. She took one, and the tea had gone cold, the bitterness overwhelming the cream. "It's been an interesting conversation," she said. "I'll count on having dinner with you the next time I'm here."

"That would be nice." Noncommittal.

She stood and placed her napkin beside the plate, and turned to the nearest server, who was clearing plates from the tables, loading them onto the buffet tray. "Thank you. It was delicious. An honor."

She did not fully notice the server's response, except that it was startled, and that he looked over his shoulder first. Lodging, a simple room of her own, was foremost, now. She looked for Dominic and Jocelyn, found them still talking and laughing with their neighbors, and their table had not begun to be cleared.

She *needed* to leave, needed the time and privacy, now.

That was an odd note. Stefan looked at it again, swiveled in his office chair so that he faced away from the screen. Real paper, thick and textured—a laid pattern, ivory with a distinctly gray cast.

Jenning Crote. He had heard the name. He strained to remember where, and the context.

She—was the one Organization had sent over to Agriculture, in charge of the recent audits. She had been in the explosion, had survived it. One of Quinn's, celebrated in that context for her knowledge of psychology, *if* that wasn't another of Quinn's machinations.

A meeting would seem desirable. He could make that out in the first short paragraph, in the spidery handwriting.

There was an attachment, folded over twice, of plain printer paper. He unfolded it and saw simple columns of numbers. Dollar figures, on closer inspection.

His numbers.

His stomach acid turned cold.

These were the most recent funding allotments to the medical graduates. *His* allotments, all here, spread out like a skeleton on a paper-drying rack.

We may be of benefit to each other, it said at the bottom of the note, above the signature.

If Jenning knew—Quinn knew. That much was certain. Wasn't it?

She had addressed him individually. The note did not come on Organization letterhead, did not bear the name of anyone other than one Jenning Crote.

Atrocious timing, with the storm coming in. He buzzed his receptionist, fought to keep his voice level. "Who brought this note? The one on my desk this morning."

"The interoffice mail courier. Why?"

He looked at it again, turned it over. "Just wondering. It arrived this morning?"

"Yesterday afternoon. I sorted it first thing this morning." There was a trace of concern in the receptionist's voice, the kind he used when he worried his duties had been deficient, nothing more. He opened his mail, opened most everyone's mail when it was not marked confidential, and distributed it. "Everything all right?"

"Yes. Thank you." He clicked off and turned back to his desk.

It was almost that close—if he brought the various researchers together, alone, they could very feasibly integrate the different parts. He would not, of course. He *could* not in this political environment, in his current position.

He had been considering—whether to bring it to Fifty. Fifty would most certainly implement it, and include him, and his spot on the council would continue to be assured, better than before.

Except that he had intended it specifically for a time when the existing powers had died away. When Quinn Rhodes, Jeri Tasco, and Meghan Truong might be the only ones remaining on the council of the current lineup, besides himself. Perhaps Marcus Gouman, too, tenaciously hanging onto the edge of old age, if he had hung onto his council seat.

But for both Marcus and himself to hang onto their seats implied Loren Fifty, who would be long gone. Except that Marcus Gouman might eventually have a shot at the leadership of Environment, *if* he would change his resourcist tendencies and maintain them long enough for credibility. Marcus would not, though, because Marcus was nothing if not contrary, no matter how solid the arguments.

The research was useless without power of the level of the Proteraiotita. Worse than useless: destructive. And if someone brought the researchers together from Medical, from the other areas—it would not stay secret.

Where Jenning Crote fell in Organization, he did not know, Quinn had never said. Of that he was certain. He *remembered* the minutes.

He read the note straight through again. Buzzed his receptionist again. "Contact Jenning Crote in Organization—discreetly. Set up a meeting in two weeks, wherever there's an open slot. Tell her that's all I've got. You have my calendar."

"Will do."

Two weeks, enough to let Jenning Crote wonder, not long enough to tempt her to publish those numbers to anyone else—which she might have to do in person, if the storm hit as badly as they were predicting. They didn't keep the power on in those circumstances.

He read it again, flipped the second page open again between his finger and thumb, and looked at the columns of numbers, and felt like he would lose all the contents of his stomach.

———————

Her own residence again—*ahhh*. Chauncey breathed a sigh coming into the breakfast room, to the glass-covered chill-plate with its tea bag ready, its hard-toasted bread, smoked kipper, and plain yogurt as she liked it in the mornings, a slight sourness. One small lemon, a luxury from the hydroponics bays, to squeeze onto the toast-and-kipper.

She heated the water while she spread the kipper onto the toast, rock-hard where she touched it with the knife, perfect.

She thought of taking breakfast on the loggia, facing east as it did. It could be at its nicest with the weather worsening as it did now—fortunate she had not extended her trip to Rue overlong. The plaster of the walls were painted an ancient yolk-yellow, and with the light from the lanterns hanging down, the dull clouds of an approaching storm tended to take on a certain cast. There'd be cool, heady air. The house sat near the top of the hill—she fancied sometimes that she could smell the needles and leaves of the forestry division. It was not far.

Far more often, of course, she could smell the water and the scent of the sea vegetation that floated atop it, near that curve of the province, and that was far less pleasant. That was a stringy, wet, astringent sort of diluted odor.

Today it was neither, it was the humidity of an approaching storm, a feeling of disturbance in the air currents, the unsettled way the wind picked up the fabric of the chair's starched slipcover and flapped it back and forth. She set the cup and saucer on the table, the tea bag steeping within, and settled into the chair with the tablet in hand, the toast-and-kipper in the other. "Notes, graduate thesis," she said, before she took a bite, and the tablet began listing all her old notes files. The list scrolled down several screens.

"Search: unionization," she said, next, and that took longer. She had three bites of the toast while it processed that.

Rue had surprised her. It really had. A higher quantity of intelligence, there: the line staff had displayed it on the lower floors of the government offices, even in the nervousness of a meeting with a government official and questions with which they were not entirely comfortable. *That* was obvious. Identity—had it been so long since they'd had any of their own, that they were not handed by the media?

For it to turn out this way, so clearly one-sided down through the years, decade after decade after decade until they had reached more than a century and a half together on this planet... Could they not have mixed better than this?

It did not have to be this way. Only—with the current powers in place, with Meghan Truong at the helm of one of the most powerful divisions on Nocturne, or if not her, someone *like* her—it did.

She could not change that. She worked within confines, no matter her options, no matter they were wider now, and that she had something far greater to defend than she had known.

The organizational structure that had worked for a few hundred residents in the very beginning, under very different circumstances, just did not work the same with this level of population, simple as that. And Jefferson talked about expansion. Oh, she knew very well, that—and that those plans would take more agricultural staff, and resources that they could only get here, from her department.

She took the last bite of the toast-and-kipper. Pleasingly acidic to the tongue, the tang of salt, the moderating mildness and scratchiness of the toast... the soft layer deep inside the hardness.

They needed her, needed Kaettegut. It was evident in the reaction to the explosion, if nothing else. The world's attention had been focused on that.

Oh, yes, she could take advantage of that, if they could. If they could skew Sophie Njelteberg's very personal tragedy until Sophie's hometown wanted to disown her—but that was a flaw in the societal structures they had built. Either that or the media image with which Kaettegut was tagged was more powerful than basic human regard, and if *that* changed, human decency won another battle, then.

Murray Lerkenlund, especially with that in mind, was a problem. This would require a fine line, when Murray Lerkenlund had nothing fine about him, nothing precise.

She had asked her staff to find all video of Murray Lerkenlund, of what he had done up in the northern province outside her notice.

That was waiting for her in the main room, and not even the prospect of a hot drink could make that palatable.

She could not put it off, not on a day off, precious, like today. It was made more so now by the prospect of the usual loss of electricity, if what they were predicting hit the southern province, and their predictions were seldom wrong.

She sighed, and went into the kitchen to refill her mug and search out another teabag.

16

There had been weather reports for days. The buoys beyond Kaettegut had been picking up agitation in the currents and yesterday then the low-level winds that often accompanied those, and now they had a weather warning.

Graham hurried home in the fits and starts of a gusty wind that smelled, even here, of rain and seawater. Thank God it was a weekend; he'd had time to get to the grocery, to get supplies. He guessed it likely there would be no walking to the restaurants, not in a storm, and he was not stocked here like he had been in Kaettegut.

He shut the downstairs door against the bite of the wind, brought the bag out from behind the protection of his jacket, and let it swing down while he climbed the stairs.

Kellan had woken: the blankets were folded at the end of the couch when he opened the door into the main room. There were sounds of water running in the sink in the bathroom. He shut the door quietly and went into the kitchen, began unloading the bag, checked the ice in the freezer.

It was getting a little low. He poured what there was into a bowl and stuck it into the back of the freezer, shoved the container back in.

Kellan came out, fully clothed, towel-drying his hair. There was a faint scent of humidity near him. "What are they saying?" he asked, having watched the weather reports the night before, when there was little else to watch.

"Just the same warning." The icemaker slowly chunked into action.

Still, this was better than their former refrigerator, which worked intermittently if at all, on that function. "It's getting gusty out there."

Kellan looked at him, at the coat. "I could have gone out and gotten things. Or gone with you."

"I was up early." On the weekends, he was always up earlier than Kellan, who usually slept in after a workweek of early mornings and long commutes. "I don't know how it'll hit here. I'm wondering. Not much to stop it, with the bay." There was bay on both sides, actually; the expanse of Jargen Bay at nearly its widest to the east, New Bay to the west, and only the mercy of the warehouse peninsula curving up, at its tip, to frame in a bit of harbor. "They must be tying down the port."

"Maybe the seawall's protection enough."

"Maybe." He doubled the bag over and stuck it into the cupboard.

"It can't be that much worse than Rue." Kellan leaned on the counter, his back to him, and began folding the towel. "Nothing to stop the wind over there, that's for sure."

Kellan's hair had grown that much longer in these months. He had kept it trimmed with scissors here at home, but he had only limited skill. It was dark, now, in its dampness.

They had barbers over here. He was the same as Kellan when it came to that: it wasn't *right* for someone to be touching his hair, doing this and that when he could do it, when everyone did in Kaettegut, at least on the northern province, where they didn't have an entrepreneurial class outside the grocers—and they were department-run. He and Kellan did not have the tools here that they had; the groceries did not sell the grooming kits, and he had not wanted to ask, had not wanted to face that kind of surprise.

"I don't know." That kind of storm coming across that kind of expanse of water—interesting, at least, no matter what. He fought a yawn. "Ugh."

Kellan looked at him. "You look exhausted."

"Nah."

"Yeah." Kellan threw the folded towel on the kitchen bar, looked at him, still. "Why don't you take a nap? I can take care of anything else. What else do we need?"

"Nothing." A Saturday spent inside these walls stretched in front of him. At home, he might work; here there was little point.

Maybe he could brush up on his relationships—who was connected to whom? Jenning with the hospital, somehow; the pricing office, almost certainly. He had not been able to find a record yet, but there might be something—a report co-authored by two parties, unlikely parties, that would help him begin to find out how those relationships worked here. Who was with who.

But that required the access he had at work. And regardless—there would be no dinner at Cisco tonight. Cisco had solidified its place as Kellan's favorite, and he didn't mind it, didn't mind waiting for a table there, by its bar. Outlandish prices for a mixed drink when he could mix it far cheaper at home, but there was the atmosphere, the noise, the anonymity that took the pressure off him that he could not find here or at work.

He opened the refrigerator, scouted for leftovers that might work for tonight in the event of a power shortage, put in ice and eaten cold with what he had purchased this morning.

"Seriously. Get some sleep. I can take care of it."

"All right." He stretched; his shoulders felt sore. He shut the refrigerator door. "An hour or so."

There was a hookup in the bedroom, something he hadn't had back at Rue. He could use that without Kellan knowing. Kellan would worry if he worked at home here; he had not, for several months, and Kellan of all others would know it wasn't for advancement, the reason he had done it back in Rue.

He brought the tablet attachment over to the bed, propped up the pillow, and brought up the keyboard function. He could type silently more than talk, would feel ridiculous whispering.

He worked for a half hour. He found nothing; they did not publish reports as readily over here. He only came across regulations, policies, and what limited access he could gain to the database from home, without using his work login, and that would require work accesses he could not transfer here.

He sighed, stretched his head back into the pillow, and it felt marvelous and cool against his neck.

Something crashed. He started, and the tablet slid from his left thigh. He made a numb grab for it. It slid away under insensitive fingers, came to rest on still-smooth sheets.

"Kellan?" A note of worry in what was hoarse and slurred; he cringed, and wished he could breathe it back in. Not fully awake; he should wait—there was a *slap* at the window, and he looked, and it was as if someone had thrown a bucketful of water at it at once, at high force.

But Kellan was at the door. A tap on that surface, and he threw his pillow over the tablet, planted his hand straight on it, and sat up.

"It's all right." Kellan's face and shoulders appeared where he had opened the door a crack. "I don't think we have much time left, with the power."

He could have bashed his head into a wall and felt the same. "How long have I been asleep?"

"A couple hours. It's a little after noon." Kellan nodded toward the window. "I closed the shutters."

After *noon*— "What?"

"Everyone started closing theirs. I tried closing the other window's shutters. One's stuck. The latch won't move. Ours isn't the only one like that."

He felt slow, and groggy. But he looked, and the shutters *were* closed, and black and flat. The streetlight outside came in only through a crack between the shutters, and that made it darker than normal in the room; he may have slept longer because of that.

Another gust of wind hit. The shutters bent inward into the glass, banged, but held.

He had better brush his teeth while there was still power and water, get the sleep taste out of his mouth. He got up, smoothed his clothes, and went into the bathroom. "You had to close them from outside?" he called into the other room, and sounded little better. His throat grated.

"Nah. You can do it from inside. There're latches on both sides, I think."

The wind sounded atrocious—angry, as if it were live, howling and spitting. He spat into the sink, dried his mouth, and went into the kitchen in search of the contents of the drinks cupboard. Plenty of Alhoa left, three-quarters of the bottle, and it was the sterner stuff. He had discovered it at one of the first restaurants they had tried after Cisco and Osiake, had asked around until he had found a supplier.

Not a reseller; this they only sold to the restaurants, but Ted had connections, Ted knew some of the personnel in the warehouse where it was stored for shipment, and a very decent donation had netted him this with the possibility of more, now and then.

Ted had only raised his eyebrows, and smiled.

There was nothing quite like it in Rue. He poured it into a shot glass: no sense wasting it, and that much ought to numb his throat some.

"A little early, don't you think?" Kellan asked—who had no idea the Alhoa's source, but liked it well enough.

"Throat's sore." If Kellan had come in and closed the shutters from inside, while he was sleeping—Kellan *knew* he had been working. Would be too polite to ask. He went into the other room, flopped on the sofa, and for once did not care if it smelled of mustiness, of service too long here or elsewhere. He had thought—if he could build up his savings again, after the hospital and all the things it took here to live, the dinners—he might try to find an easy chair, something far, far newer. There was a procurement warehouse where the used things came back, cleaned, once the Back had sent over a shipment of new furniture for Jefferson. It was used exclusively for government that he knew of, but Ted might know more.

He had not asked. He did not have sufficient funds, yet, even with the allotment Kellan was bringing in.

He took the last sip. It was working; his throat buzzed pleasantly, and then the shutter banged, and several bucketfuls of rain slammed against the window, enough to make him jump.

There was a whiteness, a flash—everything in the apartment went dark. He blinked, tried to readjust his eyes to normal, but the wall across from him was in deep shadow, now. He looked down at the shot glass, and could barely see it. Ghosts of light hovered in his eyes.

No streetlight, either, then. He looked at the window, and saw only where the sheets of rain hit it, the faint glimmer. His heart was still racing from the last bang, with the flash; pure reaction, being this close to the window.

"That's it, then," Kellan's voice said, from the direction of the kitchen.

"I bought a flashlight. It's in the drawer next to the refrigerator.

Not much, just a penlight." He waited, heard rummaging in that direction. "Can you feel it?"

A glow of light, at last. He could see its tip, blinding as it pointed toward him, coming around the kitchen bar's countertop, then Kellan's face, lit eerily from below. A smile, and the lips moved. "Ah-ha."

"Oh, good God." A *smack* of rain against the window, harder than before, and the accompanying shutter bang— "There isn't any way to get that other shutter closed?"

"If we want to try it from outside, maybe. It feels like they painted over the bottom latch a couple times."

The entire sky cracked. He started, at the sound; droplets landed on his hand, the remnants of the Alhoa. "No. No, it's fine." The window would hold; it had held in Rue, where there were few shutters. Had the storm sped up, coming across the bay? It tended to do that, coming across the water, they said—the eastern edge of the northern province got storms far harder than Rue, if the news reports were true. Whole experimental crops could be wiped out if they weren't shielded, and there were not covers sufficient for that scale.

They were on the western side now of what was effectively an island, no matter how shallow the wetlands to the north of Jefferson's residential district—but if he could remember the map, place their house on it, they were in one of the narrower sections. Thankfully they weren't on the eastern side—that side might be getting storm surge, the way the worse storms tended to have.

There was no way to tell if there was water running down the streets. It *seemed* flat, but he did not know the actual topography, if there was runoff, if water pooled. Fortunate, too, that they were on the second floor. Whether they even had a downstairs neighbor—he had never seen one, wondered now if there was some poor sap or two down there, hoping it *didn't* flood.

There was beginning to be a low-grade noise, a constant roaring in the back of his ears that was the wind as he was familiar with it from Rue, where it came across the plain and hit the sides of the structures of the town, those rare occasions. "There it is," Kellan said, and came over and put the pen light on the table, propped it so its beam widened and was hitting the ceiling. A very faint glow, on everything else. "Is there a mirror or something around here?"

He jumped, at more torrents hitting the window—God, that one sounded like it would come through, it rattled the window, and he wondered how secure were the seams, at the sides.

He lifted the penlight, took it into the bathroom, and looked at the medicine cabinet mirror.

They had no tools like they'd had at Rue, where there *were* no crews to call in for repair, except in an emergency. He pointed the pen light's beam at the joints.

It would lift out. No screws. "Kellan," he said, and he heard Kellan feeling his way over, and the light picked up the edges of him, in the doorway. "Hold the light, will you?"

Much better illumination in the bathroom, with its large mirror: Kellan had the right idea. Kellan held the light until he had lifted the posts out of their hinges, and the shelves were bared to the room— shaving supplies, toothpaste.

It took some doing arranging it right, but they got it set up in the main room so that there was a faint glow on every angle that faced them, and everything that did not face the refracted light was black and in shadow. Kellan's face had hollows, magnified and dark, that he had not noticed in any other light. The eyelids, beneath the nostrils, the line below his bottom lip. *Kellan* had Alhoa in a shot glass; they had taken refills more than a couple times.

"Kellan," he said, not sure he should go forward at a time like this, with this much alcohol involved, but it helped dim the surprise when the wind hit the window, when the sky cracked, helped muffle the constant banging of the shutters here and from the bedroom.

Kellan wasn't listening. Kellan drained the rest of the glass, reached again for the bottle. "Truth," he said, which was what he had picked every time.

He refocused on that, on the game. "Okay." He had already learned more than he had thought; it had been worthwhile, after all, the storm. His comments could wait. "Do you remember your mother? Your real mother."

Kellan rocked back, mild surprise, at that. Cross-legged, sitting on the floor on the other side of the table, where the penlight was propped. "No." A pause. "I don't *think*."

"Come on. Think."

"Maybe. I don't think so, though." Kellan put the glass down on the table, a near-miss. "A presence. Maybe. I had—hit my head on something. A table."

A loud *crack*, an accompanying gust of wind: they both jumped at it, even with the alcohol in their bloodstreams. It strained to break the window, shook it in its frame, finally eased. "Think about that," he said.

"I think someone came. Picked me up." A deep frown. He sat there, like that, a few minutes.

"Anything else?"

"No—" And finally, "No. Nothing else."

If anyone had remembered that sort of thing, it would have been Kellan, who had a mind for detail like that. Who looked at him and said, "Truth—"

"Kellan."

"What?"

"Seriously." He leaned forward, and did not pour any more Alhoa, though his cup was empty. Now *was* the right time, if Kellan was at all alcohol-fuzzed. "I've been thinking. I think—do you remember what I said about Jenning being a—a good tool? A help?"

A blink, exaggerated in the low light and the shadows there, around his eyes. The rest of him didn't move. "Graham—"

"I'm not saying she's a saint. I'm saying she might be useful. If nothing else, we can use the name." *You know how to get in touch with me*, Jenning had said. And, *Relationships. That's what it's about, on this side.*

Kellan just looked. Still, there *was* no stiffening, the way Kellan could get at mention of her.

"She signed my transfer." He expected some surprise, only held up a hand. "I found out recently. *She* signed it, Kellan. Not someone who worked with her. Not *we*." She *was* in Organization, which was the same division as Kellan, who sent the travel visas through, trickle as it sounded like to be. Similar tasks.

Kellan sat very still. Did not look away. "Why?"

"Do you know who normally does it, first? It's *not* her, is it."

Concentration in the eyebrows, the forehead, creases that were black in this lighting. "No. I don't know."

"Could you find out?" This, he *very* much wanted to know.

"I can try." Distressed. "Graham—"

"If she did it, and she doesn't normally do it—it means something else entirely. If she does it, if she normally does it, when these things aren't usually done..." He *wanted* to refill his cup. The wind gusts were maddening without it, without that one shutter to protect the whole of the window, when it might shake loose of its frame. "I filled out my application a certain way. Whoever got it—understood it."

"What do you mean?" The effects of alcohol looked to be fast fading; Kellan was focused on him, on every quirk of his face.

Damn it. He had not meant to worry him, had done it this way for a reason. He lifted the bottle and reached for Kellan's glass.

"No." Kellan held up a hand, blocked him, and there was beginning to be anger. "Damn it, Graham, do you think I'm a child? How long have you been holding out on this?"

He held up his own hands. *Slow down.* "Ease up. Don't—misinterpret me." Worse, he could *not* tell him about the meeting in Jenning's office, whose questions repeated at inconvenient times—at work, at night when he had almost relaxed into sleep. "I asked for a transfer. It doesn't matter how I got it. It still doesn't. Just that I got it, all right?"

"Did you do something wrong? Something—I don't know. Have you gotten into trouble?"

He almost laughed, at that. In relief. "No. Just listen." He poured more alcohol into *his* glass; he could use it, now. "I had found out that one of the top analysts in the pricing office over here had died, I think of age. No, I wouldn't have ordinarily known that. *They* don't know what we know over there. The way—the way they were putting things into the media. They were feelers, I think. I *think* they were testing the idea."

"Your theory. The food tampering."

"That, and maybe other things too. Maybe they were seeing if they could get a reaction, seeing if it stopped, because someone would think they were onto it. A warning, maybe."

"You don't think they—"

He shrugged. "I don't know. I don't think *they* know. I do think they suspect it. Or that they did." He held up his hand. "Maybe that's why I'm useful. Maybe it's why you're useful. Maybe they don't know what the average person knows, over there. They don't go over there themselves. Too dirty for them."

Kellan frowned, shook his head. "The audits."

"Jenning headed up the audits. She knows us—Kaetteguttans— better, maybe, than most." He didn't say, *you said she knows psychology.* "What I put on my application, maybe it made her think."

"That was the bargain? That you knew about something over here?"

"Somewhat." He did not mention the pricing office, what she must have known he would bargain if he had to.

The other things he had written—he no longer suffered under the illusion most of it meant anything; they had been static around what *had* mattered on the application, the implications he had drawn, what use he could be.

"You wouldn't have known that normally?"

"No. But she wouldn't have known that, I don't think." He could not ask, again, what she had told Kellan. Not and keep Kellan calm, looking across the refracted light of the penlight at him. But if what he had said—if she *hadn't* questioned Kellan, much if at all, could throw the wrench into it.

Kellan hadn't mentioned it. Jenning had thrown doubt on *him*, and suggested Jefferson transferred more than renovation crews. Whether that was true—he had not known of any others, not from Kaettegut, and he'd had ways to know. Something like that would not have lasted long in isolation.

Kellan sat there a full minute. The wind hissed: a gust, and another spatter against the window. The window vibrated in its frame, hard.

"I do know she's well connected. If we have even a small value to her— She wrote you that note."

Kellan shifted, ended up a little further back, and it made his face look worse in the lighting. Wariness, almost, along with the worry. "I'm settled in a department. I don't think there's any danger I'm going anywhere. They don't say anything. It's a little late to send one of us back, isn't it?"

"No. *No.*" He wasn't saying this right; he shouldn't be trying this, with his mind fuzzed. He said it anyway: "I'm just saying that it might not be bad to have an advocate on this side some time, if we need it.

—I think there's something going on, with Kaettegut. Something isn't adding up. "

He'd known this was going to be chancy with Kellan, who looked up to Chauncey Benner, who would defend Gros Morne. Still, Kellan looked at him, and did not react otherwise. "Like what?"

"I'm not sure, honestly. I'm not over there anymore, to read things like this. Just—if you weren't close to it, the media on Sophie Njelteberg wasn't subtle. Not at the beginning, but a day into it, it was all against Kaettegut, and no one could say anything that would show anything else. Put *that* with the explosion." He picked up his cup. Put it back down. "I went back and looked at all of it, a while back. When *I* wasn't so close to it. I had missed a lot of it; that helped. God, Kellan, do you realize—the way it turned? In the beginning, it was that someone had tampered with the wires, and they were trying to find that party. Now, looking back on it— do you know everyone thinks of it like it was some damned *accident*? Like a pipe had blown up, and no one had done it, and Kaettegut was at fault in its response."

"I don't know." Kellan looked toward the window, the sound of water slapping against glass. A silence, except for that. "They were like that with me from the beginning. An accident."

Oh. Damn. He could have kicked himself. "They would have been." He wanted to ask, *did you ask?* but that would bring back memories, that would bring back things, when Kellan had not worn the robe again once he had gotten to the house and away from *there*. "I'm sorry."

Kellan shrugged. "It's all right. I *should* know. I should have looked it up."

"Don't. Just don't." Kellan looking up those records, seeing those media reports—seeing the other survivors coming back home, the other few who had walked as dead as Sophie Njelteberg. "Never mind."

Kellan shifted again—closer, this time. He put his arm on the coffee table, and the change skewed the effect of the light, so that only half his face showed, and terrible shadows made the other side grotesque. "It's all right, Graham. *I'm* all right. Okay?" A small lull. "I can handle it."

He looked, and shrugged, because there was something—*concern*, there; Kellan had put his finger right on the emotion, not what he was saying, not the logical argument, and that was not something he had expected, and not something he could handle well. Not now. "Take my word for it, all right?" he said, doggedly, and tried to refocus his train of thought. God, an opening. *If* he wanted to take it, and he was even less cognizant with the alcohol. He could *not*. "It—just changed. They were all hot to find who had done it, and suddenly it was like they weren't looking anymore."

"Chauncey Benner?"

"She finally stopped mentioning it." That was honest truth, but likely to disturb—and he *needed* to think straight. "She went longer than most."

Silence, for a few minutes. The wind beat against the window, and the whole building frame creaked. Disturbing because the wind direction was not constant; it seemed to come from entirely different sources, took different routes, hit the window with its loads of water at maddeningly random instants.

"There were the audits," Kellan said, again.

Blessedly back onto topic. Blessedly. And there was possibly something to that— "For someone of Jenning's stature to lead that audit—do you know anything of Jefferson's structure, with that?"

Kellan looked at him, strange again in the lighting. But—a frown of concentration. "I—know that there's an audit department."

"What division?"

A deeper frown, thinking; Kellan's right eye socket was a mass of black shadow. "Administration." Hesitantly, but firmer on the last syllable.

Confirming what he had thought; he had not been able to determine all the structure, all the divisions. In his more rational moments, he had thought it *would* be Organization, and that he was reaching out too far, that he was losing his edge. "*Jenning* led the audit. Jenning, not even the same division." *Relationships*, he remembered her saying that, her voice. He shook it loose. "I just think, with that combination—there's something in it. And Sophie Njelteberg—that would have played into it, but it turned, too."

Kellan stared at him. Looked again to the window, and stared there a while, his hair and neck in blackened relief.

He was not in politics. He had read politics, but before this—only so far to determine power structures, and how he could move in

them, and how they affected pricing, and what would get him a promotion. But— "I just think it might not be a bad thing, having that
level of name to play with. People over here are all right for the most
part, they're polite on the face of things, but... you know the image we
have. If there *is* something wrong, and it comes out, people aren't going to be as accommodating. To any of us, renovation crews included.
They *have* to have them, though. They don't have to have us."

"You think Kaettegut's in that much trouble."

"I don't know. I just think something's wrong."

"There hasn't been anything close to that level since—what, a
century ago?"

He did not mention the explosion again. "That they write down.
We don't know what goes on. We're not at that rank."

Another bang of the shutter. Another. He looked; it had swung
loose of its latch. "Oh, great." *Bang!* Hard enough to shatter the window now that it was loose. Another swing—he cringed.

"Here, I've got it." And Kellan was over by the window, and
strained to lift it up, but it finally worked. Wind and rain hurtled in.
He stuck his head out into it.

"Kellan!" He felt his throat and tongue voice it, could barely hear
it above the screech of the wind. He swung off the sofa, was over, but
Kellan took up most of the opening. He only watched Kellan worm
his shoulders out, twist around, and rest the middle of his back on the
windowsill, shoulders working to manipulate the shutters—there was
a burst of thunder, and Kellan jumped, and finally pulled his head
in, pulled the shutter shut and latched it on the lower side, where he
could reach. Made *sure* it was in there, snug.

Another wind and rain burst; he heard the water splat against the
shutter as he felt it come through the cracks: cold, cold water, against
his skin and his clothes, on the floor beneath his feet. "Come *on!*"

Kellan slammed down the window, locked it, and wiped his hands
on his pants. Water clung to his hair, his shoulders; soaked, in the few
seconds it had taken to do it.

He only looked at Kellan, at the window, and felt that a great deal
more of the Alhoa might not be a bad idea.

17

Chauncey kept her shoulders straight, and did not show her irritation—as far as was possible.

Murray Lerkenlund did not care for her visit to the northern province, no matter it was Rue and directly under her jurisdiction. He had made it plain, and sat now in sullen silence nearly at the opposite end of the table, slouched onto one elbow.

Rene sat in place of Phoebe taking minutes, this time, and accommodating the people who were in this conference room: the tea in her mug, the coffee in the cup in front of Blair Sunsi, who had come by the taste by way of Environment's very occasional visitors and the hospitality that required.

Cabinet meetings were seldom enjoyable. Still, she had hoped for bearable, at least, for routine and procedure, a quick and efficient disposal of quarterly business.

Nothing had gone quickly once she mentioned Rue. No, she faced Murray's surliness across the table instead.

Well, she didn't care for what *Murray* had been doing in the northern province, for what her staff's search for media had turned up in great abundance in the northern-only channels. Muuray Lerkenlund had built himself a comfortable little empire, exactly that, quietly, which was *not* like him, and was worrisome.

"Was there a particular problem?" George Sunsi, head of the fish hatcheries, asked now: somewhat of a more diplomatic approach, but the equivalent message all the same.

Good Lord. "It's my right to visit anywhere in either province," she said in a tone meant to end discussion, no matter whether she had allies in the matter or not—though Rudy Benner was watching, elbow on the arm of his chair, chin on knuckles. Withholding judgment, if she knew him, but sympathetic. She visited Forestry easily four times per year. He was more familiar with her than many of the others.

More than a few of them were old enough to have administered their regions long before her tenure began, Madge Long for one, who likewise sat and only watched, heavyset and legendarily steady, gray hair streaked with white.

It had been far, far too long, then, that an administrator had stepped outside the comfort zones of Gros Morne and Jefferson al though Jefferson's comfort was certainly relative—that this was the reaction a simple visit brought.

"I'm only trying to determine if there's a problem." A reasonable tone of voice from George, imminently reasonable, but there was just the tiniest tinge of something else. She hovered a mental finger over it, prodded at it.

Damn. Nothing quite fit. "Likewise," she said, and didn't bother taking the edge off. She leaned back in her chair. "I'd *very* much like to know what the problem is."

"It's a change." That, mildly, from Geneva Long, who handled sea vegetation, younger than her. She looked, and detected nothing other than Geneva's usual desire to keep the peace. And another patented Genevan tactic: "How long did you stay in Rue? They received you well?"

"Very well, in fact," she said, and took the redirect and the hint. She had long felt Geneva might make more of her brilliance if she were more direct, but Geneva often did have a point in situations like this. She could go too far. She was not removable as administrator by anyone in Kaettegut—she might feel differently in their shoes, who *were* removable, though by a lengthy process and requiring a vote of their department's population. Too much in the way of directness could be liable to back a specific kind into a corner—if that could explain Murray's stubbornness. "I was pleased, honestly. Well run, competence extends all the way down that I saw. Some very high-caliber line staff."

"Really," Geneva said, with interest: a prompt.

She had the heightened attention of Madge and Lola, who were both in the northwestern edge of the northern province, and if Madge's territory adjoined Murray's, some of Lola's desalination plants were nearly on top of it.

"We had dinner with some of the directors," she said, and decided to press a little harder. "At the house of one of them, on the western side. Lovely place. You can see the edge of one of the first seameats settlements. The official sitting next to me had been there, and the department had evidently made quite an impression on him. Fairly— salty. Opinionated, you could say."

Several eyes turned toward Murray, whose eyes only narrowed— but the muscles in the arm and elbow grew tenser.

"Oh, quite opinionated, our Murray," she said, and would have enjoyed it, had she not seen the video. "Of course, I didn't much doubt that."

Geneva sat still and watched her.

"Representing Kaettegut has been more difficult lately, of course. I think we all know that. I'd *love* to be operating from a position of strength." She stirred her tea, idly, with the stir stick...took a sip. "With the most recent that's happened, I thought it important I make some more personal contact up there, find out how they think about things."

She touched Murray's arm coming out of the conference room afterward, timed so that she was out the door behind him. "Murray," she said, and dropped her arm. He slowed, turned and faced her, and his scowl had gone deeper.

Lola moved past, the last one. Rene had stayed in the conference room but was keeping an eye on her through the doorway, she saw, as he gathered papers.

"I don't know what you're trying to accomplish," he said brusquely. "Getting the word out that having an opinion isn't welcome in your new regime, is that it?"

He stood easily a head taller than her. *Very* much a salt-of-the-earth type, the way his workers were. It had helped in no small part to get him the post, no doubt. She was not threatened—comfortable, no, not with the way his shoulders leaned forward into her space, the way he put his physical weight into his words, but that was nothing she was not accustomed to seeing from him across the conference room table. "We should perhaps talk about *your* regime," she said, simply, and gestured forward. "My office, please. Have a drink with me." And— "Rene?"

The scowl spread into a sneer. Murray shifted some weight back to his heels, nonetheless. "That's not necessary."

"Talking? I think it is." She waited, simply ignored the density of mass and displeasure that was, after all, much closer than she preferred, typical of his kind. "And you won't mind having Rene along. I think you'll find he's quite perceptive, being so familiar with the staff."

"I'd be glad to meet with you on equal footing. Come up to *my* office, where I have staff."

She smiled pleasantly. "I'm afraid that's a luxury you don't have." With Rene on her other side, she went ahead, and felt Rene settle into place behind her, pointedly between herself and Murray. She left it to him to make sure Murray followed.

Phoebe looked up as they approached, who typically took the minutes, and no doubt had regarded the reprieve this quarter with some relief, if a little sensitivity. "Murray might like something to drink," she said, at her door, and entered.

"Of course." Phoebe followed as far as a step within the door, and looked at Murray and inclined her head, courteously. "What would you like?"

"Nothing." To her: "If you want to talk, then do it."

"More tea, for me," she said, and nodded toward Rene. "Two cups."

Rene was already turning the chairs in front of the desk. She pulled hers out from behind it, rolled it around, sat down and crossed her legs. She waited for Murray to sit, but he stood and pointedly did not look at the chair Rene had put out for him.

Rene sat and shuffled his papers. She looked at him instead. "Those reports Cliff mentioned, on maintenance. I'd like to see those."

"I was thinking the same."

She thought on that, for the moment, instead. The ships were old and getting older, that was all there was to it. Kaettegut received the hand-me-downs from the Back, whose small fleet had to transport what was far heavier, the leftovers retrofitted to food compartments and already sporting rust around the edges. Cliff Runnel eternally had his hands full keeping the fleet in operation: peak condition was a thing rarely achieved, but Cliff did a tolerable job with the constraints he was given, worked around the clock whenever he could get the ships in dock long enough for real maintenance.

Phoebe came through the open doorway with two steaming cups on saucers. She took one, and Phoebe went around, placed the other on the desk near Rene's chair. Smiled, tightly: clearly Phoebe was not comfortable.

At the doorway Phoebe stopped with her hand on the knob and looked a question at her. She opened her mouth, but Rene answered instead. "A crack," he said, firmly, and shifted his attention politely to Murray, who still stood, obstinate. Phoebe complied, left the door open an inch on her way out. Silence stood quiescent behind her departure.

"Sit down, Murray," she said, letting the patience drop from her voice, and he looked at her, but he sat, though not without a glance to the door and its inch-wide opening. She ignored that, balanced the cup and saucer on her knee. "So. You've been active up in your parts, no?"

"They're *my* parts. Of course I've been active. I run the department."

"Some might be getting the impression you're doing more than that." Murray acted to defend the interests of his operations as if they were the only thing worthwhile in Kaettegut, too damned aware of the prestige the seameats brought to Kaettegut in Prime. She trumped that, barely, by having the long term food storage—never mind the hydroponics bays. "What do you stand to gain, Murray? It does no good to have divisions. *Especially* not now. If any part of Kaettegut goes down, the rest follows. You're not isolate."

He made a good show of being set back. "I have no idea what you're talking about. We ask for our share of resources, yes, we—"

She could almost laugh. "More than your share of resources, Murray, and you know it. Every damned cabinet meeting."

He did laugh, one short bark. "Is that what all this is about? Good God, Chauncey."

Condescending, that *that*. Superior age, superior experience, those were the implications. It rankled. He had known it would, knew that she'd rather push him out of her office than deal with it, no doubt counted on it. She took a sip of tea, slowly, and put the cup back on its saucer. A little too hot—she swished it around before letting it hit her throat. "Aim to be a god, up there?"

"Surely we're not here to talk about management styles." Condescension in full force, now. "Would you mind telling me what this is *really* about?"

"Oh, we're on topic." She looked across at him, left the cup where it was. "Word gets around, you know. I'd like to know what you think you have to gain, what you've been using those resources *for.* What—is division going to bring us?"

"The way I run my department is none of your business, if it gets things done. If you have something to say, say it."

"You don't run this meeting, Murray. I do." *That* was a dig. He did not have the surname necessary to sit in her seat, that was the plain truth—and *was* the question. "Answer the question. How is division going to benefit Kaettegut?"

"I'm not trying to make division."

"Really." *God.* Like pulling teeth where there were only gums. Lerkenlund barely made it into the middle range of schools: Murray, by virtue of that alone, was second lowest on the council in terms of prestige—though she'd put Cliff Runnel well above him, if it came to that. "What *are* you trying to do?"

"Trying to run my department, damn it!"

"It's not necessary to running *any* department to appear on the media criticizing the administrator, last time I looked. Not that I don't appreciate you attempting to create some cohesion up there. We *could* use more of that. I'd just prefer the whole of Kaettegut have that kind of cohesion, and not what you're building it on."

"Is *that* what this is about?" Less artificial, this time, though—she had struck a nerve, he was clenching and unclenching his hands. Once. Twice. "*That* isn't what I'm saying. If that's how you take it, you're wrong."

She leaned back, let her spine relax into the chair. "How am I to take it?"

"Not like *that.*"

"I have some video. You can give me your interpretation. Step by step." She looked to Rene, lifted her head to nod permission.

"I don't need to see it. I know what I said. I know everything I've said. It doesn't mean that."

"I'm curious to hear your explanation." Hard, in the voice, purposefully.

"You don't know what they think up there, what they feel." Sudden emotion, a complaining timbre—past the point that was natural, in this situation, in an office. "How it is to have the same damned image slapped on you every time you turn on the television, and then this Sophie Njelteberg business, and we're killers, then, and where's our voice over there? Damn it, Chauncey, nothing new, nothing *ever* new, the same mild little denials. You don't *know* the northern province, and *that's* what we've got over there, defending us."

She let that flow by, did not let it touch her. Noted, of course, that he *was* trying to manipulate her personally, and hard, though she gave him credit for having picked up on what she would have deemed far too subtle for his type. "All very good. Very smooth. Except you were saying that sort of thing long before Sophie Njelteberg. *Long* before the explosion."

"Not like that." He was working, furiously, to put some spin on it. "We need someone over there who isn't going to lie down and take what's given. Someone with some spine! How we got into this situation at all was that, and lying down, and taking it. A seat on the Ligotera." He snorted. "We're *survival* on this planet. Let them try to do what we do. See if they can do it."

This, coming from Murray Lerkenlund, of all places—but it was all technique, which meant she had not been at all subtle, and word had gotten around.

She crossed her arms. "Which all makes sense, except that you've restricted yourself to one area, stirred up things you have no business stirring up, and did nothing, *nothing*, to change how you were represented in Jefferson. Not one word."

An open mouth and silence for a second, not long enough. "You've got to be kidding."

"I'm not."

"Then where have *you* been? Every damned cabinet meeting I speak up! I'm not hiding anything 'up there.' You ask me what I think, I'll tell you."

She felt suddenly weary. This type of negotiation—boorish, lacking subtlety *or* intelligence, and no matter the appearance of direct-ness, there was none. Misdirection, bluster, that's all it was. She had made no progress, none other than to find he could ask around, and that he had known she was in Rue, and that he was displeased about it, little more than what she had known in the conference room.

"Styling yourself a leader over more than you are isn't going to do anyone up there any good," she said. "If you're not going to tell me what you hope to gain, I can't make you. I *can* tell you I find it little amusing, and if what it takes is to go up and take up residence in Rue and start directly refuting you on those same media channels, fine. I know some people who would welcome me. I don't think that's what you want. I *would* like to know what people there are really thinking, and you know what? I've started asking, and I might keep going."

The extraneous disappeared, very quickly. The bluster disap-peared, simply heat, now, in the stare—and she had the sudden, very precise sensation that what she was seeing was the core. It gave a chill to the bones, unpleasant, and she *felt* the difference in decades, jar-ringly. She did not move, still, if only out of stubbornness, and sat in her chair, with her teacup balanced on her knee.

"Make certain what you say," he said, and the voice was searing. "You aren't in a position to absorb any more trouble in Jefferson."

"And that means?" There was anger, now, heat rising up through her sternum, her throat.

"It means I'm well aware of the value my department's efficient operations hold in Jefferson."

"And what would happen if efficiency were to slip. That's feeble, Murray. Damned feeble. If you think I've got nothing at my disposal better than what you're implying—" She turned, in her chair, and set the teacup and saucer on the desk, with precision. "Are we going to work together, or not? Just answer my question. I'm tired."

"There isn't anyone who can do what I can do in Seameats. Trust me on that. I'm not anywhere near a successor, and I haven't had any reason to train anyone in what I do. I've *got* the time. You want to put some greenhorn behind that desk, you go right ahead. *Your* reputation rests on what I do."

That early tea could have seemed downright cold in her throat. "You're asking, will *I* work with *you*."

Rene put his hands on the armrests of his chair, was tense in the shoulders, in the neck, still facing Murray—who considered, only, and *that* hung in the balance.

Finally, and diplomatically: "Not at all." A recourse to a milder tone, the heat tempered. "I'm saying that we should work together, that you acknowledge our needs, and we can look at yours."

Not so easy for her, once she was riled. "You can look at our needs, can you? Generous."

"That's not what I said. What I meant. I'm saying, we've got to depend on you to represent us in Jefferson. We have *one* option. That doesn't seem fair, but it's what we've got. I don't see how you can expect us to do anything other than make the best of it."

"I can expect you to keep your mouth shut, and come to me if you have a problem." Tightly. "You overestimate your importance, Murray. If you feel like getting yourself called in for a one-on-one with the administrator makes you that much more key to the operations of this department, you're deluding yourself. You aren't any more important than anyone else. Your seameats aren't going anywhere without the work of Cliff Runnel and his crews. More to the point, your seameats aren't lasting long without Gros Morne's food storage, and that's *my* area."

"So we can expect to see another explosion in one of those storage units, then?"

Nothing but emotion in her veins, now, pounding hot through her brain—but that's what he wanted. *And* he wanted to escalate his importance, and if she set in motion a recall, that's what it would get him. A martyr—and he would not lose at the polls, with the kind of support he had built, on *her* back.

God damn, he had known what he was doing, knew what he was doing now.

She laughed. Let it bubble up through her lungs, her throat. "Murray, Murray." She rested her hands on the arms of her chair, lightly, and looked across at him. "That's feeble. *You're* damned weak. If you haven't proved anything else in here, it's that. I don't know why I wasted my time." She rose, and Rene stood too, with far more tension in his limbs. "You've made your argument as to why I ought to give your department less of the budget, and let some of those who are clambering for it, have it. Cliff Runnel, to start. Which should help you out in the long run, so I'd hope you'll be glad. Get out of my office."

He delayed, critically: he wavered between heat and sense, it was evident in *his* face, the jowls beginning to give into gravity. "Out," she said, and went to the door and opened it, and made sure Phoebe could see her. Phoebe was standing up from her chair, her face showing uncertainty.

"I don't appreciate—" Murray began.

"I don't much care for what you don't appreciate." To Phoebe: "Phoebe—"

"The last comment was in bad taste. I admit it. Let's not be hasty."

"Damned bad taste, and another waste of my time. Phoebe, call the car. Murray will be late to the dock. He doesn't need to miss the ferry." Phoebe did not need to be told the real meaning of that, and none of the staff within hearing, either. Phoebe inserted the phone earpiece to call.

A last try, on his part: "Why don't you come up and tour the operations? See a little of what I'm talking about."

"I'll consider that," she said.

Late, Murray was at last on his feet and moving toward the door, Rene behind him—whose face had gone to a shade that was still nearer red than purple, but close, and who loomed a far sight larger in this moment.

Murray stopped in the doorway, facing her, too close. "You're inexperienced, Chauncey." Quietly. "Why *don't* you come up, take advice from some people who are a little closer to things than you are, eh? Get to know them. I'm not the only one who feels this way, you know. There are others. Dismissal of what's different than you—it's not the route to take."

"I hope you don't miss the ferry. If you'd like us to call and hold it, I will." Besides the repeated dismissal, a bit more courtesy for someone who had shown little of it: a lesson, she'd hope.

He inclined his head. Collected himself, in front of the staff. "No. I'll make it. —Think about what I said, Chauncey. You can call me."

That was nerve. She watched him walk the entirety of the path to the doors, open them and turn into the lobby and toward the stairs, without looking back, spine stiff with hurt pride—and knew that he was furious, not least at his treatment in front of her staff, when having his own staff present to match hers had been a point with him.

She knew that she had just changed the balance of things, too, and now, in the heat of her blood, very little cared.

She stepped back into the office and closed the door. Took a breath, let it out, and took a long draught of cooled tea. "I'll need his budget cut by ten percent," she said to Rene, who stood just beside the door. "Any more and it'll be ammunition for his crusade. Less than that will cover what Cliff's been wanting to do with the fleet."

Rene was close to shaking; worse, the color was still there in his face, his neck. Carefully, he said, "I don't like the way he was."

"Neither did I. It's the way it goes."

He persisted. "It wasn't safe."

"I wouldn't go that far." But she held the tea cup between her palms, and pondered that. She had been angry, could *still* feel her blood boiling. Rene, on the other hand, might have been coloring for a different reason entirely, that she'd missed, hadn't picked up on cues the way he had. He could have a different perspective, watching from the outside in. "Murray holds himself that way for a purpose. His stock and trade, to get the things he wants. It's a tactic." The sanctity of her own office, emptied of its strain, calmed her. "The rest—he'd *like* to get you boiling, where you can't think."

"It's not that." Rene held himself stiffly, hands at his sides—clenched. "I don't mean— There's a lot more to him. He *has* a temper. It's not much further to go from—leaning into someone to something more. I don't think you should meet with him again."

She massaged the mug with her right palm, looked at him.

"I think you should have staff with you whenever you go to other parts of the provinces. *Not* Joceyln and Phoebe. Dominic. Me. Two or three, at least."

She set the cup on the desk. "You think it's gone that far."

"I know what he could have done. I know what you implied in this meeting and the cabinet meeting, even if I don't know the particulars. He's stirring things up. Not everyone might welcome you like Rue did. And you said you might go back up there."

"I might," she said, and was appalled—but what Rene was saying *did* have sense to it, and if nothing happened, there would be nothing untoward in having staff with her. Rene typically accompanied her to Jefferson, Dominic had gone with her to Rue. But—*God*, was she thinking this? "No. That's going too far. You with me, that's fine. You're usually with me. I appreciate your sentiments. This is just— the sins of the fathers, that's all."

Her predecessor had not managed anything outside his immediate territory, and *this* was what had come out of it: department heads with far too much rein when only a few were suited to it, and things had almost gone too far. Much too far, if this was the level of power Murray Lerkenlund thought he had, that anyone dreamed to come into the administrator's office, who signed off on every resource his department got, and conduct himself in such a way that her own aide saw threat.

"Thank you, Rene. Don't worry." She put a hand on his shoulder and pressed once, firm. "I appreciate your help. I'll be curious to see your report. You may have seen some things I missed."

When he had gone—she pressed the intercom, swallowed the anger still simmering in the back of her throat. Elevated blood pressure, still. "Phoebe, contact Madge Long's office. Have her call me when she arrives. Tomorrow's fine, if it's too late when she gets back. I'm going to take an early evening."

Madge would be tricky. Madge was older, one of the veterans, longer by a decade and a half than Murray. If she could do it, though, she might edge her plans into favor of someone not insignificant in the northern province, where support from Rue was looking increasingly precious, and dismayingly—not large enough.

Quinn sat at the table while her drink steamed—a coffee royale, its thin layer of cream foamed and melting at the brim, good and hot and stiff below. One of the privileges of rank, this kind of drink at lunch, the table on the other side of the kitchen by the windows, all other tables empty this side of the room.

Privacy was ensured—as was a strong impression on her dining companion ensured. Gallagher Crote served on the Ligotera, had surely dined here some time or other. He had probably not seen one-third of the restaurant reserved for one guest; he had arrived first and taken a small table near the front. The waiter had quickly rectified that.

"Wonderful view, isn't it?" She gestured toward the window, leaning in to take her first sip of her drink. "Unique to this restaurant. They've done a fine job with the landscaping."

"Very lovely." An emphatic nod. From the perspective of his particular seat, one could see down the ribbon of tributary nearly to the river, dark water lit at points by the lamplights backed by deep blue sky. The grounds crews had cleaned up the storm debris, the occasional tree branch, the places where the tributary had pushed over its banks and flooded ground that could not absorb that quantity of rain and water.

Gallagher had spent no small amount of time with Chauncey Benner in the days following the news of Sophie Njelteberg. A fortunate turn of events, that: it meant an extension of the visit by several days, and if she had not been able to meet with Gallagher face to face as soon as she would have liked, she *had* received his messages.

The delay, of course, combined with several days of Ligotera sessions had also meant work piled on one natural resources administrator's desk—an administrator who oversaw the department of one peer delegate, among his other duties. She had made it her business to become familiar with Gallagher Crote's role in Environment, how close he might be to Meghan Truong.

Heady scent, coffee. She breathed it in, taking a second sip, and let the alcohol hit her stomach.

"I hope you've made some progress on that backlog," she said, the last bit of preliminaries, her nod to courtesy.

"Thank you. I have."

"I'm looking forward to hearing your thoughts." She stirred the cream into the surface of the coffee.

"She's distressed, of course, by the events back at home," he said, and took a sip of his own drink, a more tame espresso, plain. "Quite distressed, actually. Something—very personal about it."

That much was easily verified by the media coverage. Chauncey Benner had held it together, had become frustrated toward the second or third day—had seemed to realize, then. She had tried for reason at the end, had calmed it down to rational argument. Impossible, when the framework was purely emotional—but she'd had little choice, then; the emotion of the viewers had been sliding the wrong way. It had *been* a better strategy to take a different tack. Still unsuccessful, of course, but a decent move.

"How so?"

"She doesn't—view her department as a department. I know that sounds strange." He looked out the window, at the lamplight nearest them. "She sees things, acts to defend Agriculture—as *hers*. Not the way I see my staff, or the way you see yours. Protective, yes, but it's different."

Careful, she thought mildly: presumptuous to assume he knew how she saw her staff. But the point was there, and Chauncey Benner could be seen as a very real threat, possessive in a way her predecessor had not been—if she had access to the connections the rest had, in Jefferson.

That Chauncey Benner did not have those connections, did not hold a place in that web of loyalties, was something *she* was changing, slowly. The first in that line sat across a small table, here. What Chauncey did with it was an item of interest.

An Agriculture not under Fifty's perfect control remained separate, simple as that: separate and distasteful, and expansion efforts did not go far. A vast expanse of sea to the south blocked expansion that way, and wetlands made a northern route difficult; no one would propose going west into the blackness and the ice, where there was no hope of photosynthesis—when the experimental farms on the eastern side of northern Kaettegut had experienced *some* limited success, and seemed to promise more, the further east one pressed.

But she had anticipated this much, had hoped for much more. She regarded Gallagher levelly. "Do you feel this was so before the Njelteberg incident?"

"Yes." Firmly. He lifted his cup, tilted it. "I don't think—she doesn't seem to have levels. She's very straightforward, not just with the Njelteberg situation, but with the Ligotera. She doesn't try to move up, she doesn't try for relationships. She listens and she votes. She speaks once in a while. If it's ignored or someone doesn't like it, she has no qualms about it. She has the attitude—she's said it, it's been put out there, that's enough."

"She didn't seem that way about Sophie Njelteberg."

"That, yes. She was frustrated, really frustrated. She felt she was putting the truth out there, and that people refused to see it. Not just *failed* to see it, but deliberately turned and looked at something that was not true."

Gallagher *liked* Chauncey Benner. That was interesting; that might be a hint of talent that held promise, in her, if properly shaped. "She confided in you a great deal, then."

"It was a time of stress. We got to talking a bit. She was interested in the way my department runs. I had the feeling it was the first time she'd been able to see something outside her own department, in the various levels. Outside the personnel issues we review in council, of course, but there isn't as much information in that as there might seem to be." He finished off the last of his espresso, swallowed. "She operates on practicals, really; doesn't like to get into the emotions of things, even in stress. She's a lot more willing to show anger than any other emotion."

Hmmn. That was meat, that was key.

There was perhaps potential, then, what she *had* hoped. Untrained and undisciplined, that was the way the council had come to see Chauncey Benner—they still relied on Meghan Truong to keep her where she should be, and saw the media on the Njelteberg situation as proof things were on the right path.

Except that Meghan had done little to nothing to steer the media situation, and what Meghan had done had to be undone, for the most part, before it could hit residents' screens. She had gotten to most of that. *She* had Agriculture where it was now—but the food supply had not changed, there were still the anomalies nearly everywhere but hydroponics, where an administrator would be wise to maintain the appearance of propriety.

What Chauncey might be doing now, in Kaettegut, she did not have access to determine. What Chauncey might do if she saw herself with allies, if she began seeing how things worked over here—could be kept easily to this side, and easily monitored.

"You said she doesn't attempt to make alliances on the council," she said, and Gallagher nodded, over an empty cup. "Is there anyone she seems to be drawn to more than the others? Someone she seems to respect more?" Respect would be the key for someone like that, who had the propensity to focus on facts to the exclusion of feeling.

It was not that Chauncey Benner was not passionate. She did not draw that picture at all, given her previous actions, *all* of them, taken together with what Gallagher had enunciated. Great passion, funneled into action, and the only other outlet anger.

Gallagher was thinking hard, on this one. He looked over her shoulder, eyes creased. "I think—Rebecca Wright. If anyone."

Rebecca Wright. She searched her memory, briefly, for that name, and zeroed in on it. Rebecca Wright administered Durable Goods. Blond hair, built strong in the bones, in the jaw; small ears set strangely far back.

Gallagher was looking across at her. He smiled, and his eyes crinkled in the corners. "Wholesale," he said helpfully, if a little late. "Not really the warm type."

Warm. It *had* grown warm in here. Doubtless the drink was responsible, which had settled quite nicely and hot in her stomach. She looked for the waiter, over Gallagher's shoulder, and there he was, coming from some distance off.

She nodded, waited while he approached, and watched as he set each dish on the table carefully. Broiled salmon for her, steaming, decorated with curlicues of bitter but exquisite grayed herbs, some sort of white fish for Gallagher, on a bed of greens. She breathed in the scent, unwrapped her silverware. This eatery truly deserved its reputation.

"So," she said to Gallagher, taking her first bite. "Tell me about the council."

18

Jenning sat by the grate, the morning still quite early, and massaged her calf, flinching when she hit the tense spots. Muscle and slack tissue were sore and angry, made worse by the changes in weather: first the long storm, the rush of drier air that had come after it, and now, finally, the humidity, back with a vengeance.

She had almost weaned herself from the cane, damn it! Now she'd had to go back to the crutch, in the privacy of her own apartment.

The heat from the grate was a comfort. Her skin was almost too hot to the touch, sitting so close, but her muscles had gone far more pliable. She *hated* to leave it, truly did; would rather sit here today and forego going into the office at all, but Gabrielle would be concerned, and absenteeism was no way to convince anyone to consider her *or* her department.

She grimaced, getting to her feet. She left the toast sitting on its plate beside the beckoning chair, her favorite—inviting with its green fabric, made velvety and dim in its old age.

She took the ferry down to Jefferson, and stood on the lower deck with her mouth tightly closed against the moisture of the river air, of what formed on the ferry windows in droplets. She went back at last to the bar, not staffed at this hour, took two painkillers with a small glass of water drawn from the sink's limited supply.

It *was* better. She did not stop in the office, merely pulled her cape tighter and hobbled down the side block Education's offices took up, and felt immensely improved in the dryness of the main lobby, then. "Ethics," she said at the reception desk, and went the direction the young woman pointed.

Ah. Carpeted floor, a further improvement, thickly padded. She stopped in front of the elevator, stripped off the thin gloves, and brushed the cape back.

A very short trip up, and she stepped out.

Stefan Coubertin's floor was bare-bones compared to the lobby and its elevator bank. Second floor, small, old tile.

It gave her a second thought. It did. This, of all indications, told her where he was in Education's hierarchy, and she had not reckoned on quite this level.

She could turn around, simply hobble back to the elevators. *That* would be a statement, because she had a scheduled meeting with him, and it was on his calendar as well as hers—that she did not meet with those at this level, no matter whether they had wormed their way onto the Proteraiotita, and stayed.

But she liked a challenge, and she had come this far.

Stefan Coubertin was sitting in his office, and in person there were lines that did not show on the media: around the mouth, worry lines around the eyes and brows. The dark hair had the start of gray in it, for being only in his forties.

Plainly introspective. He'd be an intuitive thinker, she'd guess, high on the emotional side of the chart. Idealism easily granted, if he had obtained this post—but still, not to the point of self-sacrifice. Likely he *thought* he had that level, that he'd do it if called upon, but he would not. Most thought that, and would not.

His educational records pointed to a strong graduate focus in ancient Earth civilization—unusual, to say the least.

"Jenning Crote," she said, entering, and did not extend a hand. A simple nod would do. She willed warmth into her eyes, felt them crinkle at the corners. *Damned* that she hadn't brought her cane; she would not have used it here, but if she had used it on the relatively long walk to Education's buildings it could have saved her the splinter shooting up her calf into her knee.

She would not by any account call for the car to get to her own office from here. She had done with that, with the appearance it gave—when Jeffersonians would know it was not her importance lent her that transport, but her injury, or worse, her age.

"Please. Have a seat." He stood, extended an arm to the nearest chair. Impeccable form, if she could not say the same for his office. Cramped, tiny—the added inconvenience of an interior window only the minor supervisors typically tolerated.

But the chair was padded, and the arms were at the right height, and she lowered herself into it and placed her leg at the angle least painful and still inconspicuous.

He sat. Opened his mouth.

"You studied ancient civilization," she said, instead, and took charge. She had much to determine—that he would not reveal, wound up the way he was, nervous and trying hard not to show it—and that meant there was something in those numbers personal to him, important to him.

But today was the introduction; the numbers had only been her invitation. She considered revealing that and decided against it, here in the blue padded chair that smelled, now that she was settled, somewhat too well-used.

"Yes," he said, and sat there looking at her with his hands folded together, the fingers a little too tight.

"Interesting course of study. Why?"

Too personal, she saw in his eyes, in the glance away. He considered whether she had the right to ask it, whether he should answer it. Presumptuous, of course, to ask a personal question at this stage, in that manner; she had known that.

"It had always interested me," he said, and licked his lips, looking directly at her. Point for that. "Not the conflict so much. The way they developed. Different nations had entire collective personalities."

"Mm." She had brushed up on the subject before coming here, had been doing some research, evenings, just enough for an introduction, for a relaxation—a foot onto his turf, enough to breed familiarity. "If I remember right, I focused more on the Eastern countries in that chapter. Briefly, of course. It struck me Rome and China must have been somewhat the same, in the core. Borrowed religion, show of force—a talent for organization."

His eyebrows had lifted, slightly. "China doesn't get much press."

"Not here. I'm sure ancestry has no little to do with that, of course. I would have liked to have learned more."

"What interested *you* in that?" He was leaning slightly more forward; the anxiety had not gone far, but it *had* moved back, some.

Distraction, solely that; the anxiety would be back when the conversation turned, would still float in the room after she had left.

"I'm not sure. Perhaps it was just a such a large territory, and yet they managed to pull it off longer than anyone else had." *That* was a trigger point with him: she applied it carefully. Coubertin was expansionist, well known as that. A hell of a lot of potential as a poster boy for that party, if they chose to take advantage of it—but they had Fifty pressing palms, and Fifty's aura of power, and needed very little Coubertin's brand of intelligence to push forward the argument.

"Yes, well." He reprised the same polite smile, rubbed his nose—brought out, good God, the folded sheets of numbers, what *she* had sent, and laid them on the desk. "Naturally I'm curious about this."

Different territory entirely—which also said he didn't want to talk party politics, did not want to get at all into it. Also that he lacked any finesse; a shame, but there *was* some bravery, no matter how foolish. "In what way?"

"Oh, where it came from, why you thought it prudent to send it to me."

Not doing badly, for the level of nerves. The air fairly vibrated with them, now. "I didn't come here to talk about that. Say only that I have good sources, and disparate, and that no one has thought to put the numbers together in quite this fashion. You can be at ease."

"That's good of you to say. Any thoughts of your own as to what these numbers might mean?"

She smiled, and did not let it reach her eyes. "I'm not here to talk about that. I thought you should know, that's all." No more than that; more would reveal that she had *not* put all of it together yet, and she would not say what might have consequences when she had insufficient information, without which she could not retain control. "If you're concerned who else might know, suffice to say they don't. You're the first to see those numbers in that context. I doubt anyone else could put things together—quite the way my department can, with my staff, and my resources."

"I don't much care for people prying into my department's affairs."

"Really?" She shifted, and relaxed further into the chair. Her leg protested, sharply. "You ought to be accustomed to it, serving on the council. Comes with the privileges."

He had no answer to that. He swallowed, and moved not at all, and only looked at her. "Well, but I'm being impolite. Can I by chance offer you a drink? The weather's not at all friendly these days, especially with the river commute."

"Thank you. Coffee."

He stood, and that surprised her for an instant, that he moved past her and out of the office to retrieve it himself rather than buzzing his assistant.

Then again, it *was* early. His assistant might genuinely not have arrived. She stood her chances on the coffee, in that case.

So. He lacked finesse, had not an inkling, in private, of what he showed on the council. Deference, proper procedure—outside of the courtesies, fairly well disregarded, in his own office. He attacked directly what concerned him at the instant the small talk began to turn. Disappointing, and again not what she had expected. He showed himself and his concerns obvious, when aggression was an area in which he had precious little experience; very poorly done.

He spent no small amount of time retrieving the coffee. Point on his side, for that; she had an office waiting, and he delivered *that* disregard sharply.

She sat very still and let her calf recover, at the least. She took in the books and binders in his office, the titles, the tidy organization of most of it in secondhand cubbyholes and drawers. Everything on the desk sat precisely arranged: the screen at a certain angle, a stapler at another, easily in reach. Four inboxes, each labeled.

A working man's desk. No prima donna, at least.

He returned at last with the coffee, steaming up from the cup on a chipped saucer. He waited until she had a firm grasp before releasing it and maneuvering back into his chair behind the desk. "Our receptionist doesn't come in at this hour of the morning. At least you can know it's fresh-brewed." A quirk of the lips, too tight. He waited while she sipped. "—Is it all right?"

"Not bad." She had miscalculated and burned the tip of her tongue, when typically she *did* drink coffee hot. *Damn it.* She wouldn't be able to taste for the whole of the morning.

"We're accustomed, " she said, and ignored her numbed tongue where it hit the back of her teeth, "to arranging information we've gathered. Sometimes quite crucial. I've recently been able to participate in the agricultural audits, as I'd think you know. Really, really quite fascinating, their administrator."

She had his attention. He leaned forward. "What do you think, then? Coming from firsthand knowledge."

Possibly a slight dig. Possibly not. "It's unfortunate she hasn't more resources. Very isolated over there; almost their own world." And conversationally: "Hilly, you know, Gros Morne, and all concrete and brick. And then you go into the hydroponics bays—it makes you think what they had, originally, when they found the system and started using it."

That was fascination for anyone who hadn't been there. Distaste for Kaettegut or not, *they* didn't know where their food came from; they would have been intrigued to see the emptied hatches of a mussel hauler, with its scattered shells.

Quite apparently she would not be returning. Quinn had not asked; there had been no mention of audits.

A chance to interact with Chauncey Benner, now she knew her, knew Chauncey *wanted* to play a part on the political stage—would be invaluable. Otherwise, she could not say she was sorry, would not be sorry to never pack another bottle of water or force down another mug of Kaettegut's odious tea.

He leaned further forward. "And the explosion?" Quietly.

She turned her head and surveyed him from a different angle. Surprised, genuinely so; and that opened an entirely different can of worms. "You're the first I've talked to who hasn't referred to it as an accident, do you know that?"

"I imagine you have a different experience of it." Equally quietly, and fairly sensitively put.

"I do," she said, and then just: "I have an idea." More than she had intended to reveal, to anyone, but he deserved that, simply in identifying it for what it was. "You?"

He looked down at his hands. Refolded them, moved his thumb over the other. "I don't know. I was disturbed by it. I thought at first—the status quo. A warning to the rest of us that we *couldn't* handle things like this, and that things like this *would* happen. That we can't maintain control."

Equally honest, and equally more than he had intended to reveal, very obviously, in his hesitation. She was pleased: this was new territory. *And now?* was her next question, but better to take it another time; he had given far more than he had been prepared for, and he had come into this nervous at the first. To respond from the direction of a political leaning—would be much more dangerous.

It had grown perhaps too intimate, too quickly—and she had done, for the most part, what she had come for. She'd recalculate, next time, coming in, would adjust for the difference in his public and private personas. She might *not* have sent those numbers if she had anticipated this.

"I contacted you because I thought we might work together," she said, getting to her feet and setting the coffee cup and saucer on the edge of his desk. "A certain synergy. Truth be told, though, I found you interesting. There's a lot there, if one looks."

"Oh?" Definite interest.

"I'd rather keep it between us, of course." And at the door: "I wouldn't mind getting together—for dinner, perhaps. A few weeks. Your assistant can call mine; Gabrielle has my calendar."

She gave a last nod with the invitation; she made her way out, and passed a young man coming in, burdened with a shoulder satchel. Looking back, she saw him slide the satchel onto the receptionist's station: Coubertin's assistant, then. He had been honest, grant him that.

He *did* have some potential with her. Some shaping by her, and he'd work out just fine.

———

The lobby was the same, the pronounced clip of footsteps on the marble floor, the clean smell of spaciousness and polished stone.

Graham did not stop at the reception desk this time. Kellan had said, that long ago, to go left once in the lobby; he went past the security station, whose guard looked at him and then away.

There was an entirely different elevator bank on this side. Same marble floor, illuminated less kindly than the dim luster of the lobby—everything here glared, white and slick. Someone had burnished the silver of the elevator doors; those and the flared table against the wall, with its single vase of green leaves, were the only relief.

The interior of the elevator, when it came, was a model of traditional design. There was plain mirror on the upper walls, but the buttons glowed a warm gold in their surround of real, finely grained wood. He bent down, slightly, ran his finger across a strip of it. The protective finish had worn unevenly; he could feel dips and crevices.

Something was imperfect here, at least. He straightened, waited while the elevator pulled even with the third floor, and the doors slid open.

It took him a while once on the floor to find the travel department. He stayed to the main corridor, and that was a mistake; he finally located the department placard in the first branching corridor, nearly next to the elevators.

The reception area seemed disproportionately large, the desks and stations made of a coarser-grained wood, but dark stained and still elegant. The women and the one man enclosed in it were as Kellan had described them: polished, sleek. The women wore their hair back in smooth knots.

"Kellan Long," he said, at the counter, and tried a little to imitate their way of speaking: less crass, from their point of view.

The closest woman managed to look down her nose at him, even seated, and despite his height. "Who shall I say is calling?"

"Graham. Can I go back?" He did not know the way, but damned if he would sit out here, subject to *this*—and when she shrugged, he took the nearest hall and hoped it was the right one, and that they would not call him back.

They did not. The corridor branched immediately, twice, and turned, and the reception area was out of sight; he did remember Kellan saying he was near the back, and stayed to that path. A small part of the department, too, he had thought. He turned his head at an open doorway and saw only a storeroom, and a very small office beyond that, with an interior window. There was a T-junction ahead, dim; he approached it, heard a voice, and there were two people standing within the secondary hallway. Kellan's back and shoulder, barely in profile, dressed simply in a white shirt and pressed dark pants—talking to a man with wisps in place of hair on his pate, and a larger-than-average nose; and his heart jumped. Good Lord, Kellan, more elegant than all of them—who in the comfort of the moment could forget to be intimidated, could relax into what he *was*.

Kellan's head turned and he caught, a split-second before turning back, still in the conversation, him coming down the hall. A smile, on the instant, then the surprise. "Graham!"

"Hey," he said, and turned into the junction, and stopped. He put his hands in his pockets, looked at the man opposite.

"Are you up this way, then?" Kellan was already turning, and indicated his companion with a hand: "Graham, this is—"

But the man had already turned, had begun walking away; a strange way of standing, of walking, with the stomach almost concave. A *fading* away. "That *was* Emory," Kellan finished, and dropped his hand. He shrugged, embarrassed. "Emory's—very reserved. He doesn't talk to other people a lot."

"I see that." He smiled, to smooth the moment, and looked around at the surrounding walls, the doorway spilling out light up ahead. "No. I had the afternoon off early, just came up to see the place. We finished a project early. Wasn't any sense in trying to get started on something else."

"Oh." Kellan looked pleased, and nodded, put his own hands in his pockets. "There isn't really much to see, but—that's the floor lounge." With a gesture that way, waiting for him to go first.

The floor lounge was utilitarian. A few tables, synthetic, with metal legs so thin someone *had* to have been saving on materials cost; a refrigerator, an old coffee maker on an only slightly newer countertop. A pale green veneer, unpleasant, covered the cabinets. "Huh," he said, and followed Kellan out and down the hall. He looked at Thomas' office, to the left and still on the main corridor, but near a dead end; another storage room, stacked up with papers in the corners, but neatly organized; an office a few steps down from Kellan's, the small office he had seen earlier, with the interior window. Emory's. Emory was not in evidence, but the desk and rear credenza was spotless. A single-level inbox sat on the far left-hand corner of the desk, perfectly aligned, a few papers lonely inside.

A twin office, with matching interior window, was Kellan's. No privacy with the window, but he sat, propped his feet up on the other guest chair—grayed and as insubstantial as the tables in the floor lounge had been, but it supported the weight of his feet, at least. Kellan closed the door, came in and sat behind the desk. It was equally clean in here, but there was a multi-level inbox instead, two of those loaded far past the brim—there was something heartbreaking in that, when he *knew* what Kellan faced here, how slowly this department moved—and there were neat stacks of more paper on the credenza behind. Dun-colored and synthetic, everything in here, with the exception of the chairs.

"There's something wrong down in the peninsula, I think," he said, before Kellan offered coffee. "Some shipments due to come in."

"Like what? What kind of wrong?"

"They didn't come in. We're near the port; it filtered up."

"What kind of shipments?" Implied in that: *Kaetteguttan?*

Food. That would be first on everyone's mind, even this long after the explosion. That the existing powers had not been entirely truthful about the damage levels; that there had been some sort of chain reaction, units shutting down, units unable to handle the load they'd had to handle afterward, when a more major unit had been damaged. "Actually, manufactured stuff. I don't know what, just that it was coming from the Back, from that dock."

"This has happened before?"

He shrugged. "I don't know. I haven't been here long enough. I looked around the database, didn't see anything like this—but I don't know exactly where to look, either. They maybe don't keep the ETAs in the system, just the actual arrival times." Another shrug. "It didn't really seem good, what we were hearing."

"What do the others think? In your office."

"I don't know that they know much more about that kind of thing than I do. They probably take the word of the port workers for it." Cautiously: "There are some rumors—the Back was responsible for the explosion in Gros Morne, that sort of thing. From the more radical elements."

Kellan looked at him, face kept carefully the same. "Maybe it's just late."

"Maybe." A sideways tilt of the head, to stretch a sore neck muscle. Too much huddling over his screen, getting things done. "It was due this morning. Could be the storm knocked out a ship, and they didn't know the real damage until they tried to load it. I don't know how they rotate the ships."

"Is that why you came up?"

"No. We finished early, that's all. A couple of us have had a team project the last couple weeks. It didn't seem like anyone was getting much done, anyway. Might as well leave."

Kellan rested his chin on his hands. "When's the next shipment due?"

"Tomorrow. They don't move them in and out too fast. Twice a day is the quickest I've seen." He looked around for a mug other than the one sitting on Kellan's desk, straight and bone-colored, too large for a bistro mug. Nothing. "You have anything to drink?"

Kellan started. Stood. "Coffee, if you want some. God, I'm sorry."

"That sounds good. I can come."

"No, no, I've got it. Sorry. Back in a minute."

He sat there and surveyed the office, the neat piles of papers. No labels, but there was no doubt a system to it, safely snug in Kellan's mind. A small plant sat in the corner of the credenza, struggling in the artificial light. Next to it—lay a pair of black chopsticks, recognizable as those Osiake gave out with its meals, and that Kellan still had trouble using. *Oh.* He moved behind the desk, picked up one of the pair. Black synthetic, washed clean.

A memento, when Kellan could have few of those. Nothing from Rue; Kellan had been given no chance to bring anything from there. Few things he wanted to remember, probably, over here, with the hospital, with a colorless co-worker, and a superior probably well-described as ornery, even if Kellan defended him. Sometimes.

What had he brought Kellan to?

Kellan was at the door, coming inside; he stepped back and away from the credenza, the chopsticks. "Keeping it living, huh?" he said, only that, and indicated the plant. "That's pretty good."

"Pretty good in here," Kellan said, and did not look chagrined; rather, no little satisfied—it recalled the planter of herbs back in Rue, the way Kellan had tended *those*, with far less success. "I rooted it from a plant in the front. It's doing okay."

He could perhaps get something over here from Rue. He was next to the port, saw the shipments come in; he could easily arrange for one of the crew members of a hauler to bring something over, some photographs for the walls back at the house, maybe.

But that might only remind Kellan what he had left behind, one dead-end job for another, on a dark slip of land. Kellan still watched the media for Chauncey Benner—

Something else, then. *Think, Graham.* Kellan built familiarity, built mental and emotional structures up so that he knew where he belonged, what he was supposed to do.

"There should be a group coming over next week," Kellan said, putting his own coffee down on the desk. "Not a class. Adults."

"The old woman you were talking about?" *That* would be something.

A frown, in response. "No, not that far advanced. This group was approved a long time before I got here."

He looked at him. "You're kidding."

"Not kidding." And a try for a more positive take. "It's one of the last, though. In a month or two, I'll start seeing the ones I approved come through. Maybe enough of an increase we'll actually see *them* come through, one of these days." He pointed, with his eyes, at the pile in his inbox.

"God."

"It's okay." Kellan shrugged. He took a pen from beside his computer screen, slipped it into a drawer, set a sheaf of papers on the top of the inbox—leaned back in the chair and sighed. "Well, another day done."

"Yeah." Then: belated realization, Kellan's workday ended earlier than his; Kellan took one of the earliest commutes. This was the *end* of his workday. "Oh," he said. He took another drink, swallowed enough that there was only half the cup left, and wiped his mouth. "I won't get you in trouble being here, will I?"

"Nah. Thomas left an hour ago. He comes in at some ungodly hour. I'm surprised Emory's still here."

"Does the ferry run up this way late? We could go get something to drink. They have something like that up here?"

Kellan thought about it. "Some of the restaurants stay open. I don't know if they have bars, if they're like what Grosvenor's got. The line staff eat up here a lot of times. I only know from hearing."

"It's worth a try." He set his cup down on the edge of the desk—it would get their minds off the missing shipment, would make it so that everything was still safe.

There was a note waiting for her, carefully laid in front of her desk screen where Gabrielle put the important ones, often from Quinn, as this one was.

An immediate summons, as soon as she got in. Jenning stretched her calf, sore again from the walk from Economics and the meeting there—walked back out and past Gabrielle and Clare with only a slight limp. Gabrielle looked up, smiled a wish for luck, and bent her head back down over her work. Clare watched her with more anxiety, stood, and walked with her, and pushed open the departmental door. "How are you?" Clare asked, and meant, *should I walk with you?*

"I'm fine," she said firmly, and gave her a smile: Clare could be far more sensitive than Gabrielle. Still very competent, had caught on quickly, and was doing work some of her junior specialists handled. She added, going through the door, "Thank you."

Clare stayed, a bit reluctant; she took the elevator down to the first floor, walked the expanse of the lobby to the opposite elevator bank, took *it* up to the fifth floor and Quinn's territory. The thick pad of the carpet there was far easier on her leg. Lamps everywhere; Quinn favored indirect lighting, and had the budget for it. The hallway was a string of pools of light, cast down on wall tables from beneath dark shades.

Quinn's office was remarkably understated, very light, for all the luxury of the rest of the floor. A nicely bordered carpet, a desk and table of high quality wood and the accompanying capretto chairs, but the rest was spare, near empty. It always smelled of furniture polish, and did not disappoint today. "Coffee," Quinn said, coming around her desk, and there was already a mug steaming on the table, awaiting her. That meant Gabrielle had called ahead, Gabrielle having her own connections in Quinn's reception staff who would get coffee in when Quinn's mood tolerated it.

Ah. All this magnificence, but she'd rather have her own office, with its clutter. She lowered herself into the chair, and pulled the mug toward her. Quinn sat down opposite, and had weariness about the corners of her eyes, though her hair was groomed and smooth.

"We've been missing shipments," Quinn said, without preamble or disguise, and without her own coffee. Atypical. "Most from the Back. The third shipment from there today missing, and—a shipment from Kaettegut. Seameats and fish."

Jenning had known the first; had known after the second ship-ment had not come, had not breathed for a minute when she had heard. She had *not* known about the seameats shipment. This was worse, and far more alarming: she felt a chill, despite her coffee. There had been no food shortage since... *goodness,* the very early days, long before her time, but she had read accounts of the chaos that had resulted. Manipulating food harvests was one thing, now—this was entirely another. "Due when?"

"We haven't had a shipment since Monday." No need to exaggerate what was real crisis, and Quinn did not. "Kaettegut's was due in this afternoon. I just got word. I would have called you out of the Eco-nomics meeting, but I *didn't* want this to get out. We're not ready."

When Quinn had first known was not relevant. Quinn would share what she would, on her own timetable. Wednesday afternoon, now, and the port should have been busy, double duty on Mondays and Wednesdays, with both Kaettegut and the Back hauling in loads.

She would not bring up the experimental agricultural stations—a futile hope, and a sore point with Quinn. Besides, if the Back was not shipping, that negated that. "What's been done?" she asked instead.

A sigh. Quinn pushed back a loose strand of hair from her fore-head. "Of course we've had damage control. A communications blackout with the Back, which *is* what we've got, belated damage from the storm. The Back's regrouping, needs the manpower to make the repairs. That's the line. ...We have *no* idea. They're not answering our calls. If Kaettegut's shipments go missing—"

Quinn was stretched thin, very thin, over this. She did not have to say, the warehousing peninsula did this for a living; would not likely buy even the line about the Back's missing shipments—that if it got out, it could make a crisis of this scale far, far more desperate. There had been worse storms in the lifetime of the veterans down there at the port.

"What's Kaettegut saying?" Never mind what Meghan Truong was saying, who did not know, who did not have a grip on her own depart-ment, not since that call.

"Benner says she honestly doesn't know. I'd like to have you take a look at the recording."

So. It was a minor satisfaction, even in emergency. Quinn found herself in a scrape, the whole council in it, and found *this* to offer them. "A problem with the particular ship? *Is* it operating?" That first, that very much first.

"She doesn't know. It's not in dock at Gros Morne on Wednesdays, it's in the northern province, she says. She's having her head of shipping look at it. A Cliff Runnel."

"A *Runnel*." More for the cachet of it, for the knowledge of the little things. Quinn wanted to know she had in-house expertise: she could oblige, even in this. She had made it her trouble to learn the schools over there, early on in the audits—the way they put an administrator in office, and the department heads. Now she had Quinn's attention; Quinn was looking at her. "One of the lowest schools, I believe. One lower. I'll have to take a look at my files."

Quinn grimaced, looked as if she might swear; only rubbed one of her temples, instead.

It had to be a mistake, a late shipment; there *was* no other option.

19

Kellan sat in the office chair, spun it so that he faced the credenza, and tapped the pen on the surface.

He *wanted* to call. He wanted to turn the media on in the corner of his screen, but they did not do that here, and Thomas would walk by and it would look like he was not working.

Last week had grown far, far worse. Graham had come up on Monday, that had been the only bright spot. They had not been able to find a restaurant with much of a bar in Jefferson, not that was open into the evening—but there had been a restaurant that had served drinks to the table, a small one, silver and cold and buffed with a thousand cleanings.

He had not drunk like this in Rue. Graham had, but the collection of liquor had been so costly, he had not accepted often the invitation of a glass extended his way. Here, Graham assured him it *was* cheap, relatively, and had found more varieties than he had seen. The cabinet in the kitchen was filled with bottles.

By Tuesday the word had gotten up to Jefferson, and around, and almost everyone knew: no shipments from the factories in the Back, and now a late shipment from Kaettegut—and no ship in local dock to send either way.

They *said* it was damage from the storm, but the media implied that there had been conversations with Agriculture and the storm had wiped out only what was usual. There had been the expected losses in experimental farming and in sea vegetation, nothing else. The fish hatcheries knew to batten down their hatches; the seameats were protected in the narrowing of the bay to the north of Rue, hydroponics would be affected not at all.

It had not come, had not come by Friday, and did not come over the weekend.

That there was no ship in the Grosvenor dock to send—that was not the official media line; *that* was word getting around, that said the port had been empty since the weekend and that the ferry was the only boat moving in Grosvenor *or* Jefferson. Graham had gone by the port and verified it.

It was becoming distinctively uncomfortable. He *hoped* the Kaetteguttan shipment was on its way, that they had repaired whatever damage to the fleet there was.

He was beginning to feel—as if he had never been more Kaetteguttan, that for all his blending in, that he had *Kaetteguttan* written across his forehead. He had gotten frowns, so far, that was it, but unpleasant, and meant to be so. He had met the gazes the first two or so times, too surprised not to look, and had gotten a deliberately turned head the first time, a direct stare the next—that one on the ferry, and it had been a damned unpleasant ride in; there had been most of the journey to go, and he had spent it at the rail watching the darkness of the berm go by, the rippling of the water.

Emory and Thomas, thankfully, treated him the same, Emory limply lukewarm, Thomas irritable. His office had become a respite again, once he could get in the building and up the elevator onto his floor, past the quietness of the reception area where no one was that early in the morning.

Graham had it worse on the warehousing peninsula. Some of the warehouse staff, he gathered, did not have the manners of those in Jefferson. Graham did not describe it, not specifically—refused to do that, and that was aggravating—but he could read between the lines.

He called. He could do a decent Jeffersonian accent by now; he used it with the pricing secretary whenever she answered the phone and he could not get by using the automated system. "Graham Long," he said, and cringed at using the surname, which *did* mark them as alien—and when Graham answered: "Anything new?"

"Nothing. Port's empty."

He sighed. Rubbed his forehead, leaning onto the desk. "Damn it, what's going on? What's *really* going on?"

Graham's voice came across with an echo in the earpiece, a bit. "They giving you any problems up there?"

"No. No, just wondering." He had not mentioned the stares, that he had gotten them again now in his own department, making a delivery for Thomas. "There's just nothing on the media, and it's *been* a week, more than that." An eternity in media time.

The regular Kaetteguttan shipment *had* to come today, that was all. Agricultural shipments had come and gone like clockwork, as far as he knew, for the decades they'd had that system worked out. He looked at his watch: three o'clock, as far as his restraint had extended—and that, hard.

He kept himself from asking Graham to go out and look again, and that was almost worse.

"I'm keeping tabs on it. We'll know." And, after a pause: "Don't worry."

"Graham." He looked at the door; no one going by. Usually there wasn't, this time of day. If Kaetteguttan's shipment *didn't* come in— He should wait, should wait for the privacy of the main room and kitchen, and dinner. "What *is* it? What are they doing?"

Another pause, on the other end of the line, then: "I don't know." But Graham *was* thinking; he had that tone, and they had not talked about this possibility—had assumed Kaetteguttan's shipment *would* come in. "The storm wasn't enough to do this, that's all I know. It's what they've been saying down here, and damn it, it just *wasn't*. There's something else going on."

"Something about Kaettegut." He remembered what Graham had said during the storm. "You said it could be in trouble."

A *long* silence. "Graham?"

"Just—nothing." Another pause. "I don't know. I don't. It didn't start with Kaettegut, it started with the Back. The manufacturing shipments went missing first. There's been *that* every damned day. Kaettegut's only missed a few. That we didn't have last week's shipment—doesn't help, yes. I expect this afternoon's shipment, Kellan. They can't afford not to."

"What time does it normally come in?"

"I don't know. I don't work down there. I know things aren't easy here, but it's going to be that way until it gets here. It's been like that all day."

They *had* been looking at him. On the ferry, in the hallways. "They think something else," he said, before he thought about it. Thought better of it, instantly—but because he *had* started: "They think Kaettegut's—just that something's not right. Maybe that Kaettegut lied before. I don't know."

"There *has* been something up there. Hasn't there? They *are* giving you a hard time."

"No. Not Thomas or Emory. I've been fine at work. It's just—looks, that's all. On the way in, people I don't know. Nothing that's really going to hurt anything. It's just the *way* they look. They're getting upset, Graham."

"They need to look at the Back first, then." There was tightness in the voice, and he knew where *that* came from.

"We're an easier target." All the renovation crews were located here, and he did not know of anyone from the Back who came here, besides the councilor on the Proteraiotita.

"You need to talk to Thomas. If it's getting like that—"

"You said the shipment was going to come in. If it does, there won't be a problem." There was a shadow in the hallway, approaching; he turned toward the credenza, his back to the door. "Call me if it does. Okay? *When* it does."

One breath; Graham did that when he was trying for self-control, when things *weren't* going the way he wanted. "Okay."

He disconnected the line. He sat there looking at the piles of paperwork on the credenza, and it was not just him, there was *that*, too; there was the group from the southern province coming over in what was only days, and they wouldn't, not if the atmosphere hadn't died down, and that was enough that Thomas would cancel it or push it back. Indefinitely, probably.

Damn it. He looked at the false wood grain of the credenza, and closed his eyes.

Quinn rolled the pen between her fingers, the ivory pen made of some kind of stone that she'd received upon her promotion to the job prior to this one, when she had been young and experienced but with not near as much under her belt as now. Nothing like *this*—something to make a person wish, for a quick instant, that one wasn't in office. That one's ancestors hadn't decided to set the logistics rolling this particular way.

She looked back at the screen, at the numbers: where they were weakest when it came to manufacturing shipments, where they could hold out the longest with what was in the peninsula warehouses.

Her intercom program blipped. Michael, second to Adrienne; Adrienne must be at lunch. "Answer," she said. "Yes?"

"Councilor Daschen's coming down the hall," Michael's voice said, no preamble. Succinctly and quietly.

Kate. She was surprised; she really was. "Let her be," she said to Michael. "Thank you." She put the pen down, folded her hands; the intercom box disappeared from her screen.

A light tap sounded through the door, and it opened a crack. A section of Kate's face, one eye foremost, showed, then a hand on the door knob. "Quinn," she said. The door opened wider. She was immaculate, wearing a smooth suit of pale green fabric. "You're busy?"

She had looked up from the laptop. "No, no. Come in." She stood and indicated one of the guest chairs, at the table. "Coffee?" With a glance at her watch: "Or lunch?"

"No. Thank you." Kate sat and crossed her legs—easy, polished—smoothed the pristine fabric of her suit against her thigh. "Lunch at the desk, probably. That's how it's been."

"Yes." She reached down to re-toggle the intercom program. "Michael. Coffee for two, if you don't mind." She clicked it off, walked over to join Kate at the table—Kate had left her the chair nearest the window. Not a rainy day, but wet; there were beads on the edges of the windowsill and frame outside, parts of the glass fogging.

For an opening: "This is a surprise."

"We don't get around nearly enough." Kate smoothed her skirt again, looked to the door as it opened—Michael, in the doorway, with tray and cups and carafe, the curving white set rather than the gleaming black. He had doubtless had someone getting it ready the moment he had seen Kate step off the elevators, for that amount of time. He set it on the table.

She reached for her cup, hid the motion of her eyebrow in the movement—that was near an overture, for Kate Daschen, who stayed to her own offices, had little need for anything else.

"Thank you," she said to Michael, and he gave the tray's contents a once-over one last time, and turned and left the room, closing the door discreetly.

Her territory, too, where Kate did not know how secure it was. She could probably surmise, of course, but it was still a minor risk.

Kate poured her own cup, careful, elbow up as she held the weight of the carafe. Breathed in the steam as she did so. "Mm. Strong."

She did like it strong. Her staff could forget; they were accustomed to making it for her. But Kate settled back in her chair, glided her fingers along one padded capretto chair arm. "I have a feeling. Perhaps—" and she met Quinn's glance directly, then looked away, "a concern."

Almost straight to the point. "Oh?"

"A little background, first." Kate raised the cup to her mouth, held it there—inhaled, again, rather than drank. "You were fairly new to the council, then. It didn't impact your division so much, outside of the general idea, but when we approved the population increase for the Back for exploration purposes, much of the time for many of us was occupied with looking at increasing the infrastructure over there."

She tapped the rim of her coffee cup with her fingertip, silently, did not otherwise move, not so much as to breathe deeply.

"Energy, of course." Kate took her first sip, savored it, briefly. "I chose to locate some additional power stations deep in the Back, in line with the mines, rather than feed them from plants already at capacity. To go where the need *was*. Decheran was pleased with it. It was, I should tell you—a major project."

Resourcists, both. Daschen and Decheran had both taken advantage of a situation, then, had chosen a route that fell in very well with their philosophy. And silently; she did not remember much if any discussion, only the order to accommodate the vote. Few, after all, directed Kate Daschen how to do her job.

For Kate to tell her this—was another risk, and not an insubstantial one, to someone of her station and political party. She leaned the chair back an inch, watched Kate's face.

"I had some of my personal staff help set up the new plants, to stay with them until we could be assured things were running smoothly. Between construction and that, it took some time. Power usage had been increasing, then, for some time—before we began. Decheran said it was aging equipment, inefficiencies." She turned her head, looked toward the window. "Things looked good. I made sure of that before I withdrew any staff." And, eyes back toward her: "I expected a dip in usage in terms of the other plants. It did dip, but not as much as I thought it should have. I was surprised, honestly. I kept an eye on it, but didn't push it. We were more comfortable back then; she would have called if there had been a problem."

Quinn dared to take a sip of her coffee. Another. Polite attention still directed at Kate... more than polite, Kate would know.

The resourcists had as vested an interest as she did in the current system working, of control. No changes.

"The usage began rising again at the other plants, over time traceable to the Back. I queried more strongly, and I didn't get a satisfactory answer, a combination of things, basically, some of which made sense. Some didn't. I planned to go back over and check the plants in person. I had made some assignments, long-term temporary, with some incentives."

She rested her cup against the saucer, waited. "What happened?"

"I was shut out. Politely, of course, but that's what it was." She held her head still. "I had laid out a good chunk of budget, and I didn't have the return for it. I met with Fifty." She shrugged. "He seemed quite concerned, in fact, assured me he would see what the problem was. He took the trip to the Back."

"And?"

"I didn't hear anything for a while. I had to press it after a council meeting. He said he'd verified what Decheran had said. It was all very glossed over, but he didn't want to give specifics, that was evident. It wasn't just that he wasn't comfortable using the terminology. This time he took the stance—you accepted what he said, because he said it. A mood." She tapped one finger on the table, lips discreetly peevish at the memory. "One takes it from a different angle in those cases. I couldn't. One more conversation, but it was generalities, assurances. I couldn't get any further."

"Decheran?" she asked.

"We did lose something. Not everything, obviously. But—I highly suspected there had been an alliance made. She was not to be questioned. That's not all that unusual, not with Fifty, of course."

Quinn leaned back in her own chair. Swiveled it slightly; looked at the wall. "Energy usage." Exploration further out—but that wouldn't be enough to account for it, not on .the scale Kate implied. Resourcism in action—enough to make her stomach drop, for the instant—but Kate would not be here, for that. A higher population, on the other hand, begun long before the ink was dry on the approval, was perhaps feasible.

Alarming. Profoundly so. She felt it in her veins.

"It didn't stand out at the time." Kate put her coffee cup down on the tray, still half full. "You and I both know how Fifty operates, how alliances work." With a glance at her, eyes shrewdly appraising. A question there, too.

She did not answer it. Too caught up in this, in the idea—*God*, no, Decheran would not have been able to support something like that, something that resource-draining. Nearly every aspect of resource planning, of usage, would be affected; she could not hide something like that.

"For some time, you said, the usage had been rising. How long?"

Kate looked directly at her. "Years." She reached for her cup again, explored the handle with her fingers, without looking. "The same arguments: equipment problems, getting near the ends of the veins, having to dig deeper and deeper for less and less result. It *made* sense."

And if there were no imminent end of the existing veins?

Auditors did not have that kind of expertise. They had the minimum, learned from textbooks, from programs recorded by mining experts who *were* Backers.

Put *this* with the experimental agricultural stations...

"You think the missing shipments—?"

"I don't know how it's connected, yet," Kate said. Evenly. "It gave me the opportunity to think on it, that's all. Decheran runs things like a machine. Nothing is ever late." She frowned, and *there* was the concern, the headache, evident in the facial expression. "Maybe I'm off-base. It's fine if that turns out to be the case. But if she's doing this, it's according to design. *That's* Decheran."

And Fifty had been covering for it. Possibly, or possibly he had not wanted his judgment questioned, when he did *not* have the expertise, far less so than the auditors.

Or if there *was* a relationship in the making, back then—quite, quite possible, and Kate was right, nothing unusual.

Decheran *was* a resourcist, had been for her entire career, and had been quite vocal early on. *That* was an area she could not tread with Kate, though she had the questions. Yes, she certainly had those, measured against Fifty's nascent expansionism.

Decheran had won the experimental units, the cold-water fish program. *That* was chilling, in this light.

Decheran had not tried again for the chairmanship, after Fifty had been elected.

Kate stood. "Thank you for the coffee." She put a hand down on the table: "I'll be glad to exchange the favor."

For something of this scale, damn, yes, she'd owe a return favor. She poured herself another cup after Kate had gone, when she did not need it, did not need caffeine to further jangle already vibrating nerves.

Rene and Phoebe watched her in the office, worried, brought her small plates of snacks—in her office, in the conference room, between conversations with Jefferson. Phoebe had stayed late tonight, had brought her a cup of soup. It sat and cooled on the conference table, next to the screen.

Nothing from Murray, damn the man, nothing Chauncey could work with.

No Jenning this time, and the few on the other end were fuming, beneath a very thin surface—angrier than she had seen. There *was* no question of controlling any part of the conversation, of defending Kaettegut. She answered questions, only that, and only when they let her finish her sentences.

She would welcome Jenning, now.

There had been several questions about the Back, only a few at first, until it was very nearly every question and she had put Rene and Louis on the task of investigating things. They had turned up no unusual media mention of the Back, just the usual educational programs.

Then Rene had come in, his face empty of all natural color.

Murray was having his laugh, that was exactly what was happening. A crisis in return for a small humiliation—oh, no, he'd not miss the effect his decision would have. Murray had not taken her calls until *she* had mentioned the Back, because he could not be one to assist her with any relevant information, God forbid. No, Murray saw the battle lines drawn, obstinate man, would not cooperate even in crisis.

Damned, insufferable man. She took a sip of the soup from the spoon, swallowed hard to put it out of her mind. She could not focus on that, could not afford to waste a moment on petty, puerile mind games.

Rene had found the information in a call to one of the renovation laborers resident in Grosvenor. Not directly—a call from an acquaintance in the northern province, rather, that Rene and Louis had somehow turned up, and that call had found one renovation laborer worried, who was waiting to hear from his foreman as to whether his crew was going to work the next day, whether any of the crews were, until a shipment came from Kaettegut and things were easier.

In Jefferson and Grosvenor, there had been no shipments from the Back since the Friday before.

Kaettegut's fleet was docked at Seameats. *That's* what Murray had been doing.

A week. The mind reeled.

Councilor Quinn Rhodes was on the opposite end of the line, now, and had been twice before. Sharp, deadly sharp, and coldly furious, had cut through every honest attempt on her part to open a discussion. She wanted that shipment, and would stay on the line until the shipment pulled into dock, and had made it clear. Pure acid, this late into the evening.

"I haven't wanted to say this," Quinn said, on the screen. Folded her hands with exaggerated patience—one finger, another. All four. "I'm sure you've realized there's no possibility Jefferson does not see this as serious. I can't see how a takeover would be advantageous to you. That *is* what you're putting on the line, you know."

"If I had something to tell you—"

"I don't know how many times I can tell you that isn't good enough." More than sharp, but still very evidently restrained. The personality was palpable in every smoothed, neatly clipped hair, the immaculate clothing—this woman was not accustomed to anything *but* control. A refolding of the fingers, now, and a different tack: "This might not have anything to do with your head of shipping, might it? A Runnel, I understand."

The hairs on the back of her neck rose. She sat and stared, and tried to keep from putting her fingernails through her palms. *Jenning*. That was nothing *but* Jenning, and it was far below the belt. "You'll find the school doesn't always control the destiny, over here," she said, with gritted teeth.

"You're saying you're confident in Mr. Runnel."

Restraint was more difficult on her end this late at night, after a string of phone calls for days, at all hours. "I'm more than confident in him. Councilor, with all due respect—I've *told* others who have called that we have some—hesitation in some of our internal organization. Concerns that I can understand as well-founded from their point of view. I can tell you I'd be delighted—beyond reason—if a shipment pulled into dock over there tonight. I can tell you it's probably not going to happen, and the longer you and your colleagues keep me on the phone, the less I can do about it."

It would do little good. The council had lost its patience soon after the first missing shipment, would not recover it now. The face on the screen, pale and tight in the corners of the eyes and lips, told her that—although, thank the heavens, it was not the threats and pure anger of Meghan Truong, who saw herself publicly insulted, and whom they had put through on the phone less and less through the day before, and not at all tonight.

There came a tapping on the tabletop on Quinn's end, out of view of the camera, but not out of earshot. "That shipment comes tonight. Before the morning. I don't think I need to tell you what we're looking at over here, and I'm not going to let that happen, do you understand me? I don't have to tell you what it will mean if you see *me* set foot on your dock, or any other councilor." Another visible effort at self-restraint. A sigh. "I'd *like* to avoid that. I'd like to work with you."

"Then let me get to work on it! The longer I spend tied to this phone line, the longer those ships stay put. Do you understand *me*?"

"That—" the lower jaw came forward, a bit, and receded, "—might work if we hadn't heard the same thing all day yesterday, and all day today. The *very* same. Do you administer your department or don't you? It really comes down to that, and I think I have the answer, and it's disappointing, it really is."

She could not say what Murray Lerkenlund had said, had given as his reason, and what made *sense* in the situation: that the first ship to dock in Grosvenor faced seizure. Jefferson could not get anywhere without the ships, and the renovation laborer had said there were none in dock, which meant that all ships but hers were docked in the Back, and one rotting in dry storage in her own province, pillaged by Cliff Runnel's maintenance crews for spare parts... which was the very reason Jefferson had to resort to threats by phone, to manipulation. No ferry would make it through the currents and chop of New Bay near the Back, or through the rough water of Jargen Bay—Jefferson's ferry had been built only for the calm of a river sheltered by manmade berms. Kaettegut's own ferry would not make it.

She could not say—either—that an order from her would mean nothing to a member of her own cabinet.

"It's that, or you're playing a game much too big for you. If so, let me advise you to stop. Right now, *right* now. Something of this scale, and none of us are playing games. When I say you might see us step foot on your shore, that's not idle speculation. It might take time. I'll admit to that. It *will* happen, if it needs to." A pause, acidic—but there *was* restraint. A breath. "That's all I'll say on that end—but I've said I'd like to work with you. I still would. If we're going to do that, I need something from you that isn't the same thing you've said. You understand?"

From their end—it had to look suspicious. She could see that. "I can understand that."

"Good. Let's start here: are these your orders, or are they not?"

A trap, from the start—and what they had been dancing around, since yesterday. She *could* see Murray's point of view this time, could understand the fear. Kaettegut's property, Kaettegut's lifeline, that carried all they bargained with, their only security—but if they were *not* her orders, she admitted she did not control her department, not completely, and there was *very* little way, in her tenure, that Kaettegut would become anything other than it had been for too many years.

No. Kaettegut would have less than before. *Respect*, Murray had implied, in her office, when he had been trying to manipulate her, but—

A seat on the Ligotera. Said with disgust.

She and those ships sat, quite conceivably, at a juncture of history. What would her successors, what would every Kaetteguttan see when they looked around? When they looked back to see how it had *gotten* that way?

"I'd like to talk with Jenning," she said, and put her arms on the chair's armrests. Swiveled slightly.

A smile, contemptuous, half-formed. Quinn stopped, then, and shifted *her* position in her chair, on the screen. "Jenning reports to this council. If you think—"

"I don't think that. I'm familiar with Jenning. She's a bit more familiar with us."

"You can talk to me. I can assure you, if you need help—if something's wrong—I'll be far more able to help you than Jenning will."

"Councilor. Please." She spread her palms on the table. "Jenning. Not by videoconference. I'm going to have to be on the road. Tell her I'll contact her early tomorrow morning. Earliest I can, from the dock."

A *very* long silence.

Finally: "Is there a reason it can't be tonight?"

"I have some things to get ready. I've got to have my things in order, Councilor." She would have to, at this rate of fatigue, go to bed as soon as she could get home—get the uninterrupted sleep she hadn't had for three days. Early, early rising, when her brain would be working at a far clearer level than the slow slog she felt now. Would *have* to be. "I apologize that this has happened. You know I apologize. I'm trying to fix it, I'm going to do all I can to fix it, but I'm going to need your help. There *are* valid concerns."

"Concerns. Hesitations. Vague statements. Is that all you're going to give me?"

"Councilor." She took a breath. Her mind *wanted* to relax, wanted to sink. She kept it level, pushed a little further. "I've given you all I can right now. *You* know things can be accomplished better in person, sometimes. It looks very much like that's the case here. I do administer this department, and when I've settled concerns—with your help—you'll have your shipments. All right? We have no intention of abandoning Grosvenor, Councilor. I need a contact location for Jenning, and to know that Jenning will be there in the morning, to answer my call."

A frown, deep. "I'll think about it. You can talk to Jenning, that's fine, but I won't say it will be only her you're talking with. If she tells you to call me, you do it, you hear me? Or that bargain's off, and what I was talking about earlier—will be the next step. You understand?"

She was *not* the only one tired. She could see it in the face looking at her from the screen, from that slip, that lack of control. Not the message—the delivery.

"You know I do. You know I'll be counting on you, that I believe you." That, with the last of her negotiating skills. "Jenning. First thing in the morning, about six."

"Fine." A nod, and the screen blipped and went black.

She slumped in her chair. No energy to rub her forehead, the bridge of her nose, where it hurt. She closed her eyes instead, and counted the poundings in her head.

In the morning she boarded the ferry with Rene, and Dominic, and Louis. Foolish that she had refused that point-blank when Rene suggested the same, earlier. She had reconsidered, and Louis and Dominic sat inside the ferry, Louis having proven subject to a spate of seasickness. Rene stood next to her by the rail, watching the water go by.

Cliff Runnel and the whole of one of his maintenance crews were elsewhere on the deck. She could see a few of the maintenance personnel further down the rail. She would have thought they'd have had more pull with the ship's crews than they'd had—Murray's staff had not put through their calls, but they had gotten through by radio. Anxiety, mainly, from the other end. *They'll take the ship*, one had said, a less experienced crewman with less discretion than his seniors.

The crews lived on the ships, made their living from it, had worked shoulder to shoulder with the same crewmates for decades in some cases. They'd not take their ship into risk, did not run it in storms, would *not* run it in this kind of political situation.

"How'd it go?" Rene asked, elbows on the rail, leaning back against it. Quietly, when the ferry had come far enough out that most of the others had drifted inside or to the other end of the deck, where there was seating.

She shook her head.

She had taken a risk asking for Jenning. She had known Jenning's level of skill, what she could get out of someone who did not suspect—but she *did* suspect, and knew how Jenning operated, and how she got that information. But Jenning, too, did know Kaettegut better, disliked the local drinks and food, except what was very fresh and little touched by human hands.

Distaste, certainly—but most of Jefferson would not step foot anywhere off Jefferson or Grosvenor. Some of the higher officials might not consider even Grosvenor. That Jenning did, and Jenning had come as many times as she had, had braved trips on a hauler that she knew herself was not pleasant—said something.

"Not so good," she said, and did not turn her head away from the view of the water, and the eastern sky where the light gleamed a dim green. "She's gotten more than I wanted to tell her. Not *that* much, but some."

"She doesn't know the extent?"

"She has an idea there's dissension in the ranks. That we've a trouble spot, and where it is. That we have control—that, I hope, she buys." *Fervently* hoped. "The scope of Murray's hold—not yet. It could be just a tiny area for what she knows. They don't have much access to the local media, I don't believe."

He made a sound in his throat, hardly audible over the motor, the waves slopping against the hull. "Better that way."

"It's one break, if it's true. I'll take what I can get."

If she *could* get one ship to run, the maintenance crew would be necessary. The ships no doubt had not seen anything besides wipedown—and it would have to take an extra load, there and back.

To visit Murray Lerkenlund after the scene in her office—it grated, oh, it burned like seared skin chafed beneath a bandage. It had been bad enough to call him, to be turned away by his line staff, to keep her voice at a steady, professional cadence after he *had* answered the phone.

He kept the fleet now, when Cliff's crews ran on loyalty, and Cliff had taken no misstep. Give Murray that, that the man knew his rhetoric, could stir up fear, resentment—heighten each negative emotion, exquisitely.

I'm not the only one who feels this way, you know, Murray had said, who had long taken pains to ensure it was so.

He held the reins, whether she liked it or not.

She'd have to put their history aside, with all of Kaettegut threatened by one man's actions, and food not reaching anyone *nor* reaching safe storage in Gros Morne, further and further behind her now, and some rafts almost certainly getting beyond harvest.

One ship, at the start, was all she needed. A single seameats shipment, larger than average, all fresh—she could not afford even the hours necessary to stop in Gros Morne to take on frozen loads. A goodwill gesture, a way to bide time if things had gone further than she feared in the northern province.

As important, it would be a way out for the renovation crews in Grosvenor, who were afraid to go to work, who might by be closed in, defensive, in their apartments. Certainly there would eventually be panic in Grosvenor. Grosvenor had some food storage capacity in its warehouse district. How much, she did not know.

She would call the renovation crews back. They'd take a short trip back home, just until things settled—when there were *not* Back personnel stationed in Grosvenor that she knew.

———

It was Quinn's office again, the light beiges and polished table, the aroma of furniture wax. Coffee sat on the table for them both this time, and Quinn was maintaining calm better than before, miraculous, in the heightening crisis. Jenning *could* admire that.

No mistake, by now. There had been no shipment this morning, the beginning of another week, and continued silence on the Back's end. Manufacturing's Rebecca Wright, who regularly split her time between both sides of the bay—could not get through on channels only she knew.

There was virtually no chance of the storm knocking that out for that long, Rebecca had said. For *all* of the Back—as far back as the mountains and mining operations—not possible at all. The storms came through fiercest over the water, lost force over land, and the mountains were simply too far distant, and through increasingly chilled air.

"There *have* been inconsistencies," Quinn said, and took a sip of her coffee, and there were, at a certain angle, shadows under her eyes. "They were noted. They weren't elevated, not through the proper channels."

Meaning the Proteraiotita—or Quinn herself, if not the full council. Jenning sat with both hands wrapped around the cup, and saw, perhaps, Fifty at work, another of his arrangements, this time with Decheran—after the success of his little deal for locating the experimental agricultural stations over there. What he had *thought* he could control.

A chance like that an expansionist with a staunch resourcist in his hands, who for decades had, with Daschen, carried the weight of the philosophy, whose ideas alone influenced numbers about which Fifty could only dream.

Damn, she could see the appeal.

That, or Decheran on her own—and she had timed it for when a crisis blew. Kaettegut and the Benner call—distraction, diversion, plain and simple.

"The council approved a population increase years back. They needed to go deeper into the range, needed to find new sources of ore, Decheran told us. Production had been slowing. How much of a population increase there *has* been, in reality—" Quinn let that trail, just the hint, and handed a folder across the table. "This gets more into your area. Tell me what you see."

She opened it and saw columns, codes—sets from the genetic storge banks.

How much of a population increase— That was a jolt; not for herself but for Quinn, who took the status quo philosophy very seriously.

She set it aside, for the moment. Quinn did not want reaction, that much was clear.

"These aren't miners," she said, and ran her finger down the first column. Turned the page. "Not unless heavy analysis is in their job description. I see the explorers, here, these are very definite sets—" *God*, some of these sets had not been used since near after the landing. "A fairly high proportion—damn, this is strange—there's *artistic* aptitude, here, and they've mixed it with the analysis. Look."

"What?" Quinn pushed her coffee mug aside and leaned across. "These?" And, "Define artistic aptitude."

"I'll have to look up some records in my office to be sure. You see it a lot in craftsmen, but not nearly at this level. This was—an architect, if I remember that set. One of the particulars, ordered a lot of the ironwork, the marble layouts, that sort of thing. Detail-oriented."

"With analysis, you said. Detail and detail."

"Big-picture, too, to some extent, but yes, we're looking at—not a miner. Not an explorer. God, I don't know what they'd use this for."

That *her* department did not do aptitude placements in the Back was potentially a fatal flaw. They had, then, no idea of the real population numbers, the real proportions, only an incomplete picture from this report, and *that* what Decheran allowed them to see.

How much of a population increase there has *been...* The sets listed on this report said they did not have the science or the technology to do the combining—would not have left themselves and their choices wide open, and with that their mindset, innovation where they had reputation for none of that. They would *not* have given that away. "You think they can propagate already existing sets," she said to Quinn.

"Possibly." Which was a hard thing to admit, for Quinn; it said control was careening away from the council, that it may have been long flown. *Long* would be the key—if Quinn had caught it early enough, it could potentially be reined in. With immense difficulty. "Possibly more along the lines of Kaettegut."

Kaettegut! She looked at Quinn and shook her head. "No. Surely not."

That had been one of the coups of the early days, some thirty years after the second landing. Prime had split Kaettegut's own away: the Back had been made of Kaetteguttan stock back then, and Prime had turned the balance too far for Kaettegut to recover. Too many resources on Jefferson's side, suddenly too few numbers on Kaettegut's, when numbers had *been* the power of those descended from the second ship. Simple and brilliant, and Jefferson had only the challenge, then, to protect its much-vaunted genetic purity. It had developed the original storage bank, and Kaettegut was the only one breeding the way it did, then, haphazard and uncontrolled.

"It's a copy. Take it back with you and get me a report, soon as you can. I want to know the scale," Quinn said, and stood, and went back to her desk. She stood there with her fingertips resting on the smooth wood and looked at her, levelly. "You've been doing well, really very well, with Kaettegut. I listen to those files, not everyone, you understand, and you're pulling out amounts of information we didn't—*I* didn't expect. I don't want you burning out. Everything else—*everything* else—waits. You understand?"

Encouragement, from Quinn, did not come without a purpose. It meant herself working late and food ordered in until it was done.

It also meant she was *in* when it came to the Back, and with this kind of report—she and her department were far more indispensable.

Still, it did not keep that little edge of panic at quite enough distance, that there were still no shipments, and no word.

20

Graham put his work away same as he always did, in the system he had worked out for a desk that had no drawers—and did not look forward to the shuttle ride home. Again.

He did not know how low the food reserves were, at what date they'd be looking at a true emergency, only that it was likely very soon. Likely no one else knew either, and probably they had the same idea that he did, and he did not like to sit in close proximity to them on the shuttle or anywhere else.

He had been taking his lunches in his own office.

A lot of them, at least in the office positions, were trained to be polite, but that was perhaps all. There had been the man on the shuttle who had told him where to buy alcohol, Ted had gotten him his contact for the Alhoa; Cynthia was civil enough. That was it.

He wasn't thinking charitably, and they weren't, that's all. Something went wrong and they wanted to make *him* feel it as the only thing Kaetteguttan near them. That's all. Human nature.

He stopped at the dock after work despite it all. It was only a matter of blocks the other way, and was always the first thing Kellan wanted to know. Didn't always ask—but *wanted* to know, and hell, so did he. He assumed he'd hear about it, first thing, if any ship pulled in; still didn't trust it. He trusted his own eyes.

Nothing again, tonight, and it was only a few minutes to five. He stood there a minute and scanned the water—oily black where the light of the dock didn't hit it, without much of a wind tonight. There was a little slopping down against the seawall where the chop met concrete, rhythmic.

Well, damn. Wednesday, now, and nothing since the previous Monday, and it was going to get worse, then.

There was a sound. He was out of habit, slow—nearly missed it, and started his turn too late.

"Waiting for your ship?" Very bad breath in his face, stale, and then part of his jacket bunched and twisted; he could feel where it strained, past his neck and over his shoulder.

"It's not *my* ship." He pushed off with both hands, twisted his right shoulder away at the same time, and felt the fabric snap free. He caught his balance on his heels, and hardened that. Loosened his knees. Tried for reason, anyway—and there were others; over by the wall, who watched and did not move. "I eat over here, too. Yeah, I want it to come in."

"You come over to pollute *our* side? That it? Stay on your own goddamn side!" Voice rising; no alcohol at all on the breath—poorly cooked food eaten far earlier in the day from the smell of things, probably an empty stomach, and irritation worse.

He could still handle it. There were more coming, though, oozing from the wall like fluid. Black, nearly, in his peripheral vision.

Christ. He grabbed handfuls of fabric—abrasive against his hands, jerked, and swung around, aiming for the seawall, for the water. One shove. Not enough momentum; he didn't have the weight, not next to a laborer. First mistake. He saw legs go up, the sole of a shoe—turned, and that was too late, too; there were two already there.

He took one step back, hoping for at least a sideswipe, for *them* to take some of the momentum and force. He felt the first of a fist glancing off the shoulders, equal height—his heel came down on something other than *flat*, and something broke across the edge of his spine, his shoulder blade. Appalling force: he felt his teeth crack together; thank God, he had not bitten his tongue off, but his jaw rang with it. Bone shattered, by all sensation, back to his ear.

Sinking, briefly—a blink, just force of will; whatever that *had* been would be around again. He swung his leg back, hooked his foot, pulled, and went down with it—had known he would, had little choice, but he was prepared, and his opponent wasn't.

Cold concrete slapped against his cheek; he had his palms down and was twisting to the side, on his way up, when they had him. More than one, tremendous weight—God, how many *were* there?—something crushing his leg beneath the knee, hard on what was twisted wrong. He opened his mouth, sucked for air and sank his teeth, hard, anything to relieve the pressure, felt his teeth in his own forearm, through his jacket. Saw, in one hazed instant, part of an eye socket, a nose, reached for that, and dug his fingernails in.

A scream, not his own. The weight lifted, some, and he kept his hand locked on. He swung the other around, and his freed leg—*that* was screaming; he pulled it in and found purchase with his other hand, weighted down at the elbow. An ear. He scrabbled at it, kept the pressure on with his other hand, felt weight crush his back, roll against his shoulder blades, and then there was air, and he was on top. Another roll, and they *couldn't* get anything at him, not without risking their colleague. He felt fingers grabbing, missing; he rolled, and then the ground was sloping—*smack* against something small and round and metal, in the tissue beneath his shoulder blade, where at least it would not do damage—but he was pinned, and there was sound now, blaring, in his face, the odor of fetid food and saliva.

Hands found purchase. He felt the fabric go first; followed it, and he was upright again, and a railing behind him, and a man whimpering at his feet. There was an explosion against his face, one side—his knees staggered, but he couldn't go back over the railing, not if there was water on the other side. Could not swim.

A chin: he registered that, and let his knees sink, and the shoulders leaned in—he snapped his head, hard, against the neck, against the center. A miss: no intake, no pause between sucking for air and finding it, and they had his shoulders, then, turned him around, had his arms pinned. He lifted his feet off the ground, let his weight pull him down—no good, they'd fallen for it once, and just pushed him into the ground, now. They shoved his face into the concrete, along and against it, let *it* take skin off.

He felt himself lifted. Shoved, when he couldn't get solid purchase on the ground before he was down again, and they yanked him up. "God *damn* it!" he started, but there was no use in that; he'd gone far past that. There was something cold against one knee, and something ripped; they hauled him up again, and again, and finally, then, something smacked hard and steel-flat against his back, the back of his head, his shoulders. He kicked, squirmed; the surface gave, and he was falling, was free—he had his feet under him, his knees, crouched and didn't bother trying to rise this time; clenched his fists together, swung, hard as he could, at the nearest knees, fell and twisted the opposite direction, heard boxes go. He saw them, blurred, cardboard and mildly beige, and frost under him, slippery. There were crunches where they fell, soft, and he was getting his legs beneath him again, lost that, slid backward on one hand. Kicked.

He landed that one. "Goddamn it, get *ahold* of him, will you?" Not his voice. His skin, his clothes gathered at his chest, and they knocked his chin back, and for a second—nothing, blissfully nothing, and something slammed into his back, full on. *He* had slammed—he slid all the way back down, stung his pelvic bones landing, was twisting, but slow—*God*, too slow—

There was a thin sound, light and plaintive. Something distant slammed. His elbows and his forehead hit the floor: a crack and a shock of cold.

"Shit! What—"

They were talking. It faded in and out. He could not make them out, suddenly did not care; the floor had gone from cold to tolerable, numbed parts of his skin, and he rested his forehead on it. One minute, one blessed minute, *oh, God...*

There was nothing. Nothing. He lifted his head, and there was a throbbing—worse than—*God*, he was out of the habit, he *could* do it, *damn it, Graham*. He lifted it slower, this time, and the throbbing was terrible, but he had taken the worst in his back, that was good, that could best take it. His forehead, his jaw—he moved his fingers there, sore, too—found the jaw in one piece, nothing shattered that he could feel, both joints working.

Cold. That was next. Frigidly cold where his body came into contact with the floor, and the wall. Black, of course; he could see nothing; slipped just trying to crawl away from the wall, felt for the boxes on either side until eons later, he had found an answer to the wall, in front instead of behind him.

He felt around the surface. Got to his knees, and they shrieked at the sting, but his left fingers found purchase—he tried it from that angle, pushed and prodded and felt, finally got one knee up, and us-

ing the iciness of the metal he'd found got himself up. It took a while.
He leaned against the door, and something clicked, and the cold gave
way, and he fell forward.

Tolerably more warm. Same unforgiving hardness. He got one
knee up again, one arm on that knee, and hauled himself up. Staggered, but if he went down again, it would be worse.

He stayed there, standing, swaying, a good few minutes... maybe
longer. He wanted to close his eyes; resisted it, *just* barely. He kept
those squeezed open, and saw light—signs, here and there, emergency lights spotlighted down against metal walls, far on the other side
from where he was standing.

There was light in the crack of a door, over there. He staggered
toward that, leaned on it; it swung open with a creak, and then there
was an alarm shrieking in his ears. He covered those, got out and to
the other side of the street, leaned against the wall, and looked at the
building with its speakers piercing the air around it.

He would *not* take the shuttle. He knew that, getting down the
street; they'd not have any satisfaction, none of them. *God* damn *it*.
He was suddenly wet—it was the jacket, the frost working its way in.
He shrugged out of it, left it lying there and went on.

There *was* no shuttle. Later than seven-thirty, then, when the last
one ran—and his mind was working, then, that was good. He wanted
only hot soup, warm air; felt like his stomach had been through fam-
ine, knew that it was only that he was bruised, that a couple good
nights' sleep should do it, and a day. He had been through it before—
God, how long? There was a coppery taste in his mouth, shoving its
way to the front of his brain.

Damn it, Graham. He stopped, made himself straighten up.
Reached up, adjusted his clothes, and stood firm for a minute. Took
one solid step forward.

He could do this.

He made himself walk the shuttle route, straight line, no deviat-
ing. He felt what there was of his strength back in him, hard and
angry.

He made it. He saw the house, very little color in this light, besides
the white of the street lamp and the blue-black of the sky, familiar.

The stairs were hard to take; he had not done anything but flat, level ground. He got up them one at a time, leaned against the wall every couple treads.

The door, at last. He felt for his keycard, and his pocket, and it was still there, thank the Lord. He shoved it at the slot. Missed; it wavered. Left. Right.

The door opened. He did not expect it, fell in before he caught himself; would have fallen all the way, but then there was Kellan's face, Kellan's arms—an exclamation, *my God*, and he was tempted for a minute to let his weight go, into what was solid, finally, and not cold.

No. He'd pull his weight, could not let Kellan know what had happened. He tried for it, felt for the floor beneath his right shoe—his ankle twisted and his toes touched something else, instead. He looked down—the end of the sofa was against his foot, and the ceiling was sideways; he was disoriented, things spun—no, *get a hold of yourself, Graham*—he was on the sofa, flat on his back. Warm.

God. Kellan had thrown a blanket over him, was leaning over him; there was something frozen and acidic against his forehead. He twisted away from it, felt his heart lurch—*Easy*, Kellan said. He saw his lips move.

He blinked. The ceiling, Kellan's face, disappeared, appeared, disappeared. *Damn it*—he tried for that, but it was fading away, traitorous. There was warmth, here; there was concern in Kellan's expression, in the lips, whatever he was saying, in the eyebrows.

He reached, had the back of Kellan's neck in his fingers, and there were lips on his, warm. Pulled to him, not hard. *No*, hard; and his head was swimming. He opened his eyes. There were two eyes, wide, an open mouth, and the expression had entirely changed. "I'm sorry," he said, blurrily. Still a mumble: it sounded more inside his head than in his ears.

My God, on that mouth again; Kellan was stumbling back.

He had not done that. No, he had; he tasted it again, on his own lips. Sweet like garlic, like mussels. He closed his eyes, because now he could, he was home. He was warm again; there were cushions beneath where his shoulders were shrieking, the muscles stretched beyond what they would do.

He woke, once. The lamp was still on. There was Kellan asleep with his chin into his chest, his arms crossed, on the floor leaning against the sofa, out of reach. He rolled his eyes sideways, numb: small heaps on the coffee table. Washcloths, crumpled and drying; wrappers. A box.

"We should go to Jenning," Kellan said, and was on the other side of the coffee table, dressed for work, when he opened his eyes. The smell of *warm*—cream of rice in a bowl, steaming, on the table, with the spoon already in it.

"Oh, God." Not coherent; he cleared his throat, to try again. Came out a croak: "No. I'm okay." He tried raising himself to his elbow, to prove it, to reach for the cream of rice. His muscles screeched at every move; fibers ripped. *Christ*. Had he grown *that* old? "I've had worse. A lot worse than this."

"You maybe don't remember I've lived with you." Anger, somewhere in there.

"*You've* seen me come out of worse. At school that—"

"In school. In *school*, damn it!"

"Not everyone's so professional, outside of Jefferson." Still a croak. He tried rolling over, left shoulder first. He faced the doorway, and Kellan, and stopped. *Enough.* "Thank you. I'm fine. I'm sore. I'll *be* fine." And Kellan, who looked at him—memory came rushing back. *Oh, God.* "I'm sorry about— I didn't mean to do that."

A stubborn look away, jaw set; God, *Kellan* was unsure how to handle it. Was angry, possibly.

He could let it go. Leave it at that. *Leave it, Graham; just* leave *it.*

"I did—"

"You weren't yourself. I know." Sharp, and that wasn't like Kellan, either. He looked, closer, and saw the stress in the eyebrows, the temples. "Let's just go to Jenning. If you don't, I will."

"No." Firmer than he had thought himself capable. He wrenched himself up into a sitting position; more tendons ripped. *Agh*— "I'm fine, and we're *not* going to Jenning, and I'm not going to have you going up there and putting yourself into that position, all right? I knew better, and I went there anyway, and it's my fault. *My* fault. I'm not going crying to someone. *We're* not."

"Graham, damn it! You're not all right, I didn't spend—I'm just not doing it again. Okay? A shipment comes in and *then* you go to work. If that's what they're damn well like in the warehouse district, then that's what. *You* hear *me?*"

"Look." He closed his eyes, bent his head for a minute. Breathed, and his ribs hurt; he looked at him again. "I didn't have any right coming in here like that. Drama, that's all it was. No excuse."

"Then you're a damned good actor." Jaw set; Kellan was far past upset.

"Kellan. Just don't. All right?" Less energy, now; he could not keep at this level.

Kellan walked to the window. Stood staring out, arms crossed.

"I'm—sorry about earlier. I am." Excruciating, that.

"It's all right." Mumbled.

Kellan hadn't felt anything, then. He had *known* that would be the case; had known it, God, why did it *feel* like this, then?—blood twisted out of his heart so that it throbbed, empty. Worse, this way: he gave up everything, gave up hope, and worse, Kellan would not trust him, Kellan *knew*, now.

He should have sent Kellan back to Kaettegut. No matter what he had said, he should have put him on that hauler, sent him straight back there, should have started *over.*

"I'd rather you know," he said. *Oh, God.* Kellan did not turn, and this was it, this was *it.* His chest felt—imploding, a collapse. "I guess. I'm sorry."

A long silence.

At long last: "I'm not like that."

He kept his composure, barely. "I didn't think I was. I'm sorry."

Nothing.

He bent forward, for the cream of rice; his ribs cracked. "I can't eat. I'm sorry. I'm—going to go to sleep."

Kellan stayed at the window. Put one hand against the glass, leaned on it—crossed his arms again. Did not turn. A mumble: "All right."

Quiet after that.

He lay back, turned over—painful—pressed his arm against his chest, where it ached. There were footsteps finally, quiet, and Kellan was in the other room, and he closed his eyes, hard.

Chauncey sat in a borrowed office behind a desk that occasion-splintered if she ran her fingers across it. She had won this concession, at least, finally, had acquired the room through one of Murray's staff, who'd had some sympathy, thank the Lord. It had used every bit of skill she had. .

Damn Murray Lerkenlund. There were lines on his forehead, too, radiating away from his eyes: stress, and she sorely hoped she had helped put them there.

The office was a sad little thing, brown-paneled and old, next to one shared by Dominic and Louis, with a phone that worked but blipped while she spoke. She had kept in touch with Phoebe, who was running departmental operations in Gros Morne, who had been fielding calls from Councilor Rhodes, *trying* to assuage concerns and passing on the most insistent messages.

She'd been speaking with Jenning, too, of course, a handful of times per day, sometimes more. Yesterday it had been more, and there was little she owned of her soul that had not been pulled through the phone wire by Jenning.

Jenning was still potentially Kaettegut's best ally. Even under-handed, which Jenning was, and she found she had not known any-thing of who Jenning really *was* during the audit process, only hints. They came full bore here, now, over the phone, when Jenning had the support of the Proteraiotita behind her, and not only Quinn Rhodes.

Quinn Rhodes was Jenning's supervisor somewhere up the line in Organization. As a division Organization was one of the top three or four—she had found out that much.

That was who they had sent to do the audits. Which said some-thing very strong about the Proteraiotita's thoughts.

Tea had been hard to come by. Here the fashion was coffee, bitter and too often sludgy, and when tea *was* found, it was not the right kind. She looked up, hopefully, when Rene came into the room with a chipped, dirty-white cup.

"Sorry," he said, before he had come close to the desk, before he had begun setting it down. "Herbal again. The tan kind."

This kind tasted like cinders and always had a residue in the bottom, leaked through the teabag. She sighed, smiled at Rene anyway, and lifted the cup to her lips. "Better than nothing."

Murray was due any minure. Murray *did* come to her office. She had won that much—half of it, she strongly suspected, through his staff. He did not ever come unaccompanied by two or three of them. *Come up to* my *office, where I have staff.* Numbers and brute strength: that mattered to Murray Lerkenlund. And loyalty to his own. *That* was the way to play him, and was what she had been doing, what had gotten her this close.

He came in now, Otis and Cyrus with him this time. Second and fourth: with Murray, things were clearly delineated.

"Murray," she said, and stood, a courtesy. To the others: "Otis, Cyrus. Unusual tea. You must have a contract with Blair Sunsi in Farming. This isn't available anywhere else that I've seen."

Cyrus was pleased. He nodded in the way that they did, chin to the chest once, and done. "We test some of their things once in a while. I'll tell them you like the tea."

"A new variety would be very welcome. Blair does good work." She gestured to the chairs, only two of them, but that was fine: Murray sat, and the others stood, as a rule. She had taken care to have four chairs in the office in the beginning, crowded in front of the desk and next to the door, but had ended up removing them.

Murray did sit. Cyrus folded his hands behind his back and leaned against the wall. Otis remained upright, and had his eye on Rene as he usually did. Always alert, rather suspicious, but he had given her this office, and she had not forgotten that. She had moved Dominic and Louis into the next in recognition of it, two less for Otis to monitor during meetings.

"Thank you, Murray, for coming. I appreciate it." It was important to always start with that: Murray wanted the reinforcement, in front of staff. "I've been doing some more checking. I understand more than half the Grosvenorian crews are from this region. Oh," and she held up her hand, "a few from Rue, but a lot of them from here. *Your* department."

"Plenty from Gros Morne."

"I'm not denying that. I'm *proud* of them, Murray. They've built reputations for themselves. It's not nothing to keep Jefferson and Grosvenor in the kind of shape they do. The whole world sees their work."

A snort. "Jefferson."

"You disagree with their choice to go over."

He shifted in his chair and did not say anything for a minute, did not look at Otis or Cyrus. Finally: "No. I see why they go."

That was a surprise. She did not disguise it well, reached for her cup too late, and took a sip that seemed ill-timed and long, rather than buying time gracefully, naturally.

"You think I've got no heart, don't you?" he said. "*I* know what they've got over there is better than what we've got here, in a lot of ways. That they're living in better quarters, that they've got the budget to do what they want to do with the work, with their craft. We can't give them that, here. They've got to slop things together half-assed. *They* know it. They don't like it, and then they've got to come back a year later and do it again. I'd be frustrated with that. Hell, yeah, I can understand it."

"Then why—the disgust? The snort."

"Because." Murray's temper could rise suddenly, could fall, too. She had begun to understand that side, this trip. It began rising, abruptly, now. "Because that's the choice they've got, Chauncey! Leave everything good we've got over here, all the people they know, just for the chance to do a good job, a really good job, to live decent. Go live in the dark. And we lose the next best we've got, and the next, and the next. Kids've got to grow up to aspire to work over there, to get good enough for the damned powers that be on that side to say they're good enough for a post. It's pathetic, watching them hovering over the postings waiting for one to open. Where's the pride in that?"

She sighed, through her nose. "There isn't. You *know* I think that." This, coming from a man whose department took resources far out of proportion to his department's size—but Murray was more open than he'd been since she had come, had grown a little more comfortable with her presence, maybe... *if* she stayed to her office, if she was predictable.

Was he manipulating her? Same as before, same theme—he had found her weak spot, and used it to distract her from real issues, the way he had tried before. She wasn't willing to buy the bluster as real, not yet. It would be too damned effective with most people, who saw emotion and conflict coming down the pike, and defense mechanisms took over. It set off her own reflexes

For now: "Maybe we'll work together on that, sometime," she said, calmly, quietly, the opposite of his volume. "We can work together on this now, if you'll let me. Our last word from a renovation crew over there was that they weren't sure they could work, that tensions were that bad. *All* the crews were waiting on that word. That was several days ago." Cyrus had not heard this, not from her, not from anyone: it was on his face. *Good.* "Several *days*, Murray. I have a pretty fair idea they're not looking at anything good, by now. —One shipment. One to get in there, drop off some food, pick up our people, and get out. Bring them over here until this blows over. That's all I'm asking."

It was *not* all she would ask, but it was the crucial first step.

"They'll seize our *ship*, Chauncey. They need it worse than the food. Hell, they've got food. They've got storage capacity on their side."

"It won't last them long. It might already be gone." Evenly. "You're not thinking it all the way through. We're going to make a delivery eventually, you know that, and I know that. Our bargaining chip isn't the ships, it's the food. No food delivered, and we've got nothing. They're already talking about a takeover, did you know that?"

"And you want to give them a ship."

"They won't take the ship, Murray. They need food more than they need metal. They can live without a new jacket or tableware for a far sight longer than they can go without sustenance. It's food causing them the stress. You don't play with basic needs, Murray. We get back onto our regular shipping schedule, things will calm down very quickly. It'll *let* them focus on the Back."

"Maybe a little focus isn't necessarily a bad thing." Sullen. "They're not so self-sufficient, no?"

"No. They're not." She took another sip: taste to shrivel her nostrils, but it calmed things, gave the appearance of control, of civility. Just another meeting. "Which I think they well know, and it's what we *don't* want them acting on. You want a bargaining chip—it *is* food supplies, and it won't help if we're not in control of it."

Murray leaned forward, put his hands on his knees. "No. Let them straighten out the Back. When the Back ships, we'll ship. Not us first."

"Murray." She felt a jolt of alarm at the hint of Murray rising, and Otis and Cyrus had likewise stirred—but that was what he had designed it to do, and she kept her expression neutral. "Our renovation crews can't afford it. What are they going to do? They've got no way off Grosvenor. They're badly outnumbered. They're the face of *us*, Murray. We sit over here safe, and *they're* the ones who are going to get it in the ass—if you'll pardon me for saying so. You sit here safe."

Murray sat, no motion forward *or* back into the chair. "They aren't fools, Chauncey. They'll board themselves in. It's not going to last."

"It's going to last a lot longer if we don't let Jefferson focus where it needs to. Damn it, Murray, you ask me if I think you've got no heart. All your vaunted understanding comes to this, does it? Let them eat cake, that sort of thing?"

"Damn it!" Flare of temper, again. "We can't ship adequately without the fleet intact, you know that, and Cliff Runnel knows that. At least two of them are down half the time with maintenance as it is. Jefferson's not going to settle for temporary, Chauncey! Not after this, and it's got nothing to do with us. Oh, sure, maybe we'll get it back when they've settled all this, *after* they've had another ship constructed, which will take—how long?—and in the meantime it'll have had no maintenance, and they won't care, they'll want the same damned levels. They'll want the same levels in the meantime, I bet you anything. *That's* what we're looking at."

"Is that the worst-case scenario?" Calmly. She leaned back, consciously relaxed her shoulders. "Some extra work? I can live with that, if it means shortening this conflict, getting back to a position we can work from—and a good chance at keeping *all* of us safe. It isn't just them, Murray. It's you, it's me, it's all the departments."

"Except it's the same damned story. Not enough funds, not enough resources, even worse than what we've looked at before, and it's still that we've got to produce Grade A product at the levels they want. I'm tired of it, Chauncey. I'm not going to put up with it. I'm *not* going to risk one of the ships. Tell them that, and tell them that's why. A wake-up call."

"I've told them our concerns. *Our* concerns, Murray, not just yours. That we need all our ships to operate at schedule. I've sent over our schedules, everything to do with shipping. They *know* it."

"So damned what? They'll say what it takes to get what they want.

If they don't make good, and it happens the way I say it will, *that's* the situation we'll be in. That's what it comes down to. We've got the say now. We're using it, they don't like it, and so they put pressure on you to come put pressure on me. A damned puppet, that's what they've made you. *That's* what we've always got in charge."

Reaction—but that was what he wanted. Diversion. Distraction. She kept the coldness down in her chest, did not let it rise. "All very good, Murray. Except you won't distract me from what you've made into an emergency for every citizen of Kaettegut, here *and* over there. *You.* That's one hell of a thick skin, for the way you talk about your people, and your staff. Very noble to protect *them.* It plays well to the media, doesn't it? Except that it'll play to the media much, much better if you swing in there to get our renovation crews out of there, and if you bring food along with you, that'll buy us the luxury of time to potentially work together on the same goals. Unless, of course, you *don't* want to make it happen." In front of his staff: that was key. "If you just want the media coverage, you've already got it, after all. —You're damned well fouling up plans *I've* got to accomplish the same things you're moaning about. I've taken some very real steps, Murray, and I'm talking about the level of the Proteraiotita. Do you *really* want to get in there, throw a wrench in what could do some of the things you've been talking about?"

He looked at her. His eyes narrowed, the beginning of a scowl.

"That doesn't sound like a puppet, does it? I'm here because you forced it, oh, yes, you can be pleased with that, but it wouldn't matter whether Jefferson wanted it or not. It's what's got to be done. It isn't pleasant. It can *be* pleasant, if you'll let it. You can get out of it what you want. If we play this right, you *and* I, Kaettegut can be in a better position than we've been in before, a very much more strategic position. A place from which we can move. You want that, don't you? You've got a talent for grabbing opportunities; take this one and run with it, for goodness sake! You want to be on that ship? Maybe some of your top-level staff? *They* can keep an eye on things. I'll make sure your name is on the whole venture, and if it works, I can promise you, you'll be in the history books."

The scowl had deepened. "*If* it works." A faint attempt at mockery, ruined by the bitterness in the tone. "It's not going to."

"You're wrong. Even if they seize the ship—which it's *not* in their best interest to do—we can play it so that we're a strategic partner. Think about it. We'd offer the services of the crew. They'd stay with the ship, do the maintenance. We've got the crucial skills, and they don't. For the first time in decades, Murray, we'd have value outside one narrow arena. We've *got* directions we can go, damn it, and the only way it's not going to happen is with those ships at anchor."

"It wouldn't last. They get back on top, it'll be back to the old ways."

"It's the best chance we've got. Best we've had in years." She sat there, still, with her fingers around the handle of the cup, and left it at that.

A long silence. Murray leaned his chin into his palms, looked straight ahead. Cyrus looked at her, half shell-shocked, half thoughtful. Otis wore no expression at all, stood as still as he had when he had come in.

"I'll think about it," Murray said, finally, and grunted, getting to his feet. *Not* a pleased grunt, but that was for saving face—of course he'd insist on time, he could not give way in front of his staff. Not in front of her.

And that meant she'd have it, very feasibly, in some version.

Kellan sat in his office, sat and reread the application in his hands the twentieth time. It didn't matter; his section of Travel had been thrown into doubt with the stopped Kaetteguttan shipments—himself, Thomas Gouman, Emory. Himself, especially, he would imagine. He didn't have to hear the rumors to know that, to know that he was going to be collating papers and catching up on the rest of the department's clerical backlog for quite a while, and that if he was lucky.

Even Emory looked at him in his watery way, now.

God. His stomach roiled. It had come to this, to *this*, Graham hardly able to stand, not able to get his card in the lock, skin abraded and livid from his cheekbone to forehead.

It would have taken—more than one, unless they had caught him by surprise. It had to have been that. Graham would not have stayed where he was at risk; he was more careful than that, knew every environment he was in.

That was the way, then. One of them against anyone who damn well didn't like them, who associated anyone Kaetteguttan with personal vendetta. A handful of missed shipments, and civility was gone, and he could not trust things. *That* was all it had taken. It was a damned frail stability, this environment, and even Graham had read it wrong—who had not minded coming here in the beginning.

His hands were shaking. He straightened the paper where he had wrinkled it.

He put it down. Clenched his fists on the cool surface of the desk, and tried hard to think, to *think*. He *should* go to Jenning. Except she was part of the same system, she would be the way they were, and Graham had not wanted it, had not had the focus to make that point well enough, but he had understood it.

His face turned hot, that far in—as far as he *could* bring himself to think... what Graham had done. He turned around in the chair, picked up another application from a stack on the credenza, mechanical. Appearances, just that.

Was he that naïve? *Had* he been?

God. What was he going to do? *What?*

It was his own fault too, maybe. He had not been clear. Good God, what would anyone think? He had not ever had much, but what he'd had, he'd kept to himself. Just considerate, he had thought; less embarrassing. He didn't have anyone over when Graham was home, back in college, when he had still been exploring with a few of the girls, tortured attempts that did not end well. Each time had left him parched and hungry and frustrated, and he had shoved the last one away, and offended her. He *had* been sorry, but she had not listened.

It was not going to change. He could not gloss over it, pretend it had not happened; could not write it off to delirium—Graham had flatly turned that down. No, it was real, it had happened, would rush back every morning and rearrange everything again. *Nothing* the same.

He leaned his forehead on his palms, on the credenza.

"Kellan." A voice behind him. He started, turned, and there was Thomas Gouman in the doorway; he felt heat where had been his palms, on his forehead, and knew they were red spots. "The world's not going to end. All right?"

He hadn't been working. There was one piece of paper on his desk, *God*, he looked like Emory.

Thomas looked, for an instant, like he might sit down. He shifted his weight to the leg inside the door, instead, leaned sideways against the door frame. "Take it a little easier. I know it's hard to believe, but glitches do happen sometimes. I've been through plenty. You do, when you get older. It always goes back to normal. I'm still here, running the same department."

He—did not know what to say; felt pressure in his forehead, behind his throat. He finally picked up his pen, tapped it against the desk, looked.

"Just take it easy," Thomas said, and turned and left.

Oh, hell. He had flubbed that, too.

Still, it was nice; it was unexpectedly nice, and his stomach smoothed some, for the minute he sat there replaying it.

Chauncey put in the call, and sat and waited. Rene had gone back to his makeshift desk in the hall. It was cramped, and he had received strange looks, but he had refused to leave her door unsupervised from the minute she had procured the office, had Dominic stationed there in the hallway while he found what he needed, and assembled it into a station.

She had stopped him when he had begun to ask one of Murray's staff for schematics of the building. Politely, smoothly, so that the staff member in question had mistaken the beginnings of the request for a question about directions to the nearest coffee machine and floor lounge. *Not that far*, she had said, afterward, and reached across and squeezed his arm.

"Jenning Crote's office," said a voice, on the phone: Clare's, from the sound of it. She had met Clare fairly far back, part of the audit team from Jefferson. Close to Jenning, always.

"Clare, it's Chauncey. How are you?" She always put warmth into her voice for Clare. With Gabrielle and Jenning there was no need, rather the opposite: they responded badly.

"Not bad." After a second's thought. "Hold on for a minute, I'll get Jenning."

Another wait. After this, she and Rene and Louis would have lunch on the *Corundum* courtesy of Cyrus, with the crew in their natural environment.

Murray had turned down the invitation to take the trip himself, a surprise. Murray insisted instead on full field authority for the *Corundum* captain, to react to any situation as the man saw fit. Dangerous prerogative.

If the crew reacted, at all, even to genuine threat—relations would go straight to hell. *She* knew it. She had to make the captain know it, absolutely know it, carry it with him at bone-level.

Murray made himself vulnerable in the choice of ship, too. *Corundum* was a mussel hauler, built to haul that kind of weight. If the *Corundum* did not come back—

It had to be one of those, though, to haul the shipment they'd be sending. Still, the ship itself was message, from Murray to her—*prove what you say*. All chips on the table.

"I really hope, for your sake, you've got some good news," Jenning's voice came across simultaneous with a series of blips in the connection.

"I do, actually. It comes with some conditions."

A *very* pregnant pause, and the voice, when it came, was thin. "You're not in much of a position to be setting conditions."

She laid her hand on the desk, palm first. Fingers, then, one fingertip at a time. *Made* herself patient, calm. "I don't say that just for the sake of setting conditions, no. I *would* argue that we're the ones—but I'd like to keep working together. Let's go over what I've got. Is that agreeable?"

Another pause. "I'd like to hear what you have to say, yes." Carefully phrased.

"I can have a shipment to you by the end of the week. Not double what we normally send—our ships don't have the capacity for that—but more than what's usual. All seameats and fish, all fresh. It's going to take some doing, you understand, to get things together. We won't have time for a stopover in Gros Morne."

"We're as low on the rest."

"I know that may be the case, but it's what we can do now. Next shipment—let's just say most everything hinges on what happens with this cargo."

Quiet, then: "I'd like to know what you're implying."

"I think you have a fair idea. I've been open with you about the concerns over here. It's no small thing, Jenning. It's taken me much longer to get this than even I anticipated. I'm not the only factor over here, you know that by now."

"And I've told you those concerns are unfounded."

"For your sake, I hope they are. I know I'm counting on it, that Kaettegut's counting on it. I've put a great deal on the line for those assurances. They've got to pan out. No choice. The ball's coming to your side of the court, do you hear me?"

"Tell me the date and time. We'll have it unloaded at the same rate we always do. Your crew can stay aboard. They'll be off on schedule."

"I can't tell you." Second of Murray's conditions, and she could see it, damned well she could. What she'd end up doing—that, she'd have to mull over. A drink, out in the dark of the dock area, alone. "Not yet. I'm telling you, things are—not in upheaval over here, not so much, but schedules *have* been upset, things aren't where they're supposed to be, you understand? We'll put it together as fast as we can."

"You can't be serious." The same damned condescension in the tone, of the party with the more seniority, the far greater power.

"It's all I can give you right this minute. It's more than you've had. Give me *some* credit."

"We can't guarantee what we don't know. Surely you can understand that."

"I can understand it." She swiveled the chair, faced the back wall of the office, the atrocious paneling "Jenning—are we working together, or are we not? That's what I understood, from the beginning. It's down to basics. You don't have the capacity to get over here and get what you need. We've got it. We're working to get it to you, best we can. Some of the people over here—want to wait until you've got things settled on your side, until you've got manufacturing and mining shipments coming again. I can understand that, Jenning, I really can. Put yourself in my shoes, in the shoes of any person over here. Look at the history, for heaven's sake."

"I don't have to tell you to put yourself in *our* shoes. It's a two-way street, Chauncey."

"I can do what I can to help. I'm doing it because I understood this was to be a mutual effort. I'll do more, but first I want to know, straight from you, not from the Proteraiotita, not from Quinn Rhodes, *what* it is we're looking at. What's the relationship? —Because if it's the same as it's always been, it might be that I'm not interested, that none of us are."

A note of incredulity. "You're holding us hostage."

"*Not* hostage. Practicalities. The reason I asked to talk with you—you know us better than anyone else does, you know how we work. You'll deal straight with us. I expect that from you, Jenning. I do. It's the reason we're still talking. *Not* threats. If you think that's what motivating us, you don't know much about me. And I think you do know me. Am I right?"

Silence. The phone line blipped, once.

"I'm honored, honestly, to have ranked that level for a simple audit series. I know you haven't been isolate to the audits. You're not on this line just because I asked for it, you know damned well you're not, and I know it." Dangerous: she was approaching that line, had already come too close to it once before.

"Chauncey." Another blip, the connection could be growing worse. "If you think I'm in charge over here, you're deceiving yourself. I've got a job, and you've got a job; let's not go beyond that, and we'll keep ourselves out of trouble."

That was perhaps real. Perhaps. "Can you guarantee the safety of our ship?"

"If you let me know when it's coming, yes, we damn well can. I've told you that."

"I'll call you when I can. Best I can do with that, please understand me." A hesitation, purely strategic. "I've thought of something that might help in the meantime. I can assure your residents that it's coming, straight from the source this time, on camera. Calm things down a little."

She could *feel* the change on the other end of the line. Could feel it suppressed in the tone. "That might be of interest."

Her score, this time, then: that was information, valuable, did not tell her what she did not already know but was a precious confirmation, a weakening. "I'll film it today. I can maybe get the camera in this afternoon. Straight from the camera, you understand. The quality isn't going to be the best."

"I'll tell them to expect it. I can send you over what might help, if you can wait a half hour or so." No *thank you*, that would have been too much. "One other thing. That shipment needs to be at maximum, absolute maximum, do you understand? The more we get in, the more reassuring it's going to be, I think you understand that. If you can give me a specific idea what that will be, it *would* help. I'm talking about what's the maximum you've ever run it at, what was loaded, and where it went. Specifics."

That was strong emphasis, for Jenning. She kept still in the chair and pondered it, and still came up with nothing, no reason outside what Jenning said—when Jenning said nothing at face value. "I can find out. I'm going that way after we're done. Send me your things and I'll send that back. Good?"

"Good." Finality: the conversation was over. Jenning could *have* that tone. A click, and confirmation: she rose and stretched her neck, her shoulders. Still preferable to talking with anyone on the Proteraiotita, but the conversations drained, and she had a full day, had to have enough energy for this lunch, to assess *Corundum's* crew.

Pray they weren't excitable, that they weren't the kind which operated on instinct and that only.

21

Half past six, and there was no sign of Kellan, and Graham's stomach knotted again.

This could *not* go on.

Kellan had not come home last night until near ten-thirty, and then had gone into the bathroom and to bed without stopping in the doorway. In the morning Graham had found all the First Aid supplies on the bathroom counter, organized and re-stocked where they had been getting low. A small stack of new quick-ice packs, the worst and most painful of the lot, but what he still needed.

He could not go to work. He could cover everything else, but the scrapes on his face and knuckles would take several days to heal, and stood out like flame, now; and he would not have been able to focus in any case. And that meant hours of sleep and television.

Chauncey Benner had been on yesterday, a surprise.

For a few minutes during the broadcast, he had almost forgotten. He'd only thought that he should call Kellan and let him know it was on. Welcome to have information at all, to wring out of it what they could—but what he had been trying to put out of his head *had* happened, and came rushing back.

He felt—his internal organs had turned to sludge. And it was ludicrous to be nervous, when he had done it, when it was *done*, and then he only felt miserable and awkward, and hot-angry at himself.

Heaven knew where Kellan was now. Hopefully in Jefferson, *had* to be Jefferson, Kellan could not be out in the northern district of Grosvneor with only the streetlights and the dark and the wet, without even the minimal security inside Jefferson's buildings.

The phone blipped. He jumped; his heart kicked, too. *Kellan.* Calling in, was his first thought—the second, gut-wrenching worry that it wasn't Kellan calling in, that it was someone calling *about* him, that they had— He went across to pick it up rather than activating the speaker, stuck the earpiece in. "Yes?"

A voice he didn't know, female. "Is this Graham or Kellan Long?"

Or Kellan, she had said. He let the breath out, had not realized he had taken it. "This is Graham," he said, and managed to sound halfway aloof.

"Graham, this is Phoebe Sunsi. I'm calling from Chauncey Benner's office."

He missed the rest that she said. *Sunsi*, that was Kaetteguttan—that was status. But— *Kaetteguttan.* Chauncey Benner's office. "What is it?" he said, and interrupted her in the middle of a sentence.

A single beat, and she said, "*Corundum's* one of our seameats haulers. We need you to be at the dock by the time it gets there. All of you."

He frowned, put his hand up and rubbed his forehead. "I'm sorry. I'm *sorry.* I missed what you were saying—I just—it took me a second. Can you say it again? The whole thing."

Patience, on the other end, though not easy. She still spoke quickly. "We have a shipment coming. Now. It's scheduled to arrive at seven-thirty at your port, and we need to have all of you there by then. I apologize that it's not a lot of time, but you don't need to pack much—clothes that will hold you a couple days, if you want to take that. That's all we're anticipating this will take. Just until tensions are eased, until we can make sure the shipments are regular again. It's just safety. Just precaution. We'll have you back over there very soon."

Oh, my God. Kellan wasn't home yet, was maybe still in Jefferson, and not reachable by phone. Less than one hour. "I— All right."

It took, from what he knew—what, a couple hours to unload a full shipment?

The door clicked. There came the sound of a card withdrawing, and the door opened and Kellan came in, juggling two white, plain restaurant bags, was getting ready to slide the second into his free hand while he put away his card.

Relief surged in his throat. "My roommate just got home. We'll be there."

Kellan looked at him and in *this* moment, there was nothing but question in his eyes.

"I can't emphasize how important it is that you be on time," she said, in his ear.

"It's not a problem."

He let her end the call, heard the click. No more information, then.

"What's going on?" Kellan asked, the first words he'd heard from him since the morning before; standing there with the two bags hanging from his hands, still in work clothes and fleece jacket. Red along the edges of the cheekbones, from the cold and wind.

"That was Chauncey Benner's office. They're sending a shipment." It sounded ludicrous, and he was glad again that Kellan had walked in when he had, when he had still been on the phone with them. "We've got to go down to the port. They said to pack for a couple days if we wanted."

"Pack?"

He stood there, by the door, confused; Graham went into the bedroom and opened the closet. Called over his shoulder: "They're taking us over there for a couple days. Just safety, they said. They're saying it won't be much longer than that."

Kellan came and stood in the doorway, watched him pack, mouth still open; finally closed it, and shrugged. He held up the two bags, an attempt at levity: "Guess you'll eat on the ship."

"We've got forty-five minutes. Shuttle's not running in the peninsula, not on a Friday this late. We'll have to walk it. Couple miles."

"Okay." He disappeared from the doorway; Graham heard him in the other room, taking off his shoes. A *clunk* when the first shoe fell.

He shook his head to clear it, focused on the closet and the open bag—that he had seldom ever had a chance to use, before this year. Now it had begun to wear at the edges of the straps; it had not been excellent quality when he had first purchased it, had not needed to be for the limited use he had figured on. He threw a couple changes of clothes in, went into the bathroom, folded in his shaving kit and some of the first aid supplies. Nearly all the hated quick-ice packs; Kellan would notice, and he *could* use them.

He zipped the bag closed. Coming out, he almost bumped into Kellan coming in; his reflexes were better, and he backed into the wall where it jutted out—felt it flat and hard against his shoulder blades. Kellan only ducked his head and turned his shoulder to squeeze past.

He waited by the window, then, standing and looking out. The streetlight nearest by was still a bright white, this time in the evening; it illuminated the flat faces of the rowhouses' facades across the street. They were too low in the district to warrant the touches that the business district had, but the street had grown familiar, anyway, had grown an association better than the one in Rue. Better technology, better housing—more hope, until now.

Kellan came out with his bag at last, did not forget to scoop the restaurant bags off the counter. "Ready."

"Maybe we'd better leave those here." There would be people out, coming back from dinners at the restaurants. Two restaurant bags of their own would only help—but combined with luggage bags, probably not. His was black and structureless; he could make it conform to him, somewhat, hide it behind the bulk of his heavier coat, which *was* all he had left. Kellan's bag was beige, on the other hand, a suede fabric, more structured—something he had ordered at graduation, when he had known he would be heading to Gros Morne, and a trip like that had something of status. It would stand out more next to the darker brown of his fleece jacket.

He shifted his own bag, put the bulk of it behind him, opening the door. Kellan watched him do it, and looked back at the white bags on the counter. "Yeah. I guess so."

They had good luck, passed only a few people near the shuttle stop. He switched his bag to his left shoulder, nearing it, and adjusted the strap so that the bag hung lengthwise against his side.

Kellan followed his example, could not do it as well with the structure of his bag protesting, but Graham kept to his right, and it worked. The people walked by on the other side of the road, silhouettes in the streetlights. The white lights of the Grosvenor shuttle were shrinking, heading north again, when they got to the shuttle stop.

The narrow strip of land between the residential and the warehouse districts stretched ahead, the water lapping against its low sca-wall. After the storm it had been soggy from having flooded, so that the shuttle's tires had squished through this section. Kellan walked beside him, now, quiet, not a word after leaving the house—just one look, when they had seen the people coming from the shuttle stop.

Pleasant silence, only their footsteps—if he did not think of what the quiet meant, if he did not try to interpret it.

At the beginning of the district, walls began to loom up out of the dark and he saw silhouettes turning a corner around a warehouse where the dark of the sky was not quite as dark as the wall. They were heading the same direction, though, and his fleeting impression was of bulk in the bodies and of something lower at their sides, something carried.

He said nothing. Even so, he passed that first street and took the next, where the walls of warehouses rose on each side; better cover, and darker. The streetlight at the end of this block was off, normal for a working district with the last shuttle having gone.

Kellan looked up at both sides of the street, at corrugated walls and the few windows, glossed black. "This is where you work?"

"About a half-mile that way. On the south side." But he was pleased; it was still awkward talking, but there was interest, and that was more promising than he had let himself hope.

He shifted his bag to his other shoulder, coming around the corner into the last, shorter block—but there was dim light, flooding the walls ahead, where there should not be. He scanned the width and length of it, turned and examined the way they had come, and found both empty.

"What is it?" There was ension in Kellan's voice, more than he would have anticipated.

Nothing, he thought of saying. "It shouldn't be this light."

"Are we close?"

He nodded, and left it at that.

Someone could have turned the lights on, the port could have been brought up to full operation to receive the ship. The woman on the phone had not said anything about secrecy; he had simply assumed it in the way she had talked. *We've heard some of the things—it's just safety. Just precaution.* She had emphasized being on time as strongly as someone of her kind did.

At the corner he slowed, in what was becoming too bright. He looked, with the wall immediately to his right and his bag behind him: there were groups of figures under the port's lights on the dock, most of them bulky in the shoulders, some of them not, mostly men.

Beside him, Kellan reached back and looped his bag's shoulder strap over his head and onto his opposite shoulder, snugged the bulk of the bag against his back, and adjusted the strap so that the whole thing was solid. Unusual move—he looked at him out of the corner of his eye, and Kellan's face had tightened.

There was no untoward movement on the dock, though, was only a standing around, rather, an uneasy waiting. He looked to the water, black outside the reach of the lights, a little choppy. No ship's lights yet; he glanced at his watch. Twenty after seven.

He started out toward the dock—Kellan stepped out in front of him. Still to the side, but distinctly in front, without a word, without a look.

Defensive, he realized, late. Of *him*.

He wanted, ridiculously and for an instant, to laugh—but more with gratification, than derision. Was *touched*.

"It's all right," he said, but waited until they had come closer to the dock. A few others came out of the dark of the streets and buildings, joining them, and then there was the concrete of the dock itself under his feet. He found a spot off to the side, mid-dock, where they would be out of the way, and moved toward it. The rest were standing in uneasy groups. Crews, he guessed, who had worked together their entire time over on this side and maybe before, who knew each other that well.

In that respect, he and Kellan did not stand out; in every other way, they did not fit. He was suddenly very conscious of his coat, of Kellan's newer bag, next to the hardworn work coats of everyone else, streaked with old dust and stains—even Kellan's hair, gleaming in the port's lights, immaculate and of a length that was not practical for any of them, who either wore theirs very short or long enough to tie back.

There were only two of them, too, to the others' groups and crews, toolboxes at their feet. Not many bags that he could see; he let his drop off his shoulder, inconspicuously, caught it in his grip on its way down, and eased it to a spot beside his feet. Kellan watched him, without turning his head, then reached up and pulled the strap of his bag over his head—they watched *him* do it—and set it behind him, almost politely.

"Hey," he said, to one of the crew looking across at them. He jerked his chin, saying it, as typical a greeting as he could get. He made sure he did not cover his accent, and good Lord, it had already just a taint of foreignness to him.

They examined him, briefly. Were evidently satisfied: "Hey," the closest one responded, and turned his shoulder, quiet, back to his own group.

Kellan looked at him, finally, and there was that extra bit of worry in the eyes, of discomfort.

There was a commotion, then, and a loud voice, belligerent. He looked for the source: it came from the other end of the dock, nearer the buildings, but there was machinery in his way, sitting inactive. "What's *this*?" Not pleasant, nearer a snarl. A movement; there were others moving in among them, whose nerves and muscles fairly vibrated with tension. As bulky as some of the Kaetteguttan crews— warehouse workers, dock workers. *Christ.*

There were more than a few. He saw the crew opposite spreading back, shifting their positions behind two or three broad backs—and there were two more, coming in, who turned to look at him and Kellan and came their way, instead.

There was something else, out in the bay—two lights, white pinpoints.

Kellan took the same position he had earlier, on the instant; slightly to the front and side, but his shoulders had tautness in them, unease. He had his palms up, that fast. "What's up?" he heard him say, and then, "Take it easy. There's nothing—"

They had interpreted Kellan as the more aggressive, had centered on him. There was a crash, behind them; they did not turn to look, instead one reached forward and shoved Kellan, a hard push with all the muscles behind it. Kellan stumbled back; kept his balance all the same, put his palms back up, and said something else—he could not hear it; noise was rising, suddenly, on every side but behind him, and he put his own weight into his step forward and his shoulders and arms, and shoved the man who had gone into Kellan.

There were a couple *more* of them, suddenly, and then there were swarms, Kaetteguttan or dock workers, he could not tell—the second of the original two was on him faster than he had anticipated and he bent and rolled beneath the weight, and came out on the other side to chaos, to curses and breathing and rage, and swinging and shoving; and one of the crew across from him was on the ground, on his back, and another of his companions on his attacker, and more coming. An extraordinarily blunt-bodied man took Kellan by the front of his jacket and shoved, hard; he saw Kellan hit the wall of machinery, and his head jerk with the impact.

Damn it! Head injury, was all he could think, the nurses had *warned* him those patients could not take any further blows to the head, no matter how many years had gone by after recovery. He swung, knocked his opponent out of his path with it, saw Kellan land and look up and dodge the man's second grab at him—barely, but it was done, and Kellan *was* still going. He made for that man, almost made it, but something grabbed his coat and his shoulder and yanked him back—he jabbed his elbow back, hard as he could; connected, but someone else was already on him, carried him to the ground with a weight that seemed far greater than that of one man.

"Kellan!" he shouted, but that was no use; he could not get to him, he was trapped under the weight, and then something had his throat, rigid like metal, was pressing hard.

He kicked. Aimed, and kicked again; his vision was going dark. He felt it connect, right place, right force, and he shoved at the mass and rolled to the emptier side. Another man, behind that one, who *had* been on top of him—that explained the weight—tried to come at him from that angle and from an unbalanced position, which was a mistake. He swiveled on his back, kicked again and got the throat when the man bent down.

He had gotten almost to his feet by the time the next one got there; he had no choice but to go backward, to give himself time to get all the way up, to get his balance. He crouched, took *this* one with his shoulder, twisted, and saw more than heard the smack of human bulk on concrete. He glanced up with the instant he had, could not see Kellan anymore—saw him, then, back near the transition from dock to dock apron, near a forklift; saw him take a swing, but there were at least two on him. But *God*—Kellan swinging; he took two steps and felt the next blow in his gut, impossibly hard. He felt only agony for a second, and then air and no balance, and hit the ground and skidded backward on his back. Gasped and felt for his gut, both arms, ducked and doubled over, same time. Could not *breathe*—

Another Kaetteguttan, from the same crew as before—yanked the man back. Something went flying, clattered, metal, on the concrete and skittered away. A wet plop, then, distant; it had gone over the edge and into the water, he was that close to some edge of the dock, and *God damn*, someone had hit him with something goddamned metal! He was up, enraged, before he could breathe, was gulping for anything in his lungs at the same time he wrapped his elbow around the man's windpipe from behind. He locked on and squeezed, hard as he could, and had the other hand in the man's hair, pulling back.

Hands grabbed him from behind. Yanked him back, but he kept his grip, and the man came with him. New shouts—a roaring, in his ears, everywhere on the dock.

The Kaetteguttan man had disappeared. There was a new bulk, just inside his vision, near the roaring. "—ship!" someone yelled, *not* a Kaetteguttan, and then there was air, again; he flailed to catch his balance, found nothing—time stretched, quick, and there was just black, and a quick flash of light; he twisted in what was still not solid, and then something rose up and slapped his back, and the back of his neck, and his leg went into something. A strange noise, and the shock of cold, freezing cold, and then he could not breathe again: they were pouring something into his mouth, and there were fingers racing across his head, from the back. He twisted, and still found no purchase, but it was not air, and he still could not breathe. —Until suddenly there was air; he had thrust up into it and was already sinking.

Oh, my God! He was in the *bay*, in the water, they had thrown him off the dock and into the blackness of the bay, and there was something still blacker above his head, a weight; he glimpsed it and then he was sinking, and struggling, and there was no bottom; he reached futilely and found nothing, *nothing*, just went further down, there was only sheer terror and cold, his heart beating suddenly out of his chest, and the water silent and pressing against his ears, into his nostrils and his mouth. No sound— He reached out, thrashed against it with all his limbs, with everything; twisted, *oh God, oh God*, there was water on every side, water with a terrible weight and nothing to grab, and he could not tell which way was up or to the side or down: there was just him, a horrified flailing of his muscles and no way to breathe, and he could not vomit out what was inside him already—he felt his stomach lurch, put his hands there, twisted, and there was something against the back of his head—oh, God, it wasn't water, it was air, frigid!, but then there was the horrible weight again. He felt a last bit of frozen air against one hand, felt something hard and cold slap against it, and it was all around him again

—Something caught the collar of his jacket, solid, hard, almost cruel. Freezing air again, only this time he did not sink—he hovered there, still kicking. "Grab—!" he *thought* he heard, far away, and there was pain in his ears, but it still had him, and something came forward and struck him in the forehead, and one knee. Cold, hard—he grabbed for it, and found only cold and slippery, scrabbled fingers against it. "—Up!" he heard, through panic, and he reached for the voice

Then he had purchase, or rather, something had purchase on *him*, around his fingers, and was pulling, and he was out of the terror and the water, and swung above it. He let his head fall back with relief, but his stomach lurched and he was choking; he gripped as hard as he could with that one hand, and looked down, and that was worse, there was nothing there, there was only white chop and dizziness, and he thought for a terrible instant that they had let go. He reached up with his other hand, found nothing, tried again, and looked—there was the gleam of white against wet black, and then he found something firm, an arm, with his other hand, he gripped that and they pulled, and something hard grated across his stomach and his groin and his knees, and he fell onto something blessedly hard, and slippery. He got to his hands and knees, stomach and chest convulsing, and retched into the deck until he had it against his mouth, and there was a hand on the back of his neck. "Get one of the tarps," someone said, and a long minute later, there was something around him—cold and stiff, but he grabbed it, pulled a hunk of it into his chest, and fell back to lean against something with a bar.

"Careful," someone said, and then they left him.

He sat there, and breathed, let his heart rate slow down. Felt his hair dripping water down onto his hands, in streams down his face.

—He looked, then, and saw the infrastructure of the deck of a ship, and there was breeze, mercilessly cold against his face. A dipping; he was sitting at an angle; the entire deck was. It slanted down and away from his feet.

He twisted. Grabbed the metal bar, and it was only a thin guard rail between him and empty black space, and water below—he heard its sound, the chill sound of its slop against the hull, that far below, and clutched the bar as hard as he could. He looked up—and the dock was out there, *far*, its lights slanting and swimming in his vision.

Chauncey looked at her watch, at the ancient phone system this office had, that would not even hook up to her computer.

Dominic and Louis had gone in search of dinner. Rene had gone out to sit at his desk.

To give her space, she suspected.

The ship had left on time. The captain had assured her of his crew, that they had run the same route all their working lives. *Of course.* She had not said it again, but she had wanted to, and the captain had seen that, and nodded. She had taken the reassurance, wished she felt it.

She braced herself, putting in the earpiece, feeding in the request.

The ship would have been in dock now for ten minutes. The crew would have made a good start on unloading the shipment.

She had kept the agreement with Murray. It had been after further thought the smartest alternative—arrival after hours, no problems getting the renovation crews on board. Jenning would call the dock staff back in, would have the chance to call in controls at the same time, and they'd all see what Jefferson's honor really held.

A voice came across the line, with a bit of edge. Irritated at a call at this hour, no doubt. "Jenning Crote."

"Jenning, it's Chauncey."

"I can see that. *Haven't* seen a shipment."

"Well, you've got one. It should be in dock now. It's loaded down, Jenning. You want to call some port crews in?"

An intake of breath. Not kindly: "What?"

She took her own breath. She had *known* it would probably not go well, had still hoped— "It's food, Jenning. A lot of food. For Christ's sake, don't stand on procedure, it's what you *need.*"

"Damn it, Chauncey! You couldn't have called when it left *your* dock?" Incensed, genuinely so—but there was something behind that: a wavering in the voice.

It took her a few seconds to identify it, to get past what a furious tone did to an empty stomach sloshing with too many cups of northern province tea—and her heart sank. She sat without moving.

"It was the way I got that ship out of this port, the only way," she said, and did not try to keep her own emotion out of her voice: "I *am* sorry. Jenning?"

Nothing. She pressed the earpiece further in with one hand, listened, and heard no echo at all, none of the space of an active line.

She took the earpiece out and set it on the desk. Wanted, wanted to call the number back—knew it would do no good, that it would only provoke. She rested her head in her hands instead, leaning on the desk.

She had lost the slightest, smallest corner of a personality that had allied with her, with Kaettegut. She knew it, that instant, in the gut, and closed her eyes.

There was a tap on the door, and Rene waited a minute before cracking it, and leaning in backward on his chair, concern in the expression. "Didn't go well?"

"It's the risk I took," she said, and shook her head. "Comes with the *damned* job." She regretted that, too; she stood and rubbed her forehead, reached down for her mug of tea.

Rene's face had taken on—mild pain. "You only do the best you can do. You can't make everyone happy. *You've* told me that."

"I'll remember it tomorrow, maybe." She lifted the mug, felt the remnants of the tea slop against the side, and tried to smile for his sake. She failed. "I think I'll go out to the dock."

There were stacks of coolers on the deck, the cheap kind, ice sliding beneath his feet, an occasional person leaning prone against them, staring out at the water. Graham braced his hands against them, kept his footing most of the time, and caught himself when he did not. He had found two smaller groups when he finally came to crew, grim, each of them. "Anyone keeping a roster of who we took on board?"

One of them frowned—past him, rather than at him. "Got someone circulating. He's got the list."

"Did any of *you* see the ones who came aboard?"

The frown found him, directly this time. "It was a little crazy. I'm sure you noticed."

"You'd remember him. He'd stand out."

"Sorry. Find a guy named Carey, he's got the list."

He slid and slipped back along the rows of coolers. He found one of the men still leaning against the cooler, legs splayed, looking like he wanted nothing better than a strong drink. Ice melted from between his fingers, held in an open fist to one ear. He knelt, and felt the cold worse looking at the ice. "You okay?"

A grunt.

"I'm looking for someone. Blond. About the same height as me, a little shorter. Brown jacket."

He waited. Resisted the temptation to slap the ice out of his hand. "Look, *are* you okay?"

No answer. *Christ.* His gut felt worse, and there was bile in his throat. His nerves twanged—he would not think of that, it was no good, *no good*, he just had to find out, that was all. He stood, gripped a cooler, and reached for another with his left hand as a cold wind came down the row and blew icicles into his hair and the back of his neck.

He had begun to shiver, violently, when he finally found one of the smaller groups again, leaning against the rail. "Hey," one of them said. "You better get below deck. Warmer down there."

"I'm l-looking," he said, and willed his teeth to stop chattering, "for someone. Blond. Brown jacket. Same height as me. A lit—little shorter."

They looked at each other. "I'm going to get him below deck," the first one said.

"Damn it! Have you *seen* him?" Another shiver, near convulsion. He sucked in air. "Is he *on the ship*?"

Another one, opposite him, leaning on the rail, looked at him. "I know which one you're talking about. I seen both of you at the beginning. Didn't see him after that."

Silence, in the rest.

"Come on," the first one said, and gripped his arm, pointed. "That way."

He yanked his shoulder away. Heard a distorted *can't help some people* behind him, ignored it. He went back the way he had come—relative shelter in the rows of coolers when the wind wasn't blowing a certain direction, but it meant ice on the decking. Too slow. He finally found an opening, came out on the opposite side of the deck, and kept the guard rail hard in his right hand.

He made faster progress. He found another group, finally, two-thirds up the ship; he slowed down, coming close, and made himself still, breathing until the muscles stopped spasming in the cold.

No luck, again.

He finally found *something*, back in the rows of coolers on the other side. Two men and a woman, crouched on the watery deck, gnawing on cold mussels; the lid of one cooler was open. "Eat up," one of the men said, and jerked a shoulder toward the cooler.

"I'm looking for someone," he said, and had begun to sound repetitive and hopeless even to his ears. He gave the description anyway, and the woman looked up at him, and this time there was something there. He clutched the top cooler, braced himself, standing there.

"I saw him toward the back of the dock." She shook her head. "I can tell you he was doing fine, considering."

That was something, at least. "Have you seen him around here?"

"I don't think so." A gentle subtext of *no way in hell.* "We made it, but there were three of us. We pushed through when we saw the ship pulling away. Just made it."

He looked at her. One of his knees gave, no warning.

"Listen, they've got some of the crew cabins opened up below deck. Got a heater running down there. Blankets. You're not the only one they pulled out of the stew."

He sat, mechanically, and felt the cold surface irreparably far, far beneath his pelvic bones.

Quinn relaxed, took a sip of the drink and set the glass back on the table. *Perfect.* Excellent flavor.

The music system filled the corners of her apartment with O *Mio Babbino Caro* while she examined the household figures, her Friday night activity—her private tradition to relax with a glass of warmed sake, to get that out of the way and spend the rest of the evening on the upper balcony when the weather afforded it, as it did tonight.

This table she had found in an estate collection, the ivoried dining chairs at another, and she had been fortunate the scale had fit, better even than she had anticipated.

Her weekend cook had found a filet of salmon, still nearly frozen, but with herbs and flat on the dish without a speck of godforsaken rice, it would make a king's dinner tomorrow night. It sat in the refrigerator. She could not rely, now, even on her favorite restaurant to produce something of that level. *They* had decorated her usual entrée with only four pieces of seameats tonight, tiny mussels awash in garlic butter sauce to disguise the telltale texture that said it was frozen meat. A ridiculously small portion of vegetables and herbs sat on top of the bed of rice; mainly rice, every day until she was sick of it.

She was on the last item of household business when the phone program blipped and formed its box in the corner of her screen. *Jenning Crote, Residential* glowed in the text area. "Video on," she said, and moved the sake out of the way. She was still presentable. "Yes?"

"Sorry to call you at home." That was automatic. The rest—wasn't. The *residential* was highly extraordinary, and Jenning's face had taken on a red hue; her nose was strangely white and pinched, for all that. She thought of asking if she was well; waited, instead. "There's a shipment in dock."

"What?" She sat up, straight, in the chair.

"I just found out. I've got calls—there's riot already. There, at the dock." One palm up, calming: it did not work. "I've got people going down that way, the ones we can reach."

God damn— Quickly, calmly: "Chauncey Benner didn't communicate this?"

"No. Not until now." Equally efficient; Jenning had learned, working under her, what worked. "I got off the call maybe three minutes ago. I called Gabrielle; she's calling the others."

"Could Benner have told anyone else?"

"Not that I know of."

"Check Gallagher Crote. Find out if she called him; check Rebecca Wright, she's down that way. Get staff on it. *You* get down there." Jenning hadn't mentioned how she knew there were riots, doubtless had some source or other, but Jenning kept those close to her chest. True to form—time later to find out, not now. "Who started the riots?"

"Can't say, yet. Dock staff's involved, that's all I know at this point."

Damn Chauncey Benner! This would not stand, this would not be forgotten— "Is the ship still in dock?"

"It docked only briefly, supposedly. It pulled away once the riots started. Nothing's sure yet; I'll pick up the security recordings when I get there."

She restrained her fist; the table could take it, her fist would not. Past experience. "No shipment transferred? At all?"

"I don't know yet. I assume none."

"Find out." A glance to her watch; she *knew* what time the shifts ended, on the peninsula— "And find out how the dock staff knew to be there at the time a shipment came in, damn it."

"I'll look into it."

God have mercy on them, when Jenning arrived—Jenning was the best one to do it, when it came to that—but Jenning *had* failed, if the shipment had come in without warning. "We'll talk about the rest later. Find out *everything* you can for now, every damned little detail, you understand? I don't care what you've got to do. I'll call Media. I want everything we can damn well get on record. Tell your staff to leave them to it; they worry about *their* part."

A quick nod; the line flicked off before even that was finished. She tapped it back on, said, "Transportation, straight to the ferry. Emergency call." Waited—her next call would be straight to the media buildings, she would have to bypass Sylvie Coubertin for the instant, but would make up for it—next to Loren, and then a personal visit, probably best, if he knew she was coming. *Pray* that he was home; she could not waste time trying to track him down somewhere in Jefferson or in the residential district, but there would be hell to pay if he wasn't immediately informed, no matter that she could well handle it better, would *rather* handle it.

The ferry captain picked up. "Yes?"

"I'm rerouting you." The phone system would display her name and position, no need to waste time on that. "I need you up in the Jefferson residential district as fast as you can get there. Where are you now?"

There was a startled silence, then: "Grosvenor business district, heading south. I've got passengers."

Damn. "Drop them back off at the first stop on your way back up. You're not authorized to say anything except that there's an emergency. Nothing else. You'll take on Jenning Crote in the residential district; follow her instructions."

"Understood."

"Any problems, contact me directly." She tapped it off; fortunate that the ferry hadn't been any further south, but still not as far north as she had hoped. Jenning would arrive in time for the investigation, nothing else. Pray that she had staff far, far closer to the warehousing district.

Very possibly no food delivered, now—*far* worse, no ship.

Wait.

For the moment, she reconsidered the call to Media. She had the luxury of three minutes, perhaps, would take it. She leaned her chin on her fingertips.

That a shipment had come to dock they would not be able to suppress. There were too many involved with the dock crews alone, and the word was doubtless already out. It was possible too that word was out that the ship had departed, but perhaps not. Depending on the damage inflicted by the riot, the dock personnel involved could be taken to the hospital for observation, and might easily stay there for the space of a few days.

She did not *know* that the ship had not simply anchored in the waters off the port. Unlikely—but if she did not know, no one else knew. The next would be Kaettegut, if the ship did come home. Chauncey Benner *might* keep her hide if she kept that information repressed, might, if Chauncey Benner *wasn't* talking to the Back, as she had sworn she was not.

The Back had shut down communications. Maybe not, though, television. She had known that from the beginning, had proposed it, and the council had factored that into its planning. If so, Decheran had been watching them squirm, and she had considered that already in what she influenced of Media. Sylvie Coubertin had been willing to work with it, had kept protests down to a level better than what she had expected.

If the Back thought they had a ship, a way to their territory—it might be enough to encourage the beginnings of communication.

She reactivated the phone program. "Transportation, ferry."

22

Kellan pressed his back against the concrete of the seawall, in a portion further west of the port where the sludge and sediment had built up into a berm of sorts. The water lapped at his shoes, even so. He had pulled his knees up to his chest, had arranged himself at last into a semi-comfortable position.

His breath wasn't coming so short, now.

He had not ever—hit a man like that. *More* than once. To be so outnumbered, to have to keep going, no other option except to end up like the Kaetteguttan lying on his face and not moving, who could not have been alive, not after what they had done to him—instinct and panic had taken over, but he did remember it, what he had done.

He had wanted to throw away the— he did not know what it was, a tool, heavy iron that had mostly fit into the palm of his hand, loose from some laborer's toolbox and on the ground when he had needed it. He hated it, now; but he had kept it close to his chest and side.

Why couldn't he have memory loss *now*, when he did want it?

He'd found this spot relatively quickly. He had thrown the tool down where he thought he saw a gap between the sporadic glint of watery reflection and the wall, had heard a thud.

Graham had gotten onto the ship. Must have.

They would send another. The ship's crew would have seen there were Kaetteguttans left behind, there had been the ones near him, one with a toolbox itself, swinging *that*.

When he had regained some of his senses, he had felt for his key card. Nothing: the pocket was empty, and so were the others.

His heart still sank, at that. It meant waiting, nothing else. He could not let anyone see his face; anyone Kaetteguttan would get one reaction.

Besides, he had to be here, to be able to see a ship coming in.

He had tested the seawall. It extended above his shoulders in height, standing; it was difficult with the smoothness and the dampness of its surface but he could get back up and over it if he needed to do it.

The ship might not come until Monday, if they went through official channels this time. Two days without food, without fresh water, but he could do it. No other choice without his key card; no way to get into any building, no method of payment if he could.

He just would, that was all; he would not use any energy sitting here, except in keeping warm.

The ship had come back weighted low in the water, full of food and passengers—*passengers*, at least they had gotten that part done.

Chauncey could not blame the captain. They had all corroborated it at the dock, coming off the ship stiff and shivering with the wet cold: riot, intense, and there *were* injuries. Two belowdecks had to be carried to the train, who were now safely installed at the hotel, and with only the aid of the equivalent of medics, nothing of the level Grosvenor had.

Except—she estimated it at only a bit over three-quarters done, in actual fact. Nearly one quarter of the Kaetteguttans were still left on Grosvenor—injuries, tales of a few down, all the way down, but the rest was only speculation: the ship had pulled them out and away and they had lost sight of their comrades' fates with the fading away of the dock. The chances of a very sizeable handful of Kaetteguttans were surely now far, far worse—depending on how Jefferson chose to interpret those riots. Truth did not matter, in these instances, and she had precious little doubt whose people would take the blame for the riot, and for the missed shipment.

Her own chair and office—gave little comfort, in sight of that.

Phoebe tapped on the door and pushed it open slightly, slowly. The red hair was not pulled back into its roll today, perhaps due to it being a weekend, and it was shorter than she would have expected, the ends wispy and barely touching the shoulders. She looked for the familiar cup of tea in the hands, but it wasn't there. Phoebe stepped in, tentatively, leaned against the wall next to the door, her hands behind her back. *Melancholy,* it said, that pose. The eyes.

"You've been doing the best you can," she said.

"It doesn't matter." She gripped the arms of the chair, stood slowly and stiffly, in the joints, and came around the desk to lean against the bookshelves on the left wall. It felt good to stretch, to stand. Slowly— "We're not going to have an opportunity. Not again. I won't." *Kaettegut* wouldn't.

"There are dozens of people who are safe, who are in rooms with a warm bed and a hot meal, who are *home,* who don't have to worry about what's going on outside their walls. They might say your best was very good." Quietly.

"Who have no idea what's happening to their co-workers, their partners." Oh, yes, she was aware of that. Not many women wanted the heavy lifting and hard labor, though there were some—and Grosvenor did not mix with Kaettegut, not like that. Limited choices, and human needs *would* be needs, no matter the circumstance.

"You cared about them. You didn't know them, not one of them. Not that I know of."

"Hindsight's always easier." She shrugged, deeply, deliberately, and sighed: it expanded the lungs, offered a certain instant of relief. She should not talk to a member of her staff this way, had a responsibility for them, to help them develop. They *watched* her. "I know that. I'm glad to have gotten what we did. I am, Phoebe. It could have been worse."

"It *could* have. We have the ship, we have our people."

She made herself smile. "You didn't come in here just to talk."

Phoebe lowered her head, took a breath, looked directly at her. "One of the passengers is asking to see you. He's *been* asking. I think you'd better see him. —But I did want to talk with you. I think maybe going down to the pub or the hotel for some tea wouldn't hurt. A little something solid to eat, a change of scene."

She was touched. *Phoebe,* when Rene was the more nurturing one, and Phoebe was all business, and efficient, and competent.

"I will," she said, and made it a promise, in the back of her mind.

"Maybe after this. Tell the passenger I'll see him, if he can make it in the next half-hour."

"He will. He's in the lobby downstairs."

She waited while Phoebe ran her errand, examined the edges of the leaves of her pothos plant. Phoebe had watered it while she had been away, the soil was slightly crumbly to the touch, did not have the sharpness or dustiness of wanting care. Still—it could perhaps use a bit more water, and it *was* her plant, and her office, and she had been neglecting it.

She went out into the staff area and down the hallway, into the floor lounge. She could find no watering can, but a mug would do. She rinsed one out, filled it with water from the faucet, and carried it back to her office—walked in, intent on the plant, so that she was two steps in before she looked up and found her visitor already in front of her desk, head turned, eyes looking at her. Bruises, a vicious scrape: she registered those nearly simultaneous with the height, at least a foot higher than her.

She held up the mug and tried for a smile, walked to the plant and tried to pour the water in, smoothly, evenly. "Funny how a simple little routine can help at a time like this," she said, and the water was *not* pouring smoothly, it was sliding down the side of the mug and onto the wood of the bookshelf. She wiped it away with her hand and set the mug on a piece of paper on the next shelf. A watery ring spread from its bottom.

She looked at him more closely, coming back around the desk. Some of the bruises were new, angry looking, but some had already gone purplish, and the skin on the scrape had hardened and dried, would begin peeling off soon. "You haven't had an easy time in Grosvenor," she said, and remained standing.

"I'm fine."

Tense, very tense. She offered her hand across the desk. "Chauncey Benner."

He took her hand easily enough, gave a very firm handshake. Hesitated on his name. Finally: "Graham Long."

"I see." She sat back in her chair, leaned back as far as the tilt would take it.

"I tried to get a permit to go to the hospital, temporarily. Back then. I stayed here several days. No one would talk to me."

That was troubling, but conceivable, entirely possible. *Not* sufficient reason. She indicated the nearest guest chair with an open palm. "Who did you talk with?"

"There's a department on the first floor of this building. They wouldn't get a supervisor for me. They told me to go back to Rue. It wouldn't have mattered what I said." He sat, finally, pulled the chair up closer to the desk, so that one shoulder was partially obscured by the piles of paper. "That's not why I'm here. I just wanted you to know."

Intense, decidedly so, in the way he looked at her. There was nothing else: his posture was urgent, strained, his address fine, but the eyes said he did not give much a damn who she was outside of her potential use to him. "And?"

"My friend—the one I went over there for—he thinks the world of you. I wanted you to know that, too. He watched you every time you were on television. I think you talked with him?"

"I think I did." Guarded, before she caught herself. He elicited that response. "Is he still in Grosvenor?"

"We both went down to the dock. Someone on the ship said they had seen him, toward the end, that he was still—that he wasn't one of the ones on the ground. I don't know, after that."

God, he was controlled. "I'm sorry. I *am* sorry. It wasn't meant to turn out like this. I can tell you—I don't expect it to mean anything to you, but it *is* upsetting for me. I don't know how it happened, or why it happened. I know I haven't given up on any of them. I know it's hard to believe after—that," she pointed to the scrape on the face, "but we live in a civilized society. One breakdown doesn't mean it's anarchy. We pulled together after the explosion here, maybe not the best we could have done, but we did do it." A speech she would have to repeat several times, no doubt. "Jefferson took ours with theirs, then. Jefferson is what's in charge over there. Remember that."

"Jefferson's going to be in a damned hot rage that all the food came back with us on the ship. I'd rather not rely on Jefferson right now." With difficulty; the control threatened to break. It didn't. He held onto it. "I think your staff probably told you, I have some information you might find interesting."

She sat back, looked at him a long few seconds. "My God."

"What?"

"You think that's what it will take to make me care? You came to bargain?"

He looked away, for the first time. When he looked back, his eyebrows had drawn together. Still: "I'm not really interested in the politics, if that's okay. Hear me out. I'm not blowing smoke, here. It takes something to get up to this office."

"It takes a request."

"You might think that." He shrugged. "You might want to check with some of your departments, if you really do think so. Maybe not. I don't care. —You've seen my record? You know my career history?"

An abrupt change of subject. She frowned.

"I was in Pricing. In Rue. I did pretty well, had gone pretty high up in the ranks. I was familiar with things. The pricing office in Grosvenor, even so—it was different than I expected."

"I imagine."

"*Not* in the way you imagine. Their system, the way they think. It's almost different theory, everything built on that. They go full-bore all the time. No shifts, no reprioritizing. It's *perfectly planned*. Almost nothing lies fallow. You understand?"

She tried to follow. She did. Earnestly. "You're speaking about the farming unit?"

"Not just the farming unit."

She crossed her arms—but there *was* maybe something there, something just outside the edge of things, enough to sense, nothing more.

"We worked—in Rue—with supply and demand, constantly. With *pricing*, not with planning. Grosvenor does almost all of it just with planning, and they're damned good at it. They don't need to adjust much on their side for their own needs. If they do, it's the result of a slight shift in population or aging proportions, it's the result of long term planning. *That's* a good part of what Pricing does, over there. Nothing like we did."

Just to verify: "And what did you do?"

He gave her a disapproving look. "We watched the markets. Constantly." A frown. "You see it, don't you? In terms of raw materials, *we're* what makes short term market volatility. Kaettegut. Our agricultural operations. To a smaller extent, the Back—but mostly us."

"We produce what's ordered. What's in fashion. It's cyclical."

"That's not how they run. *We* priced Kaettegut's products. We didn't price just according to supply and demand, either, we priced according to the available funds. If metals orders fell, we could price for a bigger proportionate share of the dollar. We used what was in demand here, in Kaettegut, as a guide as to what to price highest—because that supply was short from our own usage. The problem is, they then have to order based on our prices, against what's in demand on their end."

She was humoring him. Phoebe waited to go out for that cup of tea, and she had a hotel full of ones like him, and he *could* be—could have simply thought he did have to have something to get into her office, and this was all he could use. She turned that over, a minute, decided to cut to that, and leaned onto one fist, on the desk. "I appreciate what you're trying to do, but please believe me—"

"You don't understand. I don't think they see it as a supply-and-demand issue. They see it more as a production issue, that we're not keeping up with what they want." He looked down at the carpet, stubbed a toe into it. "That—I didn't learn this over there, I just put it together. We were audited, right? There were rumors—"

This was too close to the edge. *Rumors.* She let some of the annoyance into her voice; he could handle that. "All departments are subject to audit. This was hardly the first time. Now, if you'd—"

"God." Frustration in the tone, in the clenching of the fists. "What's it going to hurt to hear me out? A few minutes of your time?"

She tried for patience, for compassion, prayed they weren't all like this, far more sympathetic in the abstract. "I've told you, you don't need to come in here and bargain. I'm not going to be able to do any more for you if you—tell me about rumors." She laid her palms on the desk. "Now. Ask me what you'd like me to do, and I'll give you a straight answer. There's not any need for any of this."

He stood up, abruptly, took a few steps, turned back around. "All right. Fine." He took a breath, and plunged ahead: "What I want is to get my friend back over here, safe. To ask you to make that happen." Frustrated—but there *was* anxiety, cringing anxiety underneath the tone and the voice, that was there in the tension of the muscles, the quickness of the steps. She *could* understand that.

"You said you didn't have any need for politics," she said. "That's fine. Let's do without them. I'll be honest with you, because that's what you want, and I think you can handle it. Am I right? I can be as direct as you can take."

Another faltering in the control. He closed his eyes, halfway—remembered himself, and stopped. "Please."

But *that* was real, at least. "There are some people one likes, and some that one doesn't. That's natural, if you're human. My first impression of you—isn't much better than the first one I got when I first found your transfer on my desk. I'll tell you that. I don't like that you've come in here with the attitude you're going to get me to do something because you've got some commodity. Maybe you did have to use that to get up here, I *don't* know, but up here it's just a tactic, and I say that in the worse sense of the word. I do like it when you're honest, and there have been spots of that."

He just looked at her, and finally—at long last—nodded.

"Good. We're doing well. What I'm going to say next, you're not going to like, but I'd say it even if you'd walked in here and been honest and perfect all the way through. I don't like that your friend transferred the way *he* did, and I'll tell you I don't much care that you might have been the reason, but he's Kaetteguttan, and for that I care about his safety as much as any of the others stuck over there. I'll do whatever I can to get him back over here, like I'll do with the rest. And I'm *not* in the position to do that right now."

A flush was growing, she noticed it in his ears first. He opened his mouth—

She'd face it with every one of them. "When I am, I'll do all that I can. I'm *not* going to leave them over there if they're not safe."

"I don't see how you're not able to do anything." No stopping the outpouring flood, and she did not try, just watched him. "With all due respect, I've been *over* there. I *know* what they're thinking, how worried they are about the food. I know they've got stocks of dried rice, but they're going to run short even of that. They're already low on the rest. They're going through the last of their frozen supplies, from the looks of the meals they serve. Forget about the groceries—they're closed."

Not bad. She had expected pure emotion. "Oh, I know they'd like the food. Who has the food doesn't necessarily have the power. When that ship was driven away—that ended what I had been trying to do. You understand me? Those men acted to protect the ship. You know the size of our fleet, I imagine. We can't afford to lose one of them. The livelihood of every person in Kaettegut is tied to those ships, and none of them, *none* of them, are going to risk sending a loaded ship over there a second time. Not when this is what happened."

"They weren't after the ship."

"Weren't they? Everyone who got off that ship told me the other side started the riot. It wasn't us."

"They were *angry*. Those kind—the warehousing district—aren't that smart unless someone put them up to it, and if that's the case, then they blew it, damn it! They went for *us*, not the ship. They were past that, they were past reason. *You* hear *me*?"

Irritation—weary of arguing, was her first reaction. She stopped, instead, had learned that much in dealing with Murray.

"They thought we were getting the hell out, and leaving them to it! That's what. That's how I got *this*." A gesture toward his face, the scrape. "A handy little gathering of a bunch of Kaetteguttans right when a ship showed up? You think they were thinking of the food? Come *on*."

Well. She stayed where she was, for the instant, thought on it.

And—*hell*. It made sense, it did make sense, it was possible, and it was—perhaps—where she had gone wrong. The fingertip put precisely on her mistake.

Had the Back done the same? If it had, if it had pulled its people in advance—it meant *its* actions had been premeditated, no less than that, which was damned ominous, and made, truthfully, her stomach suddenly roil.

The Backers were Primean, and Kaetteguttans weren't, and if the Back *had* pulled its own, it might certainly not have the same effect as her pulling every Kaetteguttan she could get.

Which meant—she had done the opposite of what she should have. She should have left the Kaetteguttan crews where they were, should have even sent a small number more, purely a good-faith gesture that said she *was* interested in getting food shipments started again, that she put her own on the line for it.

It was counterintuitive, very much so, but it might have worked; Jenning would have understood that, would have sent it up the line.

Was it too late?

She pressed the intercom pad. "Phoebe?"

Tinny voice: the speaker's quality was intermittent. "Yes?"

"Can you send Rene in? Is he still here?"

"He's still here. Just a minute."

Graham Long simply stood there, looming behind one of the chairs. He had watched her, she realized, had taken a few steps back, waiting.

It *wasn't* easy for him. A rush of sympathy ran through her veins, somewhere in her chest.

She nodded at him from her chair. Used the compliment of his name: "You do have a perspective, Graham, that I don't have. I'll say that. I do appreciate hearing it." She stood. "Rene will take you back to the hotel. I'd like it if you'd tell him what you told me, answer any questions he might have."

And he nodded. Once. But he was—pleased, or saw hope again, perhaps.

"You said you had found someone who had told you your friend wasn't injured."

"I didn't say that. *They* didn't say. They just said he had—still been going, I guess." But he was watching her, carefully, and the tension in him had changed. Not any less. Different. "Listen. We knew someone over there. She holds some power. He would have gone to her, in an emergency."

"If I can get through—*if* I can get through, which isn't a guarantee, I'll try to get a question through to her. Her name?"

"She's the head of Aptitude. Jenning Crote." Almost as an afterthought: "She was here for the hydroponics audits."

She almost started. A *department* head—of Aptitude, which was no insignificant department, and had a psychology specialization to boot. Kaettegut's version could dictate whole lives, she did not doubt that Jefferson's did any less. "You're certain?" she asked.

"We had talked about it a little, before, just a couple days ago. He wanted to go then."

I have two nurses who say it was unsolicited. Bullshit.

Quinn Rhodes was Jenning's direct supervisor. A Proteraiotita councilor, good *God*, and Jenning not someone lower down in Organization's staff at all. A department head—well versed in psychology. *That* was who they had sent.

"I'll put in the request," she said, simply that. Rene was at the door, then, leaning in. She sat, and nearly gouged her leg on the chair, was nearly shaking in her anger. She remembered to look at Rene: "If you wouldn't mind taking Graham back to the hotel, please."

Rene only nodded, Rene knew how to read her.

She leaned back in the chair after he had gone. Leaned forward again, controlled the heat rising in her throat, and pressed the inter-com pad. "I'm sorry, Phoebe. Would it be too much trouble to get some tea?" And when Phoebe had come in with it, "I'd still like to have that talk with you. It might be later."

"I understand." A smile that still held worry, but which for a split second gave her an impression of Jocelyn.

"Thank you," she added, but Phoebe had already gone, and there was only the closed door.

She put her hands around the cup, let it steam up into her nostrils. Inhaled.

Focus.

She could not take back what she had done. The renovation labor-ers sat in the hotel not far from this building, and she had promised them safety, to keep them until the trouble had passed. A few days— she could laugh, almost, at that thought.

Perhaps she could offer a choice: an opportunity for those who had left behind friends and partners, who *wanted* to return, the ones who weren't spoiling for a fight and would not make matters worse.

Jenning—damn her—could more than read that sort of state-ment.

The head of Aptitude. More than her equal, well-connected in Jefferson, and heading that kind of department, in that kind of divi-sion. *That* was *who.*

Focus! Anger served her not well at all, this minute.

Better, she might offer to send some of Gros Morne's own stor-age experts, who might serve some very good use in Grosvenor's warehouse district, where she understood they stored the limited inventory of food that was not immediately needed, and which could be made to work double-time, if Grosvenor had access to the right expertise.

...As long as they would be safe, and the council saw they were all, with their comrades still over there, put into the Jefferson hotel, where there were security features.

Except that Jefferson had not called, not Jenning, not any of the councilors. *That* had been the eeriest aspect, and the most dire—it had meant she was not in a real position any longer, that they had ceased dealing with her because of it.

She took a sip of the tea. Hot, very hot, but it had its familiar twang, and that was paltry comfort, now—but she would take solace where she could get it.

23

Avery Wright, who faced Marcus Gouman, pounded his fist on the table. Quinn felt the table shake with it but did not distinguish the sound from among the voices—nearly all raised, except for Kate Daschen, who sat in Councilor Decheran's accustomed seat and merely watched. Meghan Truong was trying to fend off Andrew Edmond, of all people, and Robert Wright, had only the width of her chair for buffer, and had pressed into the back of it, face furious. A black glare came her way, and stayed; it was easy to guess what Meghan's first attempt at diversion would be if Loren did not maintain a sufficiently tight rein on the proceedings.

Loren had gone to the back of the room, was talking intently to Stefan Coubertin. Impossible to hear them, but Stefan's eyes were intent on Loren's mouth, on taking in his words, his gestures. He was nodding. *Damn!* She was not in the right position, could not move that way without notice—and the conversation was *not* insignificant; she could see that at a glance.

She stood, anyway, began moving that way. Joseph Edmond stepped aside for her, but Avery Wright and Marcus Gouman stayed in her path, and the monstrosity of a chair had been shoved back and blocked her only other course.

Loren looked up, then, and it did not matter. He stopped, touched Stefan on the arm, and made his way up to the front of the room along the other side of the table. Message, flatly delivered: he was not interested in what she might have had to say.

No matter. She'd had her time, a long private conference in Loren's main room, Loren pacing, furious, something most of the others would have given their eye teeth to have had.

Loren's mouth was moving. Only the space of two seats away, and she could not hear him; she swiveled her chair, folded her hands on the table, and regarded him with attention. On her right, Kate Daschen did the same.

"—All *right*," finally wormed through the noise, and there was that note of irritation; she and the others had learned to never ignore it. Out of the corner of her eye, she saw gray-haired Robert Wright look at her. He moved to his seat; there were shuffles and scrapes as the rest found theirs and sat.

"Better," Loren said, though the irritation was not gone: it was there in the lines next to his mouth, his jaw drawn tight. "I see word's gotten around. *Word*. Rumors. The *last* thing we need. I won't ask how many of you knew the topic of this meeting through a source other than one of these councilors, but I will tell you that if it came from somewhere in your ranks, you'd better have squashed it, fast, and after this meeting that will be your first and continuing priority, does everyone hear me?"

Beside her Joseph tapped his pen once on the table, and snapped it into his palm.

Joseph was on her immediate left, now. Half the room had shifted since Councilor Decheran's disappearance, and not for the better: she faced a wall of expansionist power on the opposite side of the table. Thank God for Jeri, calm, logical Jeri Tasco, who made her arguments cleanly and briefly, and was the lone voice of reason on that side, fourth seat down, pure status quo. Without Decheran, too, the resourcists had lost a quarter of their membership in the room; Avery and Marcus retained their small block at the end of the table, but the sometimes-team of Kate and Decheran had gone to one—though that *did* make herself and Joseph and Jeri equal to that contingent now, and Joseph formed a small block with her. But still—together they only outnumbered the expansionists by one, and the weight of the room seemed to have shifted enormously.

Loren was looking her way; she backtracked his last few words, swiveled her chair to face the majority of the table. "Yes," she said. "We do have video. Unfortunately someone took the liberty of covering the lens early on, someone who—" and she carefully did not look

Avery Wright's way, "appears to be Grosvenorian. We can hear after that, but sound alone does not lend us much information. We hear the ship arrive and leave. We hear something falling into the water, four times. We don't know if it was food, machinery, if it was human. We have everyone accounted for on our side. We have two in critical condition still tonight, one in surgery now for severe maxillofacial injuries. The medical staff give them a fairly optimistic prognosis, considering. None have left the hospital; they'll be held for observation over the weekend." She glanced down the table, saw Jeri Tasco nod ever so slightly, comprehension in most of the others' eyes. Avery Wright had chosen to bite his tongue for the moment, but there was color in his face, in his neck.

"That's something we can cover later," she said, and clicked on the recording. With the group one short, Marcus Gouman, who had previously sat at the end of the table, for once did not have to slide over. "First take without the sound; I think you'll find it enlightening."

She let the first part play through. The camera's angle covered only a section of the dock itself, none of the apron. The arrival and movement onto the dock of the Grosvenorian dock workers was rapid, almost alarmingly so. "From the rapidity and the thoroughness of the penetration, I'd suggest something like this was expected. It's not so well-organized that any of this was premeditated to the extent of planning, but they've decided on their course of action. Watch the body language." She used the highlighter, quickly. "Here, and here—two instances, different Kaetteguttans—have their palms up, facing forward, elbows close to the chest. Almost all of the Kaetteguttans—here's an exception—are trying to put physical distance between themselves and the dock workers. Those are calming actions; they're trying to take the tension down." She saw Stefan wince at the first blows; only a few seconds left, and the face of a dock worker loomed, something then in the hand, a cloth, and the screen blacked. "It's clear to see who threw the first punch, so to speak."

Loren nodded. "With sound."

She obliged. It was worse, but it had been right to play it muted the first time; the non-verbal communication was not as easily swept under the language. Coarse words, shouts, mixed accents: Kaetteguttan, and, she had been surprised to note on the first take, Grosvenor's own dock workers. Actually conspicuous, in a heated situation.

The visuals ran out again. The sound continued, and there was finally the roar of the ship, a dull, reverberating *clunk* that shook the camera and its cover: the ship had swung into the dock, was her guess.

"I'd suggest that there was a failure on *our* part," she said, when the sound had ended, and all eyes had turned back to the front of the table, "that we on this council failed to gauge the population's reaction to the missing shipments. Also that we overestimated our own credibility with our own residents, the further south we get from Jefferson. It's not much in geographic space, but it's very significant in psychological distance. Our proof's right there." She tilted her head toward the empty wall where the video had played.

"That's pure party language." From Meghan, directly across the table, whose voice was charged.

"If you want to talk about philosophies," she said, calmly, and tapped one fingernail on the table, twice, "then yes, it's perhaps what you might see the further away you get in geographic distance. It doesn't change our failure here and now. I'd rather stay on topic."

"I saw the staff of *one* department out there," Robert Wright said, and did not hide his irritation; it was there in the voice, the face. "Don't drag the rest of us into this."

Avery flared. "They were doing what was natural for them to do! They saw every damned Kaetteguttan on this side getting ready to make a run for it, and they *reacted*. They were in the right place at the right time, that's all it was. Put your damned hoity-toity staff in that situation, see what they do."

"Regardless." She made her voice even calmer. "We had a shipment, and *we* turned it away. That's—"

"No, damn it, we're not going to gloss over this!" Meghan slammed her palm on the table. "I don't care what you want to imply about other departments, Wholesale *was* there, and Wholesale did what it did. That's fact, not speculation. We deal with the facts, here."

And Wholesale was resourcist.

"I wouldn't talk about blaming any particular departments, if I were you." Coolly neutral in the insinuation—and she saw it score, in the faces of the others. She leaned forward on her elbows, faced the others, ignored the expression on Meghan's face, the open mouth. "It's *not* about blame, this department or that. It's about addressing the problem that's made itself evident."

"Enough!" Loren's voice was loud, to her right, almost made her jump. She saw others turn, saw a scolded expression flit across Meghan's face, and composed her own expression, quickly. "Wholesale *was* there, and Wholesale did what it did. That *is* fact. I'm not going to spend all evening here discussing what might have been or what might be. We get *this* situation under control. You speak if you've got a suggestion that will help going forward. If I hear anything other than that, the speaker leaves this room. Understand?"

Damn. But she had squeezed that point in for Avery; that would be worth something in an alliance. The status quo was equal in number, now—perhaps *more* than equal in that Decheran had dirtied the resourcists' name.

"We've received one shipment." She was careful to speak first, to guard the advantage. "We can get another. We've got to have guarantees, though. Senior staff on hand."

"Which we *would* have gotten if—" Meghan shut her mouth.

She raised an eyebrow, slightly. "I'd say we first need to decide how many shipments we need to replenish our supplies. Avery, can we increase our storage capacity? What's our maximum, time-wise?"

"Thought you wanted to talk about raising our credibility," Robert Wright said, across from her and one to the left. Calmly; he was no fool.

"To which the fastest route is sufficient food. Every day that our residents don't see meat on their plates, we lose credit."

"*Kaettegut* loses credit," Andrew Edmond said. "And we're just going to let the Back slide, through all this? *That's* the real topic, can't everyone see that? This is diversion!"

"I think you know our fate is tied to Kaettegut, at this point in time." But that was dangerous territory; she had been considering it since the shipments had stopped. If Kaettegut *was* shipping to the Back—it would be disastrous, beyond what current conditions could bear. She avoided it, simply, for now. "Our options changed with that shipment. We don't have a choice but to build up our food storage. Even that's going to take some coaxing."

"We don't have to wait. We use the ferry."

Oh, God, that.

"We don't even know it would make it." Marcus Gouman's voice, from the end of the table on her side, so that she could not see him. "We can't afford to lose our own transportation, man! Last I looked, we weren't the ones manufacturing those things. We lose it, we've lost the whole commute."

"We've got the monorail. We can retrofit it."

"You want to cause panic? Change everyone's commute!"

She bent her head into her hand, groaned inwardly. A journey of that length, hugging the coast in a low-slung vessel built for the calm waters of a river, nothing to recharge it once it *did* arrive—a particular insanity of one Andrew Edmond.

"You're assuming a successful negotiation," Jeri added, cool voice of reason. "We have no actual knowledge of the situation in the Back. We can't begin to predict a success or failure rate."

She cleared her throat. "As a matter of fact, I've received some information." Loren knew, of course, even if much of it was still less than one day old to him. Jeri would have had an idea; the others had none. All eyes turned. "Some population estimates—" she held up her hand, before Meghan or Andrew could interrupt, "—that I think we'll all find fairly enlightening. Aptitude types, on top of that. Even our most basic picture of the Back looks to have been inaccurate."

"What?" That, from Andrew. Kate Daschen swiveled to face her.

"We've been doing double duty in my department these last few days. The shipment, and some matters of research. We've had access to some shipment figures from Kaettegut—yes, right there, where none of us thought to look." She did not look at Meghan, who *had* access to some of those figures; above all she did not make reference to energy usage. "Derived from that, using our own numbers—basically, we're looking at an estimated population in the Back in the range of ninety-two, ninety-three thousand. Granted, if we assume this began under Decheran's watch, we're probably talking about a fairly high ratio of young to old—but if that's off at all, I can bet you it's on the low side."

Loren's mouth stayed in its flat, grim line. The rest stared.

"That can't be right," Stefan said.

"We've no way of verifying the numbers they give us. Certainly some of us have visited. We take the traditional tour. We go where *they* lead us. Our eyes are untrained. We see a lot of people, we don't extrapolate numbers out of it. We see the departmental lists *they* supply. They report births and deaths." She shrugged.

"Decheran is resourcist," Stefan protested.

"Some of us feel more strongly than others." She had done her own analysis of Decheran from the available media record and from Decheran's file: Loren had granted that. She had asked Jenning to back up some of the portions where she was anything less than certain. "We've done a profile. It's a fairly simple guess that another goal overrode Decheran's—philosophical beliefs. With a population estimate, we've got somewhere to go."

This was high-profile, was something she'd ordinarily not discuss in the hearing of the council, even in the hearing of another councilor, outside Loren. A fair risk, this time: it kept her solidly in control, and if she handled the situation correctly, all the way through—Organization would move past Environment in rank. Perhaps a demotion for Meghan Truong, if Loren wanted to give Environment a chance at all to regain its stature, a big *if*, but that did not matter. She could hold her rank once taken. That was, psychologically, a hard barrier to cross. *She* knew that. She looked across the table, met Meghan's dark eyes.

Meghan's eyebrows drew together. Startled, very slightly in the appearance, but there.

"You said something about aptitude," Kate Daschen said, the first spoken words from her, and that gave them weight—gave her own next words the same.

A return favor, quite possibly, delivered quickly for her earlier support of Avery Wright. Or Kate wanted only to decipher the situation. It *was* a resourcist in question. "We think she's been engineering that population, nearly three decades back. Yes, it's picked up quite a bit in the last decade or so," and she did not say *since Decheran ran for election*, "but it was already there."

There was a murmuring down the table. Loren monitored it, wary; Kate kept her coolness. "In what way?"

"They've procured a fairly high number of exploration-types, proportionately. Higher than I'd think, for seeking out new veins—it'd have to mean far-scale discovery. Some unusual combinations, too, that we haven't identified a use for: some artistic aptitude, along the lines of craft, architecture. Highly detail-oriented, but still with the ability to see things at scale."

"I can verify that, given enough time." Jeri kept her hands folded on the table, deceptively lightly. "I can't support those population numbers, though. They just haven't put in requests at that level."

"Unless they've developed the ability to propagate existing sets," Loren said, evenly.

Hmn. Straight from her report, but he lent it more credibility than she could give it, on top of what else she had already said; no matter that *he* scored the points. She simply nodded.

"Impossible." Flatly, from Meghan.

"It's that, or they're doing it the way Kaettegut does," she said, as flatly. "Nearly the same end result, close term, if they do it right. The food shipment numbers say an increase in population. It's *been* verified. Three separate sources."

That Kaettegut, while Decheran had been pushing for extra funds for exploration, had not asked for funds for a population larger than reported—did not rule out its participation. It was in fact entirely feasible Kaettegut had been playing a pricing game with the Back, dealing direct in exchange for barter or additional income. The end result would be the same.

She saw a hesitation on Jeri's face, saw the decision made. "We have to consider it," Jeri said.

There was quiet for a pregnant ten seconds.

"So what have we got?" Kate looked down the table. "A split?"

Stefan's face, aghast, had frozen. "God, no," Meghan said, and there was scorn in it, unwise against a suggestion from Kate Daschen. "We control Agriculture, we've got the desalination technology. They use water in enormous quantities, all their processes. We're their *market*."

"An attempt to control the market, then," Joseph said. "Economics. Inflate the prices, that raises their standard of living."

"Control," Quinn said. They looked at her. "It's in the personality. Decheran's getting up there, age-wise. She's been defeated at election; it's not probable she'll be able to mount a more effective fight than she did a decade ago. *That* was her optimum time, and it's when this started picking up. She had the contingency plan in place long before, of course. You know what they said, then. No one from the Back has ever won election. It's got to be a part of the culture. They'd be more aware of it than we are."

"Economics could still be the motivator." Robert argued. "She had

the support from the Back during that election. She has the Back under her thumb, that's control, and this is just the next step. Raise the
quality of living, you've got a legend. Untouchable."

"It doesn't fit. She's more ambitious than that." *Come on, Robert.
Think.* "She's already got the support. Economics, maybe, but just to
guarantee her during the risk period."

"They've got no new funds coming in," Kate said, and rested her
hand on the arm of her chair, swiveled, "no food shipments—we *assume.*" A small delay for that to sink in. "That says no small amount
of planning—hoarding, or they've developed their own capacities."
She turned toward her. "What's the rest of the mix? Any increase in
administrative?"

"Not more than the usual. If they can propagate the sets, of
course—"

Kate shook her head. "They're trying for a break. It's too large-
scale for anything else."

"It's not too big for anything else," Stefan said. His voice was thin,
but he had set his jaw. "Shift of power."

Heads turned, straight down the other side. Andrew suffered a
quick paroxysm of a laugh, nearly a cough. "Good *luck,*" Meghan
muttered, but began to put her hand to her chest. Stopped.

Loren held up a hand. "We're getting too far into speculation.
We *don't* know the problem, and if we can't define it, we can't solve
it. That's the bottom line." Calming: it was the right tack to take.
Faces relaxed, slightly. "This information helps, but all it is right now
is information—in pieces. We need an action plan. The first part is
getting those agricultural shipments started. Quinn, that's your task.
The second is contact with the Back, and I don't give a damn whether
it's Decheran or if it's some poor sod of a assembly line worker. *That's*
our focus."

She looked back down the table at Stefan, appraised him in a suddenly new light.

No contact with any of the councils—made very good sense if one
meant to cut the councils out of the picture. There were few more
effective ways to send a message, in fact, than ignoring the existing
power structure. To *show* them impotent.

Who else would they contact?

Kaettegut. Cut Jefferson and Grosvenor completely out of the picture: Kaettegut had its own food storage, had its own raw materials: lumber, limestone. The two already shipped to the other; very little might remain to cut out the middleman. Pure barter, at first—yes, they could do it, at least for a while, and she felt it in her intestines, suddenly.

If they hadn't found a way to duplicate the genetic sets, if they *were* doing it simply through selective breeding—it would take time, far longer than what Decheran had to work with, but it *would* be a value shift.

Jefferson offered administration, a smoothly running system. No—civilization, a place to look to. Nearly all psychological.

"They would have heard Chauncey Benner on Thursday afternoon." Jeri was speaking, looking at her—a question in the eyes, outside her own topic. *What is it?* she read, there. "They don't know the hauler didn't stay, that we didn't take that shipment. Not unless they've got their own communication lines here, which we *do* have to consider. If they thought we had access to the ship, it might prompt a call in."

She shook her head. "It won't."

Loren looked at her. *Oh?* in the eyebrows.

"If it's a break, she doesn't need us. If it's a power shift," with an incline of her head toward Stefan, high compliment, "she's bypassing us."

He was less than pleased. Dryly, "I hope you have a better suggestion, then, because we're here to discuss solutions."

She straightened her neck, looked evenly at the faces across the table. "It's down to psychology, now, to numbers. To leverage. We campaign for our own people, and we include Kaettegut. *That's* my proposal. It won't define the problem any more than we've got it now, but I'd say we've got some pretty good conjecture—and it won't hurt us. I'm willing to be proven wrong."

Kaettegut! She saw it in the faces, the raised eyebrow, the twist of a mouth.

"Sit and wait." There was disdain in Andrew's voice.

Her palm came up, of its own power, and very nearly slapped the table. *Careful.* She laid it carefully on the smooth surface of the table-top, felt the warmth of her own skin, not far from sweating. "That's right. That's what one does when one's got no raw materials, when one can fit a very limited number of people on a ferry, and we don't have guarantee they'll even give us dock."

"Point," Kate said, unexpected quarter, when she had come dangerously near a loss of temper.

Silence spread down the table.

Loren surveyed them, slowly, dwelled longest on Andrew's face—thank God. "We're all a little frayed at the ends." He stood. "Coffee."

Yes. That was welcome, very welcome; it would give her that ten minutes to sip, to soothe nerves that had gone very tight. The room had gone to feeling tight, to close and warm, and there was strain behind even the cooler facades. She stood and turned to slip into the coolness of the hallway, to let the staff carry the coffee and the trays past her.

The meeting ended very late. Coming home nothing stirred on her street, not even wind. The streetlights had gone dimmer than she had long seen them, were the color of old parchment. Quinn let herself in the front door and took the glass-fronted elevator to her floor—turned on only the lowest of light to lead her across the marble floor of the main room, the two-story windows glossed over and reflective even at that. "Shades," she said, and her voice sounded strange and weary in the stillness; there was a slight hum as the shades slid closed. A dim panel of light crossed the surface of the drinks cabinet, lit the rim of a rocks glass, and was extinguished.

"Cancel," she amended, and the hum stopped, then smoothly continued as the panels reversed.

There was a light blinking in the dining room; she saw the greenness on the wall as she crossed to the cabinet, and lifted the glass.

She brought the glass with her, took her first sip as she pressed a fingertip to the touchpad, stood and waited for the message to load.

The screen stayed black but for the time of the call. She almost puzzled on that too long, worn from the meeting, and failed to identify the voice in the few beats before the caller herself did. "Councilor Rhodes," the voice said, overloud in the stillness, so that she moved a finger to adjust the volume, "this is Chauncey Benner. I apologize for calling you at home." A small lull. "I'd like to know if we could talk, even briefly."

Benner. She looked again at the time as listed in the corner of the screen: evening, well into the council meeting.

She sat, set down the glass, considered. No video, of course; she had considered that as little more than a tactic, early on—at best an attempt for more funds—but if so, one that had played its course. Back to that, then—but the number was not the usual Gros Morne one, could be a residence. She *hoped* it was a residence.

"Return call," she said, and waited. The status bar filled, gradually.

Damn! But: "Chauncey Benner," came a voice, finally, and there was sleep in it.

"Councilor Rhodes," she said, crisply. "I'm just out of a meeting; you know how late they can go. I received your message." No matter the Proteraiotita was not scheduled to be in session this week, very little use in hiding that there *was* a crisis; there was, and Kaettegut's failure to provide shipments was part of it. Let Chauncey squirm.

"I do know." The sleep was fading in the voice; no matter, the instincts would not be fully up to par for another few minutes. *Now* was the time. "Thank you for calling me back."

"You're welcome." She paused, deliberately. "I'd told you that I did want to work with you. I think you remember that. I'm still interested in seeing some shipments, as I'm sure you know. *With* notice."

"I told Jenning that I had misjudged—several things. I've been very up front; I'll be so with that. I'm told—that it was not a Kaetteguttan who started things."

She kept patience in her voice. "We would have assured the safety of that ship and crew if we had known the time and date of arrival. Jenning told you that. She's authorized at the highest levels."

Silence, for a beat, then: "I said that I had misjudged some things. I had reasons—there are pressures, on this side, but I'd still like to make it work. I know you can't be far from a crisis, in terms of your supplies. I'd like to help."

"Then we're in agreement."

"I'd like to send some personnel with the next shipment. We've got—very experienced, knowledgeable staff on this side, storage experts. I don't know how your raw materials stand, but they're fairly resourceful, and they're ready to help construct more storage capacity. If that's something you could get approved, of course."

She sat and looked at the black screen. Breathed, once. "I might be able to do that," she said, and thank God, the control was there; she gave nothing away.

This was no one-time offer—if it was genuine, this was nothing less than a sharing of what was a good chunk of Gros Morne's power, irrevocable. And a *real* emergency plan, not a shot at expansionism. Storage where *they* could control it. —"Can I ask what prompted the offer?" she asked. *What's the other side of it?*

"When we first talked, you said you'd like to work with us. A partnership—is something I'd find, myself, very appealing. I can't tell you everyone here would."

"Oh?" *That* was a bonus. This *was* turning into something—was very interesting, in light of her own proposal to the council tonight. Just numbers, pure numbers; Jefferson and Grosvenor could *not* stand on their own without the Back, not yet. If Decheran sought a switch— the trick was old, very old, had been used once against Kaettegut; the same could be used against the Back, if Decheran forced it.

Except that there was prejudice, carefully honed over that first number of decades, which was no simple thing. There would be no easy reversal—and here was a hint that there was a flip side to it, that Kaettegut had built up its own prejudice? She could almost laugh.

"I'm sure you can see what prompted my actions. More than I can tell you," Chauncey said: relatively smooth change of subject. "The safety of every Kaetteguttan is paramount to me. I saw them—perhaps to the exclusion of what I should have been looking at. But I think you can understand that. We *did* try for that shipment, Councilor. We never intended that you should not have it. We *were* trying to work with you. The actions of the people who started that, at the dock—is not going to make things easy for me, but I want you to know you *are* a priority for me. By choice."

Emphasis on the last. She looked at the blank screen, appraised the words in the absence of a live video feed that could tell her much, much more. *Maybe not so bad.* There was potential here, after all.

"I'd like to talk further about this—all of it. It's late now, of course," she said, and pushed her drink away. No need for it anymore. "For now, how many storage staff?"

"I can send at least twelve, next shipment. The most knowledgeable. Some of the renovation staff, too, if you can put them up in Jefferson and guarantee their safety. If you need more, let me know."

Twelve. The most knowledgeable, though: that was significant, very significant. "I'll need to know the time and date of arrival if I'm to ensure there are no problems." She hesitated, very briefly, but some *quid pro quo* was in order for something of this magnitude. "The dock staff who were present last time won't be there. We didn't take their actions lightly."

She heard the relaxation occur, slight, in the voice. "That's—very good. It will make a difference on my side. I won't tell you it won't be a challenge, but—I've got a better bead on things over here now. I won't say this hasn't been beneficial in that respect."

Tantalizing, but she had to stay on task. First priority: "Can I get a commitment to a date and time for that shipment?"

A pause. "I can try to make it Monday, normal time. I'll call you to confirm Monday morning. A good chance of it, I'd say, and full load, but it might be frozen."

Monday. Still—that was less than forty-eight hours away.

And, *It might be frozen.* That was key: that pinpointed precisely where the problems might be, additional insight. "I'd prefer it sooner, but Monday will do. I'll expect your call, then."

"Councilor." Before she could disconnect. "I have a request for Jenning, if you don't mind passing it on."

She considered saying, *Jenning will take your call*—and thought better of it. It might be preferable to keep the number of contacts minimal, from here on out, direct to her each time, unless she allowed it. "What's that?"

"We have several missing from yesterday, on our end. One in particular I'd like to ask about, if Jenning would call me. I understand she may know him. In the meantime, if you could give me an idea of the status of all of them, it would be an immense relief to some of the people over here. *I'd* appreciate it, Councilor."

Damn. There was the matter of the one, whose head injuries had proven too severe. She had received word of that during the meeting's second intermission, funneled to her through an aide in the hallway, paired with an update on the maxillofacial surgery—which she had duly passed onto Avery. She stiffened her spine. "Everyone was sent to the hospital, no matter the apparent severity of the injuries on the site. You understand. Eight—will be fine. One is on life support. Head injuries. They tell me—they don't anticipate a recovery. Too much swelling inside the skull; they weren't able to release the fluid quickly enough, didn't have access in time. I'm sorry. We haven't given up entirely."

There was a slight sucking in of breath on the other end. "Can you provide the name?"

"I don't have it with me. It's at the office. I *don't* want to provide the wrong one, you understand. I can call you back with it."

"I'd appreciate it."

When she disconnected the line, the room had gone darker. *Just tired*, she thought, and one of the lights did smear when she looked at it; she blinked, and it was as clear and gold as before. She stood, took the glass back to the drinks cabinet, poured the liquid back into the decanter and replaced the lid.

Still—she walked to the bedroom and turned down the sheets— there *was* to be a shipment Monday, on schedule, and then there was the matter of the storage staff to finesse with Avery Wright, with Loren. She took a breath, slow, let it out and simply sat, on the cool downiness of the bed linens.

24

Graham sat in the same hotel—thank God it wasn't the same room, even if it might as well be; there was the wooden armoire, a twin to the one that had so impressed Kellan—what seemed an eternity ago.

It had rained the night before. Chauncey Benner had come in with raindrops clinging to her forehead and shoulders and hair, had not given information that he had not already known—had promised to try to obtain the status of those left behind, to have news for them by the next day. He had gone back up to the room, sat in the chair and watched the rain run down in crooked rivulets on the glass. Hours—there *was* nothing else, Jefferson had not shown any of it on the media, not a single mention, and that said they would not. He had set the television to record, anyway.

So she had not rushed to call Jefferson, to inquire. *I'll put in the request*, she had said, and there had been something there—surprise that either of them would have gone to Jenning, maybe, which said she knew something of Jenning, from the audits, and that the impression hadn't been entirely good.

What *did* Kellan think of him now, if he *was* all right?

If Kellan was not—but he did not think that, not anymore; he had been through this once before. He could not have dreamed *this* in any case, any of it, same damned position, down to the same furniture, the same impossible expanse of bay—worse this time because of his own clumsiness, and now he did not know where he stood. Did not know if there was any hope at all.

Kellan would never regard him the same. It had already changed, had just not played out to its finish.

He had broken Kellan's trust, that was the worst—from this perspective, from this side of the bay. Kellan had believed something that was not quite so, would have found everything, with that, mutated, distorted.

There were some of them from the renovation crews who had talked last night, huddled standing and waiting in the lobby, refusing the tea offered them by a front desk clerk when the restaurant had long since closed—who wanted to get back to the dock, to talk the crew into taking them back over. Angry talk, *this* time they'd be prepared, this time they'd know what they were facing.

The ship likely wasn't at the dock. The ship had dropped them off, had been gearing up its engines again in the shadowed green-gray waters well before they had boarded the train.

No. Kellan would have gone to Jenning; it was what Kellan had wanted to do just two days before they had gone to the dock. Kellan would have made it to Jenning, would be there now, safe and inside an office somewhere.

Kellan had just begun to talk again, on the way to the dock. And if Kellan had started talking— It *wasn't* all over, perhaps; there was hope, maybe, small and piquant in the back of his throat.

The phone blipped in the other room while he was bent over the sink. He grabbed the hand towel and whacked his hand into a corner of the wall, trying to get out of the bathroom too quickly and into the other room. "Answer," he said; did not want to take the time to get to the unit. "Hello?"

"Graham Long?"

"Yes." Tersely; he could not stop it.

"This is Phoebe from Chauncey Benner's office. Do you have a few minutes to come up this way?"

He took a deep breath. In person—they had bad news, they did not have simple news, one or the other. "I'll be right over." *Don't go anywhere*, he wanted to say, *don't let her go anywhere*; he could not stand that, could not stand even these few minutes.

He left without his jacket, realized it when he was already out on the street and there was a wetness in the air after the rain, and puddles along the cracks on the concrete. He kept going.

She *would* have news. Kellan's faith in her had been founded on something, something he did not see so well, but Kellan had seen it. Now—it would bear out.

He had to stop in the lobby, to buzz in before he could breach the damnable second set of doors in the absence of the normal operating hours. "It's Graham Long," he said into the unit, when someone answered.

A few seconds passed, and there was a click; he pulled open the right-hand door, and there was the sharp-tasting smell of cleaner dragged through the stale rug on the limestone floor, the coolness of pale walls reflecting humid light from the doorway. The elevator was warmer, thankfully, and he tried to breathe deeply, to relax his shoulders.

Phoebe was waiting when the elevator doors opened. She offered a hand—a surprise—and pressed her palm against his when he took it, a tiny spot of warmth where he did not expect it, when he had not warranted any closeness with anyone in this department.

"She'll be right with you," she said, and turned and led the way.

Chauncey Benner was on her way out of her office, wiping her hands on a napkin—she stopped when she saw them, and he was again struck by her physical smallness, that she *could* command such presence across a desk. "There you are," she said, and he searched the eyes and the brows first for any small hint, and saw the quirk of one corner of her right eyebrow—trouble, and his stomach crowded into his throat, "I was after another plate for you, but we can share. You haven't just eaten?"

Eaten? She had changed direction; he followed her into her office, did not think to turn to Phoebe in thanks, in time; the door clicked into its doorframe before he had turned his head.

There was, on the edge of her desk, a plate of canned fish and sauce on crackers, stacked two thick in places—a few napkins. Chauncey indicated one of the guest chairs with her head, pulled up her own desk chair and sat. "I know what you're thinking," she said, and took and balanced a thinly layered cracker, carefully, "how can I eat at a time like this. Not much energy if you go too long, though. One needs to live. I imagine you haven't had much meat of any kind, yourself, for a while."

"No," he said, and pulled up the chair, and sat down. The cushion sighed.

"This is temporary, you know." She held the cracker in the air, still, and looked at him. "You're all going back." And she took the bite, and chewed.

He looked at the food, the white smarminess of the sauce, and his stomach swirled. He picked up a loaded cracker anyway, held it gingerly while its odor rose.

"Do you have a time frame on that?" he asked, even though she had framed it in a way only designed to offer comfort—that, leading to what was not good news. All doubt gone on that front, now.

"Nothing definite, but I've told everyone from the beginning that this was only intended to be a few days' length. Just enough to get the shipments regular again." She looked at him more directly. "I'm sure you know what happened at the dock didn't help. It *wasn't* our fault, but the crews aren't going to want to go back there. No one wants to endanger a ship again."

He said nothing. Nodded, finally, because it was polite.

"The shipments do have to start up again, of course. There's no alternative. Jefferson has said it will guarantee the safety of the ship, that the people involved—were operating of their own accord, and won't be at the dock when our shipments begin coming in again. I'm prepared to announce the *possibility* of Wednesday as a return date, at the hotel. Depending on how things go." She lifted a finger. "That's between you and me. It's not certain, and I've more information to obtain before I'm ready to speak to all of you. Until then, I don't want it getting out. I think you can do that."

Wednesday. Three days.

"Please eat," she said, and wiped her fingers on her napkin.

"I— I'm sorry." He looked at the cracker in his hand, finally set it back on the edge of the plate. "I can't." Something—a finger in the back of his throat, something like, kept him from asking, kept him only waiting, and hoping, and not wanting to hear the answer. Acid was already rising from his stomach, tasting rancid.

Mercifully: "I did speak to Jenning." A small pause, the barest of shrugs. "I'm afraid I can't tell you much. She hasn't seen him. I'd say she was honestly surprised to hear the question."

Oh, my God. He sat still, only watched her, watched every quirk of her face, her mouth.

"She knows who he is. She said she'd check on it, send someone down to the house." She wiped her fingers again. "She said she *was* in the office yesterday, that she didn't have any messages, that the lobby guard didn't call. —I *will* call you if I hear anything else."

"The others?" he said, and it came out uneven—but it *was* there, he had control.

"They were all sent to the hospital. All of them, no matter where they were from, no matter their level of injury. I have that from the Proteraiotita itself."

He swallowed, forced the acid back down. It surged back up, so that he could taste it again on the back of his tongue. *Oh, God.* Kellan would not have gone to the hospital, not if he was conscious. He swallowed a second time. "How are they?"

"I know one person's injuries are severe. I don't know about the others except that they expect them to recover. I've asked for names. It's the piece I'm waiting on before I address the group." She looked at him. "Phoebe or I will call you as soon as we know something. I'll do that no matter who it is."

It was a dismissal. Courteous, but there—and she had said all that she was going to say.

He stood, mechanically. Heard a distant *thank you* that was possibly his own voice, went through the door when she opened it for him, walked to the elevator, and leaned against its wall when it came.

There was a piece of cheese, aged, in her refrigerator; Jenning had been slabbing off small pieces, here and there. The vegetables she had long ago eaten, a shame, but they'd have gone bad.

She limped out to her favorite chair and settled into its welcome plushness. The limp—she had accepted that it had become part of her. It *could* become signature, lend her a certain notoriety; of course she had thought of that, had dwelled on it, hard, the day she had realized she would not send the cane back to the hospital. Symbolic, that limp; that cool, light metal of the cane. She had *not* been taken down, could not be taken down in any mere human action. That which had destroyed whole lives had not destroyed her.

She had walked down the hall with Clare at her side, and *there* were two who had survived the explosion, in view of anyone who wanted to look.

She had not forgotten. Oh, no.

To have Quinn take over the conversations with Kaettegut now—

Jenning had left the last conversation with Chauncey in the right place. She would have reentered that relationship in an infinitely precise manner; she had rehearsed the mood, the turns of phrase for the beginning, before it could turn and the conversation lost certain predictability.

Except Chauncey had called Quinn, instead. That Chauncey had routed a request for *her* through Quinn—said she had misestimated in the last conversation, that Chauncey did not have the stomach for hard negotiation.

She had been nearing the point, not where near-trust had begun to form, but where dependence had created an atmosphere ripe for it.

There *was* the Back project, even if that was almost certainly temporary. She still had the Back's aptitude codes list, was still feeding Quinn information—valuable, every speck of it. She had kept notes, this time, meticulously, would need them not only for future reference but to validate her role in the research. Quinn would not have given her much if any credit for it before the council; if she had, it would still be Quinn's department, *Quinn's* foresight to assign it.

She'd like to meet with Stefan Coubertin again. No likelihood of that anytime soon; she had sent staff, low in the department and anonymous to any outsider, to scope things. The times he had been in his office he had been barricaded in, was near-constantly on the phone.

It would be the same with all of the Proteraiotita, she'd imagine. Still, the active role was a positive sign, indeed. She had half a thought to send feelers to Marcus Gouman's department in Environment, to find out if he was taking in the same volume of calls, of meetings outside his offices.

She had come up with those population numbers. She had not given all the sources and technique to Quinn, only enough to show it plausible. She had kept to herself the reports funneled to her from her source in the pricing office, parts of the food usage reports.

Bits of Agriculture's yield, in certain departments, could not be accounted for, basically; had been going on for a long, long time. And she'd be willing to bet the Back had been receiving that extra yield, and that every bit of it had gone, somehow, through Councilor Loren Fifty.

—Oh, he *was* transparent to anyone versed in psychology, and she had perhaps the better view sitting outside the council, able to objectively pick apart the tidbits from Quinn, the appearances on the media. He played relationships too, differently than she did, but it was right there. Loren Fifty, very little doubt, was pulling the strings to some extent on both sides.

Which meant it was not agricultural *production* tampering, as Quinn had thought. Easy enough to figure, once one had enough of the pieces—unlikely as it had been for one person, outside of Loren Fifty and his staff, to have access to those. It came down to this: with a population level higher than what was reported, there must be sustenance sufficient to maintain that population. Her own audit records from her time in Gros Morne showed that what shipped, on record, to the Back was not sufficient for an increased population. Even at the highest ship capacities, at higher loads per shipment than reported, there would not be enough.

She knew from Graham Long's unwitting assumptions early on that agricultural levels were uneven—but there seemed to be no problem with limestone or forestry, which went straight to the Back.

The effect of the experimental agricultural units in the Back itself would be negligible, even if started earlier than Fifty had acknowledged. There would simply not be the scale. The experimental cold-water fish cultivation, on the other hand, could have succeeded, could have reached a scale of its own in a fairly unlimited space, depending on a variety of factors. *Could* have. How consistent it was, how consistently they were able to harvest in open water, was a question. But it could produce an unevenness in Kaettegut in certain categories—the fish hatcheries, seameats—if Kaettegut was shipping varying amounts of yield.

Fifty had merely switched tactics. A new game, an alliance with a former adversary to bypass the status quo and resourcist contingents, who inconveniently held one chairman back from what were strong expansionist tendencies, admittedly watered down for a predominantly status quo populace, and in the case of Quinn, would likely serve on that council long past the time Loren Fifty held the reins.

Fifty could not overtly act against the populace's favored philosophies and still remain popular, that was what it came down to, in an elected official's role. Could not, short of an emergency.

This qualified as an emergency. And if Decheran appeared to go out on her own and expand the population of what was already well over one-third of the planet's population, and with that transformed Jefferson and Grosvenor into a significant minority—well, that left Loren Fifty to save the day, likely by proposing to expand their own population. *Retain the proportions*: that would almost certainly be the cry.

The wholesale change of a planet's philosophy. Damn, yes, on Fifty's end it would have been worth even a slight potential for loss of control.

It was downright *convenient* that Marcus Gouman, under the authority of an expansionist known for a heavy hand, had finally succeeded in terraforming the northern patch above Jefferson. After five decades of small, strung-out successes and large failures—it was no coincidence, it could not be. Room for more population, straight up the only route available for expansion short of the Back itself.

Convenient, too, that Marcus Gouman had been selected for the second peer delegate's seat.

She stretched her shoulder over the arm of the chair and set the empty plate on the floor.

She had answered Chauncey's request as soon as she had received it, in the office, had kept out of her voice every speck of disappointment. More importantly, she had left herself the opportunity for a return call, had come back *here* for that.

She brought the laptop up to her knees and toggled the privacy-record function while it put the call through.

"I've received some word on the house," she said when Chauncey came through on her office phone. No visual, but that was normal. She had the earpiece ready; inserted it and immediately had better sound.

"Jenning," Chauncey's voice said in her ear, in greeting. "Thank you. Good news, I hope?"

"I'm afraid there doesn't appear to have been any activity," she said. "Two bags of restaurant food on the counter that haven't been refrigerated and that probably haven't been moved, judging from the rot level and the condensation on the counter beneath. Nothing in the office, either. He hasn't coded into the building."

"Oh." A long silence. "Well, thank you. It means something, that you checked on it. —I'm waiting on names from the hospital roster. Councilor Rhodes should have that to us soon. We'll hope there's something there."

An opportunity, in the first part. She heard it, took it, and framed her words carefully in case the call's contents did get out. Ambiguous, no mention of her in the individual, specifically; she could argue she had spoken for Jefferson—but Chauncey *should* get it. "Chauncey. We *can* work together. As allies, not opponents. I *know* Kaettegut." Far, far better than Quinn. "What happened before—let's correct it. That simple."

"That—" with an uncomfortable tone, as if Chauncey had winced, was scratching behind an ear. "I don't know the time yet, but it'll be there. I'm trying for tomorrow; if that doesn't work, it won't be later than Tuesday. I can promise you that. And you *will* have the time. I've been talking with the councilor about some arrangements."

Damn. She made her voice carefully neutral, let only a slight edge slip into it. "Good."

There was another long pause—that began to grow awkward, and she wanted to slap the arm of the chair in frustration. She opened her mouth, finally, when there was nothing else to do, but Chauncey at last spoke. *Very* hesitatingly: "I *was* wondering... I don't know if it's your department, though."

"Yes?"

"Just between you and me—would you be able to send me some information on those experimental agricultural units, the new cold-water fish program?" The briefest of pauses. "We've got only the most basic of information over here. We saw some on the media, of course, but it wasn't explicit."

She felt a kick inside her rib cage. *Of course.* What had Kaettegut been thinking? What had *Media* been thinking, broadcasting that to Kaettegut? Unless it hadn't. Small matter; there had been Kaettegut-tans in Grosvenor with televisions in their main rooms.

Asking that was an enormous risk, on Chauncey's part—but they had cleared, then, the hurdle of near-trust. Her own response, in terms of information, in terms of secrecy, would determine whether they stayed there, if they had the potential to move upward from there. "You know those units aren't on sufficient scale to mean anything," she said, anyway; smokescreen. "Not so much of a worry."

"Now." A great deal of meaning, in that one word.

"Decades, at least. But *you* trust me with that, I'll trust you with this much. I'll get you what I can. I won't promise it'll be much. Between us. Understood?"

"Yes." Honest, at least. "Just information that's more readily available over there, maybe. Nothing that would cause trouble."

Hmm.

"If you don't mind me asking," she said, smooth change of subject, protection of benefits already gained, "you were notably hesitant to promise anything in terms of shipment not even a week ago."

"I've been working to develop a rapport with the crew of the *Corundum*. I did—warn the councilor to expect frozen foods. I'm working on what I can guarantee. I'd rather do that at this point, get shipments going again. It's just a matter of building. Small steps. We'll get the rest up and going, don't worry."

Which, combined with the earlier delay, said there was almost certainly far more trouble in the northern province than Chauncey wanted to admit.

"Wise." A tacit stamp of approval might be going a bit far, but the warehouses *were* empty; individual refrigerators and freezers were all that held them over, now. She could not risk that. "All right. I'll get what I can for you. By the end of the week, if I can."

"I—do appreciate it, Jenning." The name as afterthought, forced technique. "I appreciate both. We'll talk soon, then."

She ended the call, sat there and looked at the grate. This was progress down lines she had not expected, and she was pleased, grimly pleased, even in the danger of this game.

25

The ship did not come.

Kellan wrapped his arms around his knees for warmth and huddled into his jacket, listened to the sound and the slop of the water lapping near his feet, and looked out into the near-blackness until he'd wondered if he had gone blind, and *hoped*.

Yesterday had been the worst. His stomach had gnawed at its own lining. He'd leaned his head back against the seawall and tried remembering his meal at the restaurant Friday evening, every bite and every aroma, the clink of the metal tines of the fork against his teeth. By the morning his muscles were cold and quivering, had cramped into the position he'd slept in—and it was Monday, he could hear movement above and behind him, could see the suddenness of lights reflected on the water and had to close his eyes against it at first.

He should not have run—but that was no use. He had run, and he was here, and paying the price. He *would* pay it, would not complain. It was where he was, simply that. He had gritted his teeth, had watched the minutes and the hours slowly tick away on his watch, watched the pale strips of light on black water.

There was no bright white dot of a ship's beacon at the last, and the district lights were clicking off, leaving less and less reflection on the water.

The air chilled, and it drizzled, again; he lifted his face to it and cupped his hands, licked the moisture from the skin when there was not enough to fill even the creases in his palms. He pulled the hood and jacket closer before he began to shiver hard, pressed back into the wall, cupped his hands and blew into them: temporary and flitting relief, but it was still blessed comfort in the dampness.

He waited until long after the last light had gone off. He stood, and a cramp seized him; he bent double and breathed until it passed. He reached up, found the cold metal bar of the railing where it went into the concrete, slick with the passing drizzle, kicked the sludge off his right shoe, and put his foot flat against the wall. Quickly; he got his other foot placed, was reaching for the lower railing bar when that foot slipped, shoe treads still filled with sludge, banged his knee hard—but he had it, barely, and reached up with his other hand, got a good grip.

First try. That was hopeful. He knocked his toe against the wall, felt more than heard the sludge rain down, and placed the foot again, higher this time. He hauled himself up, and it wasn't graceful, but he was up and over the railing, and only breathing hard.

He was filthy. There was no hiding it; if anyone saw him in any kind of light, he'd set off all kinds of alarms. He brushed off the worst of it, but most of it stayed stuck to the dampness of his clothes.

This is it, then. He started walking: openly, along the railing.

He made it into Jefferson, freezing cold and wet, at near four-thirty in the morning. The ferry did not operate in the middle of the night, and he could not have taken it in any case, in his condition, and one of the only Kaetteguttans left. The wetlands had only been passable because of the river's eastern berm, but it had not been stable, had collapsed in several places. Wading blind across those spots, feeling for solid ground in layers of frigid, slippery, underwater sludge—had been hellish, had taken hours; his skull felt like it was trying to split open.

He made it to the first of the outlying buildings, sat in the shadow of it, and let his head pound.

The pounding slowed, at least, with his pulse. He stood, finally—gingerly, without moving his head. He'd have only limited time before the ferry began running in the more dedicated from Jefferson's residential district.

He got to his building in reasonable time, and the headache had *started* to ease; the pounding had gone, but his skull still felt painfully tight. He scouted all sides, selected the western wall for the shadows behind the heating units, and wedged himself in the space between the building and the last heating unit.

He bent his head and closed his eyes for the wait. *Relax.* He let his muscles ease, around his skull.

...He slowly became aware that his left side was vibrating. He snapped his eyes open, turned his head—found a dark, dim metal sheet, his shoulder wedged against it, and the metal the source of the vibration. His mouth was dry; his teeth hurt where he touched them with his tongue, trying to muster a swallow.

He suffered a quick second of panic. He cracked his shoulder socket, bringing his wrist up: half past nine, and there were voices somewhere distant of the vibrating of the heating unit, which meant it was the morning, thank God, and he had not slept hours past the time he should have.

He worked his way out of the spot, stood, and tested every joint; felt one last time for the tool and found it had grown warm against his skin. His clothes were still wet almost to his chest, but the fleece of the jacket had dried into a sort of crunchy dampness.

He brushed off his pants, habit. It did no good, only chilled his hands more.

Now. He held up his head, walked out to the front of the building, to the stares of two women going the other direction on the sidewalk. He passed them and did not look, just turned into the entrance and got through the doors and into the lobby.

The warmth hit him first, stroked his forehead when he walked under the doorway vent, and then he was enveloped in it. Every muscle relaxed; his right knee nearly buckled.

People stopped and turned to stare. The guard behind the desk was getting to his feet. He felt something rush through his veins, hot and good; he walked over to the desk, stopped a few feet away from the counter, and looked straight at him. No nonsense. "Jenning Crote," he said.

The guard hesitated, looked instead at the woman nearest the desk, who had stopped, mouth open; he looked at her, and back at the guard. "Jenning Crote, I said." Through clenched teeth. It came out a snarl.

When the guard still vacillated: "*Call* her. She'll want to talk to me."

The man pushed the earpiece into his ear. Reached for a button. His voice, when he spoke, was cold: "Who should I say is asking for her?"

That coldness snapped something deep down in his throat. He could *sense* something crack, something faint and rare. He maintained control, still, *felt* the eyes on him, the attention. "Kellan Long," he said, clearly, and heard the silence carry his surname the width of the lobby. He reached out mentally, gauged the breadth of the emptiness around him: no one within two yards—*good*. He would not allow anyone within arm's length; he did not know what he would do, but did know in the new experience of a few days that he could do—a lot.

He kept his shoulders tense. His feet were thankfully in good position; he let his weight settle in both soles, checked mentally for flex in his knees.

The guard frowned at him. "She'll see you." A hand up, before he could move: "*She's* coming down here. You stay here."

Condescension in the tone. His ears burned; he felt heat rise up his throat, his neck, felt his hands warm. Astounding, when he had been so cold for so long, when he had sat chilled and tight just on the other side of this building. He kept his mouth closed, only looked at the guard, hard, steady.

Some of the people started moving. Not fast; the ones near the edges of the lobby, close to their exits, not at all. He turned his head toward the woman. She stood there, still, had closed her mouth. Her skin had gone tight at the corner of the eyes.

He felt his eyebrows curve, pull at his eyes. *God. He* had done this to her. His muscles relaxed, of a sudden; he saw his own change in her reaction, in the way the strain eased in her shoulders, her skin.

She put one foot back, put her weight on that foot. The guard tensed, looked— "Well!" came a voice that grated: "Look at *you*." He snapped his head that way, saw Jenning coming down the hall from the elevators, leaning her weight on her cane. She stopped several yards away. "Well, come on, then. You're not making *me* work."

There was familiarity in the voice, overmuch. He saw the wisdom of it on the instant, felt it in the loosening tension of the spectators. He consciously relaxed his shoulders and straightened. Walked toward her. No one moved to block him, to stop him.

She did not speak until the elevator doors had closed, solid. "So," she said, shortly, very differently than her demeanor in the lobby. And: "You look a mess."

In such close quarters, he could *smell* himself, suddenly: wet clothes, salt, dried and re-dried sweat. Mud. He turned and looked at the side wall. "Thank you," he said. *Not* to her comment; his tone said that.

She dredged up, from deep in her throat, a sharp syllable of what might have been a laugh. "You're welcome."

It *did* mean something. He had not been sure, would have been less sure if he had let himself think about it. For Graham and himself, when they had something else to fall back on—yes, it had been an option. An *option*. Now, he looked at the doors sliding open, at a hallway he had not seen, and felt—worry, regret, a tangle; a strange kind of warmth that she *had* claimed him, had defended him in front of everyone.

It was a last resort. He reminded himself of that. Everything changed, everything *had* changed.

Take it a little easier, Thomas had said. *I've been through plenty. You do, when you get older. It always goes back to normal.*

He was here, he had closed a door by coming here, and it *wasn't* going to be normal. No matter whether this was temporary—*God*, it had to be temporary—the balance had shifted away, had moved out of reach. In him, in everything.

Loren's executive assistant had arranged the meeting with her. *Not* where Loren ever went; this was the northernmost edge of Grosvenor, a clothing shop upscale for the town, but there was nothing on the racks that Loren would even look at, would certainly not wear.

Still, there was Moira, browsing through a rack of men's clothing: rather heavy casual wear.

Tevin came around one of the taller racks in the back before the shop attendant could assail her; Quinn could see, before he came around the corner, his light brown hair wisping away from his scalp even at his faint velocity, his pale forehead. "Councilor Rhodes," he said, with a slight nod of the head—*very* slight; it was always the proper titles with Tevin. "Councilor Fifty is that way."

Further into the back, then. She spotted a display of silken scarves already boxed, face out, one in a simple, vivid cinnabar. She stepped that way, fingered the fabric: a rougher line ran throughout. Chinese silk, fair quality. Adrienne might not mind it. The attendant had ghosted her way on the opposite side of the counter; she glanced up and caught the waiting eye. "Wrap this one up, please," she said, and lifted the box, and handed it across.

With the attendant busy, she made her way back to the dressing rooms. Gwen, familiar presence, stood in the hallway outside the first door, a man's gray field jacket lying across her arms. "Quinn's here," she said, to the door.

"Come in, Councilor," floated, muffled, through the door.

Gwen shifted the jacket to one arm and produced the key card, opened the door, and stood back with her arm still on the knob and waited for Quinn to pass.

Sizeable room. Large mirrors. Loren sat in the room's only chair, the wall hooks behind him draped with hangers and casual clothing. Charcoal-dark slacks, an open box revealing short boots—a pair of something close to sports pants, for heaven's sake. "What the hell are you doing?" she said, and added a dry nod: "Councilor."

"I've received some news." He leaned back in the chair, stretched out his legs and crossed them at the ankles. He gestured to the narrow bench built into the wall, opposite the door: "Have a seat."

Typical. She looked at the cushion of the chair beneath him, the flat surface of the bench—walked over, selected the bench's corner, sat and leaned her back into the hard *V* where the walls met.

"It appears it would be best if I take a leave of absence," he said.

She stared at him. "What?"

"I've been the recipient of some... messages. Nothing more than a nuisance," with a wave of his hand, "but my staff is convinced otherwise. I had it looked at." He abandoned the casual pose, leaned forward. "I've had the best on it. They can't determine where, yet. It could be from any direction at this point. Until it can be pinpointed, I'm considering—not taking any undue risks. After what happened in Gros Morne... the world just doesn't seem a safe place these days."

Shocking—but *that* found its mark, and she appreciated it not at all. With anyone else she'd have called it, but this was Loren—and that was an insinuation. Galling, when Loren had been the one to step in when she could still have salvaged the plan, when she *could* have had Chauncey Benner replaced as agreed—and should have. Loren had left her in one damned awkward position to be implying something like this now.

Protection of the status quo, keeping the system operating smoothly, maintaining the control—had failed, evidently, quite miserably. It would not have, perhaps, if she had been left to manage things on her own, if Loren had not cared to use her directly for his own ends.

No matter. The current Kaetteguttan situation *could* be used. If Loren was out of the way, even temporarily—

"This is news to me," she said, evenly.

"It will be to a great many people, I imagine." Just as easily. "I won't be addressing the whole council. I'll talk to a few, of course."

That meant she was one of the first, a compliment—or perhaps not, particularly with an allusion of that sort floated so early.

"It won't disrupt much, I would hope. The council is capable. There are procedures for this kind of contingency already in place."

That jolted. What *did* the law specify? Perhaps a temporary appointment—

He was still talking. "A peer delegate, of course, the first appointed. That's the law, that makes the most sense. —I'll stay away only as long as is necessary."

She stared at Loren; he could *not* be serious.

Marcus Gouman or Stefan Coubertin, in that chair.

She could not remember which had been announced first; they had been announced in the same inaugural speech. Neither even at the division level, neither in any danger of getting *near* division level. Coubertin, inexperienced and naïve, no matter his performance on the council during one evening meeting—Gouman, vocal, stubborn, habitually dissatisfied.

"I *may* not be far, depending."

Oh, hell.

But that said something else: an elaborate strategy, possibly some kind of diversion. "Well, there's that, at least," she said, and watched his face for the habitual wrinkle in the corner of the right eye, slight, the kind of manner that said he *was* negotiating with more than one party. She did not feign concern, knew she should. "These messages—there's the possibility they come from the Back?"

"There's the possibility, of course. If this thing's on the scale young Coubertin suggested the other evening—I'd not put it past them. We *don't* know who or what's over here. They've had time to put things in place. I don't count on Decheran for subtlety, for anything she could set into motion getting under *our* radar, but what we're turning up suggests otherwise, at least in some small fashion. That makes it appear, I'm afraid, that we're getting a bit out of touch."

It was criticism—but ammunition, too, for an expansionist to hand to the status quo party, and for that reason, suspect.

"That will need to stop, of course," he said. "I don't say we're perfect. The system needs refining. Any system does. If Decheran highlights that, fine. That's a favor, in my view. An opportunity. We've become too distant, too strung out. Division heads don't know a line manager from Adam, until that line manager doesn't know what *we're* about, why it's to his advantage." He tapped one finger on his thigh. "Unification. Perhaps a reorganization, if it comes down to that."

Mmn. That said, plainly, that *some* division heads were not able to control their own constituencies, that Loren had already picked them out, was toying with their divisional structures. A transfer, here and there, to someone more worthy; it would not be the first time. That he shared this information with her, here—this time, Organization stood to gain. Almost certainly.

...If she played things right. That was the stick Loren was holding out.

It also said—Loren had *not* been forced into running; Loren had simply taken it as a convenience, had designed a litmus test, and was handing an opportunity to everyone on that council. He would have his informants. Andrew Edmond and Stefan Coubertin easily came to mind. Herself, in some partial capacity.

"First things first," he said, and was glancing at his watch. He pulled the shoebox closer, took out one of the boots, slipped off a shoe. "You did very well the other night, Quinn. That's *exactly* the kind of mindset we need to have. It's down to psychology. Numbers."

Yes. But—even Kaettegut? It had been controversial; she had known it when she had thrown it out there.

"I know I can count on you to keep things headed in that direction.

It's what we need to be doing." He looked directly at her. "It's very important, Quinn."

No doubt others were being given separate, very different marching orders. She nodded.

But it *was* what needed doing, and she had the ability to do her part, more than anyone else had ability to do theirs. No, *she* had the edge; she was the one who was in here, one of the few he had called in. To know the others—would give her far more of an edge, but she knew better than to ask him that. Loren did *not* reveal his partnerships; one surmised and deduced from evidence given, the extra instant of eye contact in a meeting, the telltale partial concession on a hard-fought issue.

He slid the other boot on, had to push to get it over his heel. He tried it, put his weight on it, wriggled his foot. "One other thing." He looked at her again. "I'll need you to ensure the transition goes well. Stefan Coubertin, of course; he was the first announced. I anticipate some on the council won't take that well, and they can really take it whatever way they choose, but the law is clear. You understand? I'll trust you in that."

Her lungs deflated. *Good God.*

She had *just* begun solidifying an alliance with Kate.

To have to back an expansionist, no, more than that—to help push his appointment through, which was what it would require—would ice things over considerably with the resourcist contingent. Kate and Avery would aggressively support Marcus; Meghan Truong would almost certainly buck party and push for it. A temporary appointment, hell, why not? Marcus would be back, cozy, in Meghan's division soon enough, and he'd know it. Kate and Meghan alone—added up to a nasty battle.

But if she didn't push Stefan through, Loren would know it.

Damn Loren Fifty. He could make the announcement himself; would not, because this was a damned good way to juice up his damned litmus test.

"All right," she said, cleanly. Added some warmth: "Take care of yourself."

"Don't you worry." He turned his head toward the door. "These boots will work, Gwen. Bring in the next load you have."

The call came in the afternoon, some four hours after Jenning had received word the shipment was in dock. She took it when Gabrielle announced the caller, a department with which she was not overly familiar, but a surname she knew. Port operations, she did know, was based on the peninsula, was one small step up from the dock workers who had rioted.

"Is this Jenning Crote?" the caller asked, pitched lower and rougher than was natural for *that* voice. There was no video image: likely they did not have more than a few instances of equipment like that at the dock, and the caller had not been able to reserve it—or the caller intended it.

"Is that who you called?" she said, irritable; she had little time for games.

"I'd just like to confirm."

"Why don't you introduce yourself, and then I can confirm." It was *not* a suggestion; he had left only a surname, and there were, what, thousands of Burton graduates?—many of them in the warehouse district. She pressed the intercom pad and looked toward the door.

"I don't think so." Equally irritated. "I'll take it I *am* speaking to Jenning Crote. I'd like to discuss a few things with you."

"Specifically—?"

"*Specifically* that you've got in your possession one of the Kaettuguttans from the dock the other night. One who did damage to one of *my* staff."

Ah. So that's it. Well, she had been expecting it, or something of the sort. Had rather thought it would be snide remarks, in the halls, that Clare or Orlando or another of her staff might report it. They'd not dare say it to Gabrielle or to her senior staff. "One doesn't possess a person," she said, mildly, and relaxed back into her chair. "And there's no evidence as to who or what caused damage to anyone. Someone covered the camera." That, with sarcasm. "We do have evidence who *started* the disturbance."

Gabrielle opened the door partway, leaned her head in. She held up the phone earpiece; Gabrielle nodded, withdrew her head, and shut the door.

There had been a snort. "Tell that to the men who were stuck in the hospital all weekend. *I'd* say they felt held. You can play all you want, we know what's going on. I've got witnesses who say he did it."

She let a few seconds go by, could hear the impatience, the hostility, on the other end, in the breathing—but he held, did not speak. "Did what, exactly?"

"He bludgeoned the guy with something—some metal thing, that's what they saw. Stitches all over Carson's head, cheekbone's all shattered, and it *hurts*, he says. He's got a nice strip of hair missing."

So. She hadn't known. "I see."

"He's *going* to answer for it."

"Let me ask you a question." There was a half-second's hesitation, and she went ahead. "Good. How many Grosvenorians were there that night?"

Nothing for a beat, then suspiciously: "We *know* you were the investigating officer—"

"I'm looking for a ratio. Grosvenorian to Kaetteguttan." She picked up a pen, tapped it on the desk. "Let's say, for the sake of convenience, taking into account that some Kaetteguttans got aboard the *Corundum* before it left the dock, taking into account what *I've* heard—six to one. That's a simple enough figure, no?"

"Damn it, you're not going to argue *this* out of—"

She went on as if he hadn't spoken. "How would you feel if you had six people coming at you intending to inflict bodily harm? If you just wanted to get away, but couldn't? That's what they *were* doing, you know, getting on that ship. Because there *are* people like your staff, who want to take the first thing they see and blame it for what's on their dinner tables."

"Don't give me that! If he had wanted to get away, if he was some supposed angel like *you* want to think, he wouldn't have kept swinging on Carson! Carson was down for the count *first* hit with that thing. Self-defense, bullshit!"

If true, that was something. Damn that she didn't have a security recording! Calmly: "I'd have to see the recording, but there are always the same sorts of possibilities in that kind of situation: fear, instinct, adrenaline. There are plenty of Kaetteguttans with stitches, I can assure you of that. With more than stitches. There's one lying in a bed over at the hospital, still. That's the result of *your* staff acting on adrenaline. You can't have it both ways. Your men act on that, the

Kaetteguttans can act on it too. Fair's fair."

The breathing on the other end of the phone sent rage across the line. "You're supporting a Kaetteguttan above your own people."

"I'm not saying that. If you're asking if I'll support Grosvenorians behaving badly, then the answer is no, I won't. I won't support that in anyone." She snapped the pen down onto the desk. "Your staff drove away a ship with enough on it to put food on nearly *all* our tables. Including mine. Including every council member in Jefferson. You'd damned well better hope someone doesn't ask *your* staff to answer for that. Because I can assure you, if you think *you're* in a bad mood, you haven't seen the Proteraiotita in a loss of temper."

There was a silence. "So," finally came across the line, coldly, far different from what she had expected—which put a marker on the level of emotion across the community, these days.

"I admire you, of course, for trying to cross division lines." Another threat, inherent in that; a card she *could* play, if she felt so inclined. "I'll still need to advise you to take up any issues of concern with your division head. You're aware, of course, that any call to this office is on a recorded line."

That was enough. The line deadened. She stood, and stretched; her muscles had been particularly pliant today and the day before, a cumulative effect of a dry stretch in the weather and a consistency in her morning therapy routine, enough so that she had been using the cane only minimally. She took the cane, still, paused next to Gabrielle's desk, who looked up at her and said, "A conference room in Dock Building B."

"Find how many Burtons are in that division. Pick out all the supervisors, put both lists on my desk. With the titles."

She took the sharp left at the end of the hallway and walked past several offices. Duncan looked up from his desk as she walked past his doorway, some surprise in his eyes; she had largely kept to her office for the past several weeks. She nodded. "Duncan."

He gave a nod back, had no time to say anything.

The blinds on the windows in the second-to-last conference room had been closed but light still came in the slats, white from the glare of the building's exterior lighting, and made the shielded ceiling lights look slightly dingy. There was a chair, its back to her, over by the countertop against the right-hand wall, and an empty plate that had held salad, she knew, and a wilted one at that, but it had been all even one of Organization's departments could get.

She walked around the table, could see from that vantage point Kellan Long's head snugged into his elbow, resting on the counter; visibly uncomfortable the way the chair's arm and the edge of the countertop must be digging into skin, but he was still deep into sleep.

"Kellan," she said, and kept her distance; he was not comfortable with her, had shown it in the elevator, in her office. Louder: "Kellan."

He stirred. The neck muscles tensed, made to lift and turn the head, hesitated—began to relax again, but he shook it off, raised his head in a way that said the muscles had cramped with the awkward position.

They had cleaned him up fairly well. There were still the scrapes on the neck and hands, and the same jacket was there, folded over a chair, but the mud and the wet and rank tang of sweat and saltwater were gone. He wore borrowed clothes, of course, and these did not look like him, but it was a definite improvement.

"We're working on getting you someplace more comfortable," she said, and did not sit down, yet. A hotel room, perhaps; she'd have to rely on Jeffersonian security, which was ordinarily fine, but if word got out and someone like Avery Wright protested the decision, she might find out the hotel had released him—after the fact. And she did *not* want to bring Quinn into this, not any further than absolutely necessary.

"It's warm," he said. He did not stretch what were obviously sore neck muscles, had not moved the chair other than to swivel it; just sat there—very properly. Precise manners.

"It's better now to keep you close, that's all. I've had a few calls."

That got some small bit of alarm, in the eyes. He lowered his eyes. "I imagine."

"Do you?" She pulled out a chair, sat, and leaned her cane against the edge of the seat. "They're talking about an alliance with Kaettegut in some circles, some very high levels. That's for only you to know. This is a—tricky time for Kaettegut. As I'm sure you might also imagine."

He had looked back up, at that. "They— With Kaettegut?"

"It's not nothing. We've had a shipment today. Unloaded, no problems. I'd assume strongly it's being distributed now, that you'll have a good dinner tonight. Something better than that." She nodded toward the empty plate, at the one pale, unhealthy shred of lettuce stuck to the underside of the plate lip, something that took a certain vantage point to spot.

His face had entirely changed, went paler.

"The food's going to move off center stage in time, maybe faster than you might think. That's not Kaettegut's only value." The last, phrased carefully. His profile, once updated to take into account his work on this side, right next door—said he was far more effective when he *believed* in his work, that a significant trigger was Kaettegut. That had been in the call from Chauncey Benner. That which had overridden it, in his roommate—hadn't erased it.

"Your administrator's going to be sending some storage techs this way later this week, after things have calmed some. It's crucial, of course, how that's handled, how they're seen."

He was watching her eyes. She made them calm, tranquil. Serious. "A call I received—said you did some damage to a man. They want you held responsible. Several witnesses, apparently; some sort of metal object in your possession."

He looked away. Looked back, and even the lips were pale, now.

She leaned back in the chair, rested her palms on her stomach, and watched him.

He licked his lips. Anxiety, in every gauge— "Is he all right?"

He showed concern, of course; that was par for his profile. But there was *no* guilt. There was just necessity, which combined with a by no means risk-free trek from the peninsula, including, by all appearances, a stretch of wetlands, said there was a very specific kind of backbone in there, a turn toward utility that had *not* had occasion to manifest before. It certainly did not show in the aptitude scores, potentially because of that, and because of the low confidence level.

Ah. This was the pleasure of live study.

She laughed, dryly. "He'll live. Some stitches, I understand. Some minor cosmetic difficulty." And when he had begun to relax, when the chest and lungs began to expand: "Do you have it?"

Everything tensed, again; he held himself very still, and turned his head toward the window, at the white light coming in between the slats.

She waited.

When he turned back, he did not look at her, not directly. He reached into his right pocket, extracted it—nearly the length of her forearm, a dull steel alloy. He leaned forward, handing it across to her, and her hand sank unexpectedly with the weight.

It had a long, narrow handle, a tapered section that looked hand-forged, the entire tool weighted heavily toward the end: a sort of small, blunt knob with a four-sided, smaller cube projecting and grit worked into its crevices. She hefted it. Something of this weight, of this configuration, could easily have done worse than shatter a cheekbone, put a series of stitches into a man's skull. Hell, yes, he had wanted to get away; had maybe gone a stroke too far, but he could have done far, far worse.

What those dock workers had thought to do, what they thought they had faced, had *not* been what they had expected, that was the long and short of it. A surprise—to himself, undoubtedly, too.

She looked at him, and saw he had lost much of the conviction in his muscles, even the politeness, that he looked out the window again, and this time, there was a dullness in the expression.

She let its weight settle onto the table, slid it toward him, and withdrew her hand. He looked at it, at her; it stayed on the end of the table.

"A good symbol for you," she said, and stood, and reached for the cane. She got to the door, turned back to look at him. "You'll be safe here."

She *could* send him home with a staff member. There was no security to speak of in Grosvenor, but it would be harder to trace, certainly. People would be at the restaurants tonight, the ferry would be near empty.

She put her hand on the knob, opened the door, and walked into the hallway. No—Jefferson was the better choice, the safer of the two, and she did not intend to lose him at this stage.

26

Quinn sat with the cup warm between her palms, inhaled the heady scent of late-morning coffee—and watched the news conference on the screen against the back wall of her office.

"We've received word that indicates—well, that my office may not be safe at this time. Neither my office—nor my person." Loren began by addressing the reporter, by the river somewhere; the wind was whipping at wisps of his hair, swaying the shock of hair at the center of his forehead. "If I may—?"

It was *not* a question. Handy that he had not speculated on the source of the threat, she mused, while the camera turned and framed him squarely with the dark river behind—the white lights of the ferry to the left.

"It's a tenuous time, and I'm working on it—you can be assured that I and the entire Proteraiotita have been working on it, and will continue to do so. But it's not a time to be imprudent. We take our duties seriously, and any threat to that equally seriously, and we'll prosecute the bearer of any threat to this sovereign state." A pause, solely for drama; she did not roll her eyes, but she thought of it. "I'll be closing my office temporarily, but I will *not* be idle. I'll be working on this, I anticipate, more effectively in the absence of my usual obligations. The Proteraiotita will install a temporary appointee in office according to the procedures established by law. There's no need for pioneering new legislation, because our forebears saw the possibility of a need for this, and prepared for it. Prepared *well* for it. These procedures have been proven in history, in the same system of government, and in similar crises, and more than once. They'll work for us now."

Plenty of credit to himself, she noted; never one to pass on that when it came to the general public, not once. Well done, this time—he *was* getting untold mileage out of it, was setting himself up as nothing less than a legend. No other chairman had done what he proposed to do, not since the first century.

This kind of action brought into play associations of heroism, of sacrifice, of uncertain times ending in triumph. For *all* of Prime, including the Back—to which Loren was playing with this kind of language, just as much so. And that itself said he had information that the Back very feasibly *was* listening in, and that its leadership may have had that capability all along.

By not announcing his successor, too, he had left the Proteraiotita with the potential for significant play on the media, significant leeway in addressing the Back as he had just done—a brilliant ploy, a mere flip of the palm that returned power to the council and left them free to act, simple as that.

She brought up the phone program when the broadcast had done, when the final glory had faded. "Media," she said, and when she had gotten past the receptionists and Sylvia Coubertin's face appeared on her screen, somewhat out of breath: "Sylvie. Off the record—did that transmission also go to Kaettegut?"

Syvlie's nostrils pinched, slightly. She leaned in. "*Off* the record," she said, "yes."

Well, that was gratifying, at least.

———

Clare had made fresh coffee for the afternoon, Jenning tasted it in the first sip of the cup she had brought down the hall. Damned weather was getting ready to turn; there had been more hobble in her step, but her office was warm, and the chairs around the table had new cushions. Clare's doing; a fresh blue-and-mustard stripe, altogether too perky for her taste, but not so flat and lifeless as the last. She had padded the back of her desk chair with one, scrunched it against her lower back when she sat down, and that helped relieve some of the twinge there.

Kellan looked much more himself again, sitting at the table across from the desk. Very clean, at least, in a bleached white button-down and slacks, professional in the way of a lower-level Jefferson staffer, but the mannerisms had changed, had gone subdued and economical. The first spoke to a change of environment, simply that kind of discomfort. The second—said she had not fully sold him on the idea of a Jefferson-Kaettegut alliance, that he held reservations, maybe even suspicions. And that said at least a fair portion of Kaettegut might view any overtures, whether supported by an administrator or not, in at least partly similar fashion.

Which was not entirely unwise.

"You're sure you wouldn't like some coffee," she asked, for this second part of the session, and held up her mug. "Fresh batch."

"Thank you," he said, but shook his head.

She shrugged. "If you want something, just say it. The more I understand, the more it can help make things go more smoothly, more quickly, between us and Gros Morne. Things you take for granted."

The same carefully neutral expression, but the fingers were moving. She waited.

"I'm sorry I didn't ask this before," he said, and she thought: *finally*. "I was—it was quite a—"

"I understand," she said, and put solicitousness in the tone. "I do. Are you feeling a bit better now?"

"It's nice being settled somewhere, even if—temporarily." A valiant try: "The hotel's nice."

Honest. That was good. "I'd like to get you something a little more permanent, of course. You know—" and here she tread much more carefully, and slowly, "I do know what it's like, maybe more than you think. One less than you, of course, but I woke up in that damned hospital, too. It's unsettling. Caught up in things without your permission, that feeling. I've *known* not-home."

He looked at her, and the expression was guarded—but he *did* want to fall into it, wanted that comfort.

Powerful, that, in him. More caution called for on her part, still, in that: he was perhaps not far from becoming aware of it in himself, and without that trigger she could do far less, both for her and for him. "You'd like to know specifics. About what I said, about Kaettegut."

A bit of the guardedness dropped: not much, but there was a kind of relaxing. "Who thought of it?"

"Who *thought* of it? That's hard to say. More than one person. Councilor Rhodes proposed it formally to the council." She took a sip of coffee: good and hot. "Chauncey Benner had a hand in it. We've been talking. It was nothing formal, things simply went that way. We were amenable to the idea. Relations have been limited to too few dimensions. Food, goods. There's potential there for much more than that."

Still polite, neutral: "In what way?"

"Well, let's start with the big picture. How aware are you of the philosophies behind the political parties?"

A bit of blood, at that, in the face. "Just in general." Quickly: "I'm learning. It's not—a big thing in Kaettegut, to the average person."

She had thought so, from her visits to Gros Morne; this was a confirmation from another source. Kaettegut was isolationist, focused on the practical and the immediate. Likely it did not consider itself *able* to have an influence. Interesting, then; very key, now.

"Very well you do. It plays a part in nearly everything over here. Maybe not in the average person's behavior or everyday awareness, but it *does* affect lives, and that does very much include the average person." She leaned forward. "What's the extent of the expansionists' ambitions? A little to the north, a couple other land masses? What *happens* if we expand? Now look at Kaettegut. At the Back, even. What do you see?"

He frowned, but: "Different specializations."

"True. But you see that here, in individual departments. Kaettegut, and manufacturing and mining, are departments—nothing more, some think. What they don't see are two time bombs. Experiments, if you look at it coldly; unintentional, but experiments. What's the status quo party's primary argument?"

He hesitated. "A loss of unity, I think."

"In a centrally planned society, that means something. Means lives. A loss of unity means a loss of control. If you can't get food, if you can't get treated water, you don't live. Coordination is everything. But what have we already seen begin? What's the *theme* of the events these past few months, if you had to put your finger on it?"

He spread his hands. Shut his eyes for a few seconds. "Difference. People taking control into their own hands."

"Difference." She emphasized that. "*Culture.* People grow apart with time and space. Space means delay, and that means separation, even with our communications. We've got two narrow bays right now, that's it. Get past subsistence and survival, take more than a hundred years, add some population, and you're already seeing the branching today. *That's* the crux of the argument."

"That was—centrally planned, though. Designed from the beginning."

She looked at him over the mug, squinted one eye. *Revealing.* In more ways than one. "You're talking about the nature of power, but that's going further than we need to go right now. It's enough to say centralization won out, and *has* been successful—in a limited space, in a limited time. Not bad at all, if you know how risky a proposition colonization can be, if you have some grasp of human nature. Man is not rational in numbers. Often not rational as individuals, either, but groups are something else entirely. That's another part of the argument."

"You're saying it's ending. That expansion is already happening in some ways."

"The system is being challenged. That's quite different. If we're going to succeed in a way that we know works, *this* has got to be made to work." She leaned back in the chair. "This is all between you and me, you understand. And I don't pretend this is the only thing going. This is one part. It's not Chauncey Benner's motivation, likely, I'll tell you that. For you and me, it's a decent place to start. You understand?"

A hesitation. Finally: "We can talk more? Later on."

"If you'd like. If you're willing to learn."

He leaned back in his own chair, but he was assimilating it. Was *engaged*, for the first time.

"I have a meeting coming up. Before that happens, I'd like to talk with you a little more about the province system—the relationship between the two provinces. I've shared with you; I'm looking for a return of the favor. I'll do more. For now, does that sound fair?"

About that, he was still not sure. She knew that; he had answered the morning's set of questions economically, factually, but with a palpable undercurrent of doubt. He wondered if he betrayed Kaettegut, was it. Almost laughable, with the limited knowledge he held, but she was after cultural information, and that he had.

She was tempted to mention that Chauncey *had* been asking after him, had expressed relief when she had reported he had been located, even if that relief had been only in an official capacity. No mention of his return to Kaettegut to join the others; that would open the door to shipment certainties, for one, which Chauncey notably could not yet offer. There *was* the assertion the same renovation crews would come back: ruse or not, she was not certain. Chauncey did tend to deal in face value—but was also quick to learn.

"It's to help," she said. "It *will* be good for Kaettegut, this alliance. It'll be somewhere Kaettegut hasn't been."

"All right." The neutrality was slipping back across his face. Carefully professional, pacifistic.

Tricky. She had the triggers, though, needed only time, if she chose to invest the effort.

He did have a sense of fairness. *That* had made him answer the first set of questions, made him willing to go forward. She had defended him, had kept him in her sphere of protection; he recognized that, had given what she asked. Surprisingly utilitarian, again.

From earlier, she knew there were department heads, that Kaettegut was ordered very like Jefferson in that respect, but there—the department heads were not visible: he could name few of them. Few partnerships. He knew who held the top levels of authority in Rue.

"Who did your office in Rue serve? Not in the sense of Gros Morne, in the sense of customers."

There was *still* that hesitation. But: "I was in a section that dealt with the individual government officials across the province. The outpost offices, mostly. Some of the other government offices in Rue. There were sections that worked with the officials who were inside the different departments in Rue."

"Auditors?"

"No. Logistics, mostly. Personnel, things like that."

Hmm. She'd circle back to that one. "The pricing office. What about it?"

Caution, at that. She saw it flit across the face, in the darkening of the eyes. "It was a separate department in Rue. I didn't handle it."

Gently— "Describe what you do know."

He shook his head, looked up at a corner of the ceiling. "I

know—they watched the markets. I assume it's how they knew to price things. Supply and demand, what we studied in Economics. I don't know."

"Close to Gros Morne's heart, I suppose." The funds were funneled straight there, went out to the various departments. How the funds were allocated—she did not have the necessary access for those reports. Those were within the sanction of Environment.

"I don't know." A pause. "It was a fairly prestigious office."

"Hard to get into?"

"Rare. You had to be able to—think a specific way to be assigned there."

That was an area of interest to her—the way they tested for aptitude, how they assigned it out. Whether the schools specialized.

There wasn't quite enough time for that, though; that discussion would be in depth. She had spent too long on the convincing to wedge this in now, and perhaps it was for the best. She pushed back her chair. "I'm afraid I don't have time for much else. I regret I *don't* have more time today."

"It's okay." He stood, polite habit, no doubt because she had stood. He lowered his head in a nod when she stayed near the desk, and walked to the door, and pulled it shut behind him.

She pressed the intercom button. Gabrielle answered, and she said, "Have someone take him back over. I'd like to talk with the key staff, if you'll gather them together. Whoever's here. Include Orlando."

The inclusion of someone who was admittedly lower level might pose some minor discomfort for some of her own senior staff. Those few had, unlike the rest of the staff, *still* not quite accepted Clare, even in a peripheral role, tended to go exclusively to Gabrielle.

She might need to address that.

Of larger concern was her status in the Kaettegut negotiations. Quinn had passed the original message to her, which indirectly allowed the two subsequent calls—she had taken the opportunity that Kellan's appearance provided for one—but beyond that she had no official purview. The calls had gone well, though: Chauncey was more than open to communication from any front in Jefferson, likely thought her still officially sanctioned to negotiate.

Kaettegut was a portion of Quinn's special project, now, a project on which Quinn had hung some importance. She was not privy to the minutes of council meetings, but that much was evident.

If the project succeeded, Jenning would not benefit from being shut out early in the process—which was doubtless Quinn's point. Quinn knew to balance things; no matter how useful her department might prove, if it was not an emergency, her past participation alone precluded her involvement.

There was a light tap on the door, firmer than Clare's. Gabrielle. "Come in," she said, and turned with her hand still a support on the desk.

Gabrielle waited at the door while they filed in. Duncan and Neil took the chairs, Duncan with a look of curiosity. Audrey, Clare, and Orlando came in together, Audrey leaning against the door, Orlando hugging the wall; Clare came forward to refill her coffee mug from a carafe—which meant Clare was well aware in what role the senior staff accepted her, and where it did not. *Smart girl*, she thought, but it *would* change; Clare was fully junior level, deserved more respect than she had evidently been receiving.

They could think what they liked; Gabrielle, with an assistant's position, had her ear far more than many of the senior staff. Was privy to meetings and arrangements they'd not ever see.

"I'd like to know what you think," she said, and crossed her arms and leaned her hip, instead, against the side of the desk, "about the events of the past few days."

There was a small silence. Neil finally spoke: "You mean the Kaetteguttan."

"You know I've been involved in some of the negotiations with Kaettegut recently." That was a mark of status for the department, lent her staff confidence in her position in terms of the council—and theirs. "We've had some success. No doubt you've heard the port unloaded a shipment today." She raised a palm. "It's still tentative, but there's reason for optimism."

There was a muttering under the breath from somewhere in the room. She merely frowned her displeasure, and waited. Audrey finally spoke, though she'd wager heavily it had not been *her* muttering; Audrey frequently translated the group's feelings. "With all due respect... some don't feel they deserved the dignity of negotiation."

"Kaettegut." When Audrey nodded: "You feel they deliberately withheld shipments, knowing very well our situation."

"They saw a chance," Neil said.

"That *would* have been a unique opportunity." She held a relatively neutral expression. "Have you considered that the Back may have cut off contact with them too, that it threw *them* into somewhat of a disarray? They don't have something on the level of the Proteraiotita, may not have the capability for order that we do."

"Somewhat coincidental that their shipments stopped at the same time as those from the Back," Gabrielle said. "Doesn't that say something?"

From Gabrielle, that was a surprise. She was careful not to dismiss it. "That's possible. I don't think so, not at certain levels of Kaettegut, but I could be wrong. It wasn't perfectly timed if that was the case."

A snort from Neil. "That doesn't mean much."

She let the neutral expression slip, some. "All right. That's fine; I wanted to know. We *don't* know the circumstances for certain. We use what we've got. From what I've got, I'll tell you I don't see a conspiracy with the Back on the part of Kaettegut's administration, not at that level. I see real potential there, and I see Kaettegut in a possibly very strategic position, no matter they're different. I'd like to see this department set up to take advantage of that."

"I don't like it," Neil said. No hesitation. "I've *seen* the reports. Those were our people in the hospital afterward, too, and I'll be damned if they gave themselves those injuries. This one stopped everything in the lobby."

Audrey saw her expression changing and spoke more gently. "People do know he's here. It's a liability. We do ourselves more harm than good."

Point to Audrey—but the gist was, after all, difference; what they were too well trained to say. Disappointing. "If we're to overcome anything in terms of this situation with the Back," she said, and made her voice sharp, "it just might take a change in the way we think. If you want to be at the forefront of something, you take risks. Let others hang back, let others talk. They're not the ones leading."

There was silence again, finally broken by Audrey: "Look at his point of view. With all that's happened, he could resent things. People act strangely in times like this. It's not safe, Jenning. We don't know him well enough."

"That may well be. Some counseling may be in order. I do need to listen to you, and so far I hear two things: that you're worried a bit about safety, but mostly that you're worried about what people think. The second isn't worth my time. The first is. I've got his file, though, and some familiarity with the case. You may not know he came to this side by way of the Gros Morne explosion earlier in the year." She held up a hand. "I know. But he exhibited no aggression then; in fact, he has a decent work record in the building adjoining this one."

"We should take him." A small voice. She looked in its direction, saw Clare leaning against the door, hands behind her back, face gone slightly paler under the gaze of the group.

She raised an eyebrow: a prompt.

"It's a little too close for comfort, for me. One shipment." She looked to the side, to Neil and Duncan, but she kept on. "We set it up like this, now we've got to work with it. That's all. Maybe it's not what we might have picked, but right now they're the only thing going, aren't they?"

More silence. Neil glanced away, toward the office's bookshelves.

Jenning cleared her throat. "That appearance, how we look for having him—could work to our advantage. I can't speak more freely than that, in that respect. As to the safety concerns, I *will* look into it, but if I don't find anything worth my time, I haven't heard anything in here that has changed my mind." Firmly. "Just having access to the culture is valuable. I'll expect *your* help with that, and that means association. Interaction. I'll be watching to see how you handle it, and I'll look forward to your input. Clear?"

There was a shifting of feet, of hands, but she held their eyes. The air had begun to grow stagnant. She waited, and saw a nod from Audrey. From Duncan—a much milder expression.

"And this is, let me make this clear, confidential. You give no indication as to your feelings to anyone outside this room, and you don't let anyone overhear it. You're professional, and neutral, if someone is rude enough to push the point."

She gave a glance to Clare and nodded toward Orlando, while the others left. Clare put a hand on Orlando's arm; he stopped, waited.

"Thank you, Clare," she said, dismissal, and Clare slipped out the door, shut it behind her—under Gabrielle's watchful eye, she noticed, who stood out in the hallway. Orlando, meanwhile, stood where he had during the meeting, had bowed his head some. "Get a psychiatrist from Medical on it," she told him. "*No* hospital visit; they come to him. No medication, either."

"Anyone in particular?"

"None of them are any good. They'll probably send someone junior if it's off-site. That's fine. No more than one, and you make sure those sessions are recorded. I'll be auditing them."

He bowed his head again, lower this time, made it into a sort of nod. *Good.* She could certainly handle an audit of that kind.

"We've got to make an *announcement,*" Andrew insisted from the other side of the table, "no matter who it is. Just make the announcement."

"Oh, that's convenient." It was not Meghan Truong's finest hour; she had been backed into one corner too many, had regressed into obduracy and a painfully obvious position. Pure self-interest: she very apparently believed, far more than her counterparts, that she would hold some sway over Marcus Gouman by virtue of her position as head of his division.

In a temporary appointment, that would not be an irrational tack to take—with anyone other than Marcus Gouman.

"Agreed," Quinn said wearily. She wished she could put her head in her hands and lean onto the table, was half-tempted to do so. *Damn, damn Loren Fifty.* "All eyes are on us. We're fooling ourselves if we think they aren't. Every minute we don't announce—we lose credibility and control."

"This council isn't going to move until we're solid," Meghan snapped. "*All* of us. This isn't a partial decision." Meghan held out for a stalemate; Jeri Tasco had taken a neutral position, could not be talked out of it—she had tried herself, Joseph Edmond had been following her lead, but Kate Daschen was applying pressure there, was holding out the possibility of a not entirely ruined status quo-resourcist alliance, if the vote went the right way.

Appalling that Jeri had not followed her lead—it smeared the party's solidarity, but Jeri was no fool. Jeri did *not* want an expansionist in that seat if it could be helped, no matter the brevity of the appointment; did not want to see the first promising alliance since Fifty had first won election fall to the wayside. Jeri might have read her ambivalence, too, saw herself acting for the party when she could not—but was *not* willing to contradict her.

She *could* break with it, could help put Marcus Gouman in that seat. She had thought of it more than once. Except Meghan Truong had put the nail in her own coffin with her open support of Marcus over Stefan; when Fifty returned, there *would* be reorganization, based on these arguments in this room, over these hours, and the table would not look the same.

"Stefan Coubertin was the first one announced," she said, and forced a matter-of-factness into her tone. "It's in the language of the law. You know my views, but we can't override the law. It's what this council is built on."

"They were announced at the same time, and you damn well know it." Meghan turned her black eyes on her. "You're riding on a technicality."

"It's hard to say two names at once," she said, simply. "One did come first. We follow the law. Anything else reduces the credibility of the council further than we're already doing, sitting here delaying. The populace wants to know there's *order*. That's all. Councilor Fifty made it clear to the entire viewing public that he by no means considers himself off-duty. We're talking about temporary logistics, that's *all* this is."

Robert Wright swiveled his chair and regarded her mildly. "I'm not sure if the council isn't getting worked up over something that matters much, in fact. We *are* talking about something very temporary. Let's not forget that."

Let Stefan Coubertin not forget that, was what *that* meant.

"In all practicality," Jeri said, and most heads turned, "how much jurisdiction will the appointee hold? I'm talking about real authority, whether it's temporary or not. If Councilor Fifty is active, are we talking about a situation where there's a funneling of orders?" She folded her hands together on the table and looked at them. "I think we all know an independent decision by the appointee, whoever it may be, isn't going to matter very much in the long term if the chairman doesn't agree. We're looking at the *appearance* of order, and I agree, we're letting that slip through our fingers every minute we don't make an announcement."

"We don't know how long temporary *is*. We don't know if something will happen. How long has it been since a chairman has closed office?" Meghan was holding onto patience thinly, very thinly. "We all heard Councilor Fifty. Threat of harm. We don't need the *appearance* of a milquetoast in that seat, I don't care how temporary it is. You want order? Put someone in that seat who looks like they've got a backbone, who's had successes in his own sphere. That's what's riding on this."

She raised her eyebrows, glanced at Joseph, and made eye contact. Strategic; solidarity. She would have a talk with him during the coffee break, a break she would call if no one else did.

With Jeri—she was less sure, but Jeri's neutrality could work in their favor with Kate once things were restored.

27

Jenning watched the announcement in her office, on her screen.

The full council came out and stood on the steps of the council building, Andrew Edmond initially at the microphone in his symbolic role as acting division head of Administration, from whence Loren Fifty had come. Quinn stood next to Kate Daschen on Andrew's left, the breeze whipping their hair, eyes scrunched and resolute in the glare of the camera light.

"Stefan Coubertin," dropped from Andrew's lips, and a little icon popped up in the corner of the screen, linked to the law in question.

Stefan Coubertin. She dropped her pen. It skittered across the desk and came to rest next to her meager breakfast plate.

The media was replaying footage from Loren Fifty's original inaugural speech, then: a Loren Fifty with a less lined face, with more beige in the hair. He clearly named his appointments, one after the other: *Stefan Coubertin, Education, Ethics. Marcus Gouman, Environment, Terraforming.* One expansionist, one resourcist, strictly in line with tradition.

Hell.

A peer delegate, *not* one of the division heads, not Andrew Edmond as head of the chairman's division—what she had thought confirmed the instant she saw Andrew lift a hand to grip the microphone.

Stefan Coubertin, with all his idealism and his desire for privacy.

She could truly muse on the announcement in the privacy of her own home, but she had responsibilities first, had worked late, and now Kellan walked beside her in the blueness of the residential district, a stretch of wetlands to his side.

She had assigned Orlando to locating the apartment, to the arrangements. No detail too small: familiarity was everything, and it did not take overmuch time; not the same colors but they were warm, she understood there was a warm taupe in the main room and a sort of milk-white in the larger bedroom.

She stopped at the door of the building now, where thick ivory molding sat against the smooth gray of the façade, the way it did for the windows. Too ornate for her taste. "Go on up," she said, and held out the key card. "The inside's not so bad."

The sky was a small bit deeper here than in her quarter, but it was not distant. She'd not have far to go.

Kellan looked at her. He had tried to take her elbow to steady her when the ferry rocked leaving the Jefferson dock. She had swatted it away, hard. "Go on," she said. "Your own place. I'd like to get to mine."

He hesitated, still. "I'm not going back to Travel, am I?"

"Would you like to?" A different topic entirely. "I might arrange something there part time, until we fill it." It was preposterous just to say it, since that department had subsisted very well on two full time staff for years. "I don't think you'll have the chance to make a difference there as much as here."

He put his hands in his pockets, looked up at the streetlight. "I'd like to thank—say goodbye to my supervisor."

"I'm sure it can be arranged." She used his key card to open the door and nodded in at the long, narrow lobby. "I'm northeast of here, not far. There's an intercom system in your apartment near the front door. You can page me directly from there if there's any sort of emergency. I don't think there will be. We're civilized up here." All of which she had emphasized, in the first telling: safety. She had not said, proximity.

Well. She extended the key card; he took it, but did not make a move toward the door. She let it swing shut. "Good night, then."

She looked back when she had reached the corner, caught him still standing there, turning, examining the street, melancholy in the slope of the shoulders.

Stefan stood inside the door of what was a restauranteur's apartment, an owner who wore a bright red swath of a wrap as she circled the tables downstairs, the way the restaurateurs played with color down in the Grosvenor business district. The apartment itself was surprisingly color-free: gray, with spots of a subdued yellow—a throw blanket laid across the arm of the sofa, the vase on the dining room table behind the sofa. Cramped quarters.

He started to hang his coat on the doorknob, but Tevin was already there, and took it from him.

All lights were off, the glow of the streetlights giving the only illumination to the room. Councilor Fifty sat comfortably on the sofa cushions, an arm thrown along the sofa back, a drink in a wide, simple glass of what looked very like crystal: alcohol, golden in color. He waved a hand toward the adjacent armchair. "Sit, sit," he said. "Tevin, a drink."

It was Gwen who brought it to him, though, in a smaller glass. He settled into the chair, found it comfortably firm. "I'm glad to see you're all right," he said, trying for the correct volume, not too loud, in this atmosphere. The sounds of the diners clinked and murmured below. Someone had done a fine job in the building's construction.

"Quite all right. Very like you to say that." A smile that was *not* a smile. "How are things in the council?"

"Fine, fine." He took a cautious sip, and the liquid numbed his tongue but tingled pleasantly in his throat. Not quite cool, almost lukewarm. "A lot of sitting and waiting at first, to be honest, Marcus and I. Things have settled now. Perhaps a little *too* much. I haven't seen the division heads so—attentive, docile. I'm afraid—I suspect most of the real work is going on behind the scenes."

"Probably it is. Let them." Fifty took a long drink. "I saw your address to the people. Very well done."

Could he *expect* more of these meetings? Here, perhaps at other locales? The same confusion bubbled in his stomach as had been there the past few days. "Thank you."

"I wanted to have a good conversation with you, at least once." Fifty's face retained the same easiness, though it lost the less natural jocularity. "I know you and I share the same philosophies. What you don't know is the behind-the-scenes, what one finds in the chairmanship. You have that for now. You'll need to carry it through until I can get back into that office safely. I know you can do that. This is between you and me, believe that, but I do want you to understand."

No small talk, then. Straight to substance. He leaned forward, and held the glass between both palms, between his knees.

"Big picture, first, all the way back to the beginning. I know you studied history, that you're familiar with Earth. It's a stretch on an evening like this, but think back to—that *mindset*."

"All right," he said, and waited.

"You know that Earth didn't send everything we requested, that the way we're built now is a result of what they did send and what biodiversity capacity we didn't lose in the landing. They turned the entire circumstance of this planet, right there, with that ship—that they chose not to update our information database, with the samples it chose to send, the human stock." He raised his eyebrows, smiled. "Of course that matters. You can bet it was *not* chance. You can bet it mattered to our predecessors, and it matters every bit as much now. It's our inheritance."

"But—"

"Things drift, of course, that's natural, but we stay on the overall course. That's what's important. It's our success on this planet, how we'll stand up against time. Not just survival, *success*."

Coming from Fifty's mouth— Fifty was not a great thinker, had never shown signs of that.

"They said interest had gotten low, that Earth had turned in on its own affairs," he said. "It fits. Things go in cycles."

"After they seeded colonies." Fifty gestured toward the ceiling. "You're a student of history. It's one reason I chose you. You *know* how they operated. I think you'll come to see the centrality of it. The way history played out on this planet, the reason we're structured the way we are, economy on down. That part's worked out very well. But all of this... is only background. It's the hand we were dealt, that's all."

He had not known the part about the information database—that everything about the second ship might have been deliberate. And if he did not, the public did not either. *This* would mean Earth controlled the direction of societies far outside its regular reach, that it had not after all granted complete freedom to those colonies.

Except there had been no contact, which might look, from the outside, like a failure of that colony—that one more planet had perhaps not been so promising when it came down to it.

Fifty leaned further back. "It's still at the center of everything, that stock, those decisions. You say things go in cycles. Others think we're past it, perhaps, that it's no longer a concern. I tell you it's not, at the higher levels, that it's never left. We're looking at it again right now with what's happening, believe me—all of it, the past few months."

One could set things in motion. Except, of course, that he had no real power, that reality was that he was in much the same position as before—a puppet chairmanship, temporary, meant nothing in the long term.

Unless—he used the time to set a reputation for himself. Something people *would* remember, a legacy that might follow him through another decade or two in his post in Ethics, and get him appointments that might set him up as a contender some years down the road.

It would require boldness, real risk. A very fine balance: Fifty could have him pulled in an instant, if Fifty found his performance as an instrument insufficient. He *had* to follow Fifty's leanings, Fifty's plans, to stay in the vicinity of real opportunity—but Fifty would only claim it for himself, would add it to his own legacy. He'd still have the chance to run, then, simply under the banner of Fifty's legacy, and hope that the opinion tides had not changed. *If* he played it right, if he was not just seen as a puppet but as someone who acted the leader, who actively added to that legacy in his own right.

He examined Fifty's face, the lines, the carefully crafted expression, the way all his facial expressions were designed. "The question of Decheran engineering the population—that isn't conclusive yet."

"At this point, I don't think it's far off." Fifty held up his glass. "Tevin, I'm low. —We've got two things going on. That, and a population increase that deliberately reduces Jefferson and Grosvenor's percentage. *You* caught onto it in that council meeting. If it's an attempted shift, using the material from our genetic databanks in an inappropriate way, in an unwise way—it cannot succeed. I won't stop at much for that, Stefan. We've *got* space terraformed to the north. It's not what I'd prefer; it'll take time, it will put pressure on our educational facilities that I *don't* much think they can handle without straining the rest of Grosvenor. It'll take resources we can't get from Kaettegut without allotting the budget and population increase to them, and *that* situation is by no means in control. —You can see it's a slippery slope. It's going to mean, in that aspect, absorbing part of that population. When that happens, there will be, eventually, little use for the remainder of Kaettegut. That essential role—gone." He looked at him, levelly, glass held loosely, wrist propped on his knee. "We're in crisis, that's all there is to it. It's a turning point. You and I are at the helm. History will judge us."

False compliment, that *you and I*. With Fifty, it was just himself.

"The experimental agricultural facilities in the Back," he said.

"Yes, it's also going to mean expansion of a scale the populace hasn't really considered yet. Outside the northern patch—which I attribute directly to Marcus Gouman, by the way—we all know Environment's efforts are not much more successful than they were decades ago." Grimly. "It's known. Most of their experiments have been failing. They tell me it's to do with materials degradation. I don't know about that, but I do know we're going to outgrow Kaettegut, that's just a matter of time. Expansion isn't going to *be* an option. The question is whether it's going to go the resourcist way or if it's going to be true expansion."

Clear, from the tone, which way *he* expected it to go.

"I'll tell you this. Those agricultural facilities are a precursor. We've got plans on the drawing board. Once they work, we'll have facilities on the other side of the Jefferson residential district. The population will support it. After this, they'll support it." Fifty twirled his glass, let it dangle. "It's less well known how well the cold-water fish program has been going, Environment and Decheran cooperating. That was making good progress before any of this happened. We've *got* irons in the fire."

Which meant—he could see the lines connecting the dots, easily, now. *Little use for the remainder of Kaettegut.* More agricultural stations, north of Jefferson—Fifty would not stop there, none of the expansionists would. Facilities would go up next in the new northern patch, before or after they had that settled with a minor population, and it would go from there.

The elimination of Kaettegut, most of it, or all of it. *That's* what they were discussing.

Fifty re-draped his arm back across the sofa. "Kaettegut itself has already grown its population. No, it wasn't authorized, and their government is burgeoning just to keep pace with the population levels—and now they want more resource allocation, more budget, but they *haven't* gotten it, and so they've cut corners elsewhere, and that has already affected *us*. The agricultural fleet's in bad shape. Our lifeline." At his raised eyebrows: "But that's an old story, that's been going on since nearly the beginning, and Kaettegut grows poorer. It does it to itself. Another reason for what I've been talking about: Kaettegut goes too far. Much too far, since I've been in office, much too big for its britches."

He suddenly felt—a connection, a switch thrown. A single pinpoint, come together, the white point of a faraway light in the dark.

Fifty had announced the existence of the experimental agricultural facilities after the explosion in Gros Morne, when people had been on knife-edge, when food, tied directly to health and survival, had been threatened. Quite welcome, then, that news.

It was a *horrible* suspicion. But—the council had sat without any emotion or regret when news of the Gros Morne explosion had come through. Quinn Rhodes had sat across the table and thumbed through the stills of the aftermath, the bodies lying so visibly. He had *thought* it the work of the status quo, had assumed it was politically motivated—had shown no sophistication to do so, to automatically assign it to any party other than his.

Not political. For history, for the future. To put down any threat to what had been carefully designed, to keep things the way they were.

The populace favored the status quo because it was safe, because it did not require change. He had thought the status quo equally risk-adverse, equally complacent. *No.* Quinn and her party had put it out into the open, for anyone to see, and he had thought it only an argument, one piece of the pie—*we cannot control what is out of our reach.* Not for their smokescreens of economic coordination, *not* for unity. Just control, face value.

Except the expansionists had much more at stake in that explosion—everything he'd heard here tonight.

He sat there, and felt the cushions beneath him, the floor hard beneath the soles of his shoes—and felt cold in the pit of his stomach. His voice came uninvited: "What happened with the explosion in Gros Morne? Who *did* do it?"

Fifty laughed, leaned back into the sofa, and handed his glass up to Tevin, who had come with the decanter. "You expect too much, there. The information the office of the chairman gets isn't always perfect or complete. That's something you'll need to accept."

Too easy. An avoidance of the question—*if* he thought rationally. Emotionally, the pit in his stomach grew harder, smaller.

Strength in unity, in order, he would have said it himself a very short time ago. The structure in place, if not the individuals, worked elegantly. That was reason enough for its defense. It *could* work better, yes: it was what he had been aiming toward, in all his idealism, was to have been his greatest challenge, his greatest achievement.

He had been a fool.

––––––––

Kellan kept his back to the kitchen's empty cabinets, sitting at the table. He sat here, of late; in the main room there was the sofa, the real thing. It had the smell, must have been moved from the Grosvenor house.

And that meant it was not there, and that he wasn't going back there. Not even that—the way he had always assumed the apartment in Rue had stayed the same, in case they came back, empty and waiting, when it had surely been assigned to someone else, and someone else lived in his room, and that part was long over.

There was more than half his dinner still behind him, rapidly cooling in its takeout bag on the kitchen bar. He propped his elbows on his knees, looked up with eyes that felt too small at the dining room light—and it swam, white, in his vision.

He had made his decision. Circumstances had become what they were, had forced his hand, but *he* had let it happen.

He could sit, yes, he could answer questions, he could go where they took him, try to begin making a life out of this—and time went on, and changed things, changed things other than just himself. Reshaped everything.

Except— How *could* he be doing this to Graham? Graham had

given up Rue to know he was safe, and now he did not call, had not made even a simple phone call, had not even left a message—he did not know where, but he could have found out. Jenning would know.

Graham had not done anything to deserve this—a slap in the face, if he thought in only a limited fashion. Graham had only done something honest, had an emotion. Everything good and decent, disregarded.

That anyone could care whether he was all right, when *this* was how he was—but it wasn't his own reasoning that was the only thing that mattered, maybe.

It had felt *right*, at first, to live alone.

He understood the crisis, now. He could see it all from a different perspective, the calls, the riot at the dock, the ship swinging away. Jenning had said—and he believed it was true, that if he stayed with her department he *could* be helpful to Kaettegut. It made sense: all the information, whole chunks clicking satisfyingly, perfectly, into the gaps in others. Differences in Kaettegut and Grosvenor, the leadership structure, the way it all fit.

If he could stay—detached, give only what would help... It could not last long, surely it had its limit, and then things would go uncertain again, but for now it was what he had.

What if Graham had gone back to the house in Grosvenor, was in the pricing office, working again? He had *said* it was his part of the bargain, that he was going to keep it.

God, no. An empty place where the sofa had been, a reminder.

He didn't go that way anymore. Jenning had faced some opposition in keeping him, he knew that; that she had put him in Jefferson residential housing when that was *not* cheap or readily available, said he didn't go down into Grosvenor until things changed.

He could not go back to the way it had been. He just had to go forward, that was all.

He turned and picked up the restaurant bag, and got to his feet, slowly. Carried it into the kitchen, rinsed the silverware and left it lying in the sink—here, stainless steel with a tall arch in the faucet, blessedly different.

The bed, too, was very different: wide, with a crisp white blanket. It was early, but he lay on top of it, careful not to wrinkle it—still in his clothes from the office, and closed his eyes.

28

The hallway had the sameness of light, walking down it in the early morning. Jenning came to work early, not so much as Thomas Gouman had, but still she beat her assistants to the office.

Kellan *hoped*, took his first real breath when he saw the light under the crack of the door.

She was stirring cream into her coffee, atypical; she had taken it black every other time he had seen. She looked up when he opened the door at her *come in*. "Ah. I was wondering who it was, this time of morning."

"I'm sorry." The quick relief fled. He made himself breathe, one deep breath, an exhale. No small talk, he could not stand it now. "My friend, Graham Long. Is he still in Kaettegut?"

A small rise of the eyebrows, that was all. She drew the stir-stick out of the coffee, laid it beside the cup. "No. He came back, oh, a week ago. When they shipped the renovation crews back. He's been back in his position in the pricing office."

Oh, my God. His stomach felt as empty as it had been at the sea-wall, with the bay lapping near his feet.

———

Stefan rested his forearms on the back of Fifty's chair, *his* chair, now, changed his mind and took them off, and placed his fingertips on the warmer, unaffected wood of the table.

The council chambers had a curiously empty feeling, devoid of *souls*, pale walls and blank screen drawn up into the ceiling. All the warmness of the capretto and wood, the curve of line in the conference table and chair backs, could not take the inhumane chill out of the space.

They had *not* come any further than this. Superiority on the backs of others—of course. It was what civilizations had been built on for millennia. It was what humanity *was*. The best had taken that tendency for what it was, had not fought it—had used it. That was the furthest they had gone.

He had wanted order, order for the glory of humanity, but without humans gumming it up. Humanity in the abstract.

He had been wrong. The humans gumming it up weren't the process, they were the destination. The glory of humanity, right there, in all its self-interest and faults: what truly made them, as a race, unique. —And wrong, and against all their ideals.

His predecessors had split themselves apart so that they could have a common enemy. It was perhaps the reason they had survived, those few colonists, less than a thousand between the two ships: a drive of *us* versus *them* was more powerful than the drive for survival. One could give up, in a fight for survival, could lay one's head on the ground in peace, knowing the best had been given and still failed.

One could never give up against a common foe. No, they'd scrabble at rocks with their bare hands, but they would have a chance to win.

That was something he could not take away from them, Fifty had been right, it *was* their success. It was how Fifty was maneuvering expansion into place. Fifty had not expected it, had called it a failure, but it was enmity, and it could be used.

He could be the idealist, sitting in his office in charge of the ethics department, or he could face hard reality. He could learn how to use it. *Let* humanity in all its faults and self-interest and its scaffolding of clay become central. It was its own structure, the filling in of all the gaps, one piece needing only to be molded. *That* made it strong.

It might be that he could not do it. That he should not be in this role, not even temporarily, that it was right that Fifty should, and that Fifty should go on in it, who would let humanity go where it wanted and only protect initial positions.

No. There was perhaps a way to use humanity's propensities, but to change those initial positions, to make sure they were intrepreted *right.*

His inheritance, if he only had enough time.

Graham sat back in the chair, and looked at his screen. —It wasn't *so* bad, not as he had expected it to be. It was more—as if things had gone as planned and he *had* made a new start, had started out living in Grosvenor on his own.

He had put in for a transfer to a different apartment, an open one in the same district, closer to the ferry stop. The paperwork was still in the system, clogged up somewhere, but it was in sight. He could look to it and see a new beginning, could already see himself looking back at the old place with its malfunctioning shutter on the main room window. He would not think any further than that, just vague memory, that he had lived there with Kellan for a time.

A new start, that was what this was, was what he *needed*—Kellan's reaction had told him that, had as good as swung a door on everything he had let himself think.

He would go to Cisco tonight. He would eat and drink in the bar, so that it wasn't something he'd always avoid.

He might see Kellan on some street, in some line in an office somewhere. Kellan might not have gone to Kaettegut, might not go right away; perhaps the job in Travel was better after all than the one in Rue—but he wouldn't cringe. Would not. He hadn't been a fool; it just hadn't worked, that was all.

He *hoped* he might see him, at least once.

He gritted his teeth. *Look forward.*

There was something wrong with the numbers in the second chart on his screen, something not adding up; either that or he was still more addled than he wanted to think. He frowned, opened a file with one series of cross-references, paged down to the correct column and row.

The right speaker—the one that worked—clicked. "Phone call," the secretary's voice said, mustily; he and the secretary hadn't made much of a match, that much was settled.

"Put it through," he said—if she hadn't already dropped the call on him. She didn't identify calls for him, not the way she did for Ted, or Cecilia.

"Graham," the speaker said.

He stopped. Turned toward the speaker.

A beat. "Are you there?"

A long pause, on his part. "This is Graham," he said, finally.

"I'm sorry. I just want to say that. I'm—things have been mixed up. I've been."

No use pretending. "Kellan?" He kept his voice neutral, habit, and surprised even himself. *Good.*

There was another stretch of quiet. "I don't have much to say. I just wanted—"

God, no. He reached for the speaker before he caught himself, stopped. Calm, even tone: "Well, what's been going on with you?"

"Are you okay? The dock and everything."

He breathed. One good breath.

He knew better than to read any concern into it: too slippery a slope, and he would *not* let himself go. "Fine. We were all a little banged up, that's all. Minor, once things settled out. It was more—being displaced." A little too much, but not bad. He stopped, concisely, on the last word.

Silence stretched. He looked at the speaker and made himself think—past the surprise. This was just Kellan being decent. One last call, sensitively done. That was all this was. He made his stomach settle. *Control. Relax.*

"I know—no, forget it. I can't make it up to you. I know that. Just, I *am* sorry. I did wait. I waited until the end of the day Monday for the ship to come back. It doesn't change anything, I know—well, I wanted you to know."

"Thanks." But that he *hadn't* known, and that meant, *God,* that meant—

"Please. Don't, just don't sound like—"

An abrupt stop, steadied on the other end. *God in heaven.* He could not last through this, if it *was* only what he had thought it was. Kellan's voice kept going then, steadier, if not unruffled. "I've moved into this place up in the Jefferson residential district. It's nice, I guess. Why don't you—would you want to come up after work and see it, at least?"

He felt his brows draw together, stopped. The room was very still;

the hallway behind him, equally so. He put his hand on the desk.

"It's on Stockbridge. The street winds around for a while, then there's a stretch of wetlands on the right. It's in the gray building across, two buildings after you hit the wetlands. One-thirteen. I'm in thirty-two, third floor." Quiet, then: a waiting.

He didn't *have* to take anything from it, away from it. He could just look.

"All right," he said, finally.

It came out—sounded—reluctant. *Damn it, Graham,* listen *to yourself!* Hesitation, caution, both well warranted: he'd go, and it would be worse, it would make it much worse. It was a tie to the past when he knew what would happen, that there was nothing there for him, that he was better off this way down here, and now he did have Grosvenor to himself. A clean break. —And maybe he *wasn't* like that, after all, maybe this had only been a weakness, a match where he had not expected to find it, and he'd go on to be more himself.

"Good." Relief in the voice. And after a hesitation: "Thanks."

The line went. He lifted his hand to slap the table, quickly angry; closed his eyes instead, and leaned back in his chair, sighed.

He took one of the later ferry runs.

He had not known whether to have dinner first, had gone to Cisco, had a strong drink and a small snack that went down only because of the alcohol. His stomach still churned, stepping off the ferry into the district.

He'd had to give his name and key card when he tried to stay on past the second Jefferson dock. It hadn't helped; the wait had been nervous and then he had been irritated when they gave his card back.

He did not know how to act. That was the simple truth of it.

The street wound through a whole series of S-curves. There was, finally, a patch of wetlands coming up on the right; a small bridge, leading to another avenue on the other side, the rear of those apartments facing the wetlands. He saw balconies on some, turned his attention to the left side of the street. It was all taller, blocky buildings, still fairly elegant, a cut above Grosvenor—made Grosvenor's residential district with its small streets and pitched roofs look fairly provincial, in fact.

Oh, God. He wanted to turn around, to walk back to the ferry.

There was a gray building—the numbers in white script, cleaner than the heavy molding around the doors and the windows. Huge windows, in the front. He hesitated at the call panel near the front door; finally dropped his hand and walked out of the immediate range of the streetlight, back the way he had come.

He stopped. *Damn it!* His hands were shaking; he shoved them into his pockets, looked across the wetlands at the balconies, at the lights on in the windows. Movement caught his eye; he concentrated on that. Breathed. A woman came down a stairway, bent over to put something on a table. He could see her sweater, that it was faded and green.

She looked up, stopped. Stayed there.

He bent his head, turned, and walked back down the street toward the streetlight.

Thirty-two had a slot like the rest. No names. He lifted his hand, took a breath— slid his key card into the slot.

The door clicked. He opened it.

A narrow hall opened to him. A stairway; only one door on the right, labeled simply and discreetly *11* above the door handle. A vent blew warm air straight down onto his forehead and rustled the top few buttons on his shirt, beneath the jacket.

This wasn't right. *None* of this was right, his heart was beating too hard.

He took the stairs. He slid his hand along the banister on the way up, real wood, and oiled every week for generations from the feel of it. *Good Lord.* Jefferson's residential district—one more thing he had not had the focus, in the agitation of the afternoon, to absorb. Still could not. The banister under his palm seemed his only steady link to a tactile environment, everything else out of his control, the universe flying away from his hands.

He would not have Kellan's trust again. He knew that.

The third floor was the last, three doors grouped closely together in an L. Kellan's was on the right, toward the back. He looked back at the banister with its oiled gleam in the low light, the stairs leading down and away that said *pride*, and *salvage what you can.*

God. He stood there with his fingers clenched into his palms, and *knew* what he would do, still could not bring himself to do it.

He had just taken a step when he heard the door latch click, and then he was not facing a wall of closed doors; he could see back into a main room, and Kellan was there, hair coppery in the low light.

"Thanks," Kellan said, and looked toward the stairway, and back at him. "For coming." Awkwardly: "Really."

That was all it took. The hardness in his stomach dissolved, *all* of his organs turned liquid, warm. He moved his hand toward his stomach.

Kellan took one step and had him in an embrace, tight. *Real.* He did not react quickly enough; startled, got his arms into place and that was all before Kellan had stepped back, precisely to the same spot. "I'm glad you're all right," Kellan said, and looked away, and then it *was* real awkwardness, and he cursed himself. Tried desperately to think of something to say that would make it all natural, would be the way they had been. But: "Come in," Kellan said, and stepped back into the doorway and one step more, out of the way.

He went. Kellan moved and he followed, and he struggled against it, made himself stand away from it, to survey the apartment and its dark walls—brown, everything else light: the floors, the trim, the furniture. There sat a table very similar to what was in the Grosvenor apartment, but *this* apartment was spacious, the dining room three times the size of the old one, the main room stretching away from the door and the dining room, toward the rear of the building. "Wow," he said. "You're moving up in the world."

Kellan turned his face away, pretended to survey the same main room. "I didn't pick it."

Huh. He spotted the sofa against the wall, familiar, small in this space. "The sofa." He tried for a laugh, got maybe one syllable out of it. "I should have known they hadn't traded it out for *me.*"

Kellan had leaned back against the wall. The door, released from his grip, swung shut on its own, clicked into the doorframe. Silence stilled the air for a moment, then Kellan straightened, took a step toward the dining room. "I made some food." He went past him, into the dining room, left into the kitchen. "I didn't know if you had eaten."

There were two plates on the kitchen bar, covered in microwavable lids; he saw that as he came into the dining room. Two pans sat on the stove, scraped empty, drips and splatters on the stovetop around them. Kellan lifted the plates, and turned his head back toward him. "If you've eaten, it's okay."

"Just a snack." He looked at the cabinets, back at the main room and its low light. There wasn't much in the apartment in the way of overhead lighting. Quickly, before he could change his mind: "I could use a drink. Strong. You have anything?"

Kellan's expression deflated, some. "I don't."

"It's okay."

"I haven't—it wouldn't have been good." With hesitation. More quickly, then: "I can maybe order something in. I don't know how things work up here that well yet, but I think they do make deliveries."

"It's all right." He turned away, examined the walls, all of them blank; dark, some kind of color wash, maybe. "It's been that hard?"

"No. No." Kellan shrugged, finally. "Yes."

He turned back, but Kellan had the plates, was carrying them over to the table, setting them down. Not straight across from each other, thank God; and then he was back to the kitchen bar for the silverware, and to the coffee machine, filling two mugs. "I'm trying to learn to make this at home," he said, change of subject, and seemed more comfortable talking, more natural, when he had his back turned—which naturalness disappeared as soon as he had turned back, the two mugs in his hands, taking them to the table. A nod to the food: "I hope it's still hot enough."

Kellan had stopped beside the chair with its back to the bar. He took the other one, to Kellan's right; slipped off his coat, draped it over the chair and sat and looked at the food: a small bowl of onion soup on one side of the plate, a piece of fish, a little pile of rice. "I'm sure it is," he said, and lifted the spoon, forced a smile. He took a spoonful of the soup, and it was fairly cool, but still good, nice and acidic. "Hm. Good."

Kellan sat, picked up his napkin, his spoon. "I'm not much of a cook. No surprise, I guess." He tried the soup, too, and made a face. "It *is* too cold." He was already back on his feet. "Here, I'll microwave it."

"No, no. It's okay." He protected his plate with his hand. "Soup cools the fastest. It's still good."

Kellan sat back down, looked dubious, but he lifted his fork and knife and began cutting into the fish. There was silence again, and Kellan took the smallest possible bite of the fish, chewed mechanically.

He sliced his own piece of fish in half, and took a bite from the middle, where it was likely to be warmer.

Kellan finally set his fork down, rested both fists on the table, looked away. Hesitantly, still facing away: "I think I haven't been— unbiased. Or honest. I—I felt stupid, that I'd been so naïve."

Graham set down his fork. The bite of fish slid unopposed around his stomach.

"It was the shock of it. I know I didn't react well."

"It wasn't—"

Kellan held up his hand. "Don't. I know I didn't. —I do know I don't want to lose what you've been. I *want* to come home at the end of a day and have you here to analyze what's really happening, what I should do. And I know I shouldn't be saying that, because it's selfish, the way I've *been*. I don't know why you've put up with it. You shouldn't."

"I can—"

"I didn't consider you. Not as a person. I didn't, and I'm sorry, and I can't think of a reason you should accept it." He pushed the chair back, away from him; stood up, finally, and went into the kitchen, and faced him, with his arms straight against the bar countertop— and still looked away. "You're a person. A *person*. Just as worthwhile, feelings just as real as anyone. What does it matter if—but it," and he leaned down harder on his arms, "It just throws me into a panic."

Oh, my God. His heart was beating too hard. He *needed* that drink, needed to back up and think, to above all stay where he was, to not go into that kitchen.

It *was* possible. It was possible. He *could* do it. There was enough openness there, just an opening, more than he had dared hope.

He stood. Put his knife and fork back at the sides of the plate. "I don't think I can eat."

Kellan's face had a sick tinge at the edges. He made a try for a smile, but it didn't work, and he looked away.

He did go into the kitchen, then, carried his jacket with him, and stopped, carefully, one step away. He put his hand, firmly, on Kellan's shoulder. "All right." And dropped his hand, and put one arm into the sleeve of his coat. "Slow. We'll just try. We can just take it slow."

His chest, his heart felt impossibly light, ethereal.

Kellan looked at him, swallowed—but did not move away.

He shrugged into the rest of the coat, walked to the door, opened it; looked back once—weakness, but he *needed* the reassurance, and Kellan had turned his head, was watching him. He turned the handle, let himself out into the hall, stopped on the top stair for a moment. The smooth wood of the banister was cool against his palm, but it was solid, solid as the rest of the hall, and *not* the only thing steady around him, now.

Jus Neuce is at work on a sequel to *Nocturne.*

Acknowledgments

Many thanks to Manoj M. Joshi, R. M. Haberle,
R. T. Reynolds, Martin J. Heath, and Laurance R. Doyle,
whose works inspired the creation of
Nocturne, the planet:

*Simulations of the Atmospheres of Synchronously
Rotating Terrestial Planets Orbiting M Dwarfs:
Conditions for Atmospheric Collapse and
the Implications for Habitability*

and

Habitability of Planets Around Red Dwarf Stars

GLOSSARY

Education

Families are not part of the social unit on Nocturne but have been replaced by the educational system. There are no marriages; the closest equivalent is that of partners.

Residents bear the name of their school as their surname, and schools are firmly ranked in terms of specialty and prestige. Graduates can find their stations improved should any alumni of their school attain council level, particularly on the Proteraiotita. Only council members have the right to use the surname of their school in formal address.

Geography

Nocturne is currently in a marine transgression, which means the oceans are high and cover much of the planet's land. In comparison, Earth in 2005 was in a marine regression with ocean levels unusually low, allowing many coastal areas to exist above water.

Terminator
The terminator of Nocturne is that rim which is perpetually in twilight. A tidally locked planet like Nocturne in a synchronously rotating orbit never changes its face from the sun, so its terminator remains at a sunset, with lighting similar to Earth's "blue hour."

Prime
Prime is made up of Jefferson, Grosvenor, their residential areas, Grosvenor's warehousing district, and the Back.

Jefferson
Jefferson is the seat of government for Nocturne and the capital of Prime. Its residential district lies just north of its boundaries. It and Grosvenor sit on a thin peninsula between Jargen Bay and New Bay, with some of this rare land area taken up with wetlands. The first landing took place just north of Jefferson.

Grosvenor
Grosvenor serves as Prime's main town and is separated from Jefferson in the north by wetlands. Grosvenor's business district is located in its north and its residential districts in its south. The warehousing district, which includes the port, extends westward of Grosvenor's southern tip.

The Back
Furthest from the terminator, the Back sits west across New Bay from Grosvenor. Its manufacturing areas and port are located on that coast, while its mining operations exist in a western mountain range. It receives no light and suffers colder temperatures.

Kaettegut

Kaettegut sits east across Jargen Bay from Grosvenor and Jefferson. It consists of a hilly southern province and, across a channel, a larger, flat northern province that is part of a different land mass. Collectively, Kaettegut's geographic size dwarfs that of Jefferson and Grosvenor, while the Back dwarfs Kaettegut in turn. Gros Morne is the capital of Kaettegut and the site of a carbonate cave system, since expanded, that became the site of early hydroponics operations for the earliest colonists.

History

The first wave of colonization

At the beginning of the Colony Push, Earth's interstellar travel technology was not far advanced and each ship cycled through several generations before arriving at its designated location. These ships were stocked with Earth's informational and genetic database and with a crew made up largely of scientists. Once arrived at its target, no ship had the ability to return at the same speeds to Earth or any other destination.

One member of the original Nocturne ship's crew, a prominent scientist, suffered from a sun-adverse disease, a genetic pattern borne down through additional generations.

Nocturne's first colonists

A hazardous landing resulted in the loss of much of the exploratory ship's genetic material and communications equipment. The small population settled on the terminator to take advantage of nearby natural resources, relatively moderate temperatures, and a lesser amount of solar light. The terminator would also receive less damage from solar flares, something for which red dwarf suns tend to be known.

The second arrival

Several decades after having formed a neatly centralized system, the colonists' descendants received a second ship with some surprise. This ship came without the expected update to Earth's informational database, and Earth had not sent all requested supplies. Worse, the new colonists were of a kind different than those of the scientists' descendants: largely hardy working-class stock. These new settlers passed on the unwelcome information that Earth's interest in interstellar colonization had temporarily, at least, turned in favor of events closer to home.

A schism developed quickly between the two groups. The first group held that it was superior in intelligence and attempted to slot the new arrivals into manual industries. A major value difference lay in this: the first group had developed a genetic database to ensure the continuing quality of its population and the suitability of certain citizens for certain jobs in the correct proportions. The second group largely rejected this approach and in time retreated to a nearby land mass, forming Kaettegut; however, the two groups did cooperate in matters of subsistence. A large segment of Kaettegut's population was eventually enticed permanently to the Back to engage in mining and manufacturing operations. In a major coup which was largely economic and psychological, the first group later succeeded in splitting those working in the Back from their companions in Kaettegut. Those in the Back became citizens of Prime.

Politics

Because of Nocturne's centralized, government-based structure, politics are literally everything to Nocturne residents. Political parties are a fairly recent development on Nocturne and include three political philosophies, or parties:

Expansionist
Expansionists desire to gradually expand the population across the entirety of the planet, and to administer those populations from Jefferson.

Resourcist
Resourcists desire to exploit other portions of the planet for natural resources through the use of small outposts which would send the additional resources back to Prime, hence increasing the core population's standard of living. The resourcists do not believe a truly planetary population can be administered from Jefferson.

Status quo
The status quo contingent likewise does not believe it is feasible to either administer a geographically distant population from Jefferson nor to efficiently operate a centrally planned economy in that event. They hold that with geographic space, cultural and other changes will necessarily result which cannot be foreseen or controlled.

Nocturne is governed by three councils, with names derived from the Greek language:

Proteraiotita
The highest council on Nocturne, the Proteraiotita is in session throughout the year. Its twelve members include an elected chairman, the heads of all major divisions, and two peer delegates appointed by the chairman. Divisions exist in a firm pecking order. The Proteraiotita can veto any initiative put forth by the two lower councils.

Ligotera
The ten-member Ligotera includes the administrators of departments (departments being under divisions) related to major logistics of the economy, such as Agriculture, Mining, and Shipping. In the beginning, Agriculture held a seat on the Proteraiotita; a demotion to the Ligotera soon after Prime's coup with the Back was a severe blow.

Doma To
The eight-member Doma To includes the heads of four minor divisions and administrators of four departments, and deals with what are considered more minor issues such as those related to business, media, safety, and consumer affairs.

Find out more about Nocturne
at www.aiopublishing.com:

- Frequently asked questions about the book

- Reviews, plus the opportunity to write your own review

- Online survey (pick your favorite character, and more)

- Love it? Purchase a personally autographed copy

- Direct email link to the author

- Free reading group guide

Also...
Make the most of your reading experience at the bookstore at
www.aiopublishing.com: books, special items, and reading accessories.
We're all about the experience...

To order another copy of this book by mail, please send a request
and check or money order for $14.00, plus $4.00 for shipping
(South Carolina residents please add applicable sales tax), to

aio

Aio Publishing Co., LLC
P. O. Box 30788
Charleston, SC 29417
USA

For an autograph, please include a name and desired inscription, if any.